My Life With Tiny

My Life With Tiny

A Biography of Tiny Rowland

Richard Hall

faber and faber
LONDON · BOSTON

First published in 1987 by
Faber and Faber Limited
3 Queen Square London WC1N 3AU
Photoset by Parker Typesetting Service, Leicester
Printed in Great Britain by
Mackays of Chatham Kent

British Library Cataloguing in Publication Data

Hall, Richard, 1925–
My life with Tiny: a biography of
Tiny Rowland.
1. Rowland, Tiny 2. Businessmen – Great
Britain – Biography
I. Title
338.6'092'4   HC252.5.R6

ISBN 0-571-14737-2

Contents

List of Illustrations

Introduction

Who's Who has no entry for the man whose capricious running of his billion-pound Lonrho conglomerate often puts him into the headlines. Tiny Rowland (born Roland Fuhrhop in India in 1917) dislikes any effort to shed light on those early years which shaped his personality; he will turn aside casual questions about his background with a mixture of banter and unlikely anecdotes, but grows belligerent when feeling threatened by some more purposeful busybody. At the first hint that I thought of writing this book, a command went out to his German and English relations: they must tell me nothing.

Of course, Rowland may well ask why he should have to submit to having his past raked over. However, it is the penalty of success, of his financial wizardry; even more, of having given himself a high-profile role as a Fleet Street newspaper proprietor – first choosing to have a public slanging match with his own editor, then coaxing him into a journalistic vendetta against Lonrho's sworn financial enemies.

Like Robert Maxwell, his egregious counterpart, Tiny has had a bumpy road to fame. But whereas 'Captain Bob' is only too ready to trumpet his origins, and tell his own life story, Tiny treats any investigative journalism directed at himself as a hostile act.

This fondness for secrecy applies equally to the day-to-day activities of Lonrho. As the *Financial Times* often complains, few big companies are so uncommunicative; and likewise, Rowland reveals little about his constant political intrigues in Africa. These only surface when others talk. In the twenty-three years I have known him, he has always behaved like an expert conjuror, never letting you know what is hidden up his sleeve.

His pretences are often maddening, yet at other times endearing. He delights in that somewhat plebeian British nickname, even signing himself 'Tiny Rowland' at the end of his Chief Executive's annual statement to the 60,000 Lonrho shareholders. It is the big man having a game, playing at being a smaller one. He is also ready to take up with some rough diamonds, such as Sir Freddie Laker. For all that, he can adopt the most urbane, upper-class manner. Hearing him engage in repartee with the Honourable Angus Ogilvy (in the days before Princess Alexandra's consort had to leave the Lonrho board in tempestuous circumstances) I never failed to be mesmerized. He likewise writes immaculate English, in a style that is polished and courtly; his letters can be gems of cool logic.

Although Rowland was once quoted as saying that he voted Labour, that was probably a bit of whimsy. He gets on easily with Tories: the Rt. Hon. Lord Duncan-Sandys has been followed by the Rt. Hon. Sir Edward du Cann as Chairman of Lonrho. 'At one time, the Board was like an Old Etonians' club,' recalls the Hon. Gerald Percy. (It is a wistful recollection, because Percy was flung into outer darkness after being put forward as Rowland's presumptive successor during a disastrous attempt at a boardroom coup in the early 1970s.) Yet for all his suavity, the man who has had to live with that tag about the 'unacceptable face of capitalism' has never really belonged to the Establishment. There are good reasons for thinking that if he were ever to submit to lying on an analyst's couch (a most unlikely event) it might be discovered that his deepest motivation is to fight the Establishment, and beat it. 'Now you will have the chance to find out how vicious I can be,' he told his well-born opponents before the great boardroom struggle. They certainly did.

His past may explain a persona that seems to have been knowingly manufactured, rather than organically developed. One might almost say that Rowland's character was 'washed out' by his early experiences, leaving him free to exploit any chance that comes in front of him without the handicap of inhibitions.

But this is to anticipate the facts, always so elusive. The first autobiography ever provided by Rowland – in 1961 – amounted to six lines, scribbled unenthusiastically on a small bit of paper for Angus Ogilvy. This was an unavoidable preliminary to Ogilvy's recommendation that he was the right man to take over Lonrho and shake it into life; but it told the minimum, and was in any case shown only to a handful of people.

For decades, gossip columnists have had to rub together the same old tales, in the hope of shedding some light on the mysterious Mr Rowland; for instance, that he had spent part of the last war at Euston station as a porter, and had collected the lion's share of tips by working out where the first-class passengers would alight. Spasmodic journalistic sorties were made to flesh out such anecdotes, as Lonrho grew ever more vast, but with scant success. (It is true that he spent a few weeks as a porter, on the orders of a Labour Exchange at the end of the war, but he soon extricated himself.) The only book about Lonrho, published in 1976 by Penguin, and written by Suzanne Cronje and others, vaguely suggested that Rowland's father was a German pharmacist, but admitted that other evidence was lacking.

So in 1980, when the editorial mandarins of the *Observer* were mobilized to try and halt the Lonrho takeover, ignorance about the background of the would-be owner was nearly total. Almost the only solid fact was that his German father had run an import–export firm in India until the 1914–18 war. Editor Donald Trelford thought that Rowland might be an Old Etonian (so firmly had those boardroom associations left their mark), and ordered a search through the Eton records. All in vain – eventually the newsroom sleuths discovered that he had spent his two final years of education at an obscure establishment in Hampshire called Churcher's College. It did not, and does not, have the status of a public school, and in those inter-war years most of the boarders were the sons of junior army officers serving around the Empire. Before going to Churcher's, according to the *Observer* dossier, Rowland had been in the Hitler Youth, when his family lived in Hamburg after returning from India. During the war, he had spent more than two years as a private in the Royal Army Medical Corps, then been interned on the Isle of Man under Regulation 18B. The significance of this last discovery was never resolved; in some quarters the worst interpretation was put on it.*

However, the basic facts were discreetly fed by Donald Trelford to rival papers of influence. Rupert Murdoch in particular was a beneficiary of the *Observer*'s labours, in profiles in the *Sunday Times* and *The Times*. Even Rowland himself agreed to be interviewed, to show a more friendly face to the media world he longed to enter; he proceeded to lay some false trails for his own amusement. He said, for example, that he had had two brothers – whereas in fact there was only one, a Hamburg businessman named Raimund Fuhrhop. (Raimund was proud, incidentally, of having Everest as his second name, on account of being born in Darjeeling, within sight of the world's highest peak.)

All the *Observer* ferreting ceased when Tiny at last won his pyrrhic victory, in an atmosphere which had been unpleasantly soured, and on terms that proved increasingly vexatious to him. Jane Bown, doyenne of photographers, was hurriedly despatched to his Cheapside House office to take a portrait of Rowland; in it he looked suitably soulful, his hands raised in a position of prayer.

Even at that stage, several of the editorial staff thought that there must be a book in Tiny's battle for the paper – or perhaps a TV comedy: indeed, much of the four months' war of attrition had been fought out on the box. But everyone felt exhausted, and for a while the enmities were papered over. My own interest in picking up all the abandoned threads – of telling the full story of Rowland and Lonrho and the *Observer* was only revived by chance, when I met one of his close relations in West Africa.

I had lately become the paper's Commonwealth correspondent, and a few days before leaving on a long African trip I was invited to have lunch in the Lonrho boardroom. Rowland had sat next to me, with a dozen directors and lesser minions ranged down the table. We talked briefly about Nigeria, and Rowland assured me that if I wanted to know what was going

*See Chapter 13.

on there, I should meet Senator Joseph Wayas, president of the National Assembly. (When the subsequent military coup took place, Wayas became a fugitive, and one of Nigeria's foremost 'wanted men'.) But Rowland was far more interested in the *Observer*; after a year as proprietor, he seemed thoroughly perplexed by it. 'What are they saying about Lonrho at the paper?' he kept demanding. 'What is happening? Dick, what are they *saying*?' Everyone had watched me as I fumbled for answers and tried to steer the conversation around to my impending journey. Tiny kept returning to his question, until I was at last able to leave – conscious that I had failed to pass muster, through not having supplied whatever it was he was after. In the old days, our relationship had been far more easy-going.

So when Norbert Furnon-Roberts called at my hotel in the Gambia in the summer of 1982, and introduced himself as Tiny's nephew, I was most ready to talk. It seemed an opportunity to dissipate the memory of that gloomy lunch, by hearing about the genuine Rowland as seen through the eyes of his own family.

Norbert wore gold-rimmed glasses, spoke softly in well-phrased English, and explained that he had learned of my visit from an item on the local radio. He said he was out from Hamburg with his fiancée, who was working for an aid project somewhere up the Gambia River. I was a bit startled, after all the frantic hue and cry to trace the Rowland history, to have this unsolicited approach in such an unlikely setting, and was momentarily suspicious. After all, there had been an attempt to overthrow the Gambian President, Sir Dawda Jawara, while he was in London for the wedding of Prince Charles, and treason trials were going on. My visitor might be some kind of agent, trying to find out what I had unearthed.

That was a foolish notion. Furnon-Roberts proved genuine enough, despite his name. (Like his uncle, he had merely chosen to anglicize himself while working at a merchant bank in London – a job which Rowland's influence had helped him to obtain.) Norbert hinted that he and Tiny had fallen out, so he had chosen to return to Germany. Even so, he clearly doted on his uncle, and was now eager to hear how he was faring as a newspaper tycoon.

We talked under a thatched sun-umbrella beside the ocean.

Norbert remembered the early 1950s, when he was a small boy and Uncle Tiny would come home to Hamburg from Rhodesia for Christmas every year: 'He brought me armfuls of comics. I adored him. He told exciting stories of life in Africa, and showed me photos of himself with wild animals.' It was an endearing glimpse of the man who had seemed so remote and obsessive a week before at the Cheapside House lunch.

Norbert called on me several times in London after our first encounter. One occasion, when he came to dinner, was in the middle of 1984; and the sequel well illustrates how Rowland hates anyone else going on from where Angus Ogilvy was content to leave off. I had by then firmly decided – after the astounding 'Matabeleland row' between Rowland and Trelford – that (to use the old Fleet Street cliché) the story must be told. With the advantage of having been the editor of the first newspaper Lonrho ever owned, in Zambia in the mid-1960s, I had a lot of eyewitness material in hand.

After letting Norbert into my plans I reminisced about those distant 'wind of change' years, when Rowland began to make Lonrho's fortunes in Central Africa. Both Trelford and I had also been working there – that was where our paths first crossed. After twenty-five years, events seemed to take us full circle. So there seemed scope for more than an orthodox 'third person' biography of Rowland: it was possible to look at his career – and the growth of Lonrho – against a background of personal experience in Africa. It would likewise serve a purpose to describe life in the *Observer* during the later Astor years, since this would go some way towards explaining why there were such convulsions when Tiny took charge.

Then, towards the end of dinner, I asked Norbert: 'Who can tell me what your uncle was like as a boy? How did the family survive in Hamburg in the 1920s after coming home from India?' There was no point in trying to ask Tiny direct. In any case, he and I had fallen out badly, soon after my West African trip, over a piece I had written on Kenya.

Norbert had an idea: 'Why not try my Aunt Phyllis? She is down in Kent.' He gave me her address, and the next day I wrote to Tiny Rowland's sister, a lady nearly ten years his senior, living in Sevenoaks. Her reply, a polite refusal to tell me anything, came swiftly. But that was not all, because an anxious Norbert was on the telephone soon afterwards from Hamburg. Aunt Phyllis had passed my letter on to Cheapside House, and Tiny had launched himself into a fury. Not only his family, but even some Lonrho executives were warned to be on their guard. I was, he asserted, his 'enemy'. (That wounded me, and would have surprised certain colleagues on the *Observer* – they had often accused me of being in his pocket.)

In any case, Rowland's warning was superfluous. All the senior ranks of Lonrho's 150,000 employees go in awe of him and his impetuous ways. A former member of his close entourage looked terrified when I visited his office not long ago to ask about the background to one controversial deal in Africa. 'I'd rather not talk to you,' he said, after doodling nervously on a pad. 'Don't you realize that Tiny destroys people? I have a wife and children to think about.'

Rowland did not care to make a direct approach to warn me off. The message came through Trelford, some six weeks later. 'I've been told by a friend at Cheapside House,' said Donald solemnly, 'that you have been making inquiries about Tiny.' I nodded warily.

'You shouldn't – it's improper,' he said. In normal circumstances he might have had a point, but after the astounding quarrel he had just been through with Tiny – every detail savoured by Fleet Street – the choice of adjective merely seemed droll. Moreover, he had then been cast as the fearless editor, defying a tyrannical owner to expose the truth. Now, at the behest of the 'friend at Cheapside House', he was telling me to stop asking questions of my own.

Trelford must have guessed what was going through my mind. 'Well, I suppose you *are* the best person to write his biography,' he remarked. 'You've known him longer than the rest of us.' That was true, although I explained that there were many important points I had to find out about. It was going to be a long job to uncover those early years which seemed to have shaped Rowland's personality. We relaxed a little, and even exchanged a few recollections about Tiny. 'Tell him that I haven't sold the film rights yet,' I said on my way out of Trelford's office.

1

Golden Road from Gatooma

Rowland did not begin in the City of London, or in one of Britain's blue-chip companies, and spread confidently outwards from there. Instead, he has come to the centre of things from the financial periphery – from a distant colonial domain. Until he was well into his forties he was almost completely unknown beyond the limited arena of Rhodesia. Then at last the chance occurred for him to break out. Of course, he was never an all-conquering 'colonial' in the style of Beaverbrook or Rupert Murdoch, because he had spent almost half of his earlier life in Britain. But in the light of his flamboyant reputation today, it is worth remembering those twelve painstaking years during which he farmed and explored the African bush for mining prospects. It is in the obscure town of Gatooma that the story of Tiny's road to fortune really starts.

The people best able to give a convincing picture of Rowland during his first days in Africa are Richard and Lindy Peel. They were already living in Gatooma in 1948 when the handsome new immigrant arrived. 'He swept all the local women off their feet with his charm,' Peel remembers. 'But he did not seem interested in any of them.' After almost forty years, he has vivid memories of how Rowland stood out among the Gatooma farming community: 'Tiny obviously had no intention of spending the rest of his life growing tobacco and groundnuts. He once said to me that he wanted to "make a million". So I asked: "What then?" Tiny replied: "Oh, I suppose I'll make another."'

Rowland had bought, from London, a three-quarters share in a large farm called Shepton Estates; he had put down £40,000, a lot of money in those days. A partner named Eric Smith (also half-German) was already installed in the main house as farm manager when he turned up. Among the outbuildings was a rondavel – a round, thatched hut – and Tiny chose this as his bachelor quarters. 'It was part of his character,' says Lindy Peel. 'A deliberate show of modesty. But I noticed that he also wore a Patek Philippe watch.'

The decision to go to Africa at the age of thirty had been partly a reaction against the cramping conditions of post-war Britain, and the high taxes. This is not to say that Tiny had been unsuccessful in those years since he had been freed from detention in the Isle of Man. Within a few months of the end of the war he was operating from a flat in Brook Street, Mayfair; with the instincts of his merchant father, he was taking advantage of the post-war shortages of nearly everything. Expensive cars were his constant source of funds – he loved them, and was a shrewd dealer. He was reputedly involved in a profitable fruit importing business, flying oranges from North Africa in Dakota freight planes. Then he became the inspiration behind a refrigerator firm called Articair (presumably a misspelling of Arctic-air).

One of the directors of Articair was Lionel Taylor, an engineer, who before the Second World War had been a racing driver for Bentley cars. It was he who went out to become the farm manager in Gatooma. He was married, and had a three-year-old daughter named Josephine. Long after, having watched Josephine blossom from infancy, Rowland was to make her his bride. (This romantic ending had been long foreseen, because her friends at Arundel School in Rhodesia recall that she was always telling them: 'When I grow up, I shall marry Tiny Rowland.')

The choice of Gatooma, south-west of Salisbury on the rail route to Bulawayo, was shrewdly made by Rowland and Taylor. Although the town itself, with a white population of less than 2,000, possessed few attractions, it had around it some of Rhodesia's most fertile land – which was also dotted with small gold mines. Rhodesia itself was being hailed as the post-war eldorado, and was drawing more than 1,000 immigrants a month from Britain during the late 1940s. Most of the menfolk, coming out to settle with their families, had fought in the war: some had first been attracted to Rhodesia while posted there for RAF flying courses.

With his courtesy and Mayfair mannerisms, Rowland was unlike most of the immigrants. The new Rhodesians would say, rather defiantly, that they were 'sergeants' mess', in contrast to the white Kenyans, who were decidedly 'officers' mess'. Of course, Tiny looked the latter. But what Richard Peel calls a 'hidden steeliness' behind the façade helped to deflect questions about his own wartime career. Had it been known about, this might have made him something of an outsider.

Yet whatever the social limitations of his new country, Rowland had chosen to make a clean break with Britain. All his treasured possessions were shipped out by way of South Africa – including a prized Mercedes car. Among the most personal items was a framed photograph of himself with his mother, Muriel Fuhrhop. It showed him arm-in-arm with her on the promenade of a south-coast town, soon after he had left Churcher's College, and his parents had moved from Hamburg to London. When he became the head of Lonrho, that photograph would for many years be the only picture in his office.

Tiny's parents had both been held in the Isle of Man throughout the war, as enemy aliens – even though Mrs Fuhrhop was not German but Dutch, and her family had lived in Britain since the 1890s. She had died of cancer while a detainee, and Tiny had sat with her during the last, painful months. A few months before he had decided to start a new life in Rhodesia, his father had been remarried at Westminster register office, to the widow of another detainee.

Although his wartime years had been so full of rejection, Rowland was resolved to be thoroughly British from now on. After all, he was a British subject by birth, and he had changed his name by deed poll in 1939, just after the war began (he invented the surname by simply inserting the initial letter of his middle name, Walter, into his first name). In May 1947, while completing a document as a director of Articair, he had even chosen to write 'None' in the column headed 'Any former Christian name or names or surname'. He repeated this modest offence in a legal declaration in Rhodesia, and by the time he became the husband of Josephine Taylor he would even feel inclined to refurbish his father as William Frederick Rowland on the marriage licence (although the old man, whom he was financially supporting, was still alive and living on the northern outskirts of London as Wilhelm Friedrich Fuhrhop).

But in Gatooma in 1948, not everyone was taken in. According to Peel, Tiny's manners were 'Continental', his English too correct: 'He never used idioms – I sensed that he was afraid of getting them wrong.' There were other clues: 'Tiny shook hands whenever he met you, and when he said goodbye. There was even a suggestion of a bow.' (However, Peel had an especially keen eye for such details, because at the time he was running a small film company, and was to become one of Rhodesia's leading journalists; he later worked in Switzerland, where he now lives, for the International Press Institute.)

Sometimes, in those Gatooma days, Rowland and Peel shared a car to travel the hundred miles up to Salisbury, and Tiny would chat about various minor problems on the farm and ask 'What would you do?' or, 'Tell me if I am correct – I don't understand these things.' Peel felt that Tiny knew the answers in advance, and was just making conversation to be polite. Perhaps it also served to reduce the number of questions Rowland's companion would ask him about himself.

Peel was also struck by a certain showmanship in Rowland's nature – for example, by the way he smoked the cheapest cigarettes available, named 'Star'. Normally, only the Africans bought them. Tiny would produce a crumpled packet, take out a cigarette – then use an expensive gold lighter. 'Why do you smoke such a vile brand?' people would ask. Tiny was ready for the question. 'My bank manager won't let me buy anything else,' he would reply. He always looked well-to-do, dressing with an easy elegance. He could be equally casual about money. Once Peel met him by chance in the Meikles Hotel in Salisbury. 'Dick, would you lend me a pound?' he asked apologetically.

Another of his contemporaries in Gatooma recalls that there was a small tribe of half-wild cats on the Shepton farm. Every evening at sunset they would gather at Tiny's rondavel, where he would serve them with meals of raw meat, always making sure that each one got something. Richard Peel is emphatic about a more significant trait: 'Tiny was polite and generous to the Africans on the farm.' (In those days, in Rhodesia, this behaviour was nearly tantamount to eccentricity. It was definitely not based on any political opportunism, since black power was never thought about as a serious prospect.) When an African worker stole something, Tiny would not complain. His reaction was: 'What can you expect when we are paying them so little?'

Apart from playing the occasional game of cricket, Rowland did not mix much in the social life of Gatooma, which had the reputation of being something of a rough-and-ready Happy Valley in those years. Once the Peels persuaded him to go with them to a weekend dinner-dance, but for most of the evening he resisted all efforts to make him step on the floor. When he did succumb, it turned out that he could dance superbly. Curious friends asked oblique questions about his pre-war life, and although he revealed little, there were hints that he had been a friend of King Carol of Romania. He spoke of being in Bucharest, and in one extravagant moment talked of having hired a gypsy band – 'to follow me around and play when I wanted'.

In quite another vein, he talked of Krishna Menon, the militant Indian socialist, as an old friend. Menon had spent many years in London, and had lately become the first Indian High Commissioner to Britain. According to Tiny, the two of them had worked together after the war on a deal to sell second-hand Jeeps to India. But he never mentioned his own connections with India, and his birth there in a First World War detention camp.

At the outset, it must have been his ambition to make a spectacular entry into the Rhodesian business world. However, the going was slow and for the first five years he seems to have made scant headway. After all, this landlocked colony had only the most limited industrial base, and most of the local firms took their orders from head offices in South Africa. Admittedly, the white population had doubled since 1945, but it still only totalled around 150,000; most of the four million Africans were not even in the cash economy. The most hopeful development, for a would-be entrepreneur, was the creation of the Central

African Federation, with Salisbury – today called Harare – as its capital. This gave Rhodesia freer access to the markets, such as they were, of Northern Rhodesia and Nyasaland (now Zambia and Malawi).

Confronted by horizons so uninspiring for a man of money-making instincts, Rowland quite naturally looked towards Rhodesia's minerals. His first venture, distinctly unrewarding, was a chrome mine bought from a certain Baron Rukavina. So he turned to gold mining. There were hundreds of gold prospects scattered around the veld – indeed, it had been the lure of gold that had drawn Cecil Rhodes across the Limpopo River from the Transvaal sixty years before. Chief Lobengula of the Matabele had complained: 'The white men will never cease following us while we have gold in our possession, for gold is what the white men prize above all things.' But Rowland had come late on the scene, and there was some scepticism at his enthusiasm over the Kanyemba mine near Gatooma, which he later promoted and made into a public company – to his own considerable benefit. In the end, the scepticism was shown to be well founded, because within four years of going public the mine was a write-off. There are still investors in South Africa who hold a grudge against Rowland because of the losses on Kanyemba. A colleague who worked with him says: 'We just lost the vein – that's all.' Rhodesia is dotted with abandoned mines which had promised a lot at the start.

What made Kanyemba Gold Mine somewhat different was the quality of the directors Rowland assembled. One was the Hon. Thomas Boydell, a well-known South African politician, and another Sir John Rowland. Aged sixty-seven and living near Cape Town, Sir John was described in the records as 'a director of companies'. He was on the boards of various South African mines. Apart from sharing with Tiny the same surname, Sir John also possessed an Indian background: he had made his career as an administrator on the Indian railways and had retired to South Africa in 1942 after receiving a knighthood. With such endorsement, Kanyemba made quite an impact on the Johannesburg stock exchange – the disappointment would come later.

However, Kanyemba was just one facet of Rowland's burgeoning affairs, and Gatooma was too small a stage for his ambitions. Moreover his wanderings through the bush had given him severe malaria (a malady which still afflicts him to this day, often making him sit at his desk with his coat collar closed tightly round his throat). Soon after the founding of the Federation he moved to Salisbury, the centre of power. By that time he knew many people of influence, including the former fighter pilot and rising politician, Ian Smith; but relations between these two were always frosty.

Rowland bought a large mansion called 'High Noon', and installed as chatelaine the English wife of Eric Smith, his junior partner in Shepton Estates. This happened quietly, causing only the mildest of flutters in Gatooma. Everyone agreed that Irene Smith was exactly the right person for Rowland and 'High Noon'. She was the perfect hostess; throughout their long relationship Tiny would always insist, before introducing his business associates to her, that she was not his mistress and never had been. A woman friend from those days describes her as 'someone you might see in Sloane Street'. She was always carefully made up, a trait that marked her out from the suntanned settler wives.

The entertaining at 'High Noon' was discreet, but quite opulent: after dinner, Tiny made a point of handing around boxes of the most expensive Italian chocolates. He would sometimes point out to visitors the fine Persian carpets strewn around the drawing room. These had been bought during one of his business trips to Johannesburg, and the carpet merchant who supplied them still recalls the occasion: 'We went around to the warehouse late at night, and as I switched on the lights Tiny was astounded. I remember exactly what he said: "Good heavens, you've got more carpets here than they have at Harrods!" That was almost thirty years ago.'

By around 1958, there was some awareness in Salisbury that a formidable – and rather disturbing – personality had arrived on the financial scene. Rowland was enigmatic; he was not a 'clubbable' man. There were even rumours put about that he was a homosexual. His deals were being remarked upon in local business journals; sometimes the inferences were harsh. He paid no heed: his astuteness had earned him access to funds in Johannesburg when credit was hard to come by in Salisbury.

Moreover, he had taken care to see that not all the publicity was bad; he had struck up a friendship with the financial editor of the *Rhodesia Herald*, the main Salisbury daily.

Rowland's money-making energy was phenomenal. 'I'd go anywhere to make a deal, even for £5,' he told a friend at that time. By 1957, according to Shepton company accounts, he must have been worth at least £250,000 (which by today's values would put him well into the millionaire bracket). For a start, the Kanyemba mine had brought him a lot. He also appreciated quite early on that both companies and countries are highly dependent in their early stages of development on lines of communication. If resources are slender, a break in the flow of goods going in or out can be disastrous. His control of a small railway serving several mines was exploited to the full.

He quickly grasped the significance of Beira, the Mozambican port only a few hours' drive from the Rhodesian town of Umtali. It was plain that anyone who could somehow obtain the monopoly over a vital import passing through Beira for Rhodesia must make money. Oil was the obvious commodity – and Rowland saw that the way to control it was by building a pipeline with the exclusive right to move fuel into the country. Possessed by this vision, he set up a small company in Salisbury to negotiate for the pipeline concession. It was to be one of the most inspired moves in his entire career.

A friend he made while ferreting about in Beira was Jorge Jardim, a young entrepreneur and newspaper owner who had emigrated from Portugal to Mozambique shortly after Rowland moved to Rhodesia from Britain. A keen parachutist and big game hunter, Jardim represented Mozambique as an MP in the Lisbon Parliament and claimed friendship with Dr Salazar, the Portuguese dictator. Twenty years later, this colourful figure was to engage in a machiavellian plot with Rowland that would involve several British government ministers, some of the world's biggest oil companies – and the *Observer*.

Another friend Tiny made in the mid-1950s was a Hungarian mechanic named Varga, who owned a garage in a small Rhodesian crossroads settlement of Norton. It was with Varga that he formed the first of his many motor companies in Africa. The two teamed up after Rowland had taken his 540K Mercedes in to be repaired. The car was an eye-opener, a 1937 model of the type used by the leading Nazis.

Its owner was delighted to discover that Varga had worked for Mercedes in Europe before the war and felt it a privilege to repair a 540K. The Hungarian refused to accept any payment for his work, and Rowland suggested on the spot that they should combine; with the exclusive Mercedes franchise, Norton Motors was to become one of the biggest vehicle firms in Central Africa. (Tiny's old car is now in the Mercedes museum in Stuttgart.)

A deal marking a further watershed in his financial progress came soon after, when he bought the rich Sandawana emerald mine near Belingwe for £150,000, and immediately sold a half share at a profit to the Rio Tinto company. Rio Tinto owned some gold mines and prospecting rights around Gatooma. The sale of Sandawana had been negotiated by a young American gem-stones expert, Dan Mayers. He later tried to interest Rowland in the Chivor and Muzo emerald mine in Colombia, South America, and the pair of them flew off to look at it by way of New York and Jamaica. It was the first time that Rowland had ever seen the United States, and Mayers was impressed by the assured way he reacted. In New York they called on Mayers' parents.

However, the venture to South America proved a fiasco. Rowland and Mayers had to climb to nearly 15,000 feet to reach the mine, the last part on donkeys. But at the end of this long journey into the Andes there was no deal: Tiny decided that security was hopeless at the mine – more emeralds were being stolen than handed over to the owners.

The expedition to Colombia and the sale of the Sandawana mine in Rhodesia was to be the start of a long association between Rowland and Mayers. (It was to end in a legal dispute over a £1,000,000 hoard of Zambian amethysts.) The American was astounded by the bold way Tiny was elbowing his way into the Rhodesian mining business, notably as a consultant to Rio Tinto. Relations with Rio Tinto were not all plain sailing, however, since the newcomer was disliked by its blimpish Rhodesian chairman, Brigadier Michael Rowlandson. There were disagreements between Rowland and the brigadier on business practice. But Rio Tinto was to be the launching pad for

Tiny; it also served to introduce him to mining north of the Zambezi, since the company held a minority interest in one of the two groups running the Northern Rhodesian Copperbelt.

Rowland made plans to spread his car company interests into Northern Rhodesia. The Norton Motors garages were thriving, with the opening of a Mercedes showroom in the middle of Salisbury. There was a long struggle to persuade the Salvation Army, which had its headquarters next to the showroom, to sell the freehold and make room for an extension. The local Salvationists were unyielding to the blandishments of Mammon, so in the end Rowland had to fly to London to see the most senior commissioners and generals. He came back victorious. Apocryphal tales were told of how he had actually joined the movement and gone around the London streets with a collecting box to prove his inner godliness.

Progress was equally tiresome in his dealing with the Portuguese authorities on the pipeline plan. As his friend Jardim was to write in later years: 'Mr Rowland, for reasons which I never knew, did not enjoy the esteem of the Portuguese Government, which followed with concern his activities in Mozambique and neighbouring countries.' However, approval came through at last. *East Africa and Rhodesia* carried a small item reporting that 'Mr R. W. Rowland, a Rhodesian businessman' had been granted a concession to build a pipeline to the Rhodesian border by the Portuguese government; he was now asking for permission to extend the pipeline – should it be built – into Rhodesia.

Around this time, Tiny was starting to make overtures to the Anglo-American Corporation, whose offices in Salisbury ran all its Central African operations. He began bombarding its directors with propositions – so many that they seemed to swirl about him like corks around a whirlpool.

Tiny had his eyes on the British South Africa Company (known as 'Chartered', and founded by Cecil Rhodes). This august old firm owned all the mineral royalties in Northern Rhodesia. The local white politicians, including Roy Welensky in his earlier days, had long been agitating about the huge financial pickings enjoyed by Chartered on the basis of dubious treaties signed with illiterate chiefs in the 1890s. Now even the more educated Africans were beginning to mutter. So Tiny put forward a scheme for buying out Chartered for around £24,000,000, to be paid for in shares issued by Anglo-American and its Copperbelt partner, RST. The plan was dismissed as derisory by Chartered. In the event, it would come to sound like a splendid idea within five years, since Chartered finally lost its royalties for only £4,000,000, when Zambia achieved independence.

Another Rowland scheme was put personally to Philip Brownrigg, an Anglo director. This involved building a pipeline 700 miles across Rhodesia to Beira from the Wankie coal mine. Through this Tiny proposed to pump coking coal mixed with water. At Beira, the coal would be dried, then shipped to Japan. The attraction to Rowland was that it would complement the oil pipeline over which he was negotiating. In both instances the operating companies would expect exclusive rights.

Brownrigg recalls that he was sceptical about the technical feasibility; he also thought the pipeline would be far too long and costly for such a commodity. But he promised to look into it – and assumed he had been having a confidential, exploratory talk. However, within a few hours the Salisbury evening paper was carrying a detailed report, with enthusiastic quotes from Rowland. It struck Brownrigg as a tactless way of trying to do business. The animosity between Anglo-American and Tiny was to be long-lasting. But by the end of 1960, the *Wunderkind* of Rhodesian finance no longer needed to dangle his dreams before Anglo-American. He was close to acquiring a solid basis for promoting them himself: this was Lonrho.

It was a company he knew a lot about, because he had negotiated with it on behalf of Rio Tinto about a major gold mine, and he was well known to the directors. The most significant of these was Angus Ogilvy, who was quite a dashing businessman, despite his aristocratic connections. It was Ogilvy who had been delegated by Harley Drayton, a self-made London financier with a large slice of the Lonrho equity, to find a new supremo to revitalize the firm.

For all its Establishment pretensions, the London and Rhodesia Mining and Land Company, established in 1909, had either to take new directions or be absorbed by some more powerful rival. Bids had been made from South Africa. Yet

11

Lonrho possessed desirable assets: vast ranches and plantations in Rhodesia, as well as gold mines. The London end also held a valuable share portfolio. Its pioneering origins were proclaimed by a fine old headquarters building, just off Cecil Square in Salisbury, and built around a courtyard. (It is still lovingly preserved today.)

But Lonrho had been drifting for some years, since the departure of Sir Digby Vere Burnett. He had been the local director of Lonrho for thirty years, a post to which he had risen after his arrival in Africa in 1892 as a young army officer. Sir Digby might not have been an inspired businessman, but he was a character. This distinguished old empire-builder maintained his own light plane, in which he was flown every week between Salisbury and Bulawayo, near which Lonrho had large estates in need of regular inspection. Burnett also kept a mistress in both cities.

With his death in 1958, the most senior figure on the board was the chairman, a Brigadier Thorburn – yet another of those retired brass-hats who proliferated on the Rhodesian business scene. He was a man of doleful inclinations, and his statement to the annual general meeting of Lonrho in April 1961 was strewn with such adjectives as 'disappointing'. He reported net profits for the year of £65,000, and concluded: 'Generally speaking, I look forward with some confidence to growing prosperity for your company, but it will necessarily take time, and one must therefore not expect spectacularly improved results within the immediate future.' This kind of language was more than some City shareholders could do with any longer. Within three months, Lonrho was poised for its metamorphosis. When Tiny was offered the reins, at Ogilvy's instigation, he never hesitated.

Years later, Ogilvy gave his somewhat rueful and rather selective recollections of how he had brought in Tiny to revive Lonrho – 'just a ranching company with a couple of tin-pot mines'. He told his interviewer: 'They said he was a smart farmer, and I hoped he might be able to raise the Lonrho profits to about £300,000 a year. Shareholders have seen profits of £19 million and their five-bob shares valued at £3. Plainly Tiny Rowland was more than an ordinary farmer.' Ogilvy chose to gloss over a friendship between the two of them going back to even before the Lonrho appointment.

The deal was that Tiny would become joint managing director, in harness with Alan Ball, a languid, chain-smoking Old Etonian (who is still on the Lonrho Board with the sinecure post of deputy chairman). For quite a few years Rowland would pretend, in an arch way, to defer to Ball; but given the contrasting natures of the two, there was no doubt from the first moment who was effectively calling the shots.

There had to be, of course, the discreet inquiries into Rowland's background. Lonrho felt it could ignore the jealousies he had provoked among the Salisbury business community, but Ogilvy was deputed to ask Tiny for a brief curriculum vitae. Beyond that, somebody still at hand was perfectly placed to discover if there was anything shady in his past. He was that grandee of the Conservative Party, Sir Joseph Ball – who, like his son Alan, was also a Lonrho director. Sir Joseph had been key man in Britain's intelligence services since the 1914–18 war, when he worked for MI5. During the 1939–45 war Sir Joseph had played two roles: one was in the propaganda division, MI7; the other was as deputy chairman of the secret Home Defence (Security) Executive, set up in 1940 to control enemy aliens in Britain and co-ordinate the hunt for possible spies. A few words to the MI5 headquarters in Curzon Street, and Sir Joseph would have known if anything was recorded in the intelligence files to the detriment of the erstwhile Roland Fuhrhop. The new man must have been 'sound'. (Many years later, in the course of a government inquiry into Lonrho, it was only grudgingly decided that the Official Inspector should have access to Rowland's wartime file. Few others have seen it. Jack Lundin, an investigative reporter put on to digging up Tiny's past at the time of the *Observer*'s takeover, recalls how determined efforts to get at the file came to nothing, despite a generous offer to a private detective.)

Tiny and Angus hit it off together from the start. The aristocratic Scot was the younger of the two by almost ten years, but they looked at life in exactly the same self-assured and opportunistic way. In conversation, they specialized in raillery. Ogilvy had gone into the Scots Guards from Eton, briefly tried his luck in the Merchant Navy, and later took a degree at Trinity College, Oxford. Although just over thirty, he was a director of twenty-nine British companies and other members of his family were prominent in banking; so he was able to bring to Lonrho – and to Rowland in particular – a whole swathe of high-level contacts. At the time of Lonrho's fresh start in 1961, Angus was already courting the Queen's cousin. During his frequent visits to Rhodesia he was regularly sending home letters addressed to 'H.R.H. the Princess Alexandra'.

Ogilvy liked to divert the Princess with highly coloured accounts of his activities. He claimed to have worked as a cattle-rancher in Rhodesia: 'I lived in a shack on porridge – one had to get up to start work at four.' He almost lionized Tiny, with his adventurous style, and thought little about his unorthodox background. The disenchantment would be a long time coming.

In return for the job with a salary of £2,000 a year and 1.5 million Lonrho shares – having a market value then of about £200,000 – Rowland threw in all the assets of his holding company: the flourishing Norton Motors, with the Mercedes franchise, another motor company, stakes in his rather ephemeral gold mines, and the embryonic pipeline company. He kept the Shepton Estate farm for his future father-in-law. On paper, Lonrho was the loser – but for the fact that it was buying Rowland's immense flair.

By the end of 1962, the company was hitting the headlines in Salisbury and London through its success in winning governmental agreement to the Beira oil pipeline project. This was by far the biggest initiative ever taken by Lonrho in its fifty years of existence, and Rowland had ensured its outcome by striking up a close relationship with Frank Owen, the Minister of Transport, in Salisbury. The agreement was signed as Sir Roy Welensky was fighting a vain, last-ditch struggle to save the Central African Federation, of which he was Prime Minister. His 'Build a Nation' campaign, designed to persuade Africans to accept Federation, had received lavish donations from Lonrho.

The Salisbury journal *Property and Finance* called the pipeline deal a 'triumph' for Rowland, who it said had 'emerged from obscurity to assume preponderant executive control of Lonrho a year ago'. But was it in the national interest, the magazine demanded, to thus concede 'the sole right to transport a commodity utterly essential to a landlocked country'? It was the kind of question people would never stop raising from now on about the activities of Lonrho and Rowland. A right-wing MP called Ian Harper, who came from Gatooma, asked in the Rhodesian parliament about Tiny's self-proclaimed friendship with Krishna Menon. Perhaps sinister Indian money was backing Lonrho, hinted Harper.

But there was no halting the pipeline scheme. It made obvious economic sense to bring in oil from Beira, rather than by rail from South Africa: but looking ahead to UDI – which would prove to be only two and a half years away – Ian Smith and his Rhodesian Front colleagues saw it as a lurking threat. A pipeline is easy to sabotage and the Portuguese might one day lack the goodwill or ability to keep the oil flowing.

Rowland responded forcefully. He threatened to bring an action for £5 million damages against the Rhodesian government, for trying to renege on the Federal agreement. The threat worked: within a week, on 3 April 1963, he was able to watch benignly as a bottle of champagne was broken on the front of a bulldozer. The first great project of his life had started.

A fortnight later he was flying to London to attend Angus Ogilvy's marriage to Princess Alexandra on 24 April 1963. It was a grandiose affair preceded by a State Ball at Windsor Castle for 2,000 guests. The Queen had taken a close interest in her cousin's wedding and arranged that the newly-weds should travel in the Glass Coach – traditionally used for royal nuptials – from the ceremony at Westminster Abbey to the reception at St James's Palace. But Angus upset Buckingham Palace by declining an earldom, which the Queen thought proper for the consort of a princess. Thus did Tiny lose the chance of having his board of directors adorned by an august title.

Angus later explained that too obvious an identification with royalty would inhibit his business career. In particular, he was absorbed by the transformation being wrought in Lonrho, and did not hesitate when invited to become one of the three British directors of the Anglo-Portuguese company created to direct the management of the Mozambique pipeline. When the project was formally opened, eighteen months later, he was there, happy that the man he had chosen for Lonrho had turned up trumps.

To mark the occasion, Rowland, Ogilvy and Ball posed for a photograph, with a dozen oil company executives lined up behind them. Ogilvy struck an imperious attitude, stiffly erect, the sleeves of his open-necked shirt rolled up with Guards' precision. Ball was a little more formal; he wore, as usual, an Old Etonian tie. Tiny was just lounging, his hands thrust into the pockets of a tropical jacket, and a silk scarf tied casually at his neck. In his smile was that elusive hint of mockery.

2

Beer for the Miners

When we first met in November 1963, Rowland had been in
charge of Lonrho for little over two years; I was editing an
African newspaper financed by David Astor, the owner of the
Observer. Although neither of us were typical 'white settlers',
the label would have fitted Tiny better than me, because of his
personal stake in thousands of acres of Southern Rhodesia.
Further north where I lived, beyond the Zambezi River, the
whites had a far stronger sense of impermanence. But despite
these political gradations, we both inhabited at that time a
colonial world which is now only a faded memory.

We met at the entrance to the airport in Lusaka, capital of
Zambia – then still colonial Northern Rhodesia. Tiny had just
flown up from Salisbury. We were introduced by his companion, Gerald Percy, and I saw that they were both in a state
of excitement and expectation. Percy was an old friend of mine.
'What's up?' I asked. While Rowland stood back, smiling, Percy
pulled from his briefcase a large folio-sized volume, bound in
red leather. 'It's the report,' he said. 'We're taking it to
Kaunda.'

The report was a daringly entitled 'feasibility study' for
building a railway linking Northern Rhodesia with Tanganyika (now Tanzania) – and ultimately with the Indian
Ocean, 1,200 miles away. It is indicative of Rowland's vaunt-
ing ambition that this was his first development scheme in
black Africa – the Tazara Line, destined to be one of the
greatest aid projects ever tackled by a major world power.
When the Chinese eventually committed themselves to it in

the 1970s, the task took five years and cost around £3 billion at current prices. 'There is no way Lonrho was equipped in 1963 to build the line,' confessed Percy many years later. He added, exaggerating somewhat: 'We were just three men in an office.'

The Lonrho study was based on some cursory helicopter surveys, plus heavy reliance on a detailed report made years earlier by a distinguished British firm of engineering consultants. However, it was well got up, with multi-coloured maps printed on expensive paper. Although Kaunda was already Prime Minister of the prospective Zambia, and within a year of becoming President, he still had a lot to learn about everything, and this style of production was well calculated to impress him.

At that time, with his Mozambique–Rhodesia pipeline already under construction, Rowland was already full of bravado. When he met Kaunda he told him that the railway should be built in the pioneering manner of the Old West. 'We shall keep our surveyors only 100 miles ahead of the track-layers,' he explained. 'Then as soon as the track has settled, the locomotives will start running. That way, you don't waste any time, and the railway makes money as fast as it advances.'

Lonrho did have some slight qualifications for daring to offer its services for a venture that would ultimately test the skills of thousands of Mao Tse-tung's best technicians. It had recently acquired the management contract for the railways, such as they were, in Nyasaland. The lines there were all too fitting for what the white Rhodesians derisively called a 'rural slum', but the Lonrho stake in them did lend a degree of credibility. As he and Percy handed it over, Rowland told Kaunda that the study – which was done without commitment – had cost £150,000.

My curiosity in this venture was provoked early on, at the start of 1963, since we had already been writing in the *Central African Mail* – a pro-nationalist, anti-Welensky tabloid – about Kaunda's ambitions for opening routes to the north-east, away from Rhodesia and South Africa. I had also touched on the subject in the *Observer*, for which I was a regular freelance contributor. (According to an old office memorandum which came to light in the 1980s, I was thought on a par for reliability in those days with the Beirut stringer, who was Kim Philby.)

Rowland was coming north of the Zambezi ever more often, as he spurred Lonrho into a financial gallop. He now had the expert guidance of Percy, who became his right-hand man in April 1963. It was a shrewd appointment, for not only did the Honourable Gerald, nephew of the Duke of Northumberland, have a background – very like Ogilvy's – that opened many doors; he was also politically acceptable to Kaunda and knew all there was to know about the Zambian economy. Percy had been a senior executive in the British South Africa Company's offices in Lusaka, but had felt impelled to leave when he and his then wife Jennifer (now the Marchioness of Bute) stood as candidates for the multiracial Liberal Party in October 1962.

'The first time I saw Tiny was through a keyhole,' recalled Percy when I met him recently. 'I wanted to find out if one of my colleagues had a visitor in his office, so I bent down, looked through the keyhole and saw a handsome, fair-haired man lounging in an armchair.' Rowland was up in Lusaka to discuss the North Charterland concession, which Lonrho controlled. Some months later, when Percy was in search of funding for the short-lived Liberal Party, he called on Tiny in Salisbury: 'He did not give me a penny – he was backing Welensky then.'

It was Percy who first introduced Rowland to Kaunda in late 1962 (to this day, Kaunda remains the most loyal friend Lonrho has in black Africa). 'They talked in my house until the small hours,' says Percy. 'Afterwards, Kaunda told me that Tiny was one of the most impressive men he had ever met.' After that crucial introduction it was inevitable that yet another Old Etonian should join the Lonrho hierarchy. Tiny had said to Percy, when broaching the idea: 'The first question is, shall I work for you or will you work for me?' It was a typical pleasantry, although time would make it barbed.

One of the first tasks Rowland had set for him was to obtain discreetly from Kaunda a letter authorizing Lonrho to make a feasibility study for the railway. At around the same time, I was making my own rather ludicrous contribution to the debate over the line's potential by sending a piece to *The Economist*. My story was based on a bedside chat with Kaunda while he was laid up after straining his leg in a charity football match. Rather frivolously, I had suggested to him that it might be possible to buy up a lot of second-hand rails rather cheaply from Britain, where the future Lord Beeching was then slashing back the British system. This was considered a great brainwave, and I shamelessly decided to write it up as Kaunda's own proposition.

My *Economist* report stirred some interest in Britain, and a few weeks later Julius Nyerere sent a delegation down to Lusaka for formal talks. Next, Kaunda told a Copperbelt rally that a 'British company' was ready to build the 'Uhuru Railway' – a misleading statement in several ways. I soon discovered that the company was Lonrho, and that its commitment had some sticky conditions attached.

Casting about for more background on Rowland, I wrote to Philip Howard, then managing director of Booker Brothers in Nyasaland, where Lonrho was diversifying at hectic speed. Howard's reply, marked 'Personal and Private', reflected the general anxiety about Rowland: as an entrepreneur from the south he was suspected of being up to some political mischief. Howard wrote: 'Everybody here is asking themselves the same sort of questions as you ask me. It would appear that the man in question is a kind of "Cecil Rhodes without Vision". But is it possible for an intelligent person to be so obtuse – only perhaps if he is obsessed with his own sense of power. The aim, which is a fairly open one, is to secure a dominating position in the country's transport system.' He went on: 'They [Lonrho] appear interested in investments of any kind, providing only that they are large enough; for instance, they have told our government that they are prepared to grow sugar, they say they will start a brewery, they talk of planting 2,000 acres of tea in four years, but so far there is no evidence to suggest that they are really prepared to do any pioneering development work.' (Events were to prove him wrong, for although Lonrho soon lost control of the railways, its diverse initiatives have prospered remarkably in a warm accord with Press Holdings, the personal conglomerate set up by President Kamuzu Banda to make himself rich.)

Some personal snippets about Rowland came to me later in 1963 from Freddie van der Merwe, owner of a correspondence college in Salisbury. According to what he had heard from the editor of the magazine *Property and Finance*, which was keeping up its vendetta, Tiny was a German whose real name was

Ferkov. He fed his Siamese cat on smoked salmon and had been cashiered from the Indian army. This sounded like pretty unreliable gossip – as indeed it was, apart from the bit about the cat – but what really damned him in my eyes was that he had lived in Southern Rhodesia for fifteen years. We were all devoutly anti-Rhodesian in the *Mail*, and almost any white from south of the Zambezi River was assumed to be a double-dyed racialist.

What was Rowland's game? He was offering to build 'our' railway for £17 million – thirty times the Lonrho gross profit in 1963. We wondered if the South Africans were behind him. That was the way we were – as was inevitable, given that our funds came from David Astor; he and the *Observer* were relentlessly dedicated to black majority rule throughout Africa (some future history of decolonization will surely give both proper credit for that). The *Mail* was the *Observer*'s echo on the spot, in that very part of the continent where the drive for independence was meeting the harshest resistance. Just as Astor was so influential about Africa because of his pro-American, anti-communist stand on all other foreign policy issues, we were listened to because none of the editorial staff (I was, incidentally, the only white journalist) belonged to any political party. We were just thoroughly partisan.

My approach to Astor in the long search for finance for the *Mail* had been through Anthony Sampson, whom I first met during a trip down to Johannesburg, where he was editing *Drum* magazine. Sampson was by now working on the *Observer*, running the Pendennis column, and responded at first by urging that I should bring out a newsletter (a form of journalism towards which he has always leaned). I rejected this: the political necessity was a mass-circulation paper, lively enough to appeal to urban Africans who could understand a fair amount of English. When the idea was put to Astor, he was delighted.

On a trip to London, during which the launching arrangements were formally defined, I had gone to lunch in the City boardroom of a bank whose chairman was Lord Longford. As the guest of honour, I sat next to Jo Grimond, leader of the Liberal Party, who was to be a 'sponsor' of the *African Mail*. Several more notables were also taking on this role. It was meant to let

21

Welensky and other white politicians in Central Africa know that the paper had influential supporters in London. Furthermore, if I were put in jail – as everyone seemed to expect – Grimond would get up in the Commons and make an issue of it. My abiding memory of the luncheon is how everyone was served with grilled soles and Muscadet by deferential, grey-haired stewards; Longford was a kind of socialist with whom I was not much acquainted. But David Astor was different. In his shy way he was excited at involving himself at last in the continent he had never visited, but about which he campaigned so tirelessly.

The *Mail* made him immensely proud. He sent me a copy of a letter from Jim Rose, then director of the International Press Institute, who had been visiting Lusaka. Rose called the paper a 'good deed in a naughty world', and told how Kaunda had said to him, 'We don't know what we should do without it.' He related how we were training African journalists, and ended: 'I went in an *African Mail* van through one of the African townships, and it was a kind of passport.' David wrote on the letter, 'It makes me feel proud by proxy, so to speak.'

Despite Astor's support, the paper ran on a shoe-string, and had only one unpredictable Linotype. Much of the body-type had to be handset, and we were always struggling to meet our weekly deadlines. On publication nights, several score small boys were recruited to sit in lines and collate the sheets by hand. In the backyard of the printing works an eccentric white man kept a five-foot crocodile in a corrugated iron pen; it hissed irritably when the small boys poked it with sticks.

Astor stuck by us unwaveringly, even though the paper did not turn the financial corner as soon as we expected. Despite having the largest sale of any 'non-white' publication in Central Africa, it could never pull in enough advertising: too many big firms boycotted us because of our political opinions. We also spent more than we should have done in distributing the paper to places that were politically important but impossibly expensive to reach. Some of our selling agents turned out to be crooks; one of the most reliable was a leper.

What buoyed us up was that we knew we were on the winning side. The 'multiracial' Central African Federation of the two Rhodesias and Nyasaland was on its last legs, despite all

Britain's promises to the white minorities when it was created in 1953. The tide of history would not be turned back. In Zambia, when Northern Rhodesia became independent and Kaunda was President, the *Mail* would reap its reward. No advertisers would dare leave us off their schedules. We should have the last laugh. That was how it seemed.

So shortly after Lonrho began moving north – also in anticipation of the change – I had confidently turned down an offer to edit a new daily newspaper being planned on the Copperbelt. The man behind it was Max Heinrich, a gnome-like German who had grown rich by brewing maize beer, which the black miners consumed in huge quantities. Heinrich had been persuaded that he should start a publishing business as a sop to Kaunda. It was an attempt to direct some of the beer profits in buying political goodwill.

Within a year the operation had proved such a financial calamity that Heinrich had lost all will to go on. 'I just want to put a lock on the place,' he said sadly. By the middle of 1964 he was looking round for a buyer for his entire Copperbelt business so that he could retreat to South Africa. The buyer was ready and waiting: Tiny Rowland, who was trying to recover from his wildly over-ambitious début, the railway building project. It had soon become clear that the only way he could finance the line was by obtaining a guarantee that it would carry all of Zambia's copper exports – 600,000 tons a year – at prices fixed by Lonrho. Even Kaunda would not buy that.

Rowland and Heinrich could scarcely have been less alike, both in appearance and manner. But they did have their German origins in common, and used their native language to thrash out terms. Tiny paid Heinrich £800,000, financed from the sale of shares in the London portfolio. For that he had acquired the huge 'Chibuku' brewing concern, the modern Edinburgh Hotel in Kitwe, and other smaller properties. Although this was a total departure from Lonrho's traditional interests, he now had a solid base north of the Zambezi, with a steady cash return. But he found himself burdened with the disastrous Heinrich publishing business.

Rowland also had no experience of newspapers, except on the occasions when he wanted to use them to put up trial balloons about his own schemes. Certainly, he lacked all knowledge of journalism aimed at black readers, and his first instinct was to implement what Heinrich should have done, from any normal financial judgement, and shut the whole fiasco down.

It was not that easy. There were now two papers, a daily having been launched in the wake of the initial Sunday, and both had the sacrosanct name 'Zambia' in their titles. Rowland did not realize the affront he was about to cause to Kaunda's United National Independence Party, which was now within a few months of coming to full power. Without hesitating, he shut the daily, then prepared to close the Sunday as well on finding that the losses were still intolerable.

Kaunda complained sharply. The only other paper on the Copperbelt – the political fulcrum of the country – was the *Northern News*, owned by the South African Argus Group and aimed at the white mining community. It was staffed by white journalists who in the main were coldly opposed to the idea of black rule. By closing down his newly acquired Sunday *Zambia Times*, whatever its shortcomings, Rowland would be guilty of a politically hostile act.

This perplexed him. After all, a few months before, he had discreetly handed Kaunda's party a substantial donation. Yet newspapers have peculiar qualities that transcend all normal commercial calculations: for the first time, with a tawdry Sunday paper in the middle of Africa, he caught a whiff of the troubles he was to have, twenty years on, with an infinitely more prestigious journal in Britain.

For better or worse, he was not deterred. The solution, quite clearly, was to graft this sickly, unsought offshoot on to some healthier stock. He looked around, and his eye at once lighted upon the Astors' *Mail* – now selling 30,000, which was as many as we could print. The paper was politically 'correct' (although our frankness had made us some enemies in the coterie around Kaunda) and as managing editor I was politically acceptable. Indeed, my status was for the moment so high that the 'Republic of China' government in Taiwan had invited me on a quasi-diplomatic visit, in the hope that I might be able to persuade Kaunda to recognize 'their' China rather than the mainland Communists. (The day after I had met Chiang Kai-shek, news came through that Zambia had opted for the mainland.)

By the time Rowland was able to make his approach to the *Mail*, Zambia had just achieved its independence (24 October 1964). He was clearly eager to assert his pro-Kaunda sympathies, since the tensions between Zambia and Rhodesia were sharpening with the emergence of Ian Smith as the Prime Minister in Salisbury. As its full name, the London and Rhodesia Mining and Land Company, made all too plain, Lonrho was bound up with both the outgoing colonial power and the 'white south'. Nor was it ideal for Tiny to be principally identified with a brewery turning out about 2,000,000 gallons of alcoholic gruel a month: after all, Kaunda was a teetotaller and former Scoutmaster, always complaining that drunkenness was the bane of the country.

It was the brewery connection that made me especially uneasy when Tiny and I arranged to meet in a Lusaka hotel to discuss the possibility of a takeover. It was anathema to think of our precious paper, over which we had laboured so hard for four years, being absorbed into the 'Chibuku' empire. Before the meeting I had talked over the prospect with my then wife Barbara, who both wrote a famous advice column for the paper called 'Tell Me, Josephine' and drove a van around the townships late at night to take home the schoolboy collators. She was against such a link-up, knowing from her column what a blight alcoholism had become in the nation. 'Where would the *Mail*'s integrity be then?' she asked. Another opponent was the editor, Kelvin Mlenga, who had grown up in Southern Rhodesia, although his parents belonged to the Bemba, the largest Zambian tribe. He wanted to know where Lonrho stood on the nationalist struggle in Rhodesia. 'Does Rowland support Joshua?' he asked. (In those days we imagined that Rhodesian independence under black rule would only be two or three years away, and that Joshua Nkomo was certain to be the President.)

Yet we had to take the Rowland approach seriously, having just received a sudden shock from London. Astor wanted to sell, and sell fast. It was not that the paper was still losing money and needed an injection of funds every few months from the oddly-named Cushion Trust, the Astor privy purse; after all, it was accepted that the corner was about to be turned, now that independence had been achieved. The immediate stimulus was that the *Observer* had decided that it must follow the *Sunday Times* and launch a colour magazine. (The first issue came out in September 1964.)

Astor had been most reluctant about the 'colour supp.' project. The kind of Sunday paper he understood made no concessions to the 'swinging sixties', to the world of *Blow Up* and trendy photographers such as David Bailey. But now the management had persuaded Astor that he must walk the gaudy path behind Roy Thomson. Away in the middle of Africa we felt the backlash, since every penny might be needed to sustain this costly new venture.

So Astor would sell to Rowland, if he were willing to pay the price. I had been on the telephone to London and the stance to be taken in the exploratory talks was agreed. Slightly over £100,000 had been sunk into the *African Mail* in the course of four years and that was the selling price, in cash – unless a better offer was forthcoming from elsewhere. The paper's goodwill was enormous.

When we sat down to talk, Rowland was businesslike, yet exuded that particular charm I was to feel so powerfully in later years. He was not alone: at his side sat Alan Ball, looking like a failed nightclub owner, and wearing that familiar trademark. (I later realized that he always did so; as a friend once said to novelist Ian Fleming, surprised that he had on his Old Etonian tie, 'What's the matter, Ian? Losing confidence?')

Our meeting was brief and abortive. When the figure of £100,000 in cash was floated, they both looked dismayed. The *Mail* had no assets to strip, just its fame. I adopted a 'take-it-or-leave-it' attitude. We parted quickly, and strolling back to my office near Lusaka's Cairo Road, I felt more relieved than sorry.

As I discovered soon afterwards, it was not merely the amount that disconcerted them, but the knowledge that Astor wanted instant cash. Lonrho was temporarily on a financial tightrope and under pressure from its bankers.

But Tiny had to find some solution to his newspaper troubles and began negotiating with the Argus Group in South Africa to buy the white-oriented *Northern News*. The group had never operated in a black African country and did not relish the prospect, so it was eager to pull back across the Zambezi. Thus Lonrho had the advantage of dealing with a seller it knew was keen to quit, and eventually made a deal that involved handing out a minimum of cash. There was a joke going the rounds at the time, about one of his minions rushing up to Rowland and saying: 'It's good news! The Argus Group are willing to sell us the *Northern News*. But there's one snag – they want £500 in cash.'

A few weeks before Rowland acquired the *Northern News*, I was in London introducing David Astor to another potential buyer of the *Mail* – President Kenneth Kaunda. The meeting was at the Dorchester Hotel in Park Lane, where Kaunda was staying at the start of his first presidential world tour. The Zambian government had earlier declared that it wanted the *Mail* for 'national guidance'. We were glum to think of the paper losing its proud freedom, but several members of Kaunda's Cabinet – particularly one ex-journalist – thought it was too powerful. A minister had said bitterly to me: 'You think you run the country, don't you?'

I consoled myself that if the government took over, it would be a sure way to see that Astor got his money back safely. It would be impolitic for me to stay, but at least we had built up an unparalleled team of Zambian journalists who would never behave like stooges.

The Dorchester meeting brimmed over with mutual congratulations. Kaunda could not heap enough praise upon David Astor for having sustained the paper through thick and thin. 'I don't know what we should have done without it,' he kept repeating. He told David he was a 'true freedom-fighter', his highest accolade, and various ministers sitting around the suite added their own plaudits. My recollection is of Astor sitting there smiling, his head slightly on one side, seeming too overwhelmed to speak.

When the two of us left, we went into a pub around at the back of Park Lane for a reflective drink. Suddenly Astor said: 'Are you sure they will give us the right amount? I don't want any more – just what I have put in.'

The question staggered me. True, we had not been very specific about money: in such a large group that would have been awkward. But the paper had done so much, as Kaunda was the first to admit, that nobody was going to cavil about money. After all, the government was the buyer, and it held the financial purse-strings. 'Oh, don't worry about that,' I told Astor. 'Kaunda won't let us down.' A few weeks earlier, Longmans had published a short and laudatory biography of the Zambian President, laying great stress upon his high moral standards and devout Christianity. I had written it.

The first flicker of doubt came when we were told in Lusaka that the *Mail*'s assets were to be valued, and that an accountant from a commercial firm in the town had been commissioned to carry out the task. It was a formality, of course: procedures must be followed. But there was a little more unease when the man appeared, because like many whites he was angry at suddenly finding himself in a black-run country. He told me that he had never read a copy of the paper and looked sullenly at the Zambian reporters behind their desks as I showed him around the building.

When we learned that his valuation was £40,000 my unease became acute. It still seemed impossible that Zambia could contemplate playing such a trick on David Astor. With the white general manager of the paper, I asked for an interview at the Ministry of Finance. We were greeted by three white officials, two of whom were bitter at having been told that their jobs were soon ending. I could feel their sardonic pleasure at our plight – we had wanted black nationalism, so it just served us right. In desperation I turned to Kaunda. He told me that he was bound by the rules. It was clear, also, that some of his Cabinet who had clashed with the paper in the past were happy enough to see us hurt.

In London, this dire news was taken phlegmatically by David Astor's trust accountants. They had set a deadline for getting out with what they could, and did not think it worth trying to argue the toss. So that was the tawdry way it ended: supporting Kaunda's struggle for independence had cost David Astor almost £70,000.

I packed up at the *Mail* to turn to freelancing and book-writing: I was awaiting the publication of a long history of Zambia, which I had been persuaded to write by Colin Legum, the Commonwealth correspondent of the *Observer*. At that moment, the unexpected happened – I was visited by a small delegation from the more liberal white journalists on the *Northern News* (which was in the process of being renamed the *Times of Zambia*). They told me that Rowland had been hinting at the man he wanted as the new editor: Roger Nicholson, his contact on the *Rhodesia Herald*, the main daily paper in Salisbury. Would I allow my name to be suggested as an alternative? Much flattered, I said I would think about it.

The next day I had a call from Rowland asking me to fly down to Salisbury. When I arrived he was sitting in a somewhat ornate office, its furnishing dominated by a model of a galleon. I was still hesitant about editing a paper linked to his beer empire and talked a lot about the need to keep the editorial content well away from Lonrho's commercial interests. 'You need not think about that,' said Tiny. 'Put it right out of your mind. You must run the paper as you wish. We shall never interfere. Never.'

His personality was irresistible. The salary he named was also tempting, and so were the perks; these would include a Mercedes. By the time I was getting back on the plane in Salisbury, my mind was almost made up.

After one more meeting with Rowland in Lusaka I took on the editorship. There was a week's perfunctory handover by the outgoing editor, a good-natured South African called Stopford Brooke-Norris, who had been a pillar of the local Rotarians. Then I set about turning the paper upside down.

Kaunda had issued a statement praising my appointment. I wrote thanking him (1 June 1965), promised to do my best, then said: 'I hope that you will not think it out of place if I now turn to a matter of very deep concern to me.' The remaining ten paragraphs were an appeal for a reappraisal of the *Mail* takeover terms:

> It is tragic because I know that David Astor is bitterly wounded at the way things have gone since that happy meeting at the Dorchester Hotel. . .
> Under the terms, David Astor's existing company must pay off the creditors after collecting outstanding debts. One of the biggest debtors is the United National Independence Party itself, with approximately £1,700 owing. This

debt dates back to the hard days of 1962 when we did UNIP's printing in the face of fierce condemnation from many of our normal customers. . . We have asked UNIP for payment many times since 1962, naturally enough, but not pressing hard because we knew the position. Now the national secretary of the party has informed our solicitors that UNIP does not propose paying the £1,700.

It was I who persuaded David Astor to embark on this venture. . . The role played by the *Mail* deserves more than a ruthless study of balance sheets.

But nothing happened. After twenty years I still cannot re-read the correspondence without wincing.

3

Larks in the Côte d'Ivoire

Just as I had first encountered Tiny Rowland, future owner of
the *Observer*, at an African airport, so it was with Donald
Trelford, the future editor. We were both strolling out to board a
plane in Addis Ababa, at the start of January 1966. We hit it off
at once, which was as well since we were going to be together for
several weeks. Donald proved good company, quick and knowing, with a humour that was rather conspiratorial, making you
feel that you were sharing in his cache of light-hearted secrets.

We were up in Addis on the way to Abidjan, capital of the
Ivory Coast. The government of President Felix Houphouet-
Boigny, working through a Lebanese public relations man, was
funding the trip. It was a rare attempt to explain francophone
West Africa to the English-speaking countries that had lately
become independent several thousand miles away to the south-
east. The Ivory Coast was in those days the unparalleled economic leader in black Africa, judged from a capitalist
standpoint. But more militant states regarded it as too much
under the thumb of France, and too soft on South Africa.

So to put over its case, the Ivory Coast had invited us, the
white editors of the two main newspapers in Zambia and Malawi. Also making the trip was a rather nervous Tanzanian from
the government-controlled daily in Dar es Salaam. We had all
made our separate ways to Addis Ababa and we were flying
westward across the width of Africa.

Trelford and I lacked any real dedication about the visit. We
did not think it mattered much to our readership, down beside
the Zambezi, what the Ivoirians got up to. In any case, there had

31

been lately far more serious events in Central Africa than anything visible on the deceptively calm horizons of West Africa. Only two months earlier, Ian Smith had unilaterally declared that Rhodesia was independent, thus turning himself into a rebel in British eyes. He had promised his 200,000 white settlers that there would be no black rule 'for a thousand years'.

I had seriously wondered whether it was wise to go on the Ivory Coast trip, because Zambia was in acute economic convulsions because of UDI: with the Rhodesian stranglehold on our communications, Zambia could not get its copper exports out to the world markets and was running short of vital imports – petrol in particular. My own daily paper was being printed on some old green newsprint unearthed from the back of the warehouse and originally bought for a stillborn sports edition. (When we got back to white, some readers complained that the green was better for smoking.) Kenneth Kaunda was still demanding that Britain should use force against Ian Smith, and in return for this hostile stance the Rhodesian Prime Minister was threatening to throttle Zambia, even to the extent of cutting off its electricity supplies from the Kariba Dam. In the *Times of Zambia* we also called for Harold Wilson to use force – a vain hope.

Trelford was less worried about what he was leaving behind. He had been editing the bi-weekly *Malawi Times* for the past three years and knew that President Kamuzu Banda had no intention of involving himself in the squabbles over UDI. On the contrary, Malawi had kept on good terms with Rhodesia, and Banda had always opposed the idea of trying to bring down Smith by use of a Pan-African army. Autocratic, cantankerous and conservative, Banda ridiculed such talk. 'Africans cannot fight Rhodesia,' he said. 'Remember what a few dozen white mercenaries could do in the Congo.' That was wounding to black pride, coming from a black man.

But then, Banda was renowned for speaking his mind. Shortly after Trelford arrived in Malawi the President had made headlines at a dinner thrown for Lonrho after the company had committed itself to financing a big sugar scheme in Malawi. He said: 'Once I was sure Lonrho didn't want to turn the country into a sugar republic or a banana republic, like they have in South America and those places, then I welcomed them.' Rowland had responded wholeheartedly to what was, by Banda's standards, a fulsome seal of approval. Lonrho quickly diversified in Malawi into garages, construction and brewing.

Indeed, by the time of my meeting with Trelford the frontiers of Lonrho had been pushed well beyond Malawi and Zambia from its base in Rhodesia. Rowland was by now up to the Equator, buying garage chains, farms and tanneries in Kenya, Tanzania and Uganda. (He was also extending in the opposite direction, into South Africa, although there was less publicity about that.)

To a couple of journalists in Africa Rowland was already newsworthy because he seized any chance to buy up a local newspaper during his blitzkrieg on a particular country. Was he so naïve that he did not realize the hazards of owning such properties in newly independent states? Or did he take the risk knowingly, because of the influence newspapers could give him? I had now dismissed the popular theory that Lonrho had sinister aims, and that Rowland was an agent of the Rhodesian and South African intelligence: in any event, he was shrewd enough to give the press in Malawi a wide berth.

The *Malawi Times* was owned by the Thomson group of London, and Trelford had come out to run it from a paper in Sheffield. He worked to one overriding rule: Survive. This meant putting Banda's photograph on the front page of every issue, and on most other pages to boot, quoting every speech Banda made in full, and never allowing any breath of criticism to waft across the pages. There were no heady editorials calling for force to end UDI. It did not make for exciting journalism, but Donald was young to be an editor, and he had wanted to enjoy life in Africa.

He was, after all, contending with a tyrant who had threatened to 'detain 10,000, 100,000 – any number of people' if his authority was challenged. Trelford was also following the mode for more complaisant journalism in Africa: a white editor in Uganda, upon going on three weeks' holiday, had given his deputy a sheaf of all-purpose leaders, and told him to print one a day until his return, whatever else happened.

Trelford felt understandably remote in his Malawian

backwater from his proprietor in London. He told me how, just before leaving, he had been called to a brief interview with Roy (later Lord) Thomson. The Canadian had stared at him through his pebble glasses, then said: 'Boy, you make a dollar for me, and I'll make a dollar for you.' That was the sum total of the advice from Roy. Neither of us had difficult owners in those days – the black politicians were our preoccupation. Trelford related how one of Banda's rivals threatened to send along a band of thugs to smash up the paper's machinery unless he was given more space. Donald had finessed his way out of that, and he made no bones about leaning towards the little doctor in his dark glasses and Homburg hat.

But Trelford also saw the humour of it all. One of his anecdotes (which he has often recounted since) was about the picture caption in a party news-sheet, under a photograph of Banda casting a vote in a general election. The symbol of the ruling Malawi Congress party was – and still is – a cock crowing at the sunrise. The caption read: 'Dr Banda votes for his own cock.' That was the kind of frivolity he only aired when well away from the editorial chair.

On the plane flying across to Ghana, the eastern neighbour of the Ivory Coast, there was plenty of time to gossip. I learned that Donald felt he had been long enough running his little paper – an understandable attitude – and wanted to get back to a job in Britain.

A few weeks earlier, I had been on a quick trip to London, recruiting sub-editors, so was able to provide all the latest gossip from Fleet Street. There had been a big upheaval at the top of my old paper, the *Daily Mail*, but Donald was more keen to hear what I could tell him about the *Observer*. By this time Anthony Sampson had taken over the editorship of the colour magazine, and had done a great deal to soothe the remorse that haunted me over Kaunda's ungrateful treatment of David Astor during the sale of the *African Mail*. As usual, the *Observer* was losing money, but there was a complacent illusion that 'David could solve it by selling off a bit more of Manhattan'.

During my visit I had been on a *Panorama* programme about Rhodesia, and had provoked something of a row by describing the whites in Rhodesia as 'third-rate'; this had blocked the lines into the BBC for a while. Also on the programme had been Jeremy Thorpe, then leader of the Liberal Party, and I told Trelford of his exchange with Robin Day in the hospitality room. Thorpe said to the room at large that only a year before he had gone down into the underground power station of the Kariba Dam. 'That's the nearest you'll ever get to power,' retorted Day jovially. 'Let me know next time you're looking for a good seat,' said a slightly needled Thorpe, aware of Day's half-hearted ambitions at that time to be a Liberal MP.

By the time we were touching down in Accra I had discovered a lot about Trelford. (He confessed to being crazy about cricket and having played a lot of it at Cambridge, but never mentioned that he had also taken a double first in English.) In the RAF, doing national service, he had learnt to fly, and had put this ability to use in Malawi: he had piloted a light plane around the country to study his paper's distribution problems. 'Once I had to land on the main road through a village,' he said breezily. 'People ran in all directions.'

We had to stay a night in Ghana because our plane was late and we missed the connection. I cannot recall much except that Accra, the capital, struck us as tense. It was in the last few weeks of Kwame Nkrumah's rule, and we received a tremendous amount of harassment from immigration officials as we were leaving. It also sticks in my mind that an airlines girl, leaning over a desk in a tight white dress, had her bottom pinched by a customs man in full view of scores of passengers. That would never have happened down in Central Africa, where people are far more inhibited.

Our surprise at how different West Africa was – since neither of us had been there before – became even sharper when we were given a grandiose welcome to Abidjan and driven through the gleaming city to an hotel beside the lagoon. The stylish boutiques, the *pâtisseries*, pavement cafés, French families stepping out of their Citroëns – it hardly seemed like Africa at all. Even the blacks behaved like Frenchmen, as they sat beside the hotel swimming pool drinking Dubonnet-soda and reading *Le Monde* or *Paris Match*.

Those ten days we spent in the Ivory Coast were a whirl. Interviews had been arranged in ministry after ministry, where we tried manfully to ask all the right questions about economic development, agriculture and health. Always in the background a French adviser was ready to help out with any tricky details. President Felix Houphouet-Boigny, most powerful of all the francophone leaders, did not deign to see us. We could not blame him for that, because from our assessment of the only Ivoirian newspaper, an anodyne little sheet called *Fraternité Matin*, the Press counted for even less in the Ivory Coast than it did in Malawi.

But we were received by Philippe Yace, President of the National Assembly, in his vast office walled with light wood panelling. As we talked, a disguised door in the panelling quietly opened and a black factotum appeared in wing collar and tail coat. He bore a silver tray with glasses of iced champagne.

Trelford and I exchanged glances, and as we drank asked Yace about African Socialism (a hazy concept much more in vogue then than it is today). He smiled, fingered his gold cuff links. 'We are not sure what it means,' he said. 'Of course, I was a communist once, when I was a student in Paris. We all go through that stage. What now?' He shrugged and replaced his glass on the tray. The exchange reminded us of one of Houphouet-Boigny's best known aphorisms, that if you wanted your students to become communists you sent them to France, and if you preferred them to be capitalists, sent them to Russia.

From Abidjan we were flown up country, to be driven with practised skill around show farms growing coffee and cocoa and pineapples. Near Yamoussoukro – a highly privileged town, being Houphouet-Boigny's birthplace – Donald and I spent the evening at a big national service training camp for girls. It was run entirely by Israelis, and the commandant was a woman colonel who had served in the wartime British army before going out to fight in Palestine. Her name I forget, but remember how we were stunned by her charm as she leaned back behind her desk, smiled a little and studied us coolly as we put our questions. Later we went dancing at the camp recreation hall, whose sides were open to let in the breeze. Our partners were several buxom majors and captains, but none was as handsome as the commandant.

It is quite agreeable to remember, after all these years, that both of us (and to a more modest extent, our Tanzanian companion) got up to some mischief before we left Abidjan. At night we made sorties across to the suburb of Treichville, and patronized a frisky nightclub called *La Boule Noire*. In the course of these excursions we carried out some sociological research, and discovered that all the tarts in Treichville came from adjoining countries – Liberia, Ghana and Guinea. They had left home because there was more money to be earned in the Ivory Coast, with its markedly higher per capita income.

One evening at around midnight Trelford and I were almost arrested by a posse of Ivoirian police in a jeep. For some reason we had a consuming need to buy a crate of beer and started banging on the door of what, we fancied, was the local equivalent of an off-licence. It turned out to be a brothel which seemed to have knocked off business pretty early. While we made our excuses to the police for creating a fracas, the girls leaned out of the windows and shouted furiously.

We left Abidjan with some regret, and flew along the coast to Nigeria; our Tanzanian colleague found his way home again through Addis Ababa. For both of us Nigeria was another new experience, and the capital, Lagos, was much more relaxed than it is nowadays. Foreign oil companies had scarcely begun to reveal the extent of the wealth hidden around the Niger River delta, so the people were far less bombastic than they became a decade later.

A few days before Trelford and I flew in, Harold Wilson flew out. The British Prime Minister had been at a two-day Commonwealth conference on what should be done to end the Rhodesian rebellion. Wilson had been cagey about attending, because Britain was then maintaining that Rhodesia was a domestic problem concerning an errant slice of colonial territory. But Nigeria was very important for British trade, and Sir Abubakar Tafewa Balewa, the Prime Minister, was regarded as the most stable and moderate of all English-speaking leaders in Africa; during a recent trip to London it had been much remarked that he spoke just like an upper-class Englishman – proof enough that he thoroughly deserved his knighthood. So Balewa had to be treated with respect. To reassure the nineteen

Commonwealth nations represented at the conference on Rhodesia, Wilson had smoothly told them that sanctions 'might well bring the rebellion to an end within a matter of weeks rather than months'.

For the two of us it was to be a rebellion within a matter of hours rather than days that mattered more. Yet everything seemed placid enough as we unpacked our bags in the residence of the Zambian High Commissioner to Nigeria, the Reverend Isaac Mumpanshya. An old friend of mine, he had warmly invited us to stay when I had managed to telephone him from Abidjan (by way of Paris and London). He admitted that he felt himself far from home in Lagos, and welcomed us as though we were all long-lost brothers in a land of Martians.

Staying with a diplomat who was also a preacher put paid to our high jinks. I decided to settle down to write a feature piece for the *Observer*. In response to a telex from the Ivory Coast, the paper had said it wanted something from me on a series of military coups that had lately taken place in several French-speaking countries – Upper Volta, Dahomey and the Central African Republic. I had been mugging up about them.

By the time we went to bed I had more or less done the article. Trelford and I were sharing a room and were glad to see that it had an air conditioner, for the weather was hot and humid. But the air conditioner made a lot of noise and we had a minor disagreement about whether we could get to sleep without its being on. In the middle of the night I awoke: the air conditioner was off and the lights were not working – and in those days in Africa power failures were far rarer than they have latterly become; after a few moments of puzzlement I went back to sleep.

We had breakfast with the reverend, then he drove off to his office and I returned to my typewriter. My sententious ending said: 'The sad reality is that there never can be stability in countries such as Upper Volta and the Central African Republic without ruthless dictatorship. They are economically hopeless and survive only through massive injections of aid from France. This leads to a kind of "past-caring" irresponsibility among the leaders.' Re-reading that after eighteen years I am struck by how long the general ruin of today had been foreshadowed in Africa.

Donald offered to come along with me to the Lagos telex office so that I could send off my story, and we strolled out into Keffi Street. It is a pleasant enough thoroughfare, relatively speaking, and led then – as now – to the main army barracks in the capital. Across the road was a bus station; as ever, people were fighting to get aboard. We hailed a taxi and gave the driver his orders. As we bumped along he was laughing and singing in a most jocular fashion.

As we passed the barracks there was a lot of activity. 'They seem to be giving the tanks an airing,' said Trelford. 'Perhaps that's what they do here every morning.' We were not much interested in Nigeria, and our minds were now centred on getting back to our papers, for if Rhodesia was really going to collapse in 'weeks rather than months', we needed to be on the spot. Nigeria was just a convenient halt en route to the Congo, then on to Zambia.

But at the telex office there were more troops standing around and all were heavily armed. Nobody prevented us from going into the building, and I handed my sheets of copy over the counter.

'Sir, we are not transmitting,' said the clerk.

'Not transmitting?' I echoed in astonishment.

'No, sir,' he said politely.

'Well,' I said, 'just send it when you are.'

As Donald and I walked across the forecourt to our taxi we scratched our heads. 'This is the most bloody hopeless country I've ever been in,' I said. On the way back to Keffi Street we discussed how soon we could get visas from the Congolese embassy and catch a plane for Leopoldville. Lagos had no attractions for us; there were not even any other foreign journalists in the place to talk to, except for a couple of agency men, because everyone else had pulled out after the Commonwealth meeting.

These grumbling thoughts were swept aside just as we were paying off the taxi. The High Commissioner raced up in his Mercedes, his eyes wide in his glistening face. 'Have you heard?' he cried. 'There's been a coup!'

The news tumbled out. Sir Abubakar, the Nigerian Federal Prime Minister had been kidnapped and might be murdered.

There were reports that Chief Akintola, Premier of the Western Region was dead, and that junior officers had captured the palace of Sir Ahmadu Bello, Premier of the Northern Region. For the moment nobody knew who was in charge around the country.

We looked at one another, astounded at having blundered into such a tremendous story – the first military coup in a black Commonwealth country, and what was more, by far the most populous state in sub-Saharan Africa. There was also a ludicrous side, seeing that I had just been trying to file a piece about other coups in the midst of a coup I did not know was taking place. No wonder the telex clerk said they were not transmitting; clearly, all links with the outside world had been cut.

Our most immediate handicap was ignorance. It was not merely that we had to find out who was, literally, calling the shots. Beyond that, neither Trelford nor I had more than the most rudimentary grasp of Nigerian politics. For all the rhetoric about Pan-Africanism, the West African countries had always been as remote to us and our readers as India, for example. Perhaps rather more remote because, whereas there were plenty of Indians trading in our part of the continent, a West African was a rare bird.

The obvious place to start our investigations was the British High Commission, so we said a hurried *au revoir* for the day to our host and jumped into another taxi. As one was to notice during similar occasions subsequently, in the face of untoward events the British always alternate between tight-lipped excitement and a rather transparent pretence that nothing much is going on.

The former was the mood as we turned up. The High Commissioner, Sir Robert Cumming-Bruce, was striding up and down the corridor like a general without an army. Several girl secretaries were twisting their pearls and trying to be jolly.

We found our way to the Information Attaché, whose name was Condon. His eyes were blazing. 'We're going to get them!' he told us. He objected to our questioning, our efforts to discover who 'they' were. It was too cataclysmic a moment to waste time educating such ignoramuses.

'The bloody Ibos!' he shouted at last. It was my first introduction to the bias of the British at that period in Nigeria – they had an instinctive rapport with the Muslim northerners, who they saw as 'nature's gentlemen'. What was more, the northerners liked horses; for middle-class Englishmen whose daughters went cubbing in the Home Counties this was absolute proof of their decency. The bloody Ibos, who dominated the eastern part of the country, hardly knew one end of a horse from the other and were mostly Catholics to boot, thanks to all the Irish priests who infested Iboland. (That attitude, as broadly interpreted, was to have profound effects a few years later during the Biafran war.)

Our briefing by Condon had concluded with our efforts to be knowledgeable about Chief Awolowo, the Yoruba leader. Was he not in jail in Calabar for having spread dissension after Nigeria's recent elections? What would now happen to him? 'He'll be shot,' said Condon briskly.

We fled the High Commission and bustled around Lagos, through streets where people were dancing ecstatically at the overthrow of so corrupt a bunch of politicians. The best-informed man in town was an Associated Press staffer, conveniently living just across the road from Mumpanshya's residence. Sir Abubakar was dead, found buried in a shallow grave; Sir Ahmadu Bello was dead, shot against the wall of his harem. Chief Akintola we already knew about. It seemed that the coup had been started by junior officers, mainly Ibos (Condon had that right), but that more senior men were now in control and preventing a general bloodbath.

The young officers had made their move in the middle of the night. At the moment when I was wondering about the air conditioning, a brigadier was being shot in his hotel room along the road.

Donald and I soon realized that our imperative need was to get out of the country. The best story in the world is no story at all if you cannot deliver it. The lines were still cut and it was clear from the BBC World Service bulletins we heard that in London there was only the slimmest idea of what was happening; the bulletins were based on monitoring of the cryptic statements over Lagos radio. Getting out was a conundrum: the land borders were sealed and no international flights permitted. It was also impossible to travel as far as Lagos airport because the army had established roadblocks and the soldiers were giving a rough time to any would-be travellers.

At that moment our host, with his dog collar and diplomatic status, really proved his worth. On the Sunday morning, 16 January, he put his Zambian flag on the bonnet of his Mercedes and declared himself ready to drive us to the airport. If there was no plane to Leopoldville, as we hoped for, there might be one heading elsewhere; it was a matter of chancing our luck.

When we reached the first roadblock there was a mêlée of parked cars and lorries. Their occupants had been ordered out and were sitting in the hot sun under guard. A soldier pushed his gun and his head through the open window of our Mercedes, studied the dignified black clergyman at the wheel and the two expressionless whites, then said 'You go on.' We sailed through every roadblock in this fashion, right up to the airport entrance.

Isaac was pleased with his feat, and we shook his hand, slapped him on the back and said farewell. I have never met him again, but learned that when he finally returned to Zambia he became a member of the National Assembly, asked too many awkward questions and was forced into obscurity.

We found the airport surrounded by police trucks. Curiously, a British naval officer in tropical gear, and with a revolver on his hip, stood impassively by the main entrance. There were few intending passengers, which was hardly surprising, and nobody knew whether a plane was going to Leopoldville or anywhere. But we did have tickets, and visas obtained by bribery at the Congolese embassy from a girl with a dirty bandage around one of her legs.

It was cooler out on the old airport's verandah and we stood there waiting for signs of action. All at once a helicopter came gently down in front of us, and out stepped Archbishop Makarios of Cyprus in full Greek Orthodox regalia. He was greeted by Major-General Johnnie Ironsi, the new Sandhurst-trained ruler (who was fated to be assassinated within six months). I pulled my camera out of my shoulder bag, but the scene had been so unexpected and startling, when the film was developed it emerged that I had managed to double-expose it. The archbishop, we discovered, had been attending the Commonwealth gathering in Lagos and had decided to make an exploratory tour afterwards. He was in Enugu, in the Eastern Region, when the coup happened, and had to be told that he could not fly to meet his next intended host, the Sardauna of Sokoto, on account of his having been murdered.

Not long after Makarios and Ironsi had been escorted away in a claque of black junior officers, activity could be seen around a Fokker Friendship of Nigerian Airways on the far side of the parking apron. It was leaving soon – for Leopoldville; this was the first plane out, and we were going to be on it.

As Donald and I climbed aboard we weighed up the other passengers. It was not a heavy task since there were only four of them: two couriers, one British and one American, a Japanese and a drunken African who turned out to be a Liberian diplomat. We headed first for Douala in the Cameroons, where the couriers got out, then took off again in a storm for the Congo. It was very bumpy.

Battling through the officialdom at Leopoldville (now Kinshasa) was a tiresome affair because of the tell-tale occupations listed in our passports. When at last we arrived at the taxi rank, the Japanese was being interrogated by a knot of local journalists about what was happening in Lagos when he left. But the Japanese could not, it seemed, speak a word of any known language.

We strolled closer; then I recognized David Paskov. He had worked for me in Lusaka in the *African Mail* days, having been recruited by Anthony Sampson when there were false rumours that Sir Roy Welensky was about to have me arrested. After a couple of years Paskov had left and had since been roaming around the Congo with sundry mercenaries and girlfriends. He was writing for the *Daily Telegraph*, most of whose readers would have been scandalized by such a devil-may-care character.

'Hello, David,' I said, banging him on the back with my camera. He jumped around in astonishment, acknowledged my introduction of Donald Trelford, then dragged us away to his car before any local reporters had grasped what had happened. We were hot properties and he wanted us to himself.

At the telex office we filed and filed, with Paskov handing out bribes to the operators. They kept complaining that they were too tired, that the machines had broken down, since they knew they had a lot of leverage on an important story. In the event, we all did well out of it, although Trelford and I had the advantage of eyewitness accounts. The next day I had my picture on the front page of the *Daily Mail*, as the 'Correspondent On The Spot'.

That evening in Leopoldville we did a lot of reminiscing. I knew the place from visits a few years earlier, when the United Nations was futilely trying to see fair play. I hated the Congo – which President Mobutu has since renamed Zaire in the vain hope of making it less malodorous. As we used to say: 'The Congolese and the Belgians, they deserved one another.' Conrad had it right enough.

My most absurd memory of those earlier days was when the British embassy in 'Leo' was attacked and sacked, for some reason, by the rampaging *citoyens*. An excited servant in the hotel rushed up with the news to the room I was sharing with a man from the *Daily Express*. Through poor French on all sides, we understood him to say that they were 'throwing the typists out of the windows of the embassy'. We tore off to see this remarkable sight, but found to our dismay that the crowd had merely thrown the typewriters out of the windows. 'Fucking shame,' said the man from the *Express* aggrievedly.

Trelford and I went along to the airport for the next stage of our journey, and found ourselves assembled with a vast crowd facing a kind of sub-standard Dakota. Armed police held us back behind a barricade until the flight was called, then it was every man and woman for themselves. Somehow we got on and sat in canvas seats; the plane had no inner 'skin' since it normally carried freight, and stank a lot. Trelford and I were the only two whites apart from the pilot and co-pilot, who looked like a couple of left-overs from 'Mad Mike' Hoare's brigade.

To gain altitude the pilot had to keep building up revs., so that we climbed and fell as though going up stairs. But we made it in the end to Elisabethville, where a band played and marched up and down with absurdly exaggerated steps as we disembarked. There had been a government minister and a football team among the passengers; we could not decide who was receiving the honours.

Elisabethville was almost home. In the old days when I was editing magazines for one of the Copperbelt mining companies it was the place to go for a weekend, to eat frogs' legs and drink wine. Now it was a down-at-heel travesty of its old self. We put up for the night at the Leopold Deux Hotel, still scarred by the many battles that had raged around it, and its windows held together with tape.

It was not much of a night. In the dark I went over to the french windows of my bedroom to find out why I could hear the rain so loudly, and groping blindly forward nearly plunged out and over the balcony. There was no glass. A bit later I had an altercation with a Congolese who had left his comb and toothbrush in the room, together with a meaningful note to somebody called 'Marie B'. Finally he went off, and I lay in the darkness waiting for Marie B to arrive, but she never did.

The next morning Trelford and I hired a car and drove across the border into Zambia. He came to visit my office in Ndola. All our luggage had been offloaded back in Leopoldville because of weight problems; this rather reduced our elation at getting home (although, miraculously, it turned up several weeks later). Still, Donald and I had been through some experiences together. We parted with the warmest feelings.

Back at the *Times of Zambia*, there was the usual catching up to do, but circulation was soaring – fears about the confrontation with Rhodesia meant that we were selling as many copies as we could print. Tiny Rowland turned up on one of his sudden journeys – in those days he often travelled alone – and was all congratulations; shortly before my departure for the Ivory Coast he had made me the editor-in-chief of both the daily and the Sunday paper. I was also overseeing a business magazine bought from the old Astor group in Zambia.

By this time Rowland and I had struck up a relaxed friendship. It did not go very deep – which suited me, because I felt instinctively that relations between an editor and a proprietor should never be too close. But he remained a mystery man to my staff, who now and then demanded that I should invite him into the office for a chat. One of the few journalists who had any contact with him was Robert Cox, an economist who edited the business journal. He had sat next to Tiny on a plane flying to Nairobi. As they landed, Cox had peeped over Rowland's shoulder while he filled in an entry form, and later reported that in 'Country of Birth' he had written 'India' – which confirmed one rumour.

One morning when I arrived at the office a sweeper told me that a white man had come in very early, had stood around for a while, then hurried away without talking to anyone. It had been Tiny, making his only visit to the *Times of Zambia* during my editorship.

Even so, there were those in the Zambian political hierarchy who harboured doubts about the Lonrho role in editorial policy. One relentless critic was Mainza Chona, then secretary-general of Kaunda's United National Independence Party. He repeatedly claimed that the daily paper was engaged in a plot, directed from outside the country, to destroy stability and bring down the government. This was so enraging and harmful that I began legal proceedings, and was given £3,000 from state funds as damages. When a letter from a suspicious reader accused us of obeying Lonrho's orders about what should be published I had it prominently printed and added a footnote: 'We neither know nor care what Lonrho thinks on any subject.'

The next time Rowland appeared in Zambia he could hardly wait to make fun of this gesture. 'I don't know what to think,' he kept saying. 'You must tell me. Of course, you're very busy. When you can spare the time.' It was that particular form of feline humour at which he was so adept; the claws were always there.

In fact, his involvement with the editorial content of the papers was negligible. There were petty quarrels with the managers of some Lonrho subsidiaries, but Rowland kept his distance. I recall one story which upset the breweries, when a rumour slipped into print that a tanker-load of Lonrho beer had spilt after an accident, and had burnt a hole in the road.

The only time when Rowland did try to smooth over trouble was after we savaged the Standard Bank – with which Lonrho had an all-too-solid overdraft. The clash began when we discovered that the bank was giving basic training for its young Zambian trainees at a local centre, whereas young white trainees were still being sent down to Salisbury. (This was many months after Smith had proclaimed UDI in Rhodesia.) We proceeded to lambast this as a bad case of racial segregation, and to imply that the all-black course was second-rate.

The bank was stunned and embarrassed. It hurriedly decided to appoint a public relations man to restore its image in Zambia – and clumsily it selected a white Rhodesian who had earlier worked for the Federal information services. Once again we went into the attack, arguing that a Zambian could do the job better. The appointment was cancelled.

Three weeks later, Rowland invited me to a lunch at the Ndola Club. When I turned up, his entire entourage was there; I was seated next to Angus Ogilvy, who in his usual manner launched into a string of piquant anecdotes. Tiny was at the far end of the table. Across from me was a red-faced fellow, rather solemn, whom I took to be a Lonrho accountant. Nobody bothered to introduce us and he was tediously stiff when I tried to exchange pleasantries. Not until the end of the meal, as we were starting to get up, did Rowland hurry down to tell me that this was Mr Budge, the deeply wounded general manager of the Standard Bank of Zambia. Too late – the chance had been lost. As an exercise in hatchet-burying, it was a fiasco.

An occasion when Rowland did show some interest in the *Times of Zambia*'s handling of news was when he hoped to build a 1,200-mile oil pipeline to Dar es Salaam. The rivals were Japanese and Italian, but Lonrho's prospects looked good – it had completed the Mozambique pipeline only two years earlier (although this was no longer functioning because of international sanctions against Rhodesia). As the Zambian government moved towards making its choice, Rowland twice called me to press the advantages of Lonrho, as he saw them. He was apologetic about talking to me, and kept repeating, 'Of course, I know you'll say what you think is right.' But the contract clearly mattered tremendously to him – the pipeline would be a permanent testimony to Lonrho's economic bonds with Zambia.

If anything, Tiny's intervention made us lean away from Lonrho. We tended in our coverage to favour the Japanese. In the end, the Italians won, and in retrospect it was plain enough that Lonrho had lost because it wanted to own the pipeline, and charge a royalty, whereas the Italians merely loaned the £16 million needed for financing. Tiny had been too insensitive. Whatever the paper might have said would have made no difference to the outcome. Like the stillborn railway scheme, the lost pipeline contract was consigned to everlasting silence; Rowland gave the impression that he had plenty more ideas where those had come from.

One evening, when we were having dinner together, he was in a spirited mood. 'What can I buy?' he asked. 'Do you know anything for sale?'

'Good heavens,' I protested, 'you've bought too much up here. That's why people are so suspicious of Lonrho. You ought to try selling something.' He only laughed.

Just after he had left, I had to deal with a case of witchcraft in the *Times of Zambia* telex office. The efficient black manager suddenly grew haggard and withdrawn. On asking around among the Zambian reporters I uncovered the truth. The assistant telex manager wanted the job and had let it be known that he had obtained some witchcraft *muti* (medicine).

I had a notice put up: 'Witchcraft Must Cease in This Telex Room Immediately. By Order.' A few days later I went to see my doctor – called Hetherington, a relation to the then editor of the London *Guardian*. 'I've had one of your chaps in here,' he said. 'If I didn't know better, I'd say he's bewitched.' When I got back to the office I called in the assistant manager. 'Listen,' I said, 'I'm telling you, if the manager dies, you'll never get his job. I'll see to that. I'll send you to the far end of the country.' He looked into my face with eyes like stones.

A week later the telex manager died, so I had the assistant transferred at once to Livingstone, 500 miles to the south. (Several years later, after I had left the paper, I was back in Zambia and called in at the telex room. There he was, in charge, all affability.)

When Tiny returned I told him of this strange office drama. Another item of news was that somebody had indeed approached me with the offer of a company Lonrho might like to buy. But they refused to disclose what sort of company it was.

'Just tell Mr Rowland, and give him this telephone number,' said the caller. So when I met him I was triumphant. 'Here's something to buy,' I said. 'Here's the telephone number. They wouldn't give me the details.' He was all enthusiasm, if slightly mystified.

The next day he greeted me with a mocking smile. 'Of course, I don't mind if you have a joke at my expense now and then,' he remarked, and explained that the 'company' consisted of two men with a vague scheme of making lavatory paper on the Copperbelt. It was my last effort to provide business for him.

Shortly after this farce, which made me the butt of jokes all around Lonrho, I had a letter from John Thompson, then news editor of the *Observer*. The post of assistant news editor was vacant, and somebody in Malawi named Trelford had applied; he seemed a bit young but did I know him? I wrote back enthusiastically, mentioning our trip together to West Africa. Yes, I could thoroughly recommend Donald: 'He is intelligent and pragmatic, the sort of person the paper can well do with.'

Looking back at that, I must have been poking a bit of fun, for in those days the *Observer* was conspicuously high-minded and unpragmatic. But nobody seemed to notice. A little while later, I had another letter from John Thompson, asking me to follow up reports about sanctions-breaking in Rhodesia. In the course of it he said: 'Donald Trelford is due to come over here on Friday. He certainly sounds a good chap.'

4

Discord at the Villa Rose

Little more than a year after Donald Trelford left Malawi for London I was following him; but not, immediately, to work on the *Observer*. The wrench at leaving was considerable for me, after twelve years: I had only a Zambian passport, having renounced British citizenship, and all my preoccupations were with the hopes we had then for post-independence Africa. Even so, it had proved impossible to stay, following a quarrel when Kaunda used his presidential powers to free a minor politician jailed for contempt of court. I had attacked the decision editorially, and told Kaunda to his face: 'God knows where it will all end.'

Rowland had been reluctant to see me go on what was nominally a year's leave of absence to write a book. 'You'll never come back,' he forecast accurately. He became more willing when I told him that first moves were being made to ban the *Times of Zambia*. My concern was primarily for the African journalists who might be thrown out of jobs; but a shutdown would also be a political and financial setback to Lonrho. Letters were exchanged between Rowland and Kaunda, who wrote to say I was 'a true freedom-fighter' (that familiar phrase), but added that it would still be better if I went on leave.

The three months leading to my departure were complicated because Rowland telephoned me one day from London and said that he had finally decided to pay £1 million for the East African Standard Group in Nairobi. It was a big step at that stage for Lonrho, which remained a mixed bag of rather small companies. 'I cannot think of going ahead unless you agree to go to Nairobi and run things,' he said.

I was not averse, since it would be a neat way of bolting from the Zambian fracas. However, this soon proved out of reach, through the implacable opposition of a Major Kenneth Bolton, then editor of the *East African Standard*. Having performed the considerable feat of translating himself from being the spokesman of the white settlers in the last years of colonialism into the courtier of President Kenyatta, he had no intention of playing second fiddle to an editorial director from Zambia, of all places. As a white Kenyan woman had once said to me at a dinner party, 'Oh, Zambia! The people there are just *ants*, aren't they?' So Bolton warned Lonrho that if they persisted, he would see to it that his friend Charles Njonjo, the Attorney General, had me declared a prohibited immigrant.

Rowland went ahead with the purchase, and told me that it was my affair to get the better of Bolton, if I could. It was soon clear that I could not, and I stopped trying. Pragmatically, Lonrho settled in with Bolton, to make the best of his Kenyatta contacts. (Ten years later, after the old President's death, Rowland would cut those links with breathtaking suddenness.)

My last weeks in Zambia were marred by a dispute I had with Rowland over the financial management of the *Times of Zambia* – although it was not my direct responsibility. While on holiday in Switzerland with my family on my way back to Britain, I wrote a long letter to my mother about the recent happenings. Here is my account of the quarrel: 'At the end we were on almost nauseatingly good terms; there is something strangely feminine about Rowland. At times the meeting was very tense, with both of us standing up and shouting. Angus Ogilvy was there part of the time and listened with fascination. If he did not have so many irons in the fire I should have a very valuable ally in him.'

In London I was kept on the Zambia payroll for a year, which allowed me to get on with my long-planned book, and simultaneously to carry out a covert publicity exercise financed by the Zambian Government. From an office just off Fleet Street I ran the Central Africa Research Office, which sent out bulletins to MPs, universities and public libraries. These put the case, in sober terms, for Zambia, which was suffering heavy economic losses through being in the front line of the sanctions war against Rhodesia. These bulletins were also laced with anti-Smith propaganda. To add to their credibility, and to sow confusion, the bulletins were careful imitations, in both typography and style, of briefing papers put out by the Foreign and Commonwealth Office. I had no compunction about this subterfuge, since there was plenty of rival drum-beating for Rhodesia, and because I regarded the performance of the Wilson Government as despicably spineless.

Britain did not interest me. All my thoughts were on Central Africa. So it was quite a surprise when the *Observer* telephoned one morning and asked me to fly to Biafra. By this time, the Nigerian civil war was in full spate, although I had not paid much attention. 'You'll have to catch a plane from Heathrow to Lisbon at 2.30 this afternoon,' I was told. 'Then they'll put you on a relief plane leaving for Biafra at dawn.'

'What's wrong with Colin Legum?' I demanded, referring to the paper's august Commonwealth correspondent. 'Colin can't manage it,' was the non-committal response. I telephoned home, and told one of my sons to come to the office with my passport and a few clothes in a suitcase. At Heathrow I was lucky: there was a single first-class seat left on the only Lisbon flight that day.

After an evening around town, I was sitting at 4 a.m. in a shed at the end of Lisbon airport amid boxes of baby food from West Germany. The relief plane, it turned out, was a propeller-driven Super Constellation known as the Grey Ghost. A white-haired old man appeared and sat heavily down beside me on a trolley. 'Excuse me,' I asked, 'are you from the West German Protestants?' He looked cross. 'Hell, I'm the pilot,' he replied. 'When you get to my age, they won't even let you drive a truck in the States. So I do these Mickey Mouse jobs.' After a pause he added: 'Got my first pilot's licence in 1925.'

We were off down the runway at first light, sure enough. To my slight chagrin, I discovered that there were two other journalists aboard – Norman Kirkham from the *Daily Telegraph* and William Norris from *The Times*. We all winced as the take-off aborted. The Grey Ghost turned around and humped back to the shed where we had begun. Several shabby men came out and started to fiddle with the engines in an irresolute manner. 'If it doesn't take off this time I'm getting out,' I told Norris. But we made it, and eventually landed in Biafra in a tropical thunderstorm.

Biafra amazed me. I had never seen violence like it. The sweet smell of death hung over the place. One day I arrived in Aba just after a Federal air raid in which 112 people died. People were running about and shouting. A small boy came up and showed me several fingers he had collected in a saucepan lid. I went to the open-air mortuary to see the bodies which were heaped up as high as tables; dismembered limbs were being assembled in groups. Hordes of mourners were outside, their fingers sticking through the wire mesh. After I had taken some photographs I looked around for the gate. 'Over that side, sir,' said one of the Red Cross workers. As I left, all eyes on me, I suddenly knew: 'If these people kill me now I cannot blame them. I am white, I come from Britain, and Britain is supplying most of the arms for this war against Biafra.' But nobody touched me or said a hostile word.

Once during our stay, Norris, Kirkham and I nearly came to grief. We had gone down to a front line, despite the reluctance of a colonel in charge of the sector. The Biafrans held one side of a river, the Federals were trying to get across from the east. They had been thrown back a few nights before and there were a lot of bodies about; some were under the exposed river bank, where nobody dared collect them. The three of us climbed in and out of the trenches, then stood about on a road where in peaceful times a ferry had drawn up. The Federal troops, doubtless believing they had espied some mercenaries, started shooting – bullets began singing around us. As we scampered around the corner of the road, laughing airily, howitzer shells began crashing over.

This was more serious. We really ran, the shells falling each side of us in the thick jungle. One on the road would have been all it needed. I sprinted along behind Norman Kirkham. 'The last thing I'll see in this world is the back of Kirkham's neck,' I thought. At last we collapsed into the relative safety of a bunker.

By the time I was home again from Biafra, I had a second

African obsession. The captured shells I had seen, still in boxes marked 'OHMS', made me despise the Wilson Government all over again. An elderly Ibo professor of music, trained in Edinburgh, had asked me: 'Can you tell me, sir, why the British are doing this to us?' I looked at him, standing at the roadside in his long, old-fashioned khaki shorts. 'I can't,' I said.

My stories in the *Observer* were given good play, although my picture of the mortuary in Aba was pulled out after the first edition. Colin Legum did go into Biafra soon afterwards – with the Federal troops led by 'Scorpion' Adekunle, whose saturation shelling had turned Port Harcourt into a ghost town.

My time was now taken up with writing and lecturing about Zambia and Rhodesia on one hand, and Biafra on the other. My book, *The High Price of Principles*, was about to come out; Anthony Sampson had provided a 'quote' for the dust-jacket, calling my narrative 'a shattering commentary on British government policy'. One chapter which deeply concerned several friends of mine who were Wilson's Cabinet colleagues told in detail how he had deceived, and alienated, Kenneth Kaunda over Britain's sanctions policy. Hodders invited me to do another book, so I said I would start a biography of Dr Livingstone when there was time.

By now, I had resigned from the Lonrho payroll, but often drifted in to see Rowland at Cheapside House. Once I had words with him about the news I was getting from Zambia on the gutless way the papers were being run. As I stood up to leave, Tiny followed me out of his office, then called after me down the corridor: 'Would you like to fly out to Ghana tomorrow?' He added sardonically: 'It's a free trip.' He was not going to get the better of me like that. 'No thanks,' I shouted back. 'I'm too busy.'

When I got to the lift I stopped for a few seconds, then turned around and went back. If every man has his price, I suppose mine must be a free trip to Ghana. 'All right,' I said. Rowland smiled like a cat. 'Seven a.m. at the Pan Am counter at Heathrow. We're going in the Mystere to look at Ashanti.'

That was it, of course. Lonrho had just acquired West Africa's richest gold mine for £15 million. It was the biggest takeover Rowland had ever made, and was regarded in the City as a stunning coup. The Ashanti shareholders were offered Lonrho

Ordinary shares and Convertible stock on terms that would allow them to get out with a profit or stay with the new owners and hope for growth. For its part, Lonrho had absorbed a company of high prestige and a yearly profit of more than £3 million; it was moving in a new league. The mine was known as the 'richest square mile in Africa'.

Yet the Ashanti acquisition had not been without delicate hazards for Rowland. The foremost of these was General Sir Edward Spears, aged eighty-two. Running a close second was Miss Nancy Maurice, a virago who terrified all who met her. The general had been chairman of the mine for twenty years and Miss Maurice was his secretary-protectress; she would shortly become Lady Spears, with the death of his first wife, an American novelist.

Even the mildest of men might be expected to feel resentment if, in the November of his days, a somewhat *outré* company had snatched control of the financial domain where he had so long reigned supreme. So much fiercer, then, could be the expected response from Spears, a man of action and intellect who personified Britain's age of greatness. Much decorated for bravery in battle (he was four times wounded in the 1914–18 war), Spears had been a close friend of Churchill and had written several brilliant books about his crowded life. Perhaps his most famous feat had been to bring General de Gaulle out to England in 1940 as France was falling to the Nazis: he had pulled de Gaulle into an aeroplane as its engines were already turning.

What made Spears especially unnerving for Rowland was his intense patriotism and dislike of anything German. He had even changed his own name from Spiers, because he felt that looked too 'hunnish'. This high Tory baronet – fourteen years the member for Carlisle, first commissioned in the Eighth Hussars in 1906 – could scarcely be expected to consort with this urbane usurper, rumoured in City circles to be a recycled Teuton. So *The Times* had been well wide of the mark when it wrote (24 October 1968) that one of the reasons why the Lonrho takeover had gone through so swiftly was 'Sir Edward's opinion of Mr Roland Rowland, who he obviously considers as a potential successor as head of Ashanti'. Within a few years, Spears would be publicly stigmatizing Tiny as a 'cad'.

In truth, there were other reasons why Lonrho had pulled off the coup. One was the presence on the Ashanti board of Duncan Sandys (now Lord Duncan-Sandys), the former Commonwealth Secretary. He and Rowland understood one another well. They had links through Sandys' fellow-Scot and fellow-Etonian, Angus Ogilvy – and had found themselves on the same wavelength over the Rhodesian problem, with which Sandys had been intensely involved as Commonwealth Secretary in the early 1960s. The return of Sandys to the Ashanti board in 1966, when the Tories had fallen from office, was the crucial advantage for Rowland. The octogenarian general, his fieriness no longer what it had been, could not resist the arguments from the ex-Minister at his elbow. The historian Lord Blake – a fellow-Conservative – had characterized Sandys as 'one of the hardest, most persistent and most obstinate politicians of our day'.

The rough outline of the takeover story was familiar to me when I accepted Tiny's offer to make the trip to Ghana. On the way I picked up more details. The reason why he had been so chary about going out to see his new possession was a warning from Spears: the 20,000 black miners might start rioting again. Only a fortnight before, two had been shot dead during an attempt to storm a police station. Rowland was nervous about this – it would be a disastrous start to have a deluge of blood among the gold. Spears had obviously laid the foreboding on thick, presenting himself as the father-figure every Ghanaian had come to trust.

I was sceptical, from hints by West Africans I knew, that Spears was held in such awe as he made out. On the contrary, it seemed likely that his stewardship was regarded as a relic of colonialism, from the Rolls he had shipped out every year for his visit to the mine, to the minatory tone of his reports to the Ashanti shareholders about political events in Ghana. I put this view to Tiny when the Mystere stopped in Senegal to refuel and we sat on the steps of the airport terminal eating some absurdly expensive ham rolls. He shrugged uncertainly. 'The general is going to be out there,' he remarked. It was very clear that whereas Rowland was happy enough to include me in his entourage in the Mystere, he was constrained to let Spears go out on a scheduled flight.

When we reached Accra, a curious waiting game began. It must have reminded Sir Edward of his days on the Western Front. The Lonrho side (of which I was an uneasy member) holed up in the best hotel in town; a mile or so away, the general and his lady were entrenched in the Villa Rose, the administrative house of Ashanti Goldfields Corporation. Nothing much that I knew about seemed to be going on: neither Spears nor Rowland showed any disposition to visit the mine itself at Obuasi, 100 miles inland.

I occupied myself with going around the town, looking at the grandiose relics of the ousted Nkrumah regime. It was not without reason that Spears had written in his 1969 report that Ghana could 'ill afford the new £8 million State House, built for a meeting of the Organization of African Unity'. One old friend I encountered was Cameron Duodu, a journalist and author. He quizzed me closely about the nature of Lonrho. 'Which is stronger,' he asked, 'the Lon or the Rho?' I explained that Rowland had gone through a phase when he wanted to change the name completely, but every suggestion anyone came up with almost always turned out to have a derogatory or obscene meaning in some African language or other.

After some days of this hanging about, Rowland suddenly asked me over breakfast whether I would like to go up to the mine. 'Just take the temperature, Dick,' he said. 'Find out what people are thinking.' He was still bothered about the threat of riots. Ostensibly I would be going up to look at a paper called the *Ashanti Times*, a weekly printed and published by the mining company. The Lonrho jet, parked out at the airport, would fly me to Kumasi, the main town of the Ashanti region, then I could go by taxi down to Obuasi.

As I was being driven to the airport, I chanced to see Cameron Duodu strolling along the street. He was wearing a livid red blazer. 'Cameron,' I shouted, 'how about flying up to Kumasi with me?' He was game, and jumped in. But when we climbed aboard the plane a surprise was waiting: the general and Miss Maurice were already installed.

Spears seemed tired, defeated. He was a fine-looking man, his greying hair swept back from a noble forehead; but although he was reputed to be a great conversationalist he was not talking now. In contrast, Miss Maurice was more willing to exchange a few semi-pleasantries, and told me that she and the Chairman were going up to the mine to 'reassure' the workers, and would be staying in the residence. It was obviously a last defiant gesture and a lingering farewell. I felt a surge of pity. Miss Maurice spoke of 'Mr Rowland' with ill-concealed bitterness. Did she know that the new master of Ashanti had changed his name, from the much more patently 'hunnish' one of Fuhrhop? Even if she did not, it must still have been wounding for Miss Maurice – herself the daughter of a First World War general – to see her hero outflanked and forced into surrender by some suave stranger.

She was an astounding sight, this woman glowering across the Mystere cabin. Although close to seventy, she wore a tight-fitting white dress, drawn up well above her knees; it was really a mini-skirt, a style fashionable at that time. Her legs were covered with black fishnet stockings, elaborately 'clocked' – the sort of thing flaunted by can-can girls. On Miss Maurice's head was a high-crowned floppy hat. She had an alarmingly fierce mouth.

It was a quick flip to Kumasi, where Cameron annoyed me by saying that he would stay on the plane and go straight back to Accra. That left me responsible for our travelling companions, and I had rightly sensed that there could be difficulties. The alarming truth was that whereas a message had been tele-graphed to the mine ordering a car to meet me at Kumasi airport, there was nothing waiting for the general and Miss Maurice. I offered to give them my car and look for a taxi. Miss Maurice refused. I suggested that we shared the company car. Miss Maurice refused again. She would, on the other hand, be pleased if I arranged a taxi for them. It was not a simple request because the airport was so ramshackle; nobody wanted to hurry. While I harangued the airport staff, the old general sat in a dowdy chair, sweat running down his splendid face. People who recognized him looked on curiously.

Finally a taxi was produced and its passengers fitted them-selves in. After they had set off I told my driver to wait for a while so that Spears would have the dignity of arriving first at the mine he knew so well – where, it was said, his name was mentioned at Sunday services right after God's. My scheme went wrong, because halfway along the road we overtook the taxi, broken down. This time I persuaded Miss Maurice to relent, but she kept her lips pressed together all the way.

The mood at Obuasi was much less threatening than I had expected. The real crux was that the unions wanted 'severance pay' for all the miners because a new company had taken charge. But the expatriate staff, especially a level-headed general manager, assured me that the demise of Spears would not be a cause for all-round lamentation. The Ghanaians could recognize a real Tory when they met one. Having absorbed this message I turned to the ostensible purpose of my visit – the *Ashanti Times*. It was losing £20,000 a year, but that was not the real disadvantage: in the uncertain political climate after Nkrumah's downfall it was nothing less than reckless to have a general newspaper published directly from the mine's own printing press. Ghanaian journalism tended to be creative, to put it mildly – the American writer, John Gunther, had noticed a front-page headline in Ashanti some years before which boldly proclaimed 'Hitler Still Terrorizing Public'. So I wrote a memorandum for Rowland on returning to Accra, advising that the paper should be closed and replaced with a literary magazine. (He accepted the former proposal and ignored the latter.)

Spears had now settled himself into the Obuasi residence for an indeterminate farewell sojourn, leaving Rowland still flummoxed down in the capital. Suddenly Tiny had a brainwave, and sent a message down to Zambia ordering General 'Jock' Anderson to fly urgently to Ghana. This was to prove a masterstroke. Anderson was the former commander of the Rhodesian forces, but had retired in 1965 when he told Ian Smith that he was not willing to 'disobey the Queen' if there was an illegal declaration of independence. Anderson had then been taken on by Rowland, as a calculated snub to Smith, and put in charge of a somewhat unsuccessful match factory in Zambia.

In the Ashanti impasse Anderson had one great asset: he held the rank of Lieutenant-General, and paradoxically that made him senior, militarily, to Spears, a mere Major-General. When he arrived in Accra he was quietly amused about the role he was cast to play: rather in the manner of the Eighth Army assaulting Monte Cassino, he must go to Obuasi and take the residence. A tall and immensely handsome man, Anderson made some dry observations to me about the Lonrho 'circus' that milled around Rowland. He was critical of a Ghanaian fixer hired to promote the company's name with the military regime. 'Don't think that fellow will stay the course,' said Anderson. He was right.

The titanic 'battle of the generals' was rather a damp squib. Spears was out of ammunition, after all. Lonrho was making much play with its promise to double the ore milling rate at Ashanti within two years, which held out to the bankrupt government the bait of much-needed extra revenue. It had also promised to make a study of ways to boost output in the moribund state mines.

Anderson moved into the residence, and Tiny followed him, to survey the Obuasi panorama at last: an untidy conglomeration of headgears and surface installations against the dark green tropical hills. I was at the Accra airport when Spears and Miss Maurice flew out. The general balanced a trilby hat on his knees and gazed around forlornly. Miss Maurice was making waspish remarks, and still wearing her unforgettable stockings.

As we flew home in the executive jet our spirits were high, for Ashanti had lost its dangerous mystique. Rowland told me that Lonrho's profits in 1969 would top £13 million: in 1963 they had been less than £500,000. The company was now operating in nineteen countries and was reaching out for bigger prizes. After Ghana, Rowland had started to look at Nigeria. But the Biafran war was dragging on and in several memoranda to Tiny I had urged him to keep a neutral stance on Nigeria; he did not take the slightest notice of me, having made a cool and accurate judgement on what the outcome of the conflict must finally be.

While we chatted, Tiny suddenly said: 'We have something else on the boil, the biggest of all. It's in the Congo.' The atmosphere in the plane was suddenly electric, because several listeners knew what he was hinting at. Alan Ball, the sallow-faced Lonrho chairman, turned to Rowland, sitting next to him. 'Better keep that one quiet,' he warned. However, Tiny was now unstoppable. 'Dick's a friend,' he retorted. 'He's one of us!'

That was how I came to know of the ill-fated *Cominière*

scheme which was to end with President Mobutu sequestering £10 million of Lonrho's assets, and Rowland having to make laborious explanations to be given them back... It was not that Lonrho was trying to do anything improper – all it had hoped for was to acquire the contract to run the Congo's copper mines in Katanga, and the chance to build a railway with exclusive rights to take the metal out. It would help the Congo and help Lonrho; but that meant confronting the entrenched interests of Belgium, the old colonial power.

As Rowland unfolded the tale, like a pedlar laying out his wares, I had a strong recollection of times past. This was the same old Tiny technique: identify a country's crucial import or export, then conjure up a scheme giving a guarantee of all the vital traffic. It had come off with the Mozambique oil pipeline to Rhodesia (although UDI was keeping that out of action for the moment), but had not worked in Zambia with the proposal to build a railway if Lonrho could have a monopoly of all the copper exports. The mining companies, led by Harry Oppenheimer's Anglo-American Corporation, had scuppered that. Once again, he was challenging the big guns. As he remarked during the Mystere flight: 'Val Duncan told me never to try and beat the Establishment, because it will always win.' (Sir Val Duncan, chairman of Rio Tinto, counted as part of the mining Establishment, so this might have been regarded as sound advice.)

To establish a bridgehead in the Congo the first essential had been to buy a company operating there. Outside the ambit of the all-pervasive *Société Générale*, there was only one suitable vehicle, a conglomerate called *Cominière*. It had diverse interests, including plantations, garages and a small railway; *Cominière* also possessed a cantankerous, white-haired president named Martin Thèves. For Thèves the Lonrho connection was to prove, quite literally, fatal.

As Rowland explained to me, a Lonrho subsidiary named Anglo-Ceylon had taken control of *Cominière* through a Luxembourg holding company, Loncom. Thèves had joined the Lonrho board, while Rowland, Ogilvy and Ball became directors of *Cominière*. If Lonrho were to capture the management contract for the copper mines it was essential to work through a Belgian-based company, to avoid unsettling the Belgian technicians upon whom the 350,000 tons annual output heavily depended.

Back in London, Rowland suggested that I should go across to Belgium and meet Thèves. By this stage he had agreed that the Lonrho adventure in the Congo was a story to be written – it was of no concern to me otherwise. I told Rowland that the right medium was the magazine *African Development* (now *African Business*) which I was editing. So a few days after my return from Ghana I was in Brussels; waiting at the airport was Thèves, with his grey Rolls. We drove to a somewhat oppressive club, and he introduced me to Henri Cornelis, former Governor-General of the Congo; it turned out that Cornelis was now on the *Cominière* board – and thus, in a way, a Lonrho employee. He was a powerful man, and Thèves clearly thought highly of his influence with President Mobutu. They were also united in their hostility towards the *Union Minière*, which Rowland would have to oust if he was going to get the mines contract.

By the end of the day, I could see more clearly what Rowland was up against – precisely, that indestructible Establishment. Firstly, there was '*le petit club*', as Thèves put it: the *Société Générale* and the closely linked *Union Minière*. Then there was that grand old British company, Tanganyika Concessions (based in the Bahamas for tax reasons); Tanks owned the Benguela Railway, which took the Congo copper out through Angola – and would be ruined if Lonrho went ahead with its planned £100 million line. Finally, there was Anglo-American, with a large stake in Tanks and deep-rooted reasons for suspecting any scheme linked to Tiny Rowland.

Could Tiny beat such a *galère*? There was Lord Colyton, chairman of Tanks and a former Colonial Secretary; Harry Oppenheimer, chairman of Anglo; and Louis Wallef, chairman of '*le Générale*'. Even while I was writing my three-thousand-word piece for *African Development*, the first shots were fired. A prominent article on the City pages of the *Daily Telegraph* was headlined 'Tiny Rowland's Biggest Coup'. It was written by Nicholas Berry, son of Lord Hartwell, the paper's proprietor, and began: 'Is Lonrho's ambitious Tiny Rowland, flushed by unbroken success, now planning to gain control of the brightest jewel in Africa, the immensely valuable mining assets of *Union Minière*?' Setting aside a degree of hyperbole, this really spelled it out – even before Lonrho had been able to make a formal proposal to Mobutu. Wires to the Congo began to hum.

Rowland was still ebullient. He rested his faith in the various nods of encouragement from high Congolese sources. The Lonrho 'review of operations', put out in July 1969, spoke of a new international consortium, headed by Lonrho: the consortium was engaged on a study for railways (now in the plural) which would run more than 800 miles across the Congo. The investigations were being done at 'the invitation of the Government of the Democratic Republic of the Congo', with a view to starting construction work on the line at the beginning of 1971... It was clear that all this would more than compensate Tiny for his disappointment over the railway project in Zambia.

Then the whispering campaign started. What Lonrho was after was not just the mining management contract but the secession of Katanga. After all, Lonrho was a Rhodesian company – and was it not Rhodesia which had most openly encouraged Moise Tshombe, the arch-secessionist, to make his breakaway attempt some eight years earlier? This hint was enough to provoke Mobutu's suspicions. At once he froze all the Lonrho–*Cominière* assets in the Congo.

Rowland was stunned. He had even bought the Watergate Shipping Company, a substantial British concern, to be ready to carry the Congo's copper to Europe and the Far East. Tremendous efforts had been made to win support among the corrupt and devious clique around Mobutu. Now all was lost, as proved categorically when the *Union Minière* just signed a new twenty-five-year management contract. Tiny had a blazing row with Martin Thèves, who retreated in high dudgeon to his apartment in Nice.

What remained now was for Lonrho somehow to get its Congo assets unfrozen. But Mobutu would not listen to any overtures or protestations of innocence. Nothing could shake his belief that Lonrho had planned a real 'coup' in Katanga.

In the end, Thomas Kanza came to the rescue. A former Congolese Foreign Minister, by then living in exile, Kanza was friendly with several black francophone entrepreneurs on Lonrho's network. He suggested an interview with a Belgian journalist who contributed to a magazine in Brussels; it seemed that Mobutu had absolute trust in anything this man wrote. So the meeting was arranged – the Belgian reporter sat down with Rowland for two hours in the Dorchester in Park Lane, with Kanza interpreting. It was more like a confession than an interview, Kanza told me later: everything poured out about what Lonrho had wanted to do in the Congo. If mistakes had been made and Lonrho had, in all innocence, been too secretive, that was a tragedy. Any blame, it should be understood, must attach to Martin Thèves. He knew the Congo so much better than Rowland and his English colleagues...

When the article duly appeared, Mobutu relented. The assets were unfrozen. But there was a price to pay, because the President insisted that his uncle Litho should be appointed to the board of the Luxembourg holding company. Litho was much addicted to whisky (it killed him in the end) and insisted upon coming over to London whenever he was visiting Europe, and commandeering the Lonrho jet to fly around the distilleries in Scotland.

There was another consequence, more sombre. When Thèves, down in Nice, read the interview with Tiny, he was so mortified that he had a heart attack and dropped dead.

5

Picking Winners in Nigeria

Rather surprisingly, Rowland did not appear to hold it against me that the revelations about Lonrho's Congo project had contributed to one of his worst setbacks. It had been a costly lesson for him on the danger of handing out secrets to journalists, even those regarded as friends, and perhaps explains why the company later became so reticent about its doings. There were repercussions in the City, where one commentator cruelly remarked that Tiny had been 'booted out' by Mobutu.

But *African Development* still had access to the Rowland directors, and we printed all we could discover about the group's continuing advance northwards. Its tentacles were everywhere, groping for deals, big or small. Our month-by-month coverage led to a rumour that Tiny held a controlling stake in the magazine and was simply using it as a public relations platform, so that we felt constrained to slip a disclaimer into a leading article: 'Why do we keep going on about Lonrho? Because Lonrho is always on the go.'

That was certainly true. By the second half of 1969 Kenya was well behind the front line – Rowland was now active right up in Libya and Sudan, hunting for contracts. He had the clear aim of using these countries as gateways to the rest of the Arab world. This was in the period before the 'oil shock' – that graphic Japanese coinage – and the big American producers still seemed to have the sheikhs well under their corporate thumbs. However, Rowland was ahead of the game: with his lifelong love of cars, he had always possessed an instinct for the profits waiting to be made from a commodity so crucial as petroleum, if one had the leverage.

The potential was being demonstrated at that very moment back in Rhodesia; since Ian Smith's UDI, the big oil companies had made a covert killing out of sanctions-busting – they quickly took advantage of the enforced shutdown of the Lonrho oil pipeline through Mozambique to Rhodesia by moving in supplies by rail from the south. Rowland was chagrined by this, seeing it as a double-cross. But he bided his time and concentrated his efforts on penetrating the Arab world.

An internal Lonrho memorandum talked grandly of the 'revolutionary projects' already in mind for the Middle East, with its one hundred million people, as a natural extension of group activities in Africa and Europe. The guiding hand for Rowland's tentative steps down this new path was provided by Khalil Osman, a Sudanese millionaire. Sudan was an ideal transition point for Lonrho, since it straddled both black Africa and the Muslim world. The witty and self-assured Khalil – trained as a vet, but not much interested in delivering calves – personified this dualism. Like many other educated Sudanese, he had left the cramped Khartoum milieu to seek his fortune across the Red Sea, and in Kuwait had formed a friendship with the Emir, Prince Sabah Salim Asabah. This had given him access to funds from a Kuwaiti investment company, Gulf International, and allowed him to build up a business empire back at home in the Sudan.

Khalil was especially suited to Rowland's style of entrepreneurship; this was based – as ever – upon intimate dealings with the 'man at the top' in any country where Lonrho had ambitions. The new Sudanese ruler was a young colonel, Gaafar Nimeiri, and Khalil had swiftly made himself his personal adviser on handling foreign firms interested in the Sudan. So an introduction for Tiny was arranged. The time would come when Rowland and Khalil were to engage together in a piece of political bravura that has left its mark on African contemporary history; but for the moment their alliance was all high finance and industrial enterprise, with Colonel Nimeiri nodding his approval.

Not so long ago, Middle East potentates regarded the Nile

Valley as merely a handy source of slaves. But now, as Khalil explained, they felt it had great potential as a source of food, grown on land irrigated by the great river. The most promising crop would be sugar: exports apart, Sudan itself had a national addiction to sweet tea, and could boast the highest sugar consumption per head in the Third World. When it came to expertise in sugar-growing, Lonrho was well equipped to offer advice, since it now controlled plantations in Malawi, Swaziland, South Africa and Mauritius.

A major sugar development would give Lonrho, an unknown name in the Arab business lexicon, the necessary prestige. With Khalil as go-between it could be relied upon to draw in capital from the Gulf. The next leap would be into the oil-producing countries themselves. With such prospects, Rowland began thinking in gigantic terms – of a scheme that could produce 300,000 tons of sugar a year, dwarfing any other plantations in Africa. The Lonrho stake would be 51 per cent. Technical experts drafted in from Mauritius and South Africa finally settled on a site at Kenana, about 200 miles up the river from Khartoum.

The project has succeeded, at a price, in the face of many tribulations. The capital needs went up relentlessly, to an ultimate $700 million, and it would be as late as 1985 before the local directors could push production beyond that 300,000-ton target first set by Rowland. By then the Lonrho involvement had fallen to a minimal 0.46 per cent, as a result of disagreements with the Kuwaitis over the awarding of contracts. Somewhat nostalgically, there was a large aerial picture of Kenana in one of Lonrho's most recent reports.

That was really the beginning and the end of the Rowland dream of conquering the Middle East. As any businessman who operates there will confirm, all negotiations are tortuous and infinitely time-consuming. Perhaps Tiny, with his impetuous style of jetting from capital to capital, was simply incapable of adjusting to the Arab mind. This interpretation has certainly been supported by the way he lost Harrods to the Fayeds, years later, in the climactic battle of his career.

During those early days, however, the possibilities of Sudan and its northern neighbours had seized his imagination. When I called one morning at Cheapside he brought out a map to show me how he intended to link up the Sudanese and Egyptian railways. It appealed to me as real 'Cape to Cairo' stuff; although a sad memory stirred of his unfulfilled railway project in Zambia (and, indeed, in the Congo), I realized that somebody had been quite wrong when they called him a 'Cecil Rhodes without Vision'. He had it. The whole continent was coming to be his playground, as many new business developments proved.

Around this time he also told me about a platinum venture down in South Africa. 'It give the shares glamour,' he explained – a little apologetically, knowing my political attitude.

It has been Rowland's skill to maintain (and expand) the big Lonrho interest in South Africa, yet collect remarkably few brickbats for so doing from the rest of the continent. He relies on the ignorance of many African leaders, or his own flair for pacifying those who do feel uneasy. He has had plenty of compensation to offer them, and has made some unlikely conquests.

In his first years of power, Colonel Qadhafi became an instant – and uncritical – captive of the Rowland charm. At that time, of course, the young Libyan revolutionary was more amenable and was not yet displaying his own messianic traits.

In Kenya, several members of the ruling family were already in thrall – especially Udi Gecaga, one of the presidential sons-in-law. Such was the interwoven nature of the 'Kenyatta clan' that Gecaga's mother was also the President's niece and sister of the Foreign Minister. With connections like those, it was almost superfluous that young Udi ('John' to his white friends) had been educated at Princeton, Cambridge and the Sorbonne: within four years of coming on the Lonrho payroll he would be chief executive of all Lonrho operations in East Africa.

On the western side of the continent, Rowland had a protégé equally polished and persuasive. Gilchrist Olympio was a son of the late President Sylvanus Olympio of Togo, who in 1963 had achieved the sorry distinction of being the first head of an independent African country to suffer assassination while in office. The *soigné*, bilingual 'Gil' had worked for the International Monetary Fund in Washington before joining Lonrho.

Like his friend Gecaga, he was also a graduate of several of the best universities.

It was Gil Olympio's ties by marriage with President Felix Houphouet-Boigny of the Ivory Coast which handed Lonrho its entrée into francophone Africa. This was something of a sensation, because most British concerns gave such countries as the Ivory Coast a rueful miss, accepting that the French had them all tied up. (It would certainly have been my conclusion, after what Donald Trelford and I had seen of the place on our jaunt there in 1966.) However, Rowland was able to fix a $50 million deal – for six sugar processing factories.

The bonds with characters as able and well-connected as Khalil, Gecaga and Olympio might have been the first moves towards 'Africanizing' the Lonrho empire from the top down. Perhaps Rowland had such ideas; if so, this experiment would eventually prove far more vexing than it merited.

The break with Gecaga was to be brutal and dramatic, following close upon Jomo Kenyatta's death. There had been a murky intrigue aimed at stopping Vice-President arap Moi assuming power, and Gecaga was branded as being a driving force behind it. Although he protested his innocence, he happened to be chairman of the *Standard*, Lonrho's daily newspaper in Kenya; and the *Standard* was accused by Moi of acting as the mouthpiece of the conspiracy against him. Rowland flew out to Nairobi from London, swept Gecaga off the newspaper board and demoted several other known 'Kenyatta men'. After all, there could be no taking risks with the country that has consistently been the finest money-spinner for Lonrho in black Africa. Having performed his house-cleaning, Rowland made peace with Moi – and stuck close to him thereafter. He explained his policy succinctly: 'Even if your man out there is doing a first-class job and he falls foul of the government, then he must go.'

The intricacies of Rowland's quarrel with Gilchrist Olympio are more obscure. According to Thomas Kanza, the former Congolese diplomat, Olympio upset Tiny by calling him a racialist. But for both, money was more fundamental than words.

The operation in the Ivory Coast to supply sugar-processing factories was subjected to a painful investigation by the US

Securities and Exchange Commission. The contract went to Lang Engineering, the subsidiary of a big Texan corporation, and the SEC found that Lang had paid more than $1 million to Olympio. He was then working as a management consultant to Lonrho, and had asked Lang to deposit the money in a Swiss bank. Questioned by the SEC, Olympio said the $1 million was all above board, and given him for services rendered.

There was a long-delayed sequel to his split with Lonrho. In the High Court in London, in March 1984, it was announced that Lonrho would pay 'Mr Gilchrist Olympio, who lives in Paris', a substantial sum in full and final settlement of all claims by him. Lonrho unconditionally withdrew a counter-claim for fraud. Through their lawyers, Rowland and Olympio agreed on a total silence about the details of the dispute.

But that is looking far ahead. At the end of the 1960s, Olympio's name enhanced the Lonrho lustre, most of all in West Africa. In Nigeria, where his late father had once worked for Unilever, 'Gil' was able to sweep Tiny through the financial jungle to the centres of patronage and decision. There was plenty to play for, because although the civil war in Biafra was yet to end, the Nigerian oil industry was starting to boom. Tiny was eager to stake his claim in the country which saw itself as 'Africa's superpower'.

There was talk of a Lonrho tanker company to ship crude from Nigeria – with the involvement of Khalil and the Kuwaitis. This grandiose plan would build on the foundations Lonrho had already laid by absorbing the British textile firm, David Whitehead. This had several factories in Africa, including one in Nigeria. (The acquisition was a particular satisfaction because one factory was in Gatooma, the Rhodesian town where Tiny's African career had started; but in commercial terms, the Nigerian factory was most important.) The next move was the takeover of John Holt, a venerable trading company with head-quarters in Liverpool and activities right across Nigeria. It was a superb buy, made with assurance in the midst of the civil war when the price was at a low ebb. The purchase was done by issuing a package of Lonrho shares and trading these on a two-to-one basis with Holt shares, valued at £8 million. The benefit of this manoeuvre was to give Lonrho another ready source of cash, since Holts had a turnover of more than £30 million a year.

Rowland was totally confident that Biafra was going to be beaten, and was getting in ahead of the bonanza that was guaranteed once peace returned. He ignored my subjective view, swayed by sympathy for Biafra, that Lonrho should avoid siding with the Federal government. On the contrary, he followed his usual tactics, repeatedly flying to Lagos in the Mystere, to woo senior figures in General Gowon's administration. At the same time, he was managing to maintain his close friendship with President Kenneth Kaunda of Zambia, one of four African countries which had formally recognized Biafra. As regards the outcome of that war, Rowland certainly had a clearer view than either Kaunda or I . . .

My second trip to Biafra was in the first days of 1970, starting from Dublin in an old 'mercy mission' Stratocruiser flown by a couple of taciturn Belgians. We went into the enclave after dark on New Year's Day, after taking off from Libreville. Also aboard were several Irish priests, with hangovers from the amount of Jameson's whiskey consumed en route to Africa to celebrate the start of another decade. It was a useful introduction to these Holy Ghost fathers, who were a thousand times more partisan about Biafra than I could ever have been. The Irish features editor of a women's magazine called *Nova* had commissioned a story about them.

In the dark the Belgians got us down – at the second attempt – on the widened road called 'Uli airport'. Makeshift runway lights were switched off as soon as our wheels were on the ground, because a Federal bomber circled overhead looking for its target.

Next morning I made my way to Owerri, the last real town in Biafran hands, and was accommodated in a collection of chalets optimistically called the 'Progress Hotel'. There were few other visitors, but in the adjoining chalet I discovered the photographer Don McCullin and a rather supercilious reporter from the *Sunday Times*. They expressed astonishment at my arrival. 'Watch out, or you'll be part of the fucking autopsy,' said Don amiably. 'This place is about to collapse.' They were leaving that night, on any relief plane that would give them a lift. 'You're just trying to scare me off the story,' I said, and to change the subject we swapped some anecdotes about girls around Fleet Street.

But it was true, things were not too good. The whole place was starving, and pot-bellied kids wandered around the chalets with their hands out beseechingly. I had brought a small kitbag of tinned food, but asked if the Progress Hotel served any meals. 'One dish on the menu,' said McCullin. 'They call it goat stew, I think it's Federal prisoners.' (His little jest sank in, and when I was obliged to resort to the stew I examined the lumps of bone carefully, trying to work out what they might anatomically be.)

The next day, when the adjoining chalet was empty, life was lonely, although a renowned Japanese correspondent named Masataka Itoh was staying on the far side of the hotel compound. I had callers, however, including a young Ibo writer with a leaflet announcing a recital of work by 'Biafran war poets'. Was I interested in coming along? It was a remarkable proposition at such a moment, but then the Biafrans sustained themselves with such illusions of normalcy: a black Cambridge undergraduate had handed me, just before I left, a neat round box containing six wing collars for his father, who was a judge.

While the young writer and I were discussing the recital, a Federal MiG raced low overhead, firing rockets. The Biafran anti-aircraft guns loosed off a few of their precious shells, leaving puffs of smoke in the hot sky. The incident rubbed away my companion's veneer of eager enthusiasm. As we got up and dusted ourselves down, his thin face looked grey. He twisted his hands together. 'What is to become of us?' he kept repeating. To cheer him up I agreed to attend the recital. However, it never did take place. There was not enough time left.

Up the hill in the brooding town, messages had to be delivered. Several were from Bridget Bloom, the Africa correspondent of the *Financial Times* at that time, to various friends she had not seen since the war began. But most important was an envelope addressed to General Ojukwu, the rebel leader, from Jeremy Thorpe, then the British Liberal Party leader. Thorpe had asked me to visit him in the Commons to collect the letter, which contained his well-meant ideas for a truce in the war. My first clue to the desperation in Biafra came when I was admitted to the office of a government minister. He said there was no chance for me to hand the letter to Ojukwu personally, and shrugged indifferently when I put it on the desk and asked him to do so. There was a pair of crossed squash racquets on the wall beside his desk, but the minister did not seem the least bit sportive. I walked out in the sunlight with a sinking feeling inside me.

It was hard to know what to do. My application to go to the front line, said to be fifteen miles to the east, was refused on the grounds that the timing was 'inconvenient'. So I wandered along with Itoh, the Japanese correspondent, to see a dozen or so bodies being dug up from a cassava patch beside the Owerri jail; who could have buried them remained obscure. Then somebody mentioned that Chinua Achebe, most famous of African writers, had chosen to stay here until the bitter end; but when I found him he would not talk much – his eyes just blazed with rage at meeting somebody from the detested Britain. Most information that there was could be culled from the Irish missionaries, one of whom told me that the Biafran soldiers were now collapsing behind their guns from hunger and exhaustion. Two priests took me on a journey to a makeshift feeding centre, some thirty miles south of Owerri, and I photographed a mother with her dead twins, two little skeletons on her lap. I also called on a nun, alone in her mission, surrounded by hundreds of shell-shocked soldiers, all shouting in high-pitched voices, 'Food, food, food...' She wore a camouflaged habit, to make her less conspicuous to the MiGs, which were about all the time.

Two days after Itoh had pulled out, following a farewell meal of tinned rice pudding and whisky, the end came. I was lying in the bath in a few inches of brown water – all that would come out of the tap – when shells started falling. It seemed best to stay put, since the sides of the bath might give some protection. Anyway, the shelling soon stopped.

It was evening, and by the time I had dressed and packed my bag, night had fallen. There was no electricity. When somebody hammered on the door, I was jumpy, remembering that I only had a Zambian passport, and Zambia had recognized Biafra. But it was just the old watchman, his face glistening in the light of my torch. 'You must leave,' he yelled. 'They are coming now!

73

They near.' He kept saluting convulsively as he spoke, having once served in the British army. I gave him two tins of rice pudding, almost all I had left, and he ran off. Rather foolishly, I left another tin on the table, as a sort of peace-offering to the next arrivals, who would doubtless be Nigerian Federal officers.

Up at the reception centre for the Progress Hotel, a candle was alight on the counter, but there was nobody left to whom I could hand my chalet key. In the flickering light I could just make out the unchanging menu, chalked on a blackboard: 'Goat stew'. I turned and walked up the drive.

Suddenly I was aware of a strange muttering noise coming from the road outside. Then I saw, in the headlights of cars edging through the mass, that the road was crammed with people, in an endless procession, leaving the doomed town. They went along with basins, suitcases, boxes, bedding, all carried on their heads. Small children clung to their parents' hands. Bicycles were being wheeled along, loaded up with goods, although some had no tyres. I noticed unarmed soldiers staggering by in pairs. This was the collapse, for after Owerri there was no real place to go: although there were still two million Ibos in what was left of Biafra, those shells had sent a message, dreadful in its finality.

It took me two days, in the confusion, to reach Uli and clamber aboard an empty relief plane. In the two other canvas seats at the back were a couple of Irish nurses, crying because they had been ordered to leave and had that morning abandoned the 200 orphans in their charge, giving each one a little basin of food. When we were off the ground, the Icelandic co-pilot came back and asked: 'Things pretty bad down there?' The girls were still weeping and I looked out of the window beside me, feeling depressed. 'Terrible,' I replied. 'You won't be going back.' We landed on the island of São Tomé, and the following night Ojukwu flew from Uli to exile in the Ivory Coast.

I now found myself with another great Nigerian story to write. Just as Donald Trelford and I had been the first journalists out of Lagos after the first coup – almost exactly four years before – now I was the last journalist out of Biafra, an eye-witness to its fall. Filing from São Tomé, over its primitive radio-telephone, took hours of shouting and anguish, but I managed to send several thousands words to Gemini, the news service which then owned the magazine *African Development*. Unknown to me, they sold it to the highest bidder, the *Sunday Times*, where it led page one. But several days before I had managed to send a brief story from Owerri to the *Observer*, describing Biafra's perilous state. It was a pretty offhand piece, because I was at odds with the paper's hardline policy over Biafra. Possessing nothing better, the *Observer* ran it, so when I got home I learned about having had the unique and embarrassing distinction of my byline simultaneously on the front pages of both the Sunday 'heavies'.

Aside from that, my deeper feelings were very mixed. All the pragmatists – including Rowland – had accurately foreseen Biafra's defeat. Moreover, the fears of the Ibos and their friends that this would be followed by massacres – even genocide – were totally wrong. There was great magnanimity after the surrender.

That was to the credit of the Nigerians. But I felt there was little credit to the 'merchants of death' whose arms had kept the war going for almost three years, with the loss of a million lives. Once again, the key was that crucial commodity, oil.

On the outskirts of Owerri I had noticed a battle-scarred hoarding which said, ironically enough: 'Shell/BP Welcomes You.' British companies held the main concessions in Nigeria, and had invested £300 million there; most of that investment was within the original boundaries of Biafra. The British Government, then with 49 per cent of BP, always knew where it stood with the military leaders in Lagos; but the acquisitive Ibos of Biafra might prove much more tricky if they got away with their secession. Behind the sophistry about 'supporting Nigerian unity', the oil dictated British policy. There was no sincere effort at peace-making and the emotional political debates at Westminster were mere window-dressing.

So the Saladins, the howitzers, the seconded RAF pilots and the military advisers were ordered in. Admittedly, that might have ended the bloodshed sooner, if de Gaulle had not then decided to supply the Biafrans. The French, operating through Gabon and other former colonies, hoped they would earn the goodwill of Ojukwu and so be handed the Shell/BP concessions, but British pressure had stopped them from following this policy through effectively. The Soviet Union and South Africa also tried to get involved, but their supplies were more marginal; the British simply played up the Russian factor to justify their own actions. All this became clear as the smokescreen of war dispersed.

I wondered how far Rowland had been tuned into Whitehall's absolute determination about looking after British interests in Nigeria. Was it this which had made him so sure about the outcome? On the other hand, most Foreign Office mandarins were known to regard Tiny as a bounder, dangerously unpredictable. They would scarcely take him into their confidence.

Yet he now had some Lonrho directors with good access to the inner workings of officialdom. One in particular was Nicholas Elliott, a genial horse-racing enthusiast – formerly the third most senior figure in MI6. Elliott had won some discreet fame as the man who confronted Kim Philby, my erstwhile fellow-stringer for the *Observer*, with his guilt as a Soviet agent, after which Kim had hopped to Moscow. Pondering on the fate of Biafra, I decided that Nick would have had access to some good tips to ensure that Tiny backed the winners. But an unexpected change in my fortunes, distancing me for a while from Lonrho, served to drive such speculations from my mind.

6

David Astor and Others

It would be hard to think of two rich men less compatible than Tiny Rowland and David Astor. The former is an outsider trying to get in, the latter an insider trying to get out. One has a merciless wit, the other smiles a great deal, but lacks humour. With his chequered background, Rowland sees life as a contest in which opponents may have to be kneed in the groin now and then. For the Honourable David, born at Cliveden, it has been a perpetual stint of good works, serving the less privileged in a moral and cultural soup-kitchen. So switching loyalties from one to the other was somewhat like walking out of a casino and into a Jesuit seminary.

Still, I had always wanted a staff job at the *Observer*. It was simply hard to find a niche. My *métier* was Africa, but the paper already had Colin Legum. He was not someone to clash with, and his judgement about events in the new black nations was gospel to Astor. The prospects suddenly brightened, however, when I went to lunch one day with Anthony Sampson. He said that Astor was looking for somebody to run the colour magazine and wondered if I would be interested. It was only a few months after my Biafra experience, and in the interim I had been on a trip to the Lebanon and Egypt, but was now at a loose end. Tiny did not need me in a full-time role – lingering hopes of going to run the Lonrho papers in East Africa had withered. So indeed I was interested, even though the magazine projected values that could only seem trivial to anyone who had spent years thinking about Africa and its problems. Sampson had himself edited the magazine for a spell, and I had written for him from Lusaka. He assured me that half the pleasure lay in 'fighting the advertisements' with worthwhile features.

That afternoon I collected a bunch of old copies, studied them, then wrote a letter to Astor outlining what I thought I might be able to achieve. A week later, just before he called me to see him, I had hurt my back, and as he struggled up from his desk it was plain that he had done the same. We circled around one another like a couple of arthritic crabs, then he told me I was appointed.

There were two early complications. An agreeable and capable deputy editor, Alun Morris, believed that Astor had promised him the job. I did not discover this until I had started, and Morris took himself off to Washington to work for the World Bank. Then I had some unpleasantness with Bruce Rothwell, a former *Daily Mail* executive who had been sponsored for the magazine editorship by Arthur Koestler. With backing from so august a figure – Koestler was the archetypal *Ob* guru – Rothwell could not imagine why he had failed to be chosen (nor could I, for that matter). Rothwell eventually became one of Rupert Murdoch's senior executives, but he never forgot Astor's slight, and never forgave me.

Life at the *Observer* quickly began to remind me of my distant undergraduate days on *Isis*. It was not merely the fact that almost all senior 'Astoroids' were Oxbridge men (not to mention the mandatory woman, Katharine Whitehorn, ex-Newnham), but rather the financial insouciance of the whole affair. The paper was running at a loss, had done so for years, and did not look like ever making a profit again. The circulation was sliding down, and the *Sunday Telegraph*'s breath was all too audible at the rear, but nobody had any answers. I quickly understood that the magazine, which David Astor still tended to regard as a harlot put out on the streets, was expected to engage in anything that might help to pay the rent. Meanwhile, the standards of the paper itself were inviolate.

This is not to suggest that the magazine had untrammelled licence. When I became editor the staff was reeling from the storm over a recent feature on show jumping. It had suggested, in passing, that teenage girls gained some sexual excitement from riding a horse. This produced a clutch of letters from anxious mothers in the Home Counties, but more significantly sent David Astor into a fit of indignant fury. I made a mental note to strike out the word masturbation whenever it appeared in copy. There was obviously a need to tread carefully with anyone who had been through a course of analysis with Anna Freud.

The quintessence of the *Observer* was revealed at the Wednesday boardroom lunches, which were rather like a meeting at All Souls. The senior journalists arrayed themselves around the long table, with Astor at the centre on one side, a bottle of Malvern water near his right hand. The talk ebbed and flowed, cultivated and witty; one began to see what people meant when they likened the paper to a Renaissance court. Issues of the moment, at home and abroad, were analysed, to decide what line should be followed the following Sunday. At one of those moments when Britain was about to join the Common Market, debate grew intense about the pros and cons. At last, Astor cast his golden vote: we should set down all points of view, and let the reader make up his own mind.

These lunches were sometimes broadened to include outsiders, often a literary grandee whose book was being considered for serialization. We journalists welcomed this, because then wine was served – although once the eccentric manager, Tristan Jones, marched in and removed the carafes because he felt the guest was not of sufficient moment. One Wednesday, in the midst of a miners' strike, the guest was Roy Jenkins. 'Tell us, Roy,' said somebody, carried away by the claret, 'how would you solve the strike – you're a miner's son.' There was a silence; this was a gaffe. He had been invited as an Oxbridge equal, a first-class mind, not as an *évolué* from the working class. The nature of relationships on the paper was governed by certain assumptions.

In the first few months, my old attachments drew me back from this slightly daunting new milieu. Friends from Africa were always calling me. So was Tiny. He telephoned one day when Dick Peel was in my office. Peel was the film-maker turned journalist who had known Rowland in those remote days in Gatooma. 'Why don't you come with me to Cheapside House and say hello to him again?' I suggested.

We left the *Observer* building – which in those days

overlooked Queen Victoria Street at Puddle Dock – and strolled up past St Paul's to Cheapside. After we had sat for a few minutes in the Lonrho reception area, Tiny came striding down the corridor. He recognized Peel at once, and rushed up to him with his hand outstretched. 'The best journalist in Central Africa!' he cried.

There was then a lot of discussion about Zambian politics. Peel remembers that I said at the end: 'Don't bother about Harry Nkumbula – he's washed up.' (Nkumbula was Kaunda's rival, in as far as one still existed, six years after Independence.) The discussion ended, Tiny saw us to the lift, and we came out again into the street, mesmerized by his special charm.

But gradually I immersed myself more deeply in the Sunday newspaper world. I came to understand the dilemma of David Astor, and to sympathize. He had been editor for twenty-two years, far too long – and he knew it. But yet, he felt it impossible for him to leave. It was not merely that the paper the Astors had owned since 1911 was losing so much money – which had to be made good from the family purse – but also there were his inner fears about what might be made of it after he let go. The world was now a strangely different place from the one in which he had been given the editorship in 1948, at the age of thirty-six. Doubtless, David would have agreed with the judgement of Lord Reith, that 1956 was a turning-point for Britain; not so much because that was the year of Suez, but the year when commercial television had started. From that, much had followed – the consumer society, the relentless infiltration of American values, the erosion of the opinion-making role of the Press. Although his roots were American, and it was in New York that the Astor fortune had been made, the brash transatlantic mode of life was an affront to Astor's humanitarian and liberal instincts.

So what was to become of the *Observer*? He looked back to his 'golden age', the first years of his editorship, rather as Winston Smith had gazed into the paperweight in *1984*. But there was no escaping the reality of the present, with the impertinent Harold Evans editing the *Sunday Times* for Lord Thomson. They had too much firepower. Although David kept his fair-haired boyish looks, he was really tired. One day, soon after I joined, I sat next to Thomson at a function to give out travel writers' awards. 'Young man,' he started, peering at me through his thick lenses, 'how is that editor of yours?' I was put out by the question. 'Very well, thank you,' I said. There was a pause, then he went on: 'Let me tell you. If David Astor gives up the *Observer* it will kill him. That paper is his life. It keeps him going.' There was some truth behind his judgement, although time has had the last laugh on Thomson, since he has long been under the ground and Astor is still in good health.

There is another story about Thomson, told to me by Jim Rose, the former literary editor of the *Observer*. Astor first met Thomson at a carefully arranged dinner, when the earthy Canadian was starting to make his mark in Fleet Street. After the first course, Thomson suddenly asked: 'Mr Astor, what is your circulation?' His head on one side, David said that he could not recall the latest figure. Thomson poked out his finger triumphantly, told him the new Audit Bureau returns in detail, and added the *Sunday Times* figure, about 500,000 ahead. 'I daresay you are right,' said Astor, bleakly. There was a silence, then Thomson asked: 'Mr Astor, what is the state of your balance sheet?' After a similar reply, he went on unabashed to pour out a cascade of figures about the financial state of his own papers. David Astor suddenly turned to him and said: 'Mr Thomson, there are more important things to me than money in this world. Now let me ask you a question. What is your policy on Berlin?' Thomson looked taken aback. 'Berlin? Well, I guess I don't have a policy. But I can buy one, can't I?'

The ultimate conundrum about Astor was whether he would ever have been editor of the *Observer* if his father had not owned it. That weighed upon him as well. It was true that he could write with great clarity, even passion, on topics near his heart. As I knew from my dealings with him in Zambia, he was resolute about what he believed in. Yet he was not a natural leader. As one of his close associates said in exasperation, after another futile conference about the financial crisis, Astor would have made an excellent master in the better sort of preparatory school.

It was his contention (although no member of his staff would have been so crude as to raise the matter), that he could be sacked like any other editor. The fact that this was untrue – that the very paper which so tirelessly espoused democratic causes was itself the epitome of privilege at the top – was somehow unhealthy. The trustees could in theory dismiss Astor, but everyone knew that this titled coterie was no more likely to do so than the House of Lords would vote to scrap the hereditary principle. As magazine editor, I was invited once to that well-bred occasion, the trustees' dinner. On my right was the Countess of Albemarle, and opposite was Lord Goodman.

Goodman made a number of sententious remarks that evening about the paper, then the conversation turned to the police. I was startled to hear him say that he suspected that they sometimes planted evidence on suspects in drug cases. Pressed further, he claimed he had good reason to believe that marijuana had been planted on one of his clients. 'Good heavens,' I remarked. 'Yes,' said Goodman, 'Francis Bacon.' The idea that anyone should need to plant pot on that famous artist of such notoriously intemperate habits made me laugh. At that, the great man looked thunderous.

Although Goodman had no direct role in editorial policy, his influence was powerful. I soon learned this, because of the greater emphasis we were giving in the magazine to the arts and the coverage of major exhibitions. In this field he was ubiquitous. Once I was obliged – at the last moment – to give up my seat at a dinner held to mark the publication of an important series of William Blake lithographs, which the magazine had supported; it was explained to me that by a terrible oversight Lord Goodman had been left off the list. At another time, Goodman wanted the *Observer* to co-sponsor an exhibition in London about Jerusalem, which would have had enormous political implications at a moment when the first Israeli settlements were being made on the West Bank. The idea fizzled out – which was remarkable given the tremendous strength of the paper's pro-Israel faction, led by Nora Beloff.

This lobby had looked askance at the magazine when it printed a feature about the Palestinians in Lebanon – a product of my own visit to Beirut, where I went around Chatila and other refugee camps. As a counter-balance, David Astor proposed that we should do a series about Moses. A little baffled, I said there was not much documentary material about Moses, outside what everyone knew already. 'He's almost a joke figure to lots of people,' I said recklessly. Astor was shocked. 'I've never thought of him like that – except for the line about "Where was Moses when the lights went out?"'

In my exchanges with Astor about the magazine he declared himself pleased with its progress, but at times I found myself making belligerent remarks I did not really intend, as a kind of self-defence. I felt a need to maintain a psychological distance. The stories that circulated around the *Observer* made one afraid of letting Astor too far into one's psyche. When I had joined, somebody warned me, 'David will never really love you until you have had a nervous breakdown.' There was the classic case of the journalist who had gone to him and confessed that he was having deep emotional problems with his marriage. At once, Astor despatched him to a favourite analyst, who told the fellow that he was really a homosexual but did not realize it. Dazzled by this verdict, the patient left his wife and children, took a boyfriend, grew his hair long and returned to the paper quite transformed. Well, probably he was happier for it, but this was not much like life in the rest of Fleet Street.

Try though I might, I could not really keep my distance. One day the internal telephone gave its continuous ring, the signal that the Editor was calling. When I picked it up he proceeded to question me about my treatment of a feature about Henry Moore by John Heilpern, one of his favourite essayists. The text had run to about three thousand words, and was three paragraphs over length. After reading the piece carefully, I decided that the last three paragraphs did not add much, and cut them off. Heilpern had been to David to complain. For more than fifteen minutes I was harangued, at an ever-mounting pitch. Suddenly Astor yelled down the telephone, 'You're a philistine!' Furious, I shouted back: 'I wouldn't take that from Hugh Cudlipp!' (Cudlipp was the rumbustious editor of the *Daily Mirror*, and to be called a philistine by him would have been almost a compliment.) Shortly after this quarrel I left the office to go to lunch in Soho. As I walked up the Charing Cross Road I realized that tears were running down my face.

We often disagreed about politics, for in the closing years of his editorship Astor was moving steadily to the right. At home he was alarmed about the supposed threat to Britain from 'neo-Marxists', from Vanessa Redgrave and such phenomena as 'Women's Lib'. Abroad, he resolutely supported the United States' policy in Vietnam. Once I sent him a copy of the *New Yorker*, with a horrific account of a B-52 bombing raid; it came straight back without a comment. It was not welcomed when I ran a set of pictures, obtained with some effort, of the effects of the bombing in Hanoi.

The most remarkable disagreement was over a report from Chile by Graham Greene on the brief era of Salvador Allende. It seemed to me an honour to have Greene in the magazine, and I had latched on to him in a slightly unusual way – by spotting his name on an old list of potential contributors who had been paid but had failed to deliver. When I approached his agents and suggested that Mr Greene might like to knock us off a piece to justify the £350 he had been given several years back to do an article on Finland, they were irritated. However, Greene was game, and said he was just off to South America. He was ready to let us have something about Chile, as long as he could take the pictures as well. There was a lot of discussion on the telephone concerning the kind of film he should use, but for safety's sake I arranged a South American trip for my friend Romano Cagnoni, an Italian photographer who had been in Biafra.

When I knew that Greene was in Santiago, and about to send his story, this had to appear on the magazine's 'forthcoming' schedule. Every week or so I would discuss this list with Astor, so that there were not any blatant clashes with what was planned for the paper itself. Somebody warned me: 'Be careful – David does not like Graham Greene.' I thought that was ludicrous, but to be on the safe side just put down 'Greene', in the hope that Astor might assume it was some other Greene – even the novelist Julien Green, if he did not look too closely. It was a false hope, for Astor immediately spotted a rat. 'What's that one?' he asked, slightly tightening his mouth.

'Oh, it's about Chile,' I said with assumed breeziness. 'Graham Greene is out there. He is writing on the new Allende government.'

Astor stared so hard that I looked down defensively at my

clipboard on the low table between us. 'I should not like that,' he said. 'Greene is mischievous. He is anti-American. He is a fellow-traveller.'

It was as near as I had ever heard Astor get to giving a downright order that something should not go in. We moved on to other topics, with relief.

Soon after, the piece by Greene arrived. It was a poignant and pitiless study of the forces being marshalled to bring down Allende. In the slums of Santiago, the supporters of the new regime asked Greene whether they had a chance. There was a chance, he said. In the cathedral, he had sat behind the American ambassador and looked at the back of his head, wondering what was being planned inside it. This was a piece I knew I was going to use, somehow.

The time was around Christmas, and David Astor was due to go on holiday to Scotland. I so timed the Chile feature that when Astor went away he would have no means of knowing that it had been sent to the printers, and when he returned it could not be stopped without enormous cost. There was a cover picture, by Cagnoni, of Allende addressing a rally, with the headline: 'The New Chile – How Long Can It Survive?' Inside, we even included one of Greene's pictures, but it was the text that counted, so terribly prescient. Of all the many pieces of writing I have steered into print over the years, that is the one of which I am most proud, although it now lies forgotten in the files.

Astor said nothing, but soon afterwards the paper published a large survey of developments in Chile by Hugh O'Shaughnessy, the Latin America specialist. As a counter-blast it misfired, because O'Shaughnessy took broadly the same line as Greene. It was only a few months, of course, before Allende was brought down and replaced by General Pinochet. During the coup, the presidential palace was bombed by British-made war planes – a last, bitter irony.

Recounting such episodes, it is easy to disregard Astor's many rare virtues and the seriousness of the paper he had shaped in his own image. Bernard Shaw once wrote generously of David's frenetic mother, Nancy Astor: 'She has no political philosophy and dashes at any piece of kindly social work that presents itself. . .' The trait was inherited, and the *Observer* associated itself with countless high-minded ventures. Many have vanished in the post-Astor years, but some remain as reminders of all that was best about the paper: Amnesty International, the Minority Rights Group, Intermediate Technology, and Index on Censorship are leading examples. Once I went into Astor's office as a clergyman devoted to the uplift of a particular African tribe came out. The Editor rested his head on one hand, and said: 'Sometimes I grow tired of well-doing.'

Perhaps the most ambitious of Astor's good works is the least known. The World Security Trust was founded by him to sponsor a global 'think-tank' which would forestall wars, both big and small. The members of this exclusive group met at Boodle's, a dining club in St James's Street, and tried to devise ways of preventing conflicts. One of the most constant members in the early 1970s was Dr David Owen, a rising young Labour Party politician. Astor had been anguishing over the threat of nuclear war since the late 1950s, and had started the World Security Trust with Duncan Sandys and John Strachey. He had also floated in his leader columns the idea of some supranational body to monitor relations between nations, but the response had been slight. This was frustrating: in the years just before 1914, when the *Observer* was rescued from oblivion by the great J. L. Garvin, it had a conspicuous role in policy-making – even though the circulation was less than 20,000; but now its voice was being drowned amid the cacophony of the newer media.

Lord Harlech, Lord Chalfont, Sir Edward Thompson and Sir Paul Gore-Booth were among the high-minded diners at Boodle's. The energetic David Owen submitted discussion papers. One suggested that a World Security Authority might have to be sited in Moscow or Leningrad, to win the confidence of the Russians. So although the World Security Trust came to nothing in the end, it did play its part in the political education of a future Foreign Secretary.

In retrospect, one can see that Astor felt in harmony with those Labour Party figures who would later break away to form the Social Democratic Party, notably Owen and Roy Jenkins. He did not care for Harold Wilson, who was too devious, nor for Tony Benn, who was too extreme. Of course, the state of the underprivileged should be improved by 'kindly social work', but this should not mean turning society upside down. So the *Observer* was never a socialist paper, whatever the opinions held about it in Conservative Central Office; and its judgements on international affairs were all of a part with the domestic attitudes instilled in Astor by his background.

Revolution was not supported anywhere by the *Observer* – and no British journal was more detested in the Kremlin. I came to understand that Astor's dedication to change in Africa had not been based just on a belief that minority rule was intrinsically wrong, but also on an awareness that such a system rarely gave the blacks a square deal, and as a result made them a prey to the Soviet influence.

This trenchant anti-Communism explains the response of the *Observer* to the most important happening in Africa in the early 1970s, one whose shock waves led to the ending of Soviet influence in Egypt, and thus has a significance lasting up to the present day. That event was the Communist coup that overthrew President Nimeiri of Sudan in July 1971, followed a few days later by the counter-coup which swept him back to power. After he was restored, Nimeiri executed Sudan's leading Communists, and broke all his links with Moscow. President Sadat followed suit a few months later, ordering thousands of Soviet military advisers to leave Egypt.

This reversal for the Soviet Union was welcomed by the *Observer* – not merely because of the pressures it seemed to take off Israel. The counter-coup received effusive coverage by Colin Legum, who flew out to Khartoum for an exclusive interview with Nimeiri. Affairs of state were held up for an hour while Legum was given a presidential briefing on the 'background to the struggle against the local Communists'. Nothing was said of the wave of hangings and shootings put in hand by Nimeiri as soon as the loyal troops had freed him from jail. My personal interest in all this suddenly soared when the first hints emerged of who had shared in Nimeiri's amazing comeback.

What had not been immediately appreciated was the vital part played by the British Foreign Office. Even less understood was the role of Tiny Rowland and Lonrho. One enigma is how far these parties acted in concert, but even as far as we know it the story has all the elements of a Frederick Forsyth novel.

The Communist coup had happened on 19 July 1971, and Nimeiri was arrested by leaders of an army faction called the Free Officers Movement. Until the day before, a Sudanese trade delegation had been in London, with the Defence Minister, General Hassan Abbas, at its head. The delegation was negotiating a £10 million credit from the British Government – with the help of Lonrho officials. Also in London, by seeming coincidence, was the man the coup-leaders had chosen to succeed Nimeiri – Colonel Babiker el-Nur. Both he and Defence Minister Abbas had their ears cocked for any news from Khartoum, where the political scene was known to be jumpy.

The negotiations over, Abbas and several other ministers flew off to Belgrade to discuss investment possibilities with the Yugoslavs. It was there that they heard about the army mutiny and Nimeiri's arrest. If anything was to be done to reverse events, they had to get across the Mediterranean quickly, to muster the support of Sadat and Qadhafi. Encouraged by Khalil Osman, the Sudanese financier, Rowland came to the rescue sending the Lonrho executive jet to Belgrade. From there it flew Abbas and his colleagues secretly to Cairo, and by 21 July they were in Tripoli. Over the powerful Libyan radio, Abbas ordered troops loyal to Nimeiri to go into action.

The same evening, a scheduled British Overseas Airways plane left London. On board was Colonel el-Nur. He had told a press conference before leaving that he was returning to Sudan to take charge: although Khartoum airport had been shut down since the coup, the British VC-10 had special permission to put down there for him to disembark. What the colonel did not know was that a British secret service agent had a seat on the plane, and when it made a stopover in Rome, several more joined the flight. As soon as the VC-10 entered Libyan airspace on the way to Khartoum, the pilot was ordered to put down at Benina air base. After a brief show of indecision he did so. Colonel el-Nur and his aide, a Major Farouk Hamadallah, were immediately arrested. It was their death-warrant, for they were in due course taken back to Sudan and shot. That was also the end for the Free Officers Movement: demoralized, its forces were speedily overwhelmed by Nimeiri's loyalists.

The timing and skill of the successive aircraft stratagems

must suggest the likelihood of liaison. Commenting on 'the speed of the operation', *The Times* speculated some weeks later that 'Western intelligence agencies' had been involved. It seemed possible to me that Lonrho's MI6 man, Nick Elliott, with his Africa and Middle East background, was an intermediary. However that may be, for Rowland this feat cemented a fifteen-year friendship, only broken off when Nimeiri was finally overthrown in March 1985. Tiny was fond of calling the Sudanese President 'one of the three honest men in Africa', although he did not specify the other two. The high point of their relationship came during a state visit to Britain by Nimeiri who made time between his official engagements to visit Rowland's country home at Bourne End, near Marlow. His entire Cabinet went with him, rolling up the drive in a cavalcade of limousines.

I was to glimpse a curious aftermath of Nimeiri's hair-breadth survival during a visit to Dar es Salaam. At the university there I was invited to a farewell party for the sacked editor of Tanzania's government-owned daily newspaper. The man who had been sent packing, on the direct orders of President Julius Nyerere, was Richard Gott, now an executive on the *Guardian* in London.

I was told about the nature of Gott's offence by a left-wing black American lecturer in sociology (in those halcyon days, the Dar university must have been by far the most radical academic institution in the world). It seemed that after Nimeiri had begun slaughtering his Communist prisoners, Gott had published an angry editorial comment. It said that the lesson was plain: when a bourgeois leader had been overthrown there should be no mercy, no hesitation. The editorial was quoted *in extenso* by the official radio in its news bulletin, which Nyerere was listening to on a transistor set while laying bricks up-country at a development site. Straightening up with trowel in hand, Nyerere realized that he might be thought, by those far enough to the left, to rate as a bourgeois leader himself. He ordered his Vice-President, Rashidi Kawawa, who was also laying bricks, to hurry down to Dar and tell Gott he had to quit. Needless to say, at the university that evening, beneath the fairy lights strung among the frangipani trees, Richard was everyone's hero, a martyr for the cause.

All this was diverting to me, as an erstwhile newspaper editor in black Africa. It was clear that the passions of Latin America, where Gott had cut his political teeth, were too intense for East Africa; there was an ocean of difference between the idealism of Nyerere, a black Fabian, and the revolutionary fervour of Che Guevara and Franz Fanon. I also felt that many of the young academics in Dar had little grip on Africa's practicalities, even though they were so strong on political theory. What that vast mass of neglected people in the rural villages actually wanted out of life was not within their purview.

However, I was really back in Africa to exhume the past, not dissect the present. Somebody on the magazine had pointed out that the centenary was approaching of Henry Stanley's search for Dr David Livingstone. Would it not be a good idea to retrace Stanley's route and recreate the famous meeting – 'Dr Livingstone, I presume?' It would, and exercising my journalistic *droit de seigneur* I declared that I would do it. Several years before, my publishers had made me sign a contract for a biography of Livingstone, and I had been doing some research between times. So equipped with a copy of Stanley's century-old bestseller, *How I Found Livingstone*, I went off to trek across Tanzania. It proved exciting to look at Stanley's sketch maps of the caravan routes, and find how little had changed in many places. Outside the town of Tabora I startled a local man who was showing me the way by telling him, from one of Stanley's maps, the names of nearby hills and the direction of a path leading to a chief's village.

In Ujiji, where Stanley had finally found Livingstone, there was still a community of Arabs, dressed much as the Swahili slave-traders had been, a hundred years later. I asked to be taken to the oldest Arab in the place, and was introduced to a venerable, white-bearded character sitting on a verandah. He spoke fair English. I showed him the engraving in *How I Found Livingstone* of Stanley's arrival, with the Stars and Stripes borne behind him and a knot of Arabs looking on. The old man studied it carefully. 'Do you know anything about this meeting?' I asked. 'Oh, yes,' he replied, 'I do.' This was great. Perhaps I had stumbled upon a precious cache of oral tradition.

As unobtrusively as possible, I got out my notebook. 'Yes,' said the old Arab, 'they taught us all about that at school.'

This let-down only deterred me for a moment, because the story was so captivating. Now it was not Livingstone I was concentrating upon, but Stanley. Reading his book, getting behind the façade of his bravado, I abandoned the Scottish doctor as the subject of my projected biography, in favour of the Welsh-born journalist. It was easy to sense that there was far more to him than the brash public image conveyed in earlier books, such as Moorehead's *White Nile*.

There was something else. In more than one way, Stanley reminded me of another adventurer who had won fame and fortune in Africa. Like him, Stanley had changed his name on reaching adulthood; and as it happened, he was originally called John Rowlands. The explorer had also been obsessively secretive about his background. It was silly, of course, to look for too many similarities between Tiny Rowland and that stocky explorer who the Africans nicknamed Bula Matari – 'Smasher of Rocks'. But these personal factors they shared, the rejection of a past and the need to manufacture a public persona. Did these imbue them both with a compulsion to dominate and drive themselves beyond accepted boundaries?

Gradually, after my travels in Tanzania, the search for Stanley began to take over. Many pieces of new information fell into my hands. One of the most extraordinary was the discovery in an attic in Stow-on-the-Wold of the diaries of a Kentish boatman named Pocock. He had travelled with my hero on his greatest journey – across Africa from east to west, and down the unknown Congo River. I finally recognized that it was essential to get away from the *Observer* for some months actually to write the book. If possible, I would go abroad somewhere.

When I broached the idea to David Astor he was sympathetic. After all, no paper was more 'literary', and often enough its writers would depart on such enterprises. Admittedly, I was one of his senior executives, and there was a worsening crisis of money and morale with rumours of differences in the boardroom. But the colour magazine was riding high, and some of the initiatives we had taken were credited by the management with holding off the challenge from the *Sunday Telegraph*. We made detailed arrangements for all the series which would run through the months until my return.

Shortly before I left, however, something disastrous occurred. At a party in Belgravia I was introduced to Lady Jane Willoughby. She explained that she was David Astor's niece, and it soon became clear that she had a considerable amount of money committed to the *Observer* and was anxious about it. I had the impression that she had never met one of the paper's journalists before, and was intrigued to hear the 'inside story'. But when Lady Jane began asking about 'Uncle David' and his continued fitness to be editor, warning lights began to flash. I agreed that matters were ominous at the paper, as indeed they were: the distinguished travel writer, Eric Newby, had left after a stormy staff meeting at which he had criticized Astor to his face. Still, I was not keen on getting too close to Astor's relations, who had their own financial imperatives. We parted after a few minutes.

That was not the end. Acquaintances of Jane Willoughby telephoned after the dinner and said she was keen to see me again. These approaches were persistent. A few days before I was due to begin my book-writing leave – David Astor had agreed to six months' unpaid absence – a letter arrived from one of her close friends. It began: 'The chief point is that Jane is anxious you should get in touch before moving off.' It went on to say that she thought 'the family could really only make a move in response to an initiative from inside, and not just out of the blue'. Reading that, I began to speculate on who had conceived this plan of action. What move was the family thinking about? The inference was plain: I was being cast for a hazardous role, to set in train events that would give the 'family' – whoever they were – the chance to resolve their financial tangles concerning the paper. I now regretted having attended that Belgravia party. Fortunately, I was getting away from it all in a few days.

As a precaution I confided in Donald Trelford. In the six years since he had joined the paper as assistant news editor Donald had risen a long way. Now he was deputy editor, and regarded as Astor's closest confidant. The Editor was known to say: 'Donald is the one person I can always trust.' Trelford was not ranked as an *Observer* mandarin – he was too young for that – but he was the ideal go-between, the amiable factotum. I gave him a copy of a letter I had sent to Jane Willoughby's friend, saying that the idea of another meeting with her was 'alarming' to me: 'I fully sympathize with her anxieties, but I simply cannot feel free to offer her the kind of advice upon which actions could be based.' I told Donald that if ever, during my absence, events should make it necessary, I relied upon him to show the letter to Astor to explain the background. He assured me that I was worrying needlessly.

My destination was Deya, in Majorca, and I arrived there with a trunk full of books and notes. It felt a gratifying distance away from the troubles of the *Observer*. In an old Arab house, set above an orange orchard, I began to write.

One day I had strolled out to buy some provisions, and met Robert Graves, the father-figure of Deya's clique of writers and sybarites. He showed me around one of his houses, full of crumbling curiosities, then I went back to Henry Stanley. As I arrived a neighbour handed me a newly-arrived letter. It was from David Astor, giving me the sack.

He began by praising all I had done for the magazine. It was a meandering letter, but suddenly loosed the deadly bolt: 'I must therefore ask you to treat this letter as a formal notice from 15 February to end your existing contract of employment.' That was his prerogative, and I accepted his argument that he wanted to make urgent staff changes, so could not wait upon my return. As his letter reminded me: 'You have yourself urged the need of changes on the paper.' I could not quite see how the magazine editorship affected a reshuffle on the paper, but I wrote back at once saying that I fully understood his decision.

Then news came from London that made it all look much nastier. One of the paper's business journalists had been to see Jacob Rothschild in the City. In the course of their discussions Rothschild – whom I had never met – began asking about the state of the *Observer*, and twice mentioned my name. It seemed that the journalist in question had gone back and told Astor. The significance was, as I then learned, that Rothschild represented Jane Willoughby on the board of the paper. A close friend, leader-writer Ivan Yates, told me that rumours were flying everywhere and indignation was high on my account. One executive had warned his reporters: 'If you want to get on around here, don't talk to Lady Jane Willoughby.'

I flew back to London. It was February, and David Astor had influenza. For two hours I sat on his bed in St John's Wood, trying to overcome his suspicion. Unfortunately, Trelford had never shown him the copy of my letter saying that I had no wish to talk to Jane Willoughby. 'I don't care about the antics of my niece,' was Astor's reply when I tried to clear up that point. Finally, he agreed to appoint me as an assistant editor, to paper over the affair, but I was later told that he would never allow me into the office again.

Just before I went back to Deya to address my mind to Stanley once more, an item appeared in *Private Eye*. It said that Anthony Sampson and I were suspected of having conspired to oust Astor – who was described by *Private Eye* in typical unfriendly fashion as 'wet and ageing'.

But as I had said to Astor at his bedside: 'I would not mind getting fired for being involved in a coup that failed. Losing my job for taking part in a plot that never existed really does make me cross.' Anthony Sampson summed it all up in a note to me: 'My sympathies over the latest Ob-surdity!'

7

Falling out with Angus

After being ejected from the charmed circle of the *Observer*, I
went back to Majorca to pick up the threads of my narrative of
how Henry Stanley found Dr Livingstone. The newspapers I had
bought at Heathrow before boarding the plane were full of
breathless stories about Rowland and a quarrel he was having
with some other directors of Lonrho. It was startling to see him
on the front pages, because until that moment in the spring of
1973 he had avoided all publicity. Of course, Lonrho received
attention on the business pages, because of its phenomenal
growth, but Tiny himself was totally unknown to the British
public. That appeared to be exactly how he liked it.

Now it was about to change. The enigmatic Mr Rowland was
being transformed into a public figure, and Lonrho would from
now on become the most controversial major company in
Britain. Reading the newspapers, I could see that many of them
had not the slightest idea what lay behind the Cheapside
convulsions. It was presented as sheer knockabout stuff, the
story of a fight for power and money – for Fleet Street there was
the bonus of some well-known society names. Trying to make
sense of the drama from a Mediterranean island was impossible,
even though I knew quite a few of the leading actors; but it
seemed hard to me that Rowland's position was under threat,
considering what he had done for the company in the past
twelve years. I wrote a letter wishing him good luck, and he
replied immediately. His tone was cool and cheerful, letting me
know that he felt under far less pressure than the newspaper
implied.

The sequence of events, after the split within Lonrho, becomes clearer with the perspective of time. The first result was a massive official inquiry, ordered by the then Prime Minister, Edward Heath, into the workings of the company and Rowland's style of management. This led directly into a labyrinthine court battle between Lonrho and several august British companies, lasting until the 1980s. And from that time on, Lonrho has forever seemed to be in the toils of a governmental inquiry or commission. In retrospect, one can also look for the answers to some sensitive questions still significant today.

For example, it is occasionally asked why Lonrho, whose activities around the world bring in ever-growing profits, never wins a Queen's Award. There have also been suggestions that some honour – a knighthood, perhaps – is overdue for the man who has led the company from obscurity during the past twenty-five years; yet Rowland does not possess as much as an OBE. Indeed, he is never invited to Buckingham Palace functions for visiting African leaders, even those with whom he can claim long friendships. This royal disfavour can scarcely be on account of his chequered early years – even less because of a part-German ancestry; the Queen herself has that in common with him.

The explanation might well be traced to a telephone call made in May 1973 by Rowland to Angus Ogilvy. 'I am going to crucify you and all your family,' he said. 'I think you have behaved quite appallingly.' Ogilvy lost his temper and put down the receiver, but not before Tiny had for good measure called him a rat. It was the end of their long friendship, cemented that day in mid-1961 when Ogilvy had selected the little-known Rhodesian speculator as the best hope for shaking Lonrho into life. Their break-up, in the midst of the rowdiest boardroom battle of the century, was a deep embarrassment for the Royal Family; it likewise sent tremors through the City of London, where Ogilvy held dozens of directorships.

This was only one concealed aspect of the dispute which provoked Edward Heath to utter that savage epithet – 'an unpleasant and unacceptable face of capitalism' – in reply to a Commons question from Jo Grimond. Unfairly enough, the phrase came to crystallize the public view of Lonrho as a company and Rowland as a personality. (It has sometimes been asserted that Heath – who is unforthcoming on the matter – meant to say 'facet' and not 'face', which would have made the criticism far less devastating.)

Much that went on while his fellow-directors struggled to oust Rowland from the position of chief executive was deliberately obscured. It was rather like trying to follow the progress of a fight in an adjoining room, by listening to the thud of blows and cries of pain, without a clear idea who was enduring most punishment. Well afterwards, some contestants felt able to shed more light on what had occurred: as late as 1981, a tense chapter in his autobiography was devoted to the Lonrho battle by Sir Basil Smallpeice, who had been Rowland's foremost adversary. An essential source for any reconstruction remains, however, the 660-page report of the official inquiry ordered by Heath; never before or since has Section 165(b) of the Companies Act, 1948, been used to lay bare so much human drama. Some of the exchanges, printed verbatim, between Rowland and Allan Heyman, the QC on the investigation panel, are the true stuff of theatre.

The fuse for the explosion was lit when Rowland yielded in early 1972 to plans for strengthening the Lonrho board. Accustomed to relying upon a few cronies and yes-men, he had previously regarded the non-executive directors – in his own words – as 'Christmas tree decorations'. He ran Lonrho, and that was that in his view. So he scarcely grasped what it could be like to be *primus inter pares*, rather than just *primus*.

Still, Tiny had little alternative but to accept the restructuring proposals made by a leading firm of chartered accountants appointed to investigate Lonrho's debts. He had flown too high too fast. A first sign that matters were awry had been given by the resignation of Warburgs as the group's merchant bankers, when Tiny refused to listen to them about the mounting liquidity crisis. Even his warmest admirers knew he had been reckless to spend another £10 million on buying the rights to the revolutionary – and ill-fated – Wankel rotary engine. He had done that at a moment when Lonrho's borrowings were already running far ahead of income. But nobody could dissuade him.

He wanted Wankel and he got it. The sellers were Sakval, a subsidiary of the Israeli–British Bank, which was to collapse in dramatic circumstances in 1974.

At first, the curbs Rowland would have to tolerate as the price of Wankel and some other bold acquisitions did not look as though they were going to be too vexatious. The job of finding a non-executive chairman of high repute for Lonrho was solved by Angus Ogilvy – at that time, still Tiny's closest friend. Ogilvy had turned his persuasive powers on Duncan Sandys, the former Commonwealth Secretary and a key figure in the Ashanti takeover. The idea of Sandys as a figurehead much appealed to Rowland. This handsome and worldly top Tory was already Lonrho's principal consultant, at a remarkable yearly fee of £50,000 (more than £250,000 in 1987 terms). A large part of this was paid by Lonrho South Africa – of which Rowland was, and is, a director – into Sandys' account at a bank in Jersey.

His stipend had only been known to a handful of people inside Lonrho, since it might easily have sparked off some envy. However, Rowland felt it was money well spent, since Sandys carried weight around the Commonwealth, quite apart from his influence at Westminster. The Sandys cachet counted for a lot in South Africa; the erstwhile British Cabinet Minister had been despatched by Rowland to Johannesburg and Cape Town to polish up Lonrho's image with Harry Oppenheimer, head of the Anglo-American Mining Corporation, and with Dr Hilgard Muller, the South African Foreign Minister. To show how understanding Lonrho could be, Sandys suggested to Muller that 'South African interests' might like to infiltrate the Ivory Coast by way of the group's sugar schemes there (those being masterminded by Gilchrist Olympio).

So Sandys was clearly someone who would not rock the boat too much as chairman. However, he played hard to get: this would be a high-profile job, and its debts might yet hold the seeds of ruin for Lonrho. So he told Rowland that to give up the cosy £50,000-a-year post of consultant he needed some compensation. The figure Sandys insisted upon, after talking with Lonrho's long-suffering finance director, Frederick Butcher, was £130,000. It would be paid in three instalments in the Cayman Islands tax haven. Rowland was somewhat startled by the £130,000, but he was used to talking in millions, so this was really a bagatelle to achieve the end he wanted; still, it would raise some eyebrows if it went through the usual Lonrho books, and Butcher arranged to pay Sandys the first instalment by way of a Lonrho subsidiary, Anglo-Ceylon, with a further laundering in the Caymans.

Thus the chairmanship was settled. Then came the fatal moment in the board reconstruction. As a political figure, Sandys needed to be supported by a deputy whose probity would be beyond question in the City. His mind turned to Sir Basil Smallpeice. They had worked together briefly, back in 1959, when Sandys was Aviation Minister and Smallpeice the managing director of BOAC; more recently, Smallpeice had been chairman of Cunard, until Nigel Broackes of Trafalgar House coveted its £50 million tax allowances and made a successful takeover bid. In the way these things are done in the City, Smallpeice was first sounded out by Sir John Thomson, chairman of Barclays Bank, then given friendly encouragement by Sir Leslie O'Brien, Governor of the Bank of England. With a ritual show of reluctance, Smallpeice declared himself willing to join the Lonrho Board.

So he was swiftly voted in, at the same time as Sandys became chairman. There was another recruit, the prominent Conservative backbencher Edward du Cann; he was a keen financier whose ambition sometimes outran his skills. This reshuffle cleared the ground for a proposed share issue, to raise a desperately needed £10 million in cash. The only flaw was that Smallpeice and Rowland disliked and distrusted one another intensely from the outset.

A chartered accountant by training, Sir Basil was sixty-six, lived in Esher and was a practising Christian. When the Lonrho showdown became public, Tiny ridiculed him as a 'paper merchant, mainly interested in petty cash vouchers'. True enough, propriety was everything to Smallpeice: the peak of his pride was having been selected in 1964 as administrative adviser to Buckingham Palace, to set up an accountancy system for the royal family. Determined to earn his generous £12,000-a-year stipend as Lonrho's deputy chairman, Sir Basil began ferreting about at once in the company's finances. His prim and pernickety style was something to which the staff at Cheapside House was not much accustomed.

The first board meeting Sir Basil attended, in May 1972, quite bowled him over. Rowland went on at length about his hopes for the Kenana sugar scheme in Sudan, and was much less concerned about the impending £10 million rights issue which would help square some ot Lonrho's most pressing debts. As regards Kenana, it had seemed as though Tiny was just 'airing his thoughts'. But a fortnight earlier – as Smallpeice later discovered – he had already initialled a draft agreement by which Lonrho would finance the whole scheme ('£80 to £100 million, less any amounts he persuaded the governments of sugar-consuming countries to contribute').

It is hard to pinpoint the exact moment when the plot was hatched to force Rowland's resignation as a chief executive. But the *casus belli* was undoubtedly the discovery in early 1973 of the Cayman Islands pay-out to Duncan Sandys. As Smallpeice relates it, the 'shattering' news of this was broken to him by Sir Ronald Leach, senior partner in Peat, Marwick & Mitchell, the Lonrho auditors. Both being chartered accountants, Leach and Smallpeice talked the same balance sheet language: the £44,000 loan from Anglo-Ceylon to the Cayman Islands subsidiary had been spotted by Peats. After weeks of badgering, the harassed Fred Butcher had finally admitted what it was for – the day before the annual accounts were to be approved.

The 'pent-up feelings' of several directors broke loose when Smallpeice unveiled this revelation. Sandys swiftly promised he would repay the instalment of £44,000 he had already received, and declared the compensation deal null and void; but, says Smallpeice, 'we could no longer go on working in a company being run this way'.

Any idea that the dissident directors should just leave Rowland to it by handing in their own resignations was soon dismissed. Smallpeice had gone first to see a QC, who warned that such an action might expose them to legal action from shareholders for 'dereliction of duty'. Next he went to see his friend O'Brien, the Governor of the Bank of England, who offered sympathy but no useful advice. By now there was another piece of dirty linen coming to light, separate from

Sandys' £130,000; it was of a far more intricate weave – and for Smallpeice much more delicate, since it put Angus Ogilvy in a murky light. This concerned a copper mine in Rhodesia linked to an investment trust – based in the Bahamas and controlled by Rowland – from which Ogilvy had received a £60,000 pay-out.

The fuss Smallpeice was creating among the directors about these internal affairs only infuriated Rowland. His mind was possessed by the grandiose schemes in prospect all over Africa and the Middle East, and success in his terms meant constant movement forward. To spend time on such seemingly small matters was against all his instincts. On learning that a move was growing to unseat him, he was incredulous, when he surveyed what he had made of Lonrho. It was stunning, moreover, that one of the first people to side with Smallpeice was Gerald Percy, who had been with the company since those early days in Salisbury, when Tiny had jokingly said to him, 'Shall I work for you, or you for me?' There was never any room for compromise after the trial of strength had been mooted by Smallpeice and Percy and their fellow rebels.

One of these, predictably enough, was General Sir Edward Spears, the former chairman of Ashanti Goldfields, still valiantly holding his place on the Lonrho board at the age of eighty-six. (As Rowland would say of him: 'He cannot die happily until he sees me kicked out of Lonrho.') Another was Nicholas Elliott, the intelligence expert from MI6. The rest were relative nonentities, such as Dr Adolph Gerber, a Swiss scientist who had been acquired with the costly Wankel engine; he said stiffly that he had never been associated with such an autocrat as Rowland.

As Smallpeice marshalled his team, Rowland was not idle. He asked Ogilvy and Sandys to come down to his house at Bourne End one weekend to discuss tactics. Also there were two other directors on whom he was sure he could rely absolutely – Alan Ball, who had stood aside to let Sandys become chairman, and Edward du Cann. They all agreed that Smallpeice was to blame for 'stirring things' ever since he joined the board. They recalled how as early as the previous August he had written a long letter to Sandys, telling him: 'We are both riding for a most almighty fall (but you more than me, because you are Chairman) if we do not see that proper and full action is taken, in the very near future, wherever necessary.'

After the others had left the weekend meeting, Ogilvy had supper with Tiny and his wife, Josie. For several years the Rowlands had been on close terms with the Ogilvys, who had the use of an adjoining flat – arranged by Tiny – in Park Lane; now and then the four of them breakfasted together in their dressing gowns. But this, sad to say, was the last happy occasion they would spend with Angus, because soon afterwards Tiny realized that to win the impending battle he might well have to take it far beyond the privacy of the boardroom. In the last resort, he must make a direct appeal to the Lonrho shareholders. Not only did he own 20 per cent of the shares, which gave him a flying start, but there were also many individual holders who had come to idolize him. (He had once read out to me a letter he had just received from a widow in Hampshire, telling him how her profits from Lonrho shares had eased the evening of her life.)

But if Rowland was going to fight for his survival in the full glare of publicity, the implications for Ogilvy must be dire. He would be torn between the loyalties to a friend and the rules of discretion imposed by his marriage. . .

At first, however, only Rowland saw the possibility of a public showdown. Smallpeice put his trust in Sandys to settle matters decorously. It sounded so simple: Duncan should go to Tiny and say that eight directors wanted him to resign at once as chief executive. However, since he held 20 per cent of the shares, and had 'valuable African experience', he could stay on the board as a non-executive director. There would be no trouble about naming a successor as chief executive – indeed, the natural choice was someone who had been with Lonrho throughout the years since the profits had been pushed up from £400,000 in 1962 to £18 million in 1972. Gerald Percy had youth, breeding and experience to commend him; he also wanted the job badly. What if Rowland protested? All Sandys needed to do was to reiterate the painful truth that the rebels could muster eight votes on the sixteen-strong board, and since Rowland could not under the rules vote on his own future, the die was cast. If he refused to go quietly he would be pushed.

Nobody knew, however, that Sandys was totally on the

opposite side. He was Rowland's man. When the board met on 18 April, he reported, to general dismay, that he had made no headway with the resignation idea. It was then proposed that Rowland should be removed immediately from his executive offices; the time was past for the niceties of resignation. The most self-effacing director of all, a Major Colin Mackenzie, volunteered to be the mover, and the seconder was General Spears – at last his moment had come to extract revenge or those humiliations at Ashanti.

Down beyond St Paul's Cathedral, at the Law Courts, however, the counter-attack had begun. Rowland had taken the bold step of applying for an injunction to stop the board from voting on the resolution; all day long, Sandys managed to filibuster and avoid any pre-emptive move by his fellow directors. After dark, as the clerks were hurrying home along Cheapside, a message arrived from the court. Rowland had been granted an interlocutory injunction. Smallpeice, Percy, Spears and the rest had now lost any chance of a quick gentlemanly triumph. The battle was fated to go public, the mud-slinging was unavoidable.

The next morning, a 30-inch analysis in *The Times* was headlined 'Tiny Rowland, the Vulnerable Emperor', and talked of his 'rise and downfall'. If only Fleet Street had known what was going on inside Cheapside House at that moment it might have been even more confident about Rowland's demise. A messenger had arrived, stomping into the fraught atmosphere with an envelope addressed to Sandys in his capacity as Lonrho chairman. After tearing it open, Sandys walked down the corridor to where Rowland was sitting alone, and said, 'Tiny, I have grave news for you. Angus has resigned.'

Rowland was stunned. 'I cannot believe it,' he said. 'Angus would not do this to me.' But it was true. The contradictions of being married into the Royal Family and being on the board of Lonrho had proved too much at last. The 'Boardroom Bust-up' was now on every front page, and Angus knew his duty.

After Sandys had left his office, Rowland sat alone for fully fifteen minutes, by his own account, weighing up this turn of events. It could not have been a total surprise, because only three days before he had written Ogilvy a formidable letter, reminding him of his promise at Bourne End and dropping in a somewhat menacing reference to their private financial dealings in the Bahamas investment trust. But with Ogilvy turning tail like this, Smallpeice and his faction would be heartened – and it might fatally damage Rowland's longer-term strategy for survival.

Worse was quickly to follow. Duncan Sandys had gone into the boardroom, had called a secretary, and was dictating his own letter of resignation. When Rowland found him, he said: 'I have got to do this. It is the end, Tiny, I am afraid.' For him as well, the prospect of weeks of sordid mud-raking was too much to hear. Like Ogilvy, he had chosen to cut and run. Rowland's response was brutally candid. 'Let me make one thing crystal clear, Duncan. The publicity of Angus's resignation will be bad enough, but yours, obviously, will mean statements over the weekend which I am prepared to make, and I will have to say why we are having this argument.' He also remarked that having won his temporary injunction, he was determined to appear in court for the full proceedings and put his side, however many directors resigned. So Sandys had no hope of dodging the publicity by quitting now. 'Are you putting pressure on me?' asked Sandys miserably. He went off down the corridor and consulted one of the dissidents, Gerald Percy; but the patrician restraint of the advice he received was no match for Rowland's ultimatum. In the end, Sandys walked back and said: 'Tiny, I shall think about it this weekend, but in the meantime I shall not resign.' (As it turned out, he would stay on as chairman for eleven years, until 1984.)

In the immediate aftermath, remarkably little came out about Ogilvy's resignation. The Smallpeice faction did not feel it proper to leak this development to the newspapers, given the royal connection. Still less did they let out that Sandys was spending the weekend pondering on whether he should follow suit. All along, the rebels handicapped themselves by their scrupulous regard for etiquette. (Even in his autobiography, Smallpeice contrives to tell his side of the story without once mentioning Ogilvy or criticizing the subtleties of Sandys.)

What puzzled Rowland was Ogilvy's deepest motive for resigning when he did. The truth came out later, according to Rowland, during a stormy encounter. Ogilvy said: 'I thought that by my resigning you would resign and that would mean no publicity at all.' The inference also was that if Rowland had failed the previous day to get his interlocutory injunction and had meekly accepted dismissal, Ogilvy would have stayed on the board. 'I thought it would be in everybody's interest if there were no proceedings in court,' he told Tiny.

After his resignation, Ogilvy had literally gone into hiding to escape from Rowland's rage. Ostensibly he was suffering from back trouble, and a statement from Buckingham Palace made play of this, while dodging the Lonrho troubles: 'We do not wish to say where he is as it is important for his convalescence that he is not disturbed.' In fact, Ogilvy was in a state of nervous collapse, smoking sixty cigarettes a day and needing all the psychological back-up Alexandra could give him to weather the immediate future. The Royal Family as a whole was mortified; with her Scottish background the Queen Mother in particular was upset – and Angus's father, Lord Airlie, had been her Lord Chamberlain until a few years before. All too late did Ogilvy regret that he had not got out of Lonrho completely in 1968, when he resigned from the Rhodesian subsidiaries at the insistence of the Royal Household. Now all he could do was to lie low and contemplate the destruction of his City career. Later he complained that his back trouble stopped him getting any sleep.

Although Angus had slipped out of the limelight, affidavits were being sworn by all the remaining directors, barristers were being hired in droves, and Fleet Street was putting its best reporters on to the story. Smallpeice and his seven fellow-dissidents were nicknamed the 'Straight Eight', after a new brand of canned beer. The brewers, quick to take a public relations trick, sent them round a crate. They needed it: victory was fast slipping from their grasp.

Set against Rowland with all his panache, Smallpeice was a dowdy figure. Even his name was slightly risible, and he peered at the world through pebble-lens glasses, having just had operations for cataracts. The heir-apparent, Percy, signally lacked the common touch in meetings with journalists, and Elliott's secret service background made him reluctant to talk to anyone at all.

Spears limited himself to one gruff statement: 'Rowland's

conduct in recent months has been so uncontrolled, his language so immoderate, that I have been led to wonder whether he is entirely responsible.' It was undeniable that 'Mr Lonrho', as the papers were calling him, was giving free rein to his flair for invective against his foes.

An exotic touch was added when Rowland began to appear with an entourage of Africans. They were photographed beside him, smiling devotedly, and assured the media that Lonrho would be ruined in their home countries without Tiny's sensitive touch. It was even asserted from Zambia that all the group's assets there would be seized if he were thrown out; by the time this was denied, the propaganda had done its work.

Thousands of Lonrho shareholders were now mustering and taking sides, and it mattered little that Rowland lost his renewed case in the High Court, because the 'Straight Eight' knew they had missed their moment to sack him. An Extraordinary General Meeting had been called for 31 May; the votes of the shareholders would after all decide the issue. Rowland was already treating his opponents with contempt. He said of Smallpeice: 'I find it hard to be with this man for more than five minutes. Smallpeice and I were complete opposites, and Smallpeice and I could never live together.' He seemed to relish uttering the name. Elliott was ridiculed as 'a man who walks in the shadows', and Rowland accused him of having masterminded the conspiracy – 'that is his profession, after all'. About Ogilvy, who was keeping right out of the picture, he said not a word; but plenty was going on between them behind the scenes.

When it came to the shareholders' meeting, held in the Westminster Hall, there was no contest. Smallpeice was jeered and catcalled, Rowland cheered tumultuously, the voting was a walkover. One by one, the 'Straight Eight' were voted off the platform, and out of Lonrho for ever. As he left, Smallpeice shook hands with Rowland. Looking back, he wrote complacently: 'We had done our duty, however unpleasant it had been, and our consciences were clear.' He admitted that the three executive directors who rebelled had suffered most – and that was certainly true of Percy, whose career was wrecked; he was forty-five.

Tiny was swift to take revenge when he was asked what

compensation the sacked directors would receive. 'Compensation? What compensation?' he retorted. 'I wouldn't have expected any. They won't get a penny.' This earned a bitter parting shot from General Spears: 'It's the sort of thing we have come to expect from him. The man is a cad.' Percy said: 'I consider I am under contract and I should not think Rowland would seek to rat on a legal obligation of this sort.' In the event, Lonrho did pay.

For Rowland, though, it was a moment of total victory, a vindication of his whole career. Exhilarated, he flung himself into the drive for extending the Lonrho empire beyond Africa and into the Arab world. At the shareholders' meeting, a flamboyant speech in his support had been made by Dr Khalil Osman, his old partner in the cloak-and-dagger exercise to restore President Nimeiri to power. Now he and Khalil were constantly together. The Kuwaitis helped Rowland cure his liquidity worries with a £6 million cash injection, and as a result the first Arab joined the Lonrho board at the end of 1974. He was Sheikh Nasser Sabah Al-Ahmed, the young and somewhat naïve son of the ruler of Kuwait.

Next to join the board was an Egyptian entrepreneur with Gulf interests, Mohamed Al-Fayed, and he was followed by Khalil himself. Including the Kenyan, Udi Gecaga, there were now four non-European directors – an apparent proof of Rowland's vaunted rapport with the Third World. (Unfortunately, it could not last – and the time was to come when Al-Fayed would give Tiny a most excruciating blow in the financial solar plexus.)

Although Rowland wanted to forget – if not to forgive – as soon as the Lonrho shareholders had given their verdict, this was going to be impossible for more than three years. The two leading investigators appointed by the Department of Trade, a QC and a distinguished accountant, were already warming to their task. They were not content to look at what had happened to Lonrho in the past, but they closely monitored what was happening as the inquiry pursued its course. Some of the more dramatic developments, mainly concerning Ogilvy – to whom Rowland wrote a series of harsh letters – were sparked off by their own probings in delicate areas.

Most delicate of all was the deal by which Rowland had

deposited £60,000 in Ogilvy's family trust from Yeoman Investments, the company based in the Bahamas. It was over this that Ogilvy had feared being 'crucified'. The money had been paid in July 1970, and Alan Ball had also been a beneficiary. But it was not something that any of them wanted to talk about, even Rowland. At one point he was asked point-blank by Heyman, the QC, whether he had given £120,000 to Ball and £60,000 to Ogilvy. He replied: 'My answer is that if I did they deserved it, and if I did not it is just too bad.' Heyman was exasperated: 'That is no answer.' Rowland said: 'That is my business. That is my answer.'

There were several reasons for this evasion. For a start, just before the payments were paid, Yeoman Investments had borrowed $2 million from the Canadian Imperial Bank of Commerce, of which Ogilvy was a director. The money had apparently been used to develop the copper mine in Rhodesia, after being channelled through Switzerland, then South Africa. This was well after Ian Smith had declared UDI, so the whole financial operation went dangerously close to breaching the British sanctions laws against Rhodesia.

There was the suspicion that the £60,000 was intended to, or at least had the effect of, binding Ogilvy to Rowland and limiting his freedom of decision as a director. The time when Rowland had threatened to 'crucify' Ogilvy was just before Lonrho's Extraordinary General Meeting: he had heard a rumour that crucial blocks of Lonrho shares owned by investment trusts in which Ogilvy held executive power, were going to be used in support of the Smallpeice faction. The rumour was false, but Rowland would not believe so. In a panic, Ogilvy had gone to his solicitor, and told him about the £60,000. The solicitor said this was bad: 'It could look as if this was a bribe for you to keep your mouth shut about something.'

Before the end of the Department of Trade inquiry, the loan from the Canadian bank had been cleared by Rowland, and Ogilvy had repaid him the £60,000 with interest. But the subject kept cropping up. Rowland was derisive: 'If the inspectors are correct in saying that I purchased him [Ogilvy], then I may have a case against him under the Sale of Goods Act, 1893.' The inspectors had their own comment: 'We accept that Mr

Rowland is a strong character, that Mr Ogilvy is not.'

Tiny's own version of why the loan had been taken out from the Canadian bank was melodramatic to a degree. In a letter (2 September 1975) to Sir George Bolton, who had succeeded Smallpeice as deputy chairman, he put all the onus on Ogilvy, who allegedly said he was 'paying blackmail money to potential kidnappers of his son, James'. According to Rowland, the bank was also pressing Ogilvy – one of its directors – for repayment of a personal loan. These were the only reasons, he claimed, why the $2 million had been borrowed at all.

This letter to Bolton was written while the Department of Trade inquiry was still going on, and was part of a campaign by Rowland to make his own views known. He even threatened to take Ogilvy to court – 'It can then be decided which one of us has committed malicious perjury.' The prospect of having to face him in a courtroom was well calculated to terrify Angus because of the likely effect on his royal connections. He knew that Tiny was capable of flaunting all the titbits of information picked up in their years of friendship.

To give extra force to the letter to Bolton, a copy was sent to John Cama, the Lonrho lawyer. The knife was twisted a little more by asking Cama to retrieve 'the private correspondence between myself, Angus, and Princess Alexandra'. This corres-pondence, Rowland told Cama – who was perfectly well aware of it – had been loaned to the Department of Trade inspectors with various Lonrho files. 'While the files have, I believe, been returned to you, but not to me as yet, I understand that the letters and cards (Sheikh plus Sheikh, etc.) from Angus and Princess Alexandra to me have not been handed back to you . . .'

These were fierce tactics. Rowland was also baiting the inspectors with his discovery that Heyman, the QC, had secretly gone to South Africa to look for information about Lonrho. While there Heyman had made a call at the headquarters of the Bureau of State Security, the infamous BOSS, where he met a General Kruger and a Brigadier Buys. In letters 'for the record' to Cama, Rowland asked why Heyman was trying to keep this intriguing detail out of the inquiry records. Later, in letters to government officials, he demanded to know why the two South African security officials were not listed among the inquiry witnesses (although, it seemed, they refused to tell Heyman anything, despite his references to the British Special Branch and MI6).

Rowland also made much play, in his cascade of correspondence, with the important trust being placed in him by Prime Minister James Callaghan – at the very moment when Lonrho's reputation, and his own, were at hazard. He was able to reproduce a long telex he had sent for Callaghan to Joshua Nkomo, early in 1976. It told how Lord Greenhill was flying to Salisbury at Callaghan's instructions, and would be happy to see Nkomo if he wished. A withering five-page letter to the Department of Trade ended: 'After eleven years of public opposition to Smith, they remain so out of touch with the nationalist leaders, whose names are so often in their mouths, that this important telex message had to be routed through us, while they have, of course, maintained their channels to Smith most excellently.' Another letter, on the same topic, said: 'Ambivalence has been raised to an art.'

As the inquiry ground its way forward, an intriguing relationship had grown up between Rowland and Heyman. Sometimes there was mockery, as when Rowland was asked to go more slowly over some complex point: 'But it is so simple, Mr Heyman, your mind is so clear, much clearer than mine.' Sometimes there was anger – or a very fair simulation of it – as when Rowland suggested that the inspectors were intent on damaging Lonrho:

'I am not suggesting you should buy shares in it, but it is not a bad company, and it has a super future unless you want to kill it, because I can see things that this company can do that you perhaps cannot see. You see, Mr Heyman, the past, and I have got an idea of what the future could be, depending on whether you want to kill it. But, by God, it has got one thing, and this is it has got a protector, and that is me. In other words, anybody who wants to kill that company has got to have a machine gun, mortars, guns, all sorts of ammunition, because I am going to protect it to the bitter end. Believe me, Mr Heyman, in me you have got somebody you have got to fight when it comes to Lonrho.'

Heyman: 'Mr Rowland, I think you misunderstand the situation wholly.'

Rowland: No, I do not mean it nastily, do not get it wrong.'

Heyman: 'Whether you mean it nastily or not, you misunderstand the situation wholly. . . You are really treating me at the moment as if I am some kind of hired assassin who is out to kill the company. You are threatening using mortars and God knows what. I think you misunderstand the situation wholly.'

Rowland: 'No, I think I do not.'

At the finish, after dozens of such exchanges, the inspectors were driven to declare their admiration, in a fashion. They summed up Rowland in a paragraph: 'He is a dominating personality, an able negotiator with a record of success, and if he does not want to discuss a particular topic he has an infinite capacity to talk around the subject.' The closing sentence of their report, signed on 1 March 1976, simply said: 'We believe that Mr Rowland has a great deal to offer Lonrho and its shareholders, but his achievements will be all the greater if he will allow his enthusiasms to operate within the ordinary processes of company management.'

After anguished consideration in Whitehall, the report was released in July. At various points in the narrative, there had been sharp criticism of some of the personalities involved. Lord Duncan-Sandys (as he became during the time of the inquiry) had been notably unforthcoming under questioning, and he was condemned for being 'less than frank' about the secret agreement to give him £130,000 compensation. Ogilvy was likewise censured for being secretive with his fellow directors about the Yeoman Investments payment.

One judgement summed up what those who knew the background had long realized: 'Sir Basil and his colleagues took action against Mr Rowland alone as the originator of both sets of arrangements. This may have been just, but in our view Mr Ball, Mr Ogilvy and Mr Sandys bear a heavy measure of responsibility for allowing their respective interests in the arrangements made for them to remain hidden from the Board as a whole.' (This censure left its mark. As recently as October 1985 a London newspaper asked why Ogilvy had never received any recognition – even a knighthood – from the Queen. It asked whether she had yet forgiven him for 'blotting his copybook over a City scandal, the Lonrho Affair'.)

Although the Great Boardroom Row was long buried in the files, Fleet Street gave the 1976 report a blazoning on the front pages. Rowland and Lonrho now rated as news. Ogilvy protested that the report was 'unfair' and 'based upon simple errors of fact'. None the less, he resigned all his sixteen remaining City directorships as 'the only honourable thing to do'. Sandys said that the picture conveyed of his role was 'incomplete, unbalanced and unfair'. Rowland seemed outwardly indifferent, although he did take the opportunity for a final swipe at Ogilvy: 'We have travelled at twice the speed in the past three years, because Angus held us back.'

In an interview with the *News of the World*, of all papers, Ogilvy made his most poignant confessions. 'I have lost any pride I had,' he said. 'I wouldn't object to that, but there is one kind of pride I still have, and that is to do with my good name and integrity.' He stressed that he would not go back to the City 'until I can go back clean in everyone's mind'. His honour was what he kept returning to: 'I may have made mistakes – errors of judgement – but never dishonestly or without honour.' (As a kind of penance, it might be assumed, Ogilvy would be devoting a lot of his time in future to good works, in the manner of Profumo, the central figure in the Cliveden scandal of the 1960s; but honour aside, Ogilvy had suffered a terrible financial knock – overnight his income had fallen from £90,000 a year to less than £10,000.)

Naturally enough, the Labour Party took full advantage of the DTI report to castigate the workings of Lonrho in particular and capitalism in general. The Tories, then in opposition, were subjected to considerable raillery from behind James Callaghan's front bench. Brian Sedgemore, an inveterate hounder of financial scandals, had played a leading part, and during the adjournment debate on 5 August he startled the House with an account of what he called a 'telephone threat' from Rowland. He told how his wife – like himself, a barrister – had taken a call at their home. The man at the other end had said, 'perfectly politely', that it was his intention to 'get' her husband. Mrs Sedgemore had asked who the caller was, suggesting that he might be a member of the Fascist National Front. 'Indeed, no, I abhor them,' replied the voice. He then identified himself as

'Rowland of Lonrho'. In telling the story to his fellow MPs, Sedgemore observed: 'Just in the way one might say "I am the Empress of India".' Questioned later about the call, Tiny did not deny making it. 'But as for threats,' he said, 'that is utter rubbish.'

Yet it was another Labour backbencher, Willie Hamilton from Fife, who lashed out in the wildest fashion over the Lonrho scandal. From behind the wall of parliamentary privilege he said: 'They are a bunch of crooks who run Lonrho and every one of them ought to be in Brixton Prison. Yet here they [the Conservatives] are saying what a wonderful contribution the company has made to our export record. Lonrho has been breaking sanctions against Rhodesia for years and is in cahoots with the South African government.' Hamilton later withdrew this allegation in a prepared statement to the House.

Rowland did not reply to that charge. One aspect of the Heyman report which deeply bothered him was its strong suggestion that Lonrho had been sanctions-busting in Rhodesia.

A successful prosecution against the company might be disastrous throughout black Africa, where the guerrilla assault led by Nkomo and Mugabe on Smith's white citadel was being followed with passionate sympathy. Any individual or any organization identified as helping Smith's survival would be branded as an enemy.

This had to be the moment, Rowland decided, when he would expose the true traitors in the sanctions war.

8

Oil Villains – and a Hero

The decision Rowland took in the spring of 1976 to begin an all-out legal war with Shell and British Petroleum sprang from a short-term defensive need. He was aggrieved at the charge that Lonrho might have been sanctions-busting in Rhodesia, when he felt that the oil companies merited the real obloquy. There was also the need to divert attention. The results of his calculated aggression were to be far-reaching, however. He had set himself on a tortuous and costly path – and the further he travelled along it the more 'hypocrisy' became his favourite term of abuse about those in power in Britain. The frustrations he came to feel made him all the more obsessive in his urge to 'get even' with the Establishment. As a letter-writer he was tireless: James Callaghan was on his list, and so was the new Foreign Secretary, David Owen. Eventually he brought this correspondence together as photocopies in three bound volumes, for handing out to sympathetic MPs.

Reading through these volumes it is impossible not to be struck by the stylishness of Rowland's prose and the clarity of his thoughts. Often he adopts a tone of high Victorian solemnity, then suddenly tosses in an informal phrase like a firecracker. Given the level of output, the unflagging standard is astounding. At one point, in a long letter to Edmund Dell, then Minister of Trade, he invents a hilarious – and all too authentic-sounding – exchange of signals between the Admiralty and a Royal Navy ship patrolling off Mozambique. Most of the replies he received were leaden and evasive.

GOVERNMENT OF KARNATAKA
ಕರ್ನಾಟಕ ಸರ್ಕಾರ

CHIEF REGISTRAR OF BIRTHS AND DEATHS
ಜನನ ಮತ್ತು ಮರಣಗಳ ಮುಖ್ಯ ರಿಜಿಸ್ಟ್ರಾರರು

(FORM No. 9—ಪತ್ರಿಕೆ ಸಂ. ೯)
(See Rule 9)—(೯ನೇ ಸಂಯಮದಂತೆ ನೋಡಿ)

CERTIFICATE OF BIRTH
ಜನನ ಪ್ರಮಾಣ ಪತ್ರ

~~Issued under Section 12~~
Issued under Section 17 of the Registration of Births & Deaths Act, 1969.

This is to certify that the following information has been taken from the original record of birth which is in the register for *November 1917* of Taluk *Cantonment* (local area) District *Belgaum* of State *Karnataka*

Name _____
ಹೆಸರು

Sex *male*
ಲಿಂಗ

Date of Birth *27th of november 1917*   Registration No. *197*
ಜನನದ ತಾರೀಖು   ನೋಂದಣಿಯ ಸಂ.

Place of Birth _____   Date of Registration *30·11·1917 / 4·12·1917*
ಜನನದ ಸ್ಥಳ   ನೋಂದಣಿಯ ತಾರೀಖು

Name of Father/Mother *Roland walter*   Permanent address of Father/Mother _____
ತಂದೆಯ/ತಾಯಿಯ ಹೆಸರು   ತಂದೆಯ/ತಾಯಿಯ ಖಾಯಂ ವಿಳಾಸ

Nationality of Father/Mother *of German*
ತಂದೆಯ/ತಾಯಿಯ ಜನಾಂಗ

Signature of Issuing Authority,
BELGAUM CANTONMENT

Seal
Date *02·2·1985*

GPB—08505

Roland Walter Fuhrhop — the future Tiny Rowland — was born in an Indian detention camp for enemy aliens during the First World War. His birth certificate lists his father as being 'of German birth'.

The Isle of Man camp where Rowland spent part of the Second World War. Confined with him, under Regulation 8B, were Sir Oswald Mosley's Fascists. *(Crown copyright, Public Record Office, HO 215/302)*

Together with Angus Ogilvy *(centre)* and Alan Ball, his old Etonian fellow directors of Lonrho, Rowland posed in 1964 for a photograph at the completion of his first great triumph, the Mozambique oil pipeline. The men standing behind them are Shell executives.

Tiny at the time when eight dissident directors were trying to oust him. *On the left* is the Nigerian entrepreneur, S. W. K. Ogungbade; *on the right*, Tom Mtine, Lonrho's chairman in Zambia.

Signing a contract in the early years of his dramatic expansion of Lonrho. His charm was to prove one of Rowland's prime assets.

Addressing shareholders during the 1973 'boardroom battles'. A despondent Sir Basil Smallpeice, who led the revolt against Tiny, faces the camera.

Tiny's most loyal ally was Lord Duncan-Sandys, chairman of Lonrho for a decade. Secret consultancy payments to Sandys through a Cayman Islands bank led Prime Minister Edward Heath to speak of 'the unacceptable face of capitalism'.

In 1984, at the height of the 'Matabeleland row' with editor Donald Trelford, Rowland was threatening to sell the *Observer* to Robert Maxwell.

There is a sense that the recipients are scared of trying to 'mix it' with such an opponent.

Undoubtedly, David Owen was best able to cope; perhaps in some areas the two have a lot in common. Owen was firm with Rowland, but always amiable. He did not go in for the usual Foreign Office obfuscation. One of his letters began by taking note of Rowland's 'strong personal feelings' about the way sanctions-breaking should be investigated, and suggested a meeting 'if you think it would be helpful'. Rowland replied that Owen's sentiments struck him as being 'so kindly expressed' that he would be at his disposal whenever the Foreign Secretary wished. On the very same day Tiny had sent a long letter to James Callaghan, eloquently defending Lonrho's record and enclosing for the Prime Minister's guidance several volumes of argument countering the findings of the recent Department of Trade inquiry.

Yet for a time the 'Oilgate' scandal was just a political sideshow, even though Rowland said he possessed all the facts to prove why Britain's promise to bring down Ian Smith with sanctions had been such an utter fiasco. He recalled how Harold Wilson had promised in 1965 that UDI would end in weeks, not months; fully ten years later, after Labour had been voted out of office and come back again, 'Smithy' was still there. Oil was the commodity without which the white Rhodesians could not survive for a fortnight, yet they always seemed to have plenty of it. According to Rowland, Shell and BP were supplying more than half of Rhodesia's illegal oil. 'I have the railway wagon numbers to prove it,' he said. The Foreign and Commonwealth Office dismissed his claim as 'absolutely without foundation'. It ignored his sarcasm about the 'meaningless formulae' of British sanctions.

Relations between the oil companies and the FCO had been close ever since the Nigerian civil war, when they had combined their energies to ensure a Federal victory; there was an official resolve to stonewall Rowland if he tried to make more trouble.

The FCO had been guided on the matter by Lord Greenhill, its erstwhile Permanent Under-Secretary; since retiring from Whitehall he had become the government-nominated director on the board of BP. This was the very same Greenhill who in

1968 – while still a civil servant – had been an emissary to advise Angus Ogilvy that he might do well to leave Lonrho 'because of rumours about the group's involvement in Rhodesia'. A BP spokesman now said the suggestion that it or Shell could have been sanctions-busting was 'rubbish'.

From the good listening-post of the *Financial Times*, which I had joined after finishing my book on Henry Stanley, I followed the growing sanctions-busting debate in the mid-1970s with incredulity. To anyone who knew Africa it was absurd to say that the oil companies had clean hands. Their South Africa subsidiaries were absolutely brazen – they scarcely bothered to paint out their names on the sides of the rail tankers. As early as 1967, when I was still editing the *Times of Zambia*, there had been talk of a lawsuit by Lonrho against Shell/BP, on the grounds that they had contracted to send fuel into Rhodesia only by way of the Mozambique pipeline, but after UDI had reneged and were using the railways from South Africa instead. Rowland's argument was, and always would be, that by giving secret assurances in advance of UDI to supply Rhodesia, the oil companies made Smith's rebellion possible. An incidental consequence was to deny Lonrho the profits from its pipeline.

What we did not know in Zambia at the time was that Rowland had been obliged to drop this proposed action, because it would also mean suing the British Government, which held almost half of BP shares. This was intolerable to Ogilvy, who had consulted Sir Michael Adeane, the Queen's private secretary. The word from the Palace was that if Lonrho took such action Ogilvy would have to leave the main board, not merely the boards of the Rhodesian subsidiaries.

However, I discovered that Rowland quickly handed all his documents to his friend Kenneth Kaunda, the President of Zambia. At a press conference Kaunda then dismissed Wilson's claims that sanctions were really biting – 'even a flea bites'. He said he had written proof that the British oil companies were breaking the embargo. The documents he held were in a foreign language, but he would not say which for fear of disclosing the source; in fact, as later emerged, the language was Portuguese. Yet it was to take a time for Rowland's inside information on the undercover activities of the oil companies to be given the attention they merited.

My relations with Tiny were to be somewhat cool during the five years I was on the *Financial Times*. I was annoyed that he had ignored my detailed proposals for setting up a Lonrho public relations unit – I had even gone to the trouble of interviewing candidates to run it. For his part Tiny thought, fairly enough at the time, that the paper was disdainful of his style, and held up a mirror to all that was most snobbish and conservative in the City. In the aftermath of the Department of Trade inquiry he was in a rampaging, provocative mood. 'I vote Labour,' he said. 'I have always voted Labour. I consider that I am a revolutionary capitalist.' On another occasion he said: 'There is no jungle in the whole of Africa like the jungle of the City of London.' Once I called him to suggest that he might like to come to lunch in one of the Bracken House dining rooms. But after putting down the telephone I had to confess to several colleagues who were hoping to meet him, and had thought I could do the trick, that he had just harangued me about the *FT* and the City, then ended by saying: 'I'm not going down there. You come up here.' (It was not much of a challenge, seeing that we were in buildings only about 250 yards apart.)

Although Rowland had a point about the *FT*'s reverence for the merchant bankers and the Mansion House brigade, I wondered how he would have taken it if the paper had done a proper hatchet job on his friend Jim Slater. When Slater crashed, and the Bank of England dashed in with £100 million of the taxpayers' money, there were many journalists on the *FT* who thought too many punches had been pulled. The *Wall Street Journal* would have taken Slater to pieces without mercy had his financial tricks come unstuck in the United States.

So for the moment I turned my back on Tiny and his 'sanctions war' to look down Queen Victoria Street instead, and follow the dramas on my previous paper – where oil was also to play a decisive role.

Many pessimists had feared by the mid-1970s that the *Observer* was on the verge of death. It was a tragic prospect for its newly appointed editor, Donald Trelford, who had just acquired the post in the face of some august opposition. The slate of seven candidates had included Anthony Sampson and David Watt, whose weekly political commentary in the *Financial Times* was one of the benchmarks of British journalism. But the money troubles were so desperate that one of those rejected was told by Lord Goodman, chairman of the trustees, that Trelford had been chosen because it was thought unfair to bring in an editor who might have to give up a secure job.

This was a gentle deception, because when David Astor finally retired after twenty-seven years he was quite single-minded about wanting Trelford to take over. Donald was young, alert, would be guided by the editorial mandarins, and not make impetuous changes. Before Astor left there was a great show of consulting the paper's sixty journalists, in a manner unheard of in the rest of Fleet Street. Many had been with the paper for most of their writing lives, and were sensitive to the wishes of the *grand seigneur*; they were assured that Donald stood for continuity, the abiding qualities. So he won, just ahead of Sampson on editorial votes.

But now what? The circulation of the *Observer* by the middle of 1976 was less than 680,000, more than 10 per cent down on what it had been in 1970. It was lying third in the weekend quality field, slightly behind the *Sunday Telegraph*. The *Sunday Times* was almost out of sight, with sales about equal to those of the other two combined. Weakened by a wave of voluntary redundancies, too penurious to pay for television promotion, using presses that stood expensively idle for six days out of seven, Britain's oldest Sunday paper looked ready for the graveyard. At long last the flow of Astor funds had simply dried up, and the overdrafts were mounting ominously. True, the family did still have wealth – including 11 per cent of London Weekend Television – but this was all tied up in trusts.

So while Trelford got on with bringing out the paper on a skinflint budget, Goodman and Astor and a coterie of liberal well-wishers began to hunt around for white knights. What they wanted was somebody of enormous wealth who would prop up the paper, but would never demand a say in editorial policy. Such people are scarce, certainly in Britain. There was one place abroad where easy money could be found – in the Middle East, whose sheikhs were almost literally rolling in it after the leap in oil prices after the Yom Kippur War of 1973. But Goodman, an avowed Zionist, blackballed the Arab proposals (most of all, one from Colonel Qadhafi). So in the end there was no white knight. There was only Rupert Murdoch. At that time he merely owned the *Sun* and the *News of the World* in Fleet Street.

The approach to Rupert was made in deadly secret, for once the advertisers know a paper is up for sale they take fright and start pulling out. Furthermore, although it was plain that something or other had to happen, the possibility of the 'Dirty Digger' as an owner only came to *Observer* journalists in moments of hysteria. There were jokes in El Vino's about having a Page Three Bum, to maintain the 'essential character of the paper', but Murdoch was never seen as a serious option.

The realities were only unveiled to Trelford after negotiations had been going on for several weeks. He was told to fly to New York and talk matters through with Murdoch himself, because the management was already close to a deal. News International, the Murdoch newspaper company, was willing to put in several millions; it would also put in a new top editorial team.

It was generally supposed at the time that Astor, who had scarcely been able to countenance the vulgarities of a colour magazine, was horrified at the thought of Murdoch. He was alleged to have told Goodman: 'You will not sell my paper to that pornographer.' It was untrue. Murdoch also happened to own 11 per cent of LWT, and they got on well during their meetings. As the *Observer* later explained, David felt it was 'better to have an efficient Visigoth than nothing at all'. (Not merely an efficient Visigoth, but one who had also been at Oxford.) When the 'pornographer' anecdote appeared in an American news magazine, Astor quickly wrote in to deny it and say how much he admired Murdoch.

The feelings of Trelford were rather different. The man Murdoch proposed to install as editor-in-chief was Bruce Rothwell, my principal rival six years before in the contest for the editorship of the colour magazine. As I knew, having once worked on the *Daily Mail*, Bruce was in the toughest Northcliffe House tradition, and five years with Murdoch could only have made him that much more ruthless. Trelford knew it, too. Although Astor had insisted that Donald be retained, Murdoch had come up with the ambiguous title of editorial director for him. It was the kind of job from which it was all too easy to be fired.

After several meetings with Murdoch in New York it seemed to Trelford that the prospective new owner had agreed after all to tiptoe around the sensibilities of the editorial staff. Far from it: Murdoch was merely incredulous at the suggestion that the journalists would not 'accept' sudden changes at the top. The reality was simple to Rupert: he was putting in the money to save the paper, and anybody who did not like it could waltz right out of the door. That was precisely the message Rothwell gave Trelford when they had lunch the following week at the Garrick Club in London. Another Murdoch stipulation was that there should be no 'time-wasting' inquiry by the Monopolies Commission. When they parted Trelford was very thoughtful.

In the middle of the next week the story of Murdoch's intentions broke in every Fleet Street paper, with plenty of supporting detail. Until that moment the *Observer*'s financial crisis had been kept out of the headlines, except for a report a month earlier that it was seeking government help to settle redundancy pay-offs. Now Fleet Street began to doorstep one of its own fraternity, just as much as it would any vicar who had run off with a choirmistress. Everyone was immediately interviewed – Goodman, Astor, the management, the unions. Only Trelford could not be contacted: he was away 'lecturing'. In his absence, the paper's journalists began a furious agitation. The thought of Murdoch, 'for real' and not mere bar-table gossip, gave them palpitations. It was understandable enough. In the Commons, media-watching Labour MPs demanded to know what would be done to stop such an outrage.

As the telexes from his London lieutenants began cascading on Murdoch in New York, his mood turned uncompromising. Suddenly the headlines were saying: '*Observer*: Murdoch Pulls Out'. At the end of a dignified account of the approaches made to him and the progress of the confidential negotiations, his statement said: 'In view of the breach of confidence that has taken place, together with the deliberate and orchestrated attempt to build this into a controversy, News International is no longer interested.' Trelford surfaced, and said he was utterly surprised:

'The leak certainly did not come from our side and I don't know where it came from.' Showing tremendous sang-froid, he explained that the paper was not really in a position of crisis: 'We would like the money that Murdoch has to offer. But we can carry on without it.' In contrast, the *Observer*'s management said it was alarmed that the negotiations had collapsed, and even some of the journalists began to lose their nerve and said they wanted to talk to the Digger. One of his aides responded drily: 'The editor has indicated they have no financial troubles.'

Once again, Fleet Street began to shovel out the *Observer*'s grave, while rumours of possible buyers flew around. The *Daily Mirror* group disclosed that it had twice been asked by the Labour Party to think of a takeover, but had refused. Briefly, Tiny Rowland was mentioned. Then other names were bruited about as saviours, even including that of the militant right-winger Sir James Goldsmith.

One of the most outlandish was Olga Deterding, whom I had got to know well when her lover, Jonathan Routh, had contributed to the *Observer* colour magazine. Olga lived in a Piccadilly penthouse overlooking Green Park, and had inherited £23 million at the age of ten from her father, Sir Henri Deterding, the founder of Shell. Apart from working for a while in Dr Albert Schweitzer's leper colony in the Congo, Olga had never had a job in her life. She was a reckless alcoholic. I called her up and urged her to push ahead with her plans to become a press baron, feeling that she might now have a purpose in life. She was drunk and frisky. 'I'm serious,' she said. 'I want to make the *Observer* more whimsical.' I said I thought it could do with a bit of that.

Although oil money would ultimately fend off the *Observer*'s bankruptcy, sadly it was not going to be Olga's. At the very moment when Murdoch had, despite Trelford's opposition, been lured back into negotiations – Astor had a draft contract on his desk – a genuine white knight appeared wearing a ten-gallon hat. He was Robert O. Anderson, chairman of Atlantic Richfield, seventh biggest oil company in the United States. Without a word to anyone, least of all to the journalists, Astor as proprietor flew off to Los Angeles to meet him: in less than two hours it was all settled – and the *Observer* had a new owner.

Up at the *Financial Times* I wrote a slightly satirical feature, entitled 'American Sir Galahad Rescues Elderly Damsel'. The story of how Anderson had been ensnared was certainly worth recounting, beginning as it did in Rules, that somewhat staid restaurant which had known racier days (Edward VII liked to meet his mistresses there). Rules had always been a haunt of Kenneth Harris, one of the old hands at the *Observer*, and it was there he suggested having dinner with an American academic named Douglass Cater when he called up to say he was in London. The two had known each other in the 1950s in Washington, and Cater had unearthed Harris's name from his address book when he found himself with an evening to spare. Over dinner Harris poured out the financial predicament of his paper, and Cater – who directed a cultural centre in Colorado, which Anderson backed out of philanthropy – saw that the *Observer* might be just the challenge to take his patron's fancy. Back at his hotel, Cater made a call to America. By the next afternoon, after going for a good lunch with Roy Jenkins, the professor had received his answer: Anderson was quite ready to hazard a few of Atlantic Richfield's millions on sustaining a fine old British institution.

At the *Observer*, the news was greeted with relief, tempered by bewilderment. None of the staff knew anything about Anderson, but the deal was done so fast that there was little chance to work up a philosophical debate about the rights and wrongs of being owned by a multinational oil corporation. It was only certain that Trelford would stay on as editor, and there would be no frightful Murdoch to endure. (As one executive put it: 'That would have been like giving your beautiful daughter to a gorilla.') There was even a selfish satisfaction at the *Sunday Times*, which had been bracing itself for an onslaught from a re-invigorated rival – which, as matters were turning out, now seemed likely to trundle along as before.

That cosy prospect was assured by Kenneth Harris's central role in the rescue, and his consequent elevation in the paper's hierarchy. He was a pundit from the past, brought out now and then to perform his special accomplishment: Ken had a corner in long, question-and-answer interviews with royalty and similar dignitaries – the kind of avuncular journalism that never gives offence. He also ran a school debating competition, for a prize known as the 'Observer Mace'. Even at university, where I had been a contemporary of his, he liked to greet everyone as 'old boy'. It was a long time since he had been taken seriously at the *Observer*, but now he was the hero of the moment.

There were only a few questioning voices about what had been pulled off. For a token £1 payment, Atlantic Richfield had acquired 90 per cent of the paper's shares, and in return promised to plough in as much as £5 million to protect editorial freedom. Would it matter that Anderson was just as right-wing as Murdoch, and had been a big contributor to Richard Nixon's presidential campaigns? Could ARCO's oil interests in Iran be a complication, given liberal distaste for the Shah's regime? A *Washington Post* commentator, Charles Seib, added other speculations: 'What happens when ARCO's stockholders tire of supporting a fine but unprofitable newspaper? What happens when an investigative reporter for the *Observer* starts to dig into the world-wide operations of the oil companies?'

The verdict of *Time* was more cynical: 'The *Observer* has lost much of its vigour in recent years under Editor David Astor ("the editor's indecision is final", an Astor deputy once quipped). But the paper is still firmly plugged into the Old Boy network of Oxbridge dons, senior civil servants and other privileged subjects who have helped to run Britain – and the *Observer* – for decades. Ownership will give Anderson a box seat in the select circle, a valuable asset in a business as politically sensitive as oil.' Such remarks were thought to be in thoroughly poor taste.

The losing suitors had a variety of reactions. Olga Deterding said she felt 'terribly disappointed', and thought that a British institution should not be allowed to fall into American hands; it was her last effort to make something of her fragile world, and she did not have long to live. Murdoch said he went through a 'gamut of emotions', deciding in the end that it was all for the best.

One almost unpublicized contender said nothing: Tiny Rowland, who had made an offer in collaboration with his Middle East partners. This was one of the four 'Arab bids' thrown out by Goodman.

9

A Tip from Tiny

It was just as well, as matters turned out, that Rowland's consortium did not buy the *Observer* in 1977. By that time the Lonrho advance into the Middle East was running into the sand. Indeed, it could be put much more strongly – the entire initiative had been a succession of failures. He had hopes of making a 'killing' in a region suddenly rich because of high oil prices, but these came to nothing. Perhaps the quick and tigerish style Tiny had of doing business was too unsettling for the Arabs; more likely, the main Arab investors were disappointed with their profits from Lonrho. In any event, Sheikh Nasser Sabah Al-Ahmed – later to become Kuwait's Minister of Information – resigned as a Lonrho director in November 1976, just as Anderson was buying the *Observer*. The Sudanese millionaire, Khalil Osman, left with him, after less than a year on the board. They were soon followed by Mohamed Al-Fayed, the Dubai-based Egyptian financier who had come into Lonrho as an executive director for 'shipping and construction'. On leaving Al-Fayed had bought back his large slice of shares in Costains. One matter which had deeply embarrassed the Arabs was the proposal that the Wankel engine should be made in Israel; because of this Lonrho was, for a time, threatened with being put on the Arab League boycott list.

As far as anyone knew, the partings were amicable – although the *Financial Times* did remark that it had cost the Sheikh £38 million to build up his 23 per cent holding in Lonrho, and that was double the market value when he resigned. Never again would an Arab become a Lonrho director (or any other

124

non-European, for that matter), and Rowland's reports to the shareholders fell silent about the limitless potential of the oil-rich Middle East.

He was still thinking about oil, none the less – but not in a sense that would bring any profit to the Lonrho shareholders. It was the vendetta against Shell and BP – and a score more oil companies for good measure – which took up an unconscionable part of the chief executive's time. Tiny had the evidence in his hands, and quite apart from issuing High Court writs to claim £116 million in damages he was determined to extract the greatest publicity value from it. This is how the *Observer* came to publish, in June 1978, one of the most sensational exclusive stories in its history.

There was one obvious reason why he chose the *Observer* as the best shop-window for his cache of revelations. It was the great 'Africa paper', tireless in its coverage of Rhodesia. No publication was more important to him. He could be confident that the inside story of how the British oil giants, with the connivance of British ministers, had made a mockery of British sanctions would be given the fullest treatment in its pages. Rowland did not insist, however, that his own name, or even that of Lonrho, were mentioned in the story; he simply let it be known, among people who mattered in Africa, that he had been the *deus ex machina*.

The tip-off was given to Colin Legum, as the Africa correspondent; he was told to go to a London hotel, where he could find Jorge Jardim, the Portuguese politician and businessman, who until the end of colonialism had been one of the most influential figures in Mozambique. Jardim was just about to publish a book on sanctions-breaking, based on the official Portuguese sources to which he had possessed total access until 1974.

On other topics this protégé of Salazar, this opponent of Mozambican independence, would have been a suspect source. But on sanctions, Jardim more than lived up to Legum's expectations. As instructed by Rowland, he handed over an advance copy of the English version of his book, entitled *Sanctions Double-Cross*. It had been published in Lisbon by the firm of Intervencao (with financial help from Lonrho, although Jardim did not mention that). Without exaggeration, the book was a bombshell, and the *Observer* printed extracts from it across the top of page one, then down three columns inside.

There was a wealth of devastating facts, showing how the South African subsidiaries of Shell and BP had worked with other suppliers, notably Total, to keep Rhodesia's petrol tanks full. Worst of all, for the companies, were extracts from confidential memoranda from inside BP, proving that the London headquarters knew exactly what was going on but had made little effort to intervene for more than ten years.

The book put a finger in particular on George Thomson, a colourless Commonwealth Secretary in the second Wilson Government, who was later given a life peerage. At a secret meeting with the oil company bosses, Thomson had been briefed on what was happening – why Ian Smith was never short of fuel – and had promised them that he would be very careful in the way he answered questions about sanctions in the Commons. Set against Harold Wilson's assertions, time and again, that it was the French who were helping Smith, and how De Gaulle had refused to listen to British protests, it made the politicians look quite as devious as the oilmen.

To drive the message home, the *Observer*'s story was adorned with the emblems of Shell, BP and Total, in place of cross-headings. All in all, it must have been an intriguing read for the *Observer*'s new proprietor, on the fifty-first floor of ARCO House in Los Angeles.

Jardim's book had been frank about the Rowland connection. It described a meeting in the Ritz in Lisbon, soon after UDI, at which Jardim had explained to Tiny that quite apart from Lonrho's own wishes, the Portuguese dictator, Dr Salazar, would not allow any oil to be pumped through the Beira–Rhodesia pipeline. This was in case of embarrassment to Angus Ogilvy, on account of the high regard Salazar had for the Queen.

The book brought together all Jardim knew from the Portuguese side together with what Rowland had been able to unearth. The most sensational material had been acquired from a file full of correspondence 'leaked' from the BP head office, Britannic House, near London Wall. It was this which made plain the complicity of successive Cabinets, both Tory and Labour.

Two months later, the *Observer* came out with still more

damning material, headlined 'Rhodesia's Oil Pledge from Shell'. This was also organized by Rowland, but once again there was no hint of his involvement – in marked contrast to a long exposé on the same day in the *Sunday Telegraph*. Written by Ivan Fallon, then one of Rowland's closest friends in Fleet Street, this spelled out how Lonrho was dedicated to 'exposing the sanctions-busters', and had been hounding the oil companies for years – not merely out of altruism, but from anger at all the pipeline profits Lonrho had been denied during the eleven years of UDI.

There were some elements in the story which Fallon either did not know, or preferred to slide over: for instance, that the decision to issue writs against the oil companies had been opposed for a while by Lord Duncan-Sandys, the Lonrho chairman. Duncan-Sandys was still recovering from his bruising by the Department of Trade inquiry, and was reluctant to get into a new brawl with companies whose boards were sprinkled with some of his best friends. But the article did spell out Rowland's close alliance with Jardim, and how both ministers and civil servants had tried to pigeon-hole all the letters and memoranda Rowland had submitted to them.

Perhaps it was modesty – hard though it is to believe – that had restrained Tiny from telling Fallon that it was his campaigning behind the scenes which had forced the hand of Dr David Owen, the Foreign Secretary. As the volumes of photocopied correspondence make plain, the evidence pressed upon him had obliged Owen to order an official inquiry into the oil companies' activities in Rhodesia. This was not quite what Rowland was seeking, however, since he believed that the material he had handed over was more than enough as a basis for criminal proceedings without further ado.

Such a blaze of public condemnation of Shell and BP would have suited him ideally. Not only would it have greatly improved his chances of winning a civil action against them, but it would also have dwarfed Lonrho's own manoeuvrings over sanctions; this was being laboriously investigated by Scotland Yard, as a sequel to the Department of Trade inquiry. The possibility that Lonrho itself might be prosecuted was a constant worry to Rowland, because of political scars it would leave.

He was still getting ominous criticism from the collapse of a scheme by which Lonrho would have become oil consultants to the whole of black Africa, working through the Organization of African Unity. The company would have had a monopoly of buying, shipping and distribution. After Idi Amin, of all people, had drawn attention to Lonrho's links with South Africa, the attacks had begun to gather such momentum that Rowland was forced to cancel the contract he had signed with the OAU; its secretary-general, Nzo Ekangaki, resigned in disgrace. It had been a bad experience, convincing Rowland that he must try his utmost to be on the side of black nationalism (while quietly pressing ahead, of course, with Western Platinum and similar South African ventures).

When Rowland learned Owen had agreed, under pressure from the oil companies, that the sanctions-busting inquiry would be in camera without any guarantee of the results being published – he was disgusted. 'It's a non-starter,' he wrote to Owen, 'particularly as I know that many of the witnesses will be intimidated, either by fear of losing their livelihoods or by more direct threats.'

Having a lot to hide, the oil companies relied heavily on the government's promise of secrecy. A written statement to the inquiry by BP said: 'Lonrho has by some means unknown to BP obtained possession of some of the documents in BP's possession and these may be submitted [as evidence] by Lonrho.' In the event, it took a subpoena from the QC in charge of the inquiry, Thomas Bingham, to make Rowland come to give evidence and produce his documents. Bingham had told him, in a letter accompanying the subpoena, that he 'had a public duty to perform'.

It was his expectation that the Bingham Report would let the oil companies off the hook which had impelled Rowland to serve up Jardim's evidence to the *Observer*. There was even a possibility that the report would not be released at all, or at best in summarized form. Once again, Rowland was daring to pre-empt an official inquiry, to Whitehall's annoyance.

Eventually, when Owen did release it in full, in late September 1978, Bingham's report was seen to have gone some way towards unveiling a distinctly murky episode. The oil companies had clearly been much less than honest, both with successive British Governments, then with Bingham himself. Their predictable defence was that they could not dictate to subsidiary companies in South Africa, who would have been prosecuted if they had tried to impose their own embargo on Rhodesia. The defence of the British Government, in so far as it had one, was that the only real way of stopping oil reaching Rhodesia would have been to engage in total sanctions against South Africa itself, and that it would not be able to do alone. (A logical extrapolation from this argument might have been that it would be unwise to encourage further British investment in South Africa since the time was surely coming when international sanctions against South Africa would be inescapable; but nobody cared to extrapolate.)

The release of the Bingham Report was marked by a squalid public quarrel between Harold Wilson, the former Prime Minister, and George Thomson, his one-time Commonwealth Secretary. According to Thomson, his old boss had been told everything about the covert doings of the oil companies. Wilson, typically adroit, said he only knew that 'oil sold by British companies to South African agents was in some cases diverted to Rhodesia'. For some reason, Bingham never asked Wilson to give evidence before him, and the Cabinet papers which would have nailed the truth were not available under the thirty-year rule. The archives may well reveal that one reason for Wilson's sudden and unexplained resignation in 1976 (as Rowland began releasing his bombshells) was a desire to dodge having to admit that the sanctions policy had been an unscrupulous farce.

After the Bingham Report came out, the *Observer* published a cartoon by Trog showing the Houses of Parliament being drowned in a flood of dirty oil pouring out of two office blocks marked 'Shell' and 'BP'. But unlike all its competitors, the paper gave Rowland no credit whatsoever. A compliment to the Tamberlaine of Africa, the unacceptable face of capitalism, would have died on Colin Legum's lips. At least one knew where one was politically with the oil company chiefs – the likes of Lord McFadzean, chairman of Shell and an 'ultra' of the Conservative Party. They were not rivals for the friendship of President Kenneth Kaunda.

On the other hand, it was impossible to avoid any mention of

Rowland at all in the *Observer*, because he would never stop involving himself in the efforts to bring about a settlement in Rhodesia. Whenever a promising black nationalist surfaced, after Smith's hold had begun to weaken, Rowland would rush forward with offers to pay for air tickets, hotel suites, medical examinations – whatever was wanted. So great was his enthusiasm that he did not seem to discriminate, and Lonrho funds were showered in turn upon Bishop Abel Muzorewa, the Reverend Ndabaningi Sithole, and finally Joshua Nkomo. (While writing the 'Men and Matters' column of the *Financial Times* I once went to interview Nkomo as he was passing through London; he was in a suite at the Savoy, and was just going on to Moscow to meet Brezhnev – all at Tiny's expense.)

Yet it was in the provision of his executive jet that Rowland made the biggest splash as a 'merchant-statesman' (which was how he now saw himself). It exactly suited his impulsive nature and love of sudden, mysterious gestures to fly African leaders about on secret missions. He often lent his jet to Kaunda, as he had once used it to help Nimeiri's counter-coup in the Sudan. More recently he had made an aircraft available to a new friend, the Angolan rebel, Jonas Savimbi.

So as the pace quickened in the negotiations to transfer power in Rhodesia, his home for so long, Tiny was in his element. Twice the Lonrho jet was involved in secret missions across the Zambezi, taking Ian Smith from Salisbury to Lusaka, the Zambian capital. The first time was in November 1977, when Smith and ten officials were flown to meet Kaunda. They talked for six hours, while Rowland strolled around the grounds of Lusaka's State House. Their aim was to find a formula by which Joshua Nkomo could be brought into a national government. When the news leaked a week later, there were recriminations on every hand. Robert Mugabe, who had an uneasy pact at the time with Nkomo, believed – quite correctly – that this was a conspiracy to outflank him, and quite wrongly that Nkomo had actually been present at the meeting. The second Rowland initiative was almost a year later, when he did fly Smith up to Lusaka for direct talks with Nkomo. There were plans for a further encounter, this time involving Mugabe, but he refused to attend on discovering that Smith and Nkomo had already met without him. A message was sent down to Smith, telling him not to leave Salisbury.

A slightly garbled account was written by the *Observer*'s correspondent, David Martin, saying that Mugabe had 'angrily walked out' of the meeting before Smith could make any proposals to him. But it did correctly report that Rowland had been involved.

The net result of all this slipstream diplomacy was, unfortunately, to sharpen the animosity between Nkomo and Mugabe. Any warmth that might have been generated between Smith and Nkomo was quickly dissipated when a band of the latter's guerrillas, armed with a Soviet ground-to-air missile, shot down a civilian airliner near the Victoria Falls. The plane was full of holiday-makers, and thirty-eight died as it crashed; of the eighteen survivors ten were 'executed' by the freedom fighters.

Rhodesia was earning headlines almost daily, and Rowland enjoyed recounting his role in events. He told me of his turbulent relationship with Smith, and how the Rhodesian leader had once threatened to arrest him. When he was flying Smith up to Lusaka he might have ordered the plane to swing east and land in Mozambique. 'We could have handed Smith over to Mugabe,' he said. 'It would have been a quick way to end UDI.' This was a nice flight of fancy, because it overlooked the ten-strong team Smith had with him. More interesting, I thought, was that Smith trusted Kaunda to let him leave Lusaka.

Rowland tended to see himself at this time as a rival to David Owen, who he thought was rather jealous of his contacts with the black nationalists. On the contrary, Owen admired Tiny's complete lack of racial prejudice, although privately calling his unofficial mediating 'a bit of a nuisance'. But Rowland accused the British government of 'harassing Lonrho', because he had refused to halt his legal action against the oil companies. Owen was publicly lambasted by Rowland for promising that the investigation of Lonrho's alleged sanctions-busting would be dropped, in return for help in ending the Rhodesia crisis, then failing to honour his word. This was a misunderstanding, caused by the careless talk of Foreign Office 'contacts'.

At last, in November 1978, there was a terse statement from

the Government that it was not proceeding against Lonrho over its investments in the Shamrocke copper mine. The news lifted a cloud which had hung over Cheapside House for more than three years: Lonrho had survived the UDI years in Rhodesia without any indelible stain on its record, yet had kept its businesses flourishing there. It was no more, or less, culpable than several other leading British companies. Only a handful of smaller firms were prosecuted, to give an illusion of official seriousness about sanctions.

In preparation for the day when the country became Zimbabwe, there was now an assiduous drive by Rowland and his underlings to make friends with the men who might wield power after independence. The most obvious target for such attentions was Nkomo, who was widely regarded as sure to become the national leader. That was the opinion of big business, and it was equally the judgement of the Foreign and Commonwealth Office. He looked the part of 'Father Zimbabwe', with his huge girth and imperious manner. It mattered little, in practical politics, that the Rhodesian whites regarded him as a murderer, far worse than Mugabe, after his guerrillas had brought down a second civilian airliner, killing all fifty-six people on board.

Nkomo is fulsome in his memoirs about the help Rowland gave him. 'As I got to know Tiny I came to trust him. His charming wife Josie is Zimbabwean-born [*sic*] and Tiny became one of us. I began to regard him as a son-in-law, what we call the *mkweenyana*, one of the family by marriage.' In return, Rowland called him by the nickname 'Lloyd', a kind of *nom de guerre* when they talked on the telephone.

Rowland was always ready with air tickets. 'I was constantly travelling,' recalls Nkomo, 'usually with two or three assistants: all I had to do was to ring up Tiny's office and the tickets would be ready. I was travelling between Belgrade and Moscow, or New York and Havana, on tickets provided by this great capitalist. He knew where we were going, but we never discussed it.' Sometimes, when the hotels were full, Nkomo would stay in Rowland's flat in Park Lane.

The extent to which Nkomo was being subsidized by Rowland was no secret in Fleet Street, but was viewed with some disapproval by papers such as the *Observer* as a type of corruption, a blatant attempt to buy goodwill. In the event it was a misfire, a classic example of the way Rowland's personal enthusiasms come in the way sometimes of his business instincts. During the post-independence election campaign, early in 1980, Nkomo's ZAPU party was given help worth more than £150,000, including a plane-load of electioneering material hurriedly printed in Britain and a campaign helicopter, complete with pilot. But Mugabe's ZANU won fifty-seven seats, and ZAPU only twenty. Anybody with an understanding of the tribal alignments in Zimbabwe – which Rowland should have had, after living in Gatooma for years – must have known that Nkomo could never win. Yet it would be a long time before Tiny finally abandoned him; when he did, I was to be an eyewitness, on behalf of the *Observer*.

My return to the paper had come at the start of 1980. Donald Trelford and I lunched at the Garrick, and talked about those remote days, fourteen years before, when we had been in the Ivory Coast. Then we discussed my proposal that I should fill the *Observer*'s vacancy for a diary editor; for two years I had been running the *FT*'s 'Men and Matters' column.

Donald and I soon came to terms, with the aid of the Garrick's claret. The thought of returning to the *Observer*, where I still had many friends, was exciting; although David Astor remained on the board, he had nothing to do with the day-to-day affairs, so he would not be an obstacle. It was impressive how Trelford had grown into the editorship, because Astor's twenty-seven years was a hard act to follow. But Donald now seemed audaciously confident, his mind as quick as a whippet.

He had just been through an exhilarating year, with the sales of the paper well over the million mark – far higher than ever in its history. Admittedly, this had not been solely due to the *Observer*'s virtues; the *Sunday Times* was out of action for most of 1979, along with *The Times*, on account of a confrontation between the incompetent Thomson managers and the avaricious Fleet Street printers, which the latter won. Other people's troubles had been a happy windfall, giving the *Observer* an operating profit of £1.4 million. It was the first time the paper had been effectively in the black for well over a decade.

This turn-around had done a lot to reinforce Trelford's position: there had been, one knew, a half-hearted attempt by Lord Barnetson, the deputy chairman, to replace him, but Donald had outwitted this quite easily. The appointment of that veteran Irish word spinner Conor Cruise O'Brien as editor-in-chief was no threat – the Cruiser was rarely seen on the editorial floor, and his main occupation was to dictate a column of dazzling casuistry once a week over the telephone from Dublin.

However, by the time I had served my notice at the *FT* and taken the short walk down Queen Victoria Street to the *Observer*, the outlook there was suddenly looking more unsettled. With the *Sunday Times* back in business at last, the easy profits disappeared like air from a pricked balloon. What was worse, the printers were reluctant to return to normalcy: for a year they had become used to midweek printing, and plenty of overtime, because the ancient presses had been unable to cope with the inflated issues when the *Sunday Times* was absent. The mood was threatening, the sense of anticlimax acute.

The row with the printers, and forecasts that the paper was heading for phenomenal losses after the brief interval of sunshine, let loose the disenchantment of ARCO. After four years, Anderson was thoroughly regretting his quixotic gesture in 1976, and he was having to fend off awkward questions about the paper's policies from ARCO's more right-wing stockholders in the United States.

At the start, of course, it had all seemed like thoroughly good fun. Anderson had been photographed with a copy of the *Observer* in one hand and his cowboy hat in the other. Lord Goodman had laid on banquets and introduced him to a galaxy of British aristocrats. Kenneth Harris, an assiduous courtier, was often over at Anderson's home in New Mexico, and gave a lot of pleasure with his plummy British ways. But then, two awful truths began to dawn on Anderson: it would be a long time, if ever, before the *Observer* was going to turn in a regular profit; and secondly, it inclined towards socialism (which in his West Coast political terminology was about the same as Communism).

The watershed in Anderson's relations with his London paper plaything came with the 1979 British election, which Mrs Thatcher won. The editorials in the *Observer* had effectively supported James Callaghan and the Labour Party. Too late, Trelford and his senior colleagues saw that they had taken all the elevated talk about the editorial freedom a bit too literally. Sporadic efforts were made to please from then on. Kenneth Harris did his bit with two long question-and-answer interviews with Ronald Reagan, the Republican candidate, whom Anderson was backing heavily. Less blatantly, a short story was published on the *Observer*'s 'review front' – something of an innovation. Written by the literary wife of one of the ARCO directors, it appeared under a pen name, and described being made love to in Claridge's, then peeping out through the bedroom curtains and seeing Henry Kissinger arrive.

Such efforts were not enough. In the middle of 1980 the American directors had suddenly turned tough with the printers. They threatened to shut the paper down for good at the start of October unless production changes were accepted, and the entire staff was given notice as a proof of their determination. We received individual letters, setting out the details of the closure. This was a terrific shock to many of the journalists, who had complacently assumed that the oil subsidy would go on to eternity.

Although the fact was little noticed, ARCO by now had absolute control: at the start of 1980 it had acquired the remaining 10 per cent holding by the Astor family in the *Observer* for £250,000, under an option arrangement made in 1977. Astor and Goodman were now only 'courtesy' directors, totally without power, and the Americans had full freedom of action. Apparently they had never been asked why ARCO wanted this change so badly that it was willing to pay out £250,000, on top of millions the paper had already cost.

The showdown with the printers and the formal dismissal notices further rattled the mood on the paper. What would happen when the oilmen had finally had enough? Once more, the old hue-and-cry began, to find someone to save the *Observer*. Murdoch was again mentioned with the ritual shudder; he looked most likely because he was known to still be eager to expand his Fleet Street stable. Then there was Vere Harmsworth, owner of the *Daily Mail*; plans were being discussed at Northcliffe House for launching a middle-brow Sunday paper, so Harmsworth might save a lot of money by taking over the *Observer* and revamping it. Neither of these possibilities was hailed with joy, because both Murdoch and Harmsworth used their papers dogmatically in support of the Conservatives, and would never let the *Observer* go on in its liberal way. It was agreed that Murdoch was the worst possible option, since he understood how newspapers worked – he would march into a newsroom and know precisely whom to order about to achieve the result he had in mind. Nobody wanted an owner like that.

Several people came up to my desk and said: 'What about your old friend Tiny?' It was well known by this time that Rowland wanted to buy a national paper, and when Lonrho had taken control of Sir Hugh Fraser's Scottish Universal Investments in 1979 it acquired two daily papers in Glasgow and a score of local papers. So the suggestion made some sense.

Without expecting much from it, I typed a short letter, telling Rowland that events seemed to be 'moving towards a precipice at high speed'. Unless somebody was ready to step in, the *Observer* might vanish. I ended: 'You may not be in the least interested in braving Fleet Street's troubles. But if the worst happens here next week and you want to know more about the internal scene, I shall naturally be ready to help.' I sent this off gloomily, with regret at having left the buoyant *Financial Times*. For all that, I felt better placed than most of my younger colleagues, with children and big mortgages – my last book had been on the bestseller lists. But just as suddenly as it had developed, the threat to the paper from the unions receded, and Rowland never replied to my letter. Later I understood why – at the time when I wrote to him he already knew Anderson. They had been talking about the *Observer*.

His link with Anderson was through Daniel K. Ludwig, one of the richest men in the world. It happened because Tiny was looking to the Americas for Lonrho's continuing expansion – the crumbling economies of black Africa were less and less rewarding, and Britain was stagnant. The starting-point for his new departure was Mexico, where for years he and his family had gone on holiday each Christmas. (He once said to me, 'If it wasn't for Lonrho I'd spend the rest of my life walking beside the sea in Acapulco in a pair of shorts.') Among his string of interests around the world, Ludwig owned luxury hotels in Mexico, and in 1979 he had sold a half-share in them to Lonrho for £40 million. This was something of a sensation in the business world, because the eighty-three-year-old recluse was not in the habit of selling anything to anyone – or even of talking to anyone. But he and Rowland had struck up a friendship. They got along so well that when a photographer took a picture of them together Ludwig was smiling; usually he lashed out at any cameraman who came near him.

Rowland was glad of Ludwig's introduction to Anderson, because the oil world still fascinated him. Up to now, admittedly, there had been scant satisfaction of any kind – his lawsuit against Shell and BP was foundering with a legal bill for Lonrho of more than £1 million. But he felt that Lonrho and ARCO could arrange joint ventures. Angola was a place where he had particular interests, and there was plenty of oil there, waiting to be exploited.

While Tiny nurtured his relationship with Anderson, affairs at the *Observer* went on bumping downhill. By the end of 1980 the loans pumped in by ARCO had soared to more than £8 million, plus another £1 million or so in unpaid interest on them. (We journalists sometimes wondered what the accumulated losses were in the previous twenty years.)

So Anderson yearned to get rid of the paper, as soon as a good excuse presented itself. Perhaps he had decided in principle at the start of 1980, when he bought out the remaining 10 per cent of Astor's shares. Or it might have been during the dispute with the printers in July 1980. But undoubtedly the purchase of *The Times* and the *Sunday Times* by Murdoch for £12 million at the end of 1980 concentrated his thoughts still further.

Murdoch had come in with his characteristic brusqueness when the Thomson family had announced that they would shut both papers down in March 1981 unless they could find a buyer. As when he almost bought the *Observer* in 1976, Murdoch simply said he would abandon the whole deal if the government tried to drag him through a Monopolies Commission inquiry. He was clearly not bluffing.

In any case, Rupert made no secret of his politics – in the United States, a right-wing group had just handed him an award for the support his papers had given to the newly elected President

Reagan. For that reason, Mrs Thatcher was not disposed to frustrate an owner who would surely make *The Times* more Tory than it was already. Murdoch's purchase was nodded through, with a bevy of virtually powerless 'independent' directors as a fig leaf for the integrity of *The Times*.

We recognized with dismay that under a dynamic new ownership the *Sunday Times* was likely to hustle the *Observer* more than ever; and Murdoch did not disguise that the way he had been thwarted in 1976 would harden his resolve to inflict the maximum punishment. That would mean still more losses for ARCO to shoulder. (The animosity of Murdoch towards Trelford was reciprocated: thus the *Observer* serialized Harry Evans's scarifying memoirs of his departure from *The Times*.)

Another factor making a sale more probable was the resignation of Anderson's right-hand man, Thornton Bradshaw, whose wife had written the romantic tale about Claridge's. In January 1981, Bradshaw accepted the presidency of the RCA Corporation: until then he had done most of the travelling for ARCO between Los Angeles and London to keep an eye on the *Observer*'s troublesome doings.

Rumours were now abounding in the *Observer* that something was afoot. In the middle of February, Astor and Goodman had lunch with Anderson in London, and asked him about reports that he was planning to sell the paper to Vere Harmsworth. No, he said, he did not intend to do that. It seems that they did not ask him if he meant to do anything else.

Then there was a fatal board meeting, at which Anderson suddenly proposed that Kenneth Harris should become vice-chairman of the *Observer*. Everyone objected to the idea, feeling that sycophantic Kenneth was being promoted above his station. The proposal was voted down. This was the moment when Anderson finally decided to rid himself of the whole business, of these querulous Limeys and their lack of gratitude.

The next evening, 25 February 1981, Donald Trelford bounded into the newsroom, stood on a table, and announced: 'We've been sold.'

We later heard that when Anderson entered the ARCO boardroom in Los Angeles to spell out the details of the sale, his fellow directors rose as one man and gave him a standing ovation.

10

Fine Game of Snooker

A few minutes after Donald Trelford had finished telling the journalists that the *Observer* had been sold to Lonrho, my telephone rang. Tiny was on the line. I congratulated him, remembering that it was fifteen years since I had first heard him saying that he wanted to buy a British newspaper. On the surface he sounded his usual cool and faintly mocking self, but I knew that really he was delighted by the suddenness of the coup. 'What are they saying?' he asked. 'Are people pleased? You can tell them I want to make it the best paper, with the best writers. Tell them we shall take on the *Sunday Times*.' Already he was using the proprietorial 'we', I noticed. 'Nobody is saying anything,' I replied. 'They are just flabbergasted at the way it has been done. You must come down here as soon as you can and talk to everyone about the future.'

Before that could happen, the future was being widely prejudged. The most damaging predictions were made from within Lonrho's own camp, by Sir George Bolton, its octogenarian deputy chairman. A retired banker, Bolton had been brought on to the board in the wake of the 1973 imbroglio, as a respectable 'Christmas tree decoration' with good friends in the City. By 1981 he was on the verge of being quietly discarded: this was plainly not before time, because the interview he gave, that evening after the news had broken, left an impression of geriatric tipsiness. 'Effectively, the *Observer* will be run from Scotland,' he said. 'The editor of the *Glasgow Herald* will have as much say in its running as anyone. We think London is a very bad place to run a newspaper from. In

Scotland there are fewer difficulties. They work harder.'

Sir George told the agency reporters, who doubtless could scarcely believe their luck: 'Although we don't propose to change the staff in the immediate future, I suppose there must be some editorial staff who would be having kittens tonight.' He signed off by warning: 'If we can't make a profit, we shall close it down.'

These gaffes were quoted everywhere the next morning, to Rowland's shocked dismay. They swamped his own simple promise: 'I will take on Rupert Murdoch head on.' Whatever hopes there were of a welcome from Trelford and the other editorial executives had been instantly wrecked by Bolton with a few ludicrous sentences. Yet perhaps it would have made no difference in the end, because reflex responses from the *Observer* camp were as instantly bleak. I watched unhappily while my old friend Anthony Sampson castigated Lonrho on TV as a predatory multinational and Rowland as an unprincipled tycoon who would be bound to interfere with the paper's freedom – especially on African affairs. David Astor said he did not imagine that he would be staying on the board, and admitted he was 'very, very surprised' at the speed in which the sale had been rushed through. This remark was less a measure of Astor's credulity than of the extent to which he had been beguiled. It later emerged that Rowland and Anderson had been talking over the deal for at least a year – since the moment when ARCO had exercised its option to buy the last 10 per cent of the *Observer*'s shares. By selling out, Astor had lost all legal right to be consulted about a change of ownership. However, he has always been a notably high-minded person, and could not fathom how Anderson was morally able to entertain him to breakfast at Claridge's Hotel on the previous Sunday, talk earnestly about long-term editorial plans, and keep silent about the contract he was on the point of signing with Rowland. Anderson had merely promised that he would not sell to Associated Newspapers.

Few people blamed Astor for being duped. What seemed amazing (and still does) was the beguiling of Lord Goodman, so long the chairman of the trust. Astor had relied totally upon his acumen, his solicitor's mind, his unequalled grasp of company law. So why did Goodman allow the former editor-owner to be manipulated into a position where his intellectual birthright was hawked off to a man he detested? The question was never answered. It can only be speculated that six years as Master of University College, Oxford, had changed Goodman from a legal eagle into an academic dove. Certainly, he seemed perplexed by the sale, and brushed aside all attempts to interview him on what had gone wrong.

Another senior figure who felt justifiably pained was Donald Trelford. After all, when he had been given the news by telephone from Los Angeles, the caller was not even Anderson himself but Kenneth Harris; as a member of the editorial staff, Harris was his subordinate. Of course, Trelford had felt much in his debt in 1976, when the legendary dinner at Rules had saved the paper from Murdoch and his hit squad, but such warm feelings were long since dissipated. Now there was a sensation of having been double-crossed, because Harris was clearly in on the negotiations between the two tycoons, but had said nothing to his own editor. (Immediately after giving the news, Harris retreated with Anderson to the latter's New Mexico ranch, where both were incommunicado.)

The crestfallen admission by Trelford that he had been kept in the dark was seized upon with glee by Murdoch's *Sun*. This treatment was clearly part of a long vendetta, which had recently reached a peak – or more accurately a nadir – in a crude attack upon Trelford for having criticized the Fleet Street tabloids. This tirade called him 'possibly the most inconsequential journalist of our times', described the *Observer* as 'wordy, pompous and self-righteous', and said that it had 'recklessly squandered the resources of its American parent company'. When the news of the sale broke, the *Sun* was intent upon having as much sport as possible. Murdoch's new possession, *The Times*, was more restrained, limiting itself to a sober analysis under the headline 'Third "Observer" owner in five years'. The popular papers, almost without exception, recalled Edward Heath's rebuke about the 'unacceptable face of capitalism'. It was a classic reach-me-down cliché.

After surveying the morning's papers Trelford made his way up the hill, past St Paul's, to Cheapside House. Anxious to apologize for Bolton's ill-considered words in the name of Lonrho was an almost obsequious Tiny Rowland. He and Trelford had never met before. There was no thought, insisted Rowland, that the paper would be run from Glasgow, or that there would be changes in the staff. Bolton had just been airing some quaint ideas of his own. Paul Spicer, the most acerbic of the Lonrho directors, was far more cutting: 'If you're eighty-two years old and in bed, you can make mistakes.'

All this was not enough. The groundswell against Lonrho was already gathering, and Trelford felt able to resist the Rowland charm, despite the promises of much Lonrho money without strings. When Donald returned to his office he called in his trusted friends and said: 'Let's be clear, we're not bound to have Lonrho.' It was his cool self-assurance which gave this remark its credibility. There was also some truth in what he said, assuming that Anderson was willing to ditch Rowland, because Sir James Goldsmith was a possible buyer; so, of course, was Vere Harmsworth of Associated Newspapers. This hypothesis, that nothing irrevocable had happened, was likewise fostered by David Astor, in hurried calls to his former acolytes. 'I was led up the garden,' he confessed. 'But Rowland is not the right man. I object to the way he has called Donald up to his office – he's behaving as though he has already taken over.'

So even by that first afternoon, when he came to the *Observer* to meet the journalists, the idea that Rowland was simply on approval had begun to take root. His arrival was curiously furtive – after an elaborate manoeuvre with decoy cars he slipped in through the back door, to dodge a phalanx of TV cameras around at the front. Then he was hurriedly led down a grubby staircase to the basement, where the seventy journalists sat waiting in the canteen. Tiny was put behind a canteen table, flanked by two of his directors and several executives from Outrams, the Scottish newspaper firm owned by Lonrho. There was a terse round of introductions by Trelford, and for the first time in all the years I had known him, I saw that Tiny was visibly nervous. He had just agreed to pay Anderson £6 million for the *Observer*, and the allegiance of this notoriously fractious crowd now staring at him was a large part of what he had bought. He was peering around for someone he recognized –

probably for me. But I had hidden myself at the back, loath to be identified as the 'boss's man'. Later I wished I had been nearer the front, to play a better part.

Perhaps Tiny had a speech prepared, but he did not deliver it. Instead he made some rather awkward apologies for the 'unusual' way in which the staff had been told about the sale. He told how he had met Bob Anderson of ARCO a week before and had been asked if Lonrho was still interested in buying the paper, since a bid had been received in Los Angeles from Lord Rothermere. They had met again forty-eight hours later and reached a verbal agreement. Soon afterwards, Anderson had telephoned to say that he wanted everything tied up at once. They had come to terms there and then.

This was heard in silence, then somebody asked from the floor why Rowland wanted the *Observer*. He replied, 'It is the one paper we've always wanted to own in the UK.' This was plainly meant as a compliment to all the journalists present, but some put a more sinister interpretation on it, as the next question showed. What guarantees would there be that he would not interfere with the editorial content? At once, Rowland answered: 'Ask Dick Hall, not me. I've made it quite clear there'll be no interference from the proprietors.' (All quotations are taken from the record made by the National Union of Journalists.)

There were some more questions, about whether Lonrho meant to make money out of the paper; Tiny quickly said that it certainly did, then added: 'I want to make the *Observer* competitive and enter the circulation battle with the *Sunday Times*.' Everyone perked up and waited to hear more about his plans. But Colin Legum, the Africa and Commonwealth correspondent, announced: 'I have three questions.' Colin was right up beside the table where Tiny was sitting, and had the remains of his lunchtime cigar between his teeth. As the Africa expert, he regarded it as his prerogative to put the new owner through his paces, and let him see that from now on his actions would be under close surveillance.

An intricate debate then started, in front of a mystified gathering, about Lonrho's role in Kenyan politics. Names of black politicians, most of whom were significant only to

Rowland and Legum, were tossed to and fro. Eventually, the new proprietor grew impatient and heated; his interrogator leaned back, puffing on his cigar, the visible winner. Since most of the audience could not follow the arguments, they could not judge the merit of Rowland's answers. Somehow the mood had been fatally clouded and Rowland's chance to win the respect of the bulk of the staff had been squandered.

Several more questions were piled in about editorial integrity, and in the end I spoke up, because Rowland was so obviously craning his neck from side to side to pick me out. 'I can understand everyone's anxiety,' I said. 'But Tiny never did me a bad turn when I was editor of the *Times of Zambia*.' This was true, although events were to teach me how crucial it was for an editor to set down hard and fast guidelines.

Time would teach us all a lot about the way our editor's instinct for retaining power might motivate him. Donald Trelford took the floor after Rowland had left, to assure us that nothing was finally settled regarding the paper's ownership: the bid – as he adroitly termed it – would certainly have to go to the Monopolies Commission, despite Murdoch's easy ride with the *Sunday Times* and *The Times*. That would take time, and there were, he reminded us, other bidders standing by. But if Lonrho did carry the day, we could rely on him to keep Rowland at bay. 'What is important,' he said engagingly, 'is to keep Tiny Rowland out of Tiny Trelford's editorial conferences.' After he had departed, the rest of took a vote, and there was an overwhelming majority in favour of accepting Lonrho's ownership, as long as the written safeguards for non-interference were strong enough. That was not, however, how the editorial heavyweights were thinking.

From then onwards the onslaught on the sale to Lonrho was relentless, both outside the paper and within. Once again, the future of the *Observer* became the subject of 'think pieces' and editorials, then began to fill the letters columns of *The Times* with solemn sentiments. The loudest protester was David Astor, more and more dismayed that his old paper, his life's work, had changed hands like a tin of baked beans. He said that Anderson had 'behaved very badly', and sadly recalled his own gratification five years earlier at the sale to ARCO – when he had flown to Los Angeles and been so reassured by all the works of art in the chairman's suite. That aura of culture had deceived him.

In those first days after the sale to Lonrho, the Astor house in St John's Wood became the tactical headquarters for the diverse 'Stop Tiny' factions. Old confidants on the editorial staff mingled with liberal academics and politicians. The unease at Westminster, among many Liberals and Socialists, was compounded by continuing alarm over Murdoch's newly-won grip on Fleet Street. His takeover of the Thomson empire was being followed by the resignation of some distinguished journalists, led by Hugo Young and Hugh Stephenson. The opposition parties at Westminster were less bothered at the idea that Rowland would use his new acquisition to promote Lonrho's business abroad than by the thought that he would probably shift the paper to the right at home. That would leave the *Guardian* as the only serious national paper which did not back the Conservatives. This certainly seemed a possibility, because although Rowland's own politics were hard to pin down, he was surrounded on the Lonrho board by such vintage Tories as Duncan-Sandys and Edward du Cann. But in their appeals to the Government to intervene, the opponents of Lonrho had to be discreet about this fear: Mrs Thatcher approved of any paper which espoused her monetarist philosophy, and had begun showering honours upon editors who danced to her tune. She could scarcely be relied upon to keep the *Observer* on the left just in the interests of fair play.

All such factors were debated in the increasingly feverish mood of conspiracy inside the *Observer*. The obvious aim was to play for time, by having the purchase investigated by the Monopolies Commission. If this happened, the sale would be 'frozen' for several months, and it might be possible to produce evidence that Lonrho was simply too unsavoury to be entrusted with the running of a national organ of opinion. So within twenty-four hours, Goodman and Astor had called at the Department of Trade to make this classic 'Establishment' proposal. Although their status was rather fragile, since it was not buttressed by any shareholding, they none the less felt confident that the commissioners would come down on the side of tradition and decency. They also had various pieces of legislation on their side: the Fair Trading Act and the Monopolies and Mergers Act give force to the rule that the sale of any newspaper with a circulation above 500,000 must be scrutinized in the public interest. There could be exceptions, of course, as Murdoch had so recently proved, and the hopes of this delaying tactic depended upon Anderson's reply to the simple question: 'Will you close the paper if you cannot sell it to Lonrho?' (Either because Anderson failed to understand the implications, or because he preferred to be honest, when it came to the point he answered 'No'.)

As the alignments among the journalists became clear-cut, I found myself increasingly alienated. Apart from a handful who argued that Lonrho would bring a more enterprising management to the paper, Rowland now had few open supporters. About half of the editorial strength was entirely apathetic, willing to swim with the tide, but a score or more were passionately hostile and eager to go to the rhetorical barricades. Most militant among them were the associate editors, the 'mandarins' of the paper. Trelford was keeping in the background, making no statements as hostages to fortune. His nerve, as ever, was admirable.

My instinctive objection to the anti-Lonrho campaign was not solely founded upon my long friendship with Tiny, but sprang from a feeling that there was too much egotism around the office. After all, the *Observer* was operating in a capitalist society, and by its editorials did not show any particular desire fundamentally to alter that society. But the most voluble of the staff seemed to assume, without question, that they were on a paper which had some miraculous exemption from normal economic laws. They could make a loss, year in and year out (as they did), yet grandly assume that the unique qualities of the *Observer* – its liberal intellectualism – could never perish. This illusion had, of course, been nurtured in the long years of Astor's hegemony: the paper had seemed so special and inviolate. At an earlier moment of crisis, one associate editor had said with a mixture of pride and defiance that he had never worked on a paper that made a profit and had no wish to do so. Then, in 1977, when reality had almost burst in, when the wolves were howling outside, seeming proof of this mystical power was given by the eleventh-hour summoning-up of Bob Anderson with his ever-open wallet. In short, if the *Observer*'s mandarins did not like the style of a potential new owner, they were free to reject him.

The paper was hardly looking for an owner, rather for a patron. This concept was not of the Renaissance kind, wherein princes and popes told their subsidized artists the topics to paint, but something more impersonal. The Arts Council would have been an ideal patron.

I came to realize that the *Observer*'s view of itself, as being rather outside the commercial arena, was also influenced by its closeness to the academic world. After all, professors are not called upon to show a profit. Yet there was a paradox, because logically the *Observer* should have been dedicated to teaching that British newspapers should be subsidized by the state, as in some other democratic countries. It did not do so. Even less was there any sympathy for the Communist way of running newspapers, in which the journalists did not need to think about balance sheets. Astor had imbued his creation with an abhorrence of the militant left. Germaine Greer was anathema to him. He much preferred Mary Whitehouse. These were the paper's contradictions.

There had always been plenty of avowed socialists on the staff, but their ability to raise the clenched fist of revolution was inhibited by the need to hold out the other hand to the benefactor of the moment. It seemed to me, looking back, that the *Financial Times* had been more healthy: the owners were out-and-out capitalists, and nobody had any illusions about that, and the socialists on the *FT*'s editorial floor – there were quite a few – got across as many home truths as they could to a readership that really mattered. (Purists may regard this as a 'cop-out', but it is arguably more worthwhile to sow some doubts in the minds of merchant bankers than grind away at pamphlets for distribution to the faithful in the Workers Revolutionary Party.)

My contention was that my left-wing *Observer* colleagues either had to get out of Fleet Street entirely or stop living a fiction. Rowland presented them with a challenge. They were lucky, it seemed to me, to have acquired another owner who was promising not to alter the character and politics of the paper, rather than someone like Harmsworth or Murdoch who would assuredly have tossed it straight into Mrs Thatcher's handbag. As one of the younger journalists was quoted by *The Times* as saying, shortly after the takeover: 'We are sitting on a melting iceberg, and if someone offers us a lifeboat, we should jump into it.' The real way to ensure that a future owner left the paper in peace, and allowed it to speak its own mind, was to make it profitable. That was playing the capitalists at their own game – to be able to say, 'Leave us alone, because although the editorials may be red, the balance sheet is black.'

Financial success cannot give any guarantee, of course, of editorial freedom. An owner may like to argue that the profits are absolutely splendid, but none the less he had put up the money and taken the risk, so he still had a right to make a contribution to what goes into 'his' paper. Sheer pride must persuade him that he is expert on some subjects.

After all, journalism is not a profession. Anyone can play at it. Whereas a financier putting money into a mining venture would not dream of telling the shaft sinkers how to do their job, he has little reason to be inhibited about dictating his paper's policy on economic issues. Lord Beaverbrook never had doubted his own competence to give orders to his editors, and they knew just what to expect, as he made clear in some succinct evidence to a Royal Commission on the Press.

We all agreed, talking about Tiny, that the owner–editor relationship was influenced by many factors – especially the personalities of the people involved. I explained that I had managed to define the boundaries quite easily on the *Times of Zambia*, and that Rowland had never tried to cross them. It seemed to me that Trelford should be able to do the same. Even though the *Times of Zambia* was a tinpot paper by comparison with the *Observer*, making it less tempting as a plaything, the contrast also meant that Trelford had much greater prestige and so was better able to defend himself. But I could not carry the day with the mandarins. Rowland was simply the 'wrong man', as David Astor was telling everyone.

The debate soon lapped out into other channels. What if Lonrho was caught up in some great scandal – would this not besmirch the paper's own reputation? This is always the risk with a conglomerate – the disgrace is contagious. It was also assumed that Lonrho was forever handing out bribes to black politicians: there was a conviction that almost single-handed, Rowland was corrupting the entire African continent. This struck me as absurd, given the behaviour of some other companies with august reputations. Even Lonrho's support for Joshua Nkomo was quoted as an example, and my rejoinder that most leading British companies gave money to the Conservatives carried little weight.

Of course, Lonrho did give hand-outs, known as 'special payments', and doubtless still does. The wheels of business are greased with varying degrees of subtlety in many countries. As Angus Ogilvy told the Department of Trade inquiry in 1975: 'I was not against the principle, or would not be against the principle of bribery, because I think it has probably got to be done in certain countries.' One cannot know for sure whether Lonrho goes in for this as much as other multinationals in Africa, because by its nature 'commission' is a very secret affair, with as little as possible committed to paper. But there is no doubt that the most esteemed British companies, their boards sprinkled with the well-born, have often shown themselves to be the most apt in corruption. This emerged clearly after the downfall of Kwame Nkrumah in Ghana, when judicial commissions laid out the evidence with total precision. Luckily for the companies concerned, these revelations went unpublished in Britain, owing to doubts about the legal privilege bestowed by a Ghanaian court. More recently, damning evidence has been seeping out of Nigeria about the business methods of some leading European firms operating there.

Nigeria has always strained to the limit the moral elasticity of foreign companies; the rapacity of its politicians is notorious. Whereas the worst of Ghana's corruption was ended before Lonrho won its stake in that country through Ashanti Goldfields, the company was heavily involved in Nigeria during the oil boom years. In private conversation, Rowland did not hide his distaste for some of the Nigerian notables he was forced to deal with. He made the 'special payments' through his personal bank account, without giving Lonrho's non-executive directors the pain of knowing too much about such necessary evils. Many companies follow a different pattern, by laundering the bribe through the account of a middle-ranking executive, such as an assistant finance director; he then passes the money on in cash or through a bank transfer. But Tiny liked to handle the 'special payments' directly.

He kept a tight rein on them. During his first fifteen years with Lonrho the amounts he handed out totalled slightly over £500,000 – rather a modest figure for a company of such a size, operating in so many new places. Lonrho did not create the moral climate, it went along with what it encountered.

Quite understandably, Rowland hates to be reminded of the 'unacceptable face of capitalism' jibe, and he talks about the 'smiling face of development'. Without pretending that Lonrho is guided by altruism, there is no denying that it has put its weight in Africa behind many constructive ventures that have helped ordinary people. Energy and imagination, rather than bribery, have won Rowland his friends in Africa. He rightly says that he is not a 'paper merchant', like people in the City of London.

As such arguments were volleyed to and fro in the *Observer*, I was sometimes told that I was too romantic about Rowland. Perhaps it was true. But at least I had worked and travelled with him in Africa, whereas a lot of my opponents just believed what they read. Less agreeable were the hints that I was supporting Rowland because I hoped to gain personally: Auberon Waugh did me a bad turn by writing in the *Spectator* that I would soon replace Trelford. Once this seed was sown it became widely assumed that I was after the editorship. I knew, on the contrary, that I was fatally compromising myself.

All this was during a month of phoney war, when Astor strove to ensure that the Monopolies Commission would be brought into play, and Rowland vainly tried to outwit him. One brainwave Tiny had was to buy control of the paper personally. This seemed like a winner, until a university expert in company law, writing to *The Times*, ruled that this would be improper. Finally, after some shuffling of the terms of the sale between ARCO and Lonrho, a detailed submission was put to John Biffen, the Trade Secretary. On 17 March the inevitable happened: the Lonrho bid for the *Observer* was put before the Monopolies Commission.

By this time Trelford had joined the anti-Rowland camp. He showed his hand in a leader attacking Rowland's abortive efforts to circumvent the Monopolies Commission inquiry, calling such 'clandestine devices' the 'unacceptable face of multinationalism'. Although this was nominally aimed at Anderson, the adaptation of that notorious phrase made the real target plain enough. For good measure, the leader was leaked in advance of publication. Rowland reacted angrily, saying that he did not regard the remarks as fair.

A few days later, he invited me up to Cheapside House. I went reluctantly, aware that although he was anxious to know what was happening inside a property for which he had just staked several millions, this was tricky ground. As I expected, there was much questioning about Trelford's position and who was exerting pressure upon him. Suddenly Rowland threw out a remark to one of his directors, sitting in on the meeting: 'We have an editor, don't we? What's his name? Oh yes – Hugh Stephenson.'

I was startled, but pleased. Although he looked a bit dour on television, Hugh Stephenson had a good record as the business editor of *The Times*. He was also a socialist. If Rowland really had made up his mind to sack Trelford, this was perhaps the best choice he could make for a successor. From what little I knew of Stephenson, he was not the person to be pushed around, by Tiny or anyone. If Rowland realized that, all credit to him. If not, it was our luck.

However, this was a titbit for sharing with nobody, and I walked back down to the *Observer* feeling compromised. The journalists as a body declared their support for the Monopolies Commission inquiry, and their backing for Trelford. As a union member, that was going to be my position. My only course was to keep away from Rowland, keep my head down, and let events take their course.

This soon proved to be a difficult goal. The conspiracy at the heart of the paper was too provocative. A group of senior executives were fanatical in their resolve to uncover anything bad about Rowland – one even assured me that he had spent most of the war in Colchester prison, which was a complete invention. Former Lonrho employees were sought out at home and abroad, and invited to reveal any dirt they knew (few obliged). Then the rumour was spread around that a wonderful alternative buyer was standing by – another Bob Anderson, as it were. This drove me to abandon my determination to keep quiet.

Finally, I wrote a letter to *The Times*, after the general fashion, saying that the orchestrated campaign was no longer about editorial integrity, but about ownership: 'I believe that the external anti-Rowland faction (which exerts considerable pressure internally through some of my colleagues) should now name the prospective alternative buyers. We have lived too long on hints and rumours . . . If a better buyer than Mr Rowland can speedily be produced, that is splendid. If not, we should extract from Mr Rowland all possible guarantees and press on with the business of producing a newspaper.'

It was a vain effort to make somebody admit what was common knowledge inside the *Observer*: the Aga Khan was being wooed. This did make a certain amount of sense, because he was certainly rich enough, and owned several newspapers in Kenya. Moreover, he had Michael Curtis on his staff in Geneva, and Curtis was remembered in Fleet Street for having been the editor of the *News Chronicle* at the moment when the Cadburys so brutally axed it. However, the Aga suffered many calls on his millions, so he was a difficult fish to net. (Almost twenty years before, when I was editing the *African Mail*, Astor had tried unsuccessfully to persuade the Aga to take a share in it.) His critics also asserted that he was an autocrat, and exceedingly conservative in his political views.

My letter won no response, although some weeks later there was a report in the *Financial Times* that the Australian group owning the *Melbourne Age* was tentatively interested in making a bid for the *Observer*. Soon there were leaks about a 'dream consortium': the Aga and the *Age*. The reaction from Anderson to this news was truculent, and when a delegation of the paper's executives flew to see him in America they were given a dressing down. 'I have promised the paper to Lonrho, and that's settled,' he said. 'The deal is done.' Rowland was equally adamant – he hated the prospect of a Monopolies Commission inquiry, but would go through with it, and win.

But would he? The procession of witnesses soon began trooping up to the Commission's offices in Carey Street, starting with the main contestants, Rowland and Astor. Asking the questions was the Commission's permanent chairman, a QC with the resounding name of Sir Godfray Le Quesne. He was flanked by seven members of the Commission, who occasionally chipped in; among the three specially co-opted for this inquiry was one journalist, Alastair Burnet, as yet unknighted. A long slate of interested parties also made submissions, including various trade unions. The National Union of Journalists spent a lot of time condemning the capitalist domination of the Press; admirable though these sentiments were, they did little to help Sir Godfray and his team solve the central conundrum about Lonrho's fitness to own the paper.

Re-reading after several years the report the Commission presented to Parliament in June 1981, it seems a rather tired and amateurish document. It shows how quickly the debate had narrowed down – or, perhaps, widened – to the Africa connection. As Legum had accurately defined it at the start, this was the heart of the matter. If Lonrho owned the paper, would Rowland let it speak freely about the Dark Continent? Naturally, he promised the Commissioners that they need have no fears on that score. (But as Mandy Rice-Davies had said in another Astor-related investigation, 'He would, wouldn't he?') Almost everyone else said the opposite.

Astor and Goodman made a joint submission, listing Lonrho's past role in the politics of various African countries. It argued that Rowland had interfered so much in such places as Kenya and Zimbabwe that he had often come in for criticism. For sheer financial survival, he would have to restrain any newspaper he owned – and the *Observer* in particular – from being totally honest about what it might uncover in the black states.

This thesis was extended by Donald Trelford in a 10,000-word document which distilled the findings of the paper's correspondents throughout Africa and beyond. It was a very personalized view. As an old Africa hand myself, I knew that Donald was fascinated by the relationships Rowland had developed with African leaders; these were the cornerstones of the Lonrho empire. He said: 'The *Observer* carries influence in the very places where Lonrho's interests are most extensive and most at risk.' If the company gave the paper editorial freedom, it would be granting it *carte blanche* to do commercial damage. Could there be safeguards? He dismissed the idea, pointing out that the influence of the 'national directors' appointed to protect the freedom of *The Times* had been negligible: even during the Thomson era they had been pretty much ignored, and their prospects seemed even less encouraging under Rupert Murdoch.

More heavy artillery was trundled up to Carey Street to bombard the impassive Sir Godfray and his colleagues. Conor Cruise O'Brien and Colin Legum both stressed that they were planning in any event to leave the staff shortly (although O'Brien was to go on writing a weekly column), so they could see things quite impartially. In precise detail, Legum recounted some of the games Rowland had played in Africa, and said that he did not think any foreign correspondent operating in the Middle East or Africa could keep an independent status if Lonrho owned the company. O'Brien went further, asserting that Lonrho wanted positively to determine how the *Observer*'s influence would be exerted in Africa.

All this evidence was being given in confidence, and while many of the attitudes were predictable enough, there was nothing to disclose the total enmity being shown to Rowland by his adversaries. However, there were some revealing leaks while the Commission was still in the throes of its task. One followed a party at the Garrick Club, that invariable venue, to mark O'Brien's departure from the editorship-in-chief. Amid the bonhomie, as the wine flowed, the 'Cruiser' suddenly let fly with the whole armoury of his notable invective. Tiny was his target. 'You must fight him off at all costs,' the gathering was told in the course of a Cassandra-like monologue. He urged his listeners to recognize that death was better than dishonour. By the end of it, said one spectator, O'Brien's face was even more puce than usual. Some of those around him felt he was going too far, and felt that a modicum of dishonour might be preferable to the death of the paper – which would entail the loss of their jobs and an end to vinous evenings at the Garrick. As for O'Brien, he could go off again to an American university. A quarrel ended the evening. This was duly reported in the *Sunday Times*. From then on, Rowland set his heart on erasing O'Brien's name from the columns of the *Observer*.

He also set his heart on erasing a few other names when he realized that not a good word was being said on his behalf to the commissioners. Like Murdoch five years before, Rowland grew obsessed with the notion that he was the victim of an 'orchestrated campaign' from within the *Observer*. Hoping to be welcomed as the saviour of a chronic loss-maker, he instead found he was being reviled. He also found he was being pursued by the *Sunday Times* and some other papers on the sidelines, to confirm details about his early life. (These details had, of course, been dredged up by the *Observer* and discreetly passed on to its rivals.)

A lot was being written about the way Rowland operated as a tycoon, restlessly moving around the world in his Gulfstream jet. More than that, Fleet Street began burrowing into his family life, which he had always tried obsessively to keep from the public gaze. Readers were told how he and his wife Josie had three children; the eldest, Toby, was at Westminster School. They went by Rolls every weekend to Bourne End, near Marlow, to relax in the mansion he had bought from Lonrho for £250,000 after the DTI inspectors had remarked in 1976 that he was living in it rent-free. It was further revealed that the family dined 'very simply', and that their favourite dishes were fillet of plaice and lamb chops. They had a staff of five, including a butler-cum-chauffeur, and there were ducks and geese on the lawns running down from the house to the Thames. All this exposure, which many rich men would have accepted with more aplomb, was the unexpected price Tiny was having to pay for being tempted to put £6 million into a Sunday paper.

Six senior journalists decided to add yet more. They felt that the submission from the editorial staff as a body had not been trenchant enough, even though it declared keen doubts about Lonrho and said it should only be allowed to own the paper with the strongest safeguards. The self-styled 'Gang of Six' (led by John Cole, the deputy editor) concluded that Rowland was not a suitable owner whatever the conditions, and that independent directors would not be any safeguard at all.

At this point I grew so angry that I decided to put my own head above the parapet, and wrote the Commission a three-page memorandum, pointing out that Cole and his colleagues did not speak for all the journalists, as they claimed. After observing that I was the only person on the paper who had worked for both Astor and Rowland, I stressed that all the staff were in the former's debt, for the values he had imbued. ('It was also true,' I went on, 'that the impetuous way in which the paper was sold without reference to him was wounding and provoked needless suspicion.') But I believed that once the dust had settled, Rowland would prove to be a good owner. The nub of my argument was that he had not interfered when I was editing the *Times of Zambia*; and I thought he still had a clear understanding of the damage caused when an owner tried to dictate to an editor. 'Mr Rowland must also be aware, from the debate during the past two months, that Lonrho could rely on a lot of uproar from the *Observer*'s journalists if he did.'

As it happened, Rowland himself was propounding this line to Le Quesne. In a letter he had sent in a few days after my memorandum, but which I only saw much later, Tiny wrote: 'If I were a Commissioner, I would have in mind the alleged suppression of articles about President Giscard d'Estaing by the proprietor of the defunct magazine *Now*! The first people to publicly complain were the journalists themselves. This gave the magazine massive adverse publicity. I think it was a major dent in the magazine's appeal to the public, and one which a more experienced owner could have recognized as suicidal.' (Apart from pressing his own suit, Rowland was having the pleasure of running down his old adversary, Sir James Goldsmith, whose disastrous news-magazine had recently collapsed with a loss of £5 million.)

To my astonishment, the Monopolies Commission responded with eager interest to my overture. They called me in for two long sessions, and Le Quesne went into my experiences as editor of the *Times of Zambia* with solemn persistence. It was obvious that the inquiry felt it at last had something tangible to weigh up, after all the airing of opinions and prejudices. Suddenly, the fate of the *Observer* in 1981 was hanging upon what had happened in the remote African country more than fifteen years before. As Rowland assured me later, my evidence had 'won the day' – a phrase he repeated several times, although it was not a responsibility I much cared to accept single-handed.

When it appeared, the Commission's report would be seen to devote a whole chapter to Zambian matters. The significance of Zambia had also been accentuated when Donald Trelford stuck on the end of his submission the highly coloured recollections of one of my former staff, claiming that Lonrho interfered almost daily.

After I had started giving evidence, there was another development. A one-time manager of the *Times of Zambia*, tracked down in South Africa, wrote in that he remembered Rowland ordering me to write that the Italians in Mussolini's day had been in the habit of pushing rebellious Ethiopians out of aeroplanes; that was said to be part of Lonrho's efforts to discredit the Italians, during vain efforts to win a Zambian pipeline contract. A lot of this ludicrous make-believe rebounded: to explode one convoluted allegation, a tattered 1966 cutting was unearthed, showing a Lonrho executive shaking hands with the newly elected black mayor of the Zambian town of Ndola, under the heading, 'Well done, Sir!'

After a good deal of pondering, the Commission accepted my version of Lonrho's behaviour. Its conclusions said: 'As regards the general experience of editors, we attach importance to the evidence of Mr Hall, because he had experience as editor of a newspaper owned by Lonrho.'

Immediately after the report was released, Trelford and I were invited to appear on a BBC television programme, *The Editors*. Also under the arc lights were Hugh Stephenson (who by this time was known to Trelford as Rowland's choice as his successor) and Adam Raphael, political editor of the *Observer*. The fifth panellist was an Irish journalist named Cosgrave, who spoke of Rowland with nothing but syrupy reverence.

Apart from generating much heat, the programme answered one big question: would Donald resign? After his outspoken rejection of Lonrho, his reference in a tough editorial to 'acceptable alternative owners', and his continuing allegiance to David Astor, this had seemed on the cards. Only two days before 'The Editors' went out Astor had written a *cri de coeur* in *The Times*, starting: 'If the Government agrees to Lonrho acquiring the

Observer it is hard to see how that paper can avoid being dead or unrecognizable within three years.' He had pressed the case for the 'alternative owners' – the Aga Khan and the *Melbourne Age*. It was the first time they had been so categorically named, although the *Age* had sent a management team to London in case Lonrho was turned down, and Trelford had told me how impressed he was on meeting them. But now the die was cast in Lonrho's favour, Donald was not going down in a blaze of idealism. He quickly made that clear on the programme. 'The editorship of the *Observer* is the best job in the world,' he said crisply.

His aim was not to give the job up, but to make the safeguards so cast-iron that there would be no way in which Rowland could put pressure on him. It was a remarkably dextrous volte-face: he was no longer arguing that Rowland was an unacceptable owner, but that the guarantees of editorial freedom being offered were 'illiberal and unworkable'.

In the head-on TV argument, I suggested that everyone had been squealing before they were hurt. The long public wrangle had done the paper no good commercially, and the best way to deal with any owner was to spell out some basic rules, face to face, and stick to them. Then independent directors became superfluous. The other essential, in my view, was to make a profit. By the end of the programme tempers were high. The producer, Jeremy Bennett, wrote to me afterwards: 'General consensus was that it was not only "good television", but that it shed some light on the personalities and issues involved as well.'

Rowland called me the next morning. He said he was particularly amused by one exchange, in which I had pointed my finger at Adam Raphael and said: 'You may be luckier than you think!' Emboldened by Rowland's praise, I decided to tell him that he would do well to accept the proposal of the rank-and-file journalists that two of their strength should be made 'working directors', in addition to the editor. Immediately, I could see he was against the principle – for all the talk of voting Labour, his instincts were just like those of any other capitalist when it came to power-sharing.

However, Tiny had one suggestion: 'We should be delighted to have *you* on the board,' he announced. I replied that I was the last person he wanted – after so much controversy, the board needed a few solid neutrals. Tiny seemed nonplussed that I had so hurriedly turned aside the offer, then said there was somebody else who wanted to speak to me. The telephone was handed over to Lord Duncan-Sandys, the Lonrho chairman. 'I want to thank you,' said Duncan-Sandys. 'It came across well.' He paid me some more compliments, but I felt uneasy after putting down the receiver. The new owners of the paper were congratulating me for having had a verbal duel with my own editor in front of several million viewers. Matters had gone badly awry. Somehow or other, we all had to live together.

The last convulsive phase of Rowland's takeover saw Trelford at his most brilliant, showing all those characteristics which have made Harold Evans, former editor of the *Sunday Times* and *The Times* call him a 'master politican'. It is no accident that while Trelford excels as a cricketer and enjoys rugby, the game that he really loves is snooker. He delights in the soft, artful shot, leaving an opponent in a hopeless quandary, in the opportunity shrewdly seized for a winning break, the careful calculations each time before you aim the cue.

Trelford's intention now was to get Rowland well and truly snookered. He wanted the independent directors given such powers that the editor could only be dismissed with their approval, and that the owner had no control over the hiring or firing of any member of the editorial staff. If there was a dispute between the editor and the owner, the independent directors would have to adjudicate, and their decision would be final. For good measure, the owner would only be allowed to communicate with any member of the editorial staff with the consent of the editor. Trelford was by now feeling sure enough of his control of events that he quietly turned down the offer of a senior position with the Aga Khan Foundation. The offer was made because the Aga thought Donald's position had become untenable through his support for the anti-Lonrho group.

There were some lingering hopes among the 'Gang of Six' that Rowland might blow up at the prospect of being so hog-tied and say the deal was not worth having after all. He did not, although neither did he show much jubilation at having won through on such irksome terms. It had been a wounding war of attrition – a bad augury. The finale was a week of horse-trading between Rowland and Trelford about who should be appointed as the five independent directors. Each one struck off on the other's list those which he deemed unacceptable. The only journalist proposed by Lonrho was Hugh Stephenson; not surprisingly, Trelford put him at the top of his 'unacceptable' list.

The time was opportune for Trelford to identify completely with the journalists. This had not been possible when he was striving for an outright rejection of Lonrho, because the rank-and-file had never taken quite such a hardline attitude. Now he went to see Rowland at the head of a delegation from the union, and at one tense moment sent in a briefing to one of his spokesmen in the midst of a staff meeting. By a happy chance, two Labour MPs with close newspaper connections spoke in the House about Trelford's 'great courage' and spirit. Asked to endorse these encomiums, Trade Secretary John Biffen was somewhat enigmatic: 'I gladly pay tribute to the skills of Mr Trelford.' After some nudging he said: 'I shall not disparage the role of any of those who have been working to try to secure the future of the newspaper.' These exchanges were duly published in the *Observer*, beneath a picture of Rowland; quite appropriately, it was the portrait in which he was holding up his hands in an attitude of prayer.

By the middle of July 1981, the names of five independent directors of impeccable repute were published: Lord Windlesham, Dame Rosemary Murray, Sir Geoffrey Cox, William Clark and Sir Derek Mitchell. With some asperity, Rowland told me that they would each be paid £4,500 a year. I tried in a letter to persuade him to ask David Astor to stay on the board: 'It would save him from going to his grave bitter about the new era.' But there was no reconciliation. Along with his *éminence grise*, Lord Goodman, the former editor-owner resigned as a director. 'I feel that the paper has been betrayed,' said Astor.

As though to give Lonrho a warning that it had bought itself a deal of trouble, the takeover was accompanied by a rash of labour problems. With the appearance of the new owner, the printing unions decided to flex their muscles a little. After all, they did not give a damn about editorial integrity, and they regarded the rumpus caused by the journalists as 'wanking'.

One of them used that expression, quite amiably, while he was making up my column on the stone one Saturday. 'Nobody asks us what we think,' he said. 'What we do think is that our wage packets come first, whether we're turning out *Comic Cuts* or the *Observer*.'

Trelford soon flexed his muscles as well. John Cole had resigned as deputy editor to become the BBC's political editor, and Rowland was given no chance to offer his opinion on who should fill the gap. It might have created a dangerous precedent. In the middle of Africa, in the midst of one of his high-speed trips, he received a telex message from Trelford, saying that Anthony Howard was to be the new deputy editor, unless there were any objections. On his return, Tiny called me and said bitterly: 'What could I do? I had to send back my approval. But I had never heard of Howard until that moment. Who is he?' Embarrassed, I put in a few warm words for Howard, then decided to be out whenever Tiny telephoned again.

Having shown his strength, Trelford knew he must establish a *modus vivendi* with the holder of the purse strings. Although he still regarded me with suspicion, as might be expected after the takeover quarrels, he was keen to solicit my views, as someone to whom Tiny was not a personal stranger. One day, when I was in his office, he suddenly said: 'I was talking to Rowland, and told him that since he might not see much financial reward from the paper for a few years, I hoped he could derive some satisfaction from the section he understands best of all.' I was startled. 'Oh,' I said. 'What section's that?' Trelford smiled conspiratorially. 'The business pages, of course.'

Snooker is a game for two. But if you once give a maestro the chance to pot a red, can you be sure he will not start sinking all the colours on the table?

11

The Kenya Rift

Looking back, I can see that it served me absolutely right when I found myself in the midst of the *Observer*'s first big row about interference by Rowland. My role in the Monopolies Commission inquiry had led many of my journalistic colleagues to assume that I was constantly in touch with him, forever engaged in intrigue. 'How's your friend?' they would ask, with varying degrees of sarcasm. Now I was to become the butt of his anger.

Going back to Africa was my undoing (if that is the right term for what happened). One could also say that my experience simply confirmed the apprehensions of all those people who had opposed the Lonrho takeover in the first place. That may be true, but the way matters would fall out was to depend considerably on the tactics of all concerned.

Yet, taking over as the Commonwealth correspondent – a job which has Africa at the top of its priorities – had first struck me as a splendid turn of events. After all, the *Observer* was *the* Africa paper in Fleet Street, and over a quarter of a century my predecessor, Colin Legum, had given the post a unique prestige. He was on first-name terms with a dozen or more black Presidents, took a front seat at international conferences, and gave confident judgements on everything that had happened, was happening or might happen anywhere between Cairo and Cape Town. Colin reminded me of the great Professor Malone in Harold Nicolson's *Some People*.

I did not get the job through being 'Tiny's friend'. On the contrary, that rather weighed against me, through the fears that even if I tried to be objective, my stories would be grinding some hidden Lonrho axe. The *ad hoc* committee set up by the paper to make a choice had seen a number of outside candidates, including Lord Soames's stylish nephew, James MacManus – who had been flown from Cairo for an interview. In the end, my long experience of Africa carried the day. The appointment also pleased Anthony Howard, who was anxious to bring in Peter Hillmore to write a new kind of diary and was happy to see the obstacle of my own column thus amicably removed.

To play myself in, I made two long swings down the continent, firstly on the eastern side from Sudan to Zimbabwe, then along the west coast from Senegal to Cameroon. In almost every capital I was asked what had happened to Mr Legum: there was a suspicion that Rowland had given him the sack. I had to explain that he had long been thinking of retiring, and the Lonrho takeover merely accelerated events. It was also fascinating that in every country I visited, Tiny's name was almost a household word: this, of course, was because Lonrho had big interests in them all.

My mode of behaviour was less grand than Legum's had been, largely because I did not follow his habit of conducting interviews with Presidents. In Nigeria I decided to travel around in mammy wagons, lorries and buses, to get to know the people; when I crossed what had once been Biafra, I hunted around nostalgically for the places I had known in the war, but the oil boom years had changed everything; all I found, beside the road which had been Biafra's last link with the outside world, was a ramshackle café entitled 'Uli Airport Motel'.

Although I was then unaware of it, my way of tackling Africa was not much to the liking of Rowland. He believed that the most becoming conduct for a correspondent was to meet Heads of State, ask their opinions, then report these faithfully. Such a view was natural enough, and in a way almost a compliment, because it was an extension of his own policy of only dealing with the 'man at the top'. (In this he also stood closer to Colin Legum, despite their other differences.) But the extent to which I was a disappointment to Rowland only emerged later, because I was at pains to keep away from him, to avoid any accusations that I was taking his orders. At the one meeting we had, before my trip to West Africa, he did say that interviewing some Presidents would 'add status' to my position, but I thought little of it.

So in the six months before we fell out, I was satisfied with my plunge back into Africa. What shocked me most about the continent, reappraising it after a decade, was the headlong economic decline, and the acceptance of violence for solving political differences. In Uganda I reported on the struggle to recover from the barbarities of Amin's years, in Sierra Leone on the reign of terror imposed by President Siaka Stevens's police, and in Ghana on the murder of four judges by an aide of the new revolutionary leader, Flt-Lt. Jerry Rawlings. I also wrote about the problems of famine, over-population and urbanization. But there were only two interviews with Presidents.

The bloody coup attempt in Kenya at the start of August 1982 was to be the watershed of my relationship with Tiny. When the air force mutinied, as part of a botched plot to throw out President arap Moi, I had happened to be back in London. Everyone there was astounded, given Kenya's glowing reputation as a haven of good sense, free enterprise and racial reconciliation. It was certainly a shock to Lonrho, which at that time was earning around a quarter of its African profits from Kenya alone. After the manoeuvres needed a few years before to distance himself from the discredited 'Kenyatta clan', Rowland understandably did not want to see the malleable Moi replaced by some lower-rank revolutionary.

Kenya had a narrow squeak, but with some external help the forces loyal to Moi managed to crush the self-styled People's Redemption Council. The task when the looting, raping and shooting stopped was to explain why it had happened. On that I had fairly clear-cut opinions, and offered to write for the *Observer* a leader-page analysis for the coming Sunday. My thesis was that behind the glossy façade of Nairobi, as seen by visiting businessmen and tourists, Kenya had long harboured festering social troubles. The gulf between rich and poor was too blatant, and this is what had been exploited by the plotters. Moreover, there was resentment among the intelligentsia in the universities (many of them Marxists) at the way Moi was giving bases to the United States and making Kenya the 'bastion of the

West'. The series of arrests in the weeks before the coup attempt was a clear signal to anyone watching carefully that trouble was at hand.

It had always been my view that Kenya was seriously under-reported, despite having seventy foreign correspondents based there from all over the world. They all liked the life too much to want to risk being thrown out. The conspiracy of semi-silence reminded me of Lebanon, before that country blew up. However, I forbore to take up space in castigating my old friends in the Nairobi Press Centre, but tried to give a balanced picture of Kenya's political frailties.

A few hours after my piece had gone down to the printers to be set I was called in by Trelford. He was all compliments, but made a surprising comment on my reference to foreign bases in Kenya. 'You didn't say anything about the threat from the Cubans in Ethiopia and Angola,' he said, and added: 'Perhaps we could slip a line in.' Although slightly nonplussed – especially about the mention of Angola, almost 4,000 miles from Kenya – I agreed. 'Don't worry,' said Donald, 'I'll see to it.'

As the deadline neared, one or two curious things happened. Somebody told me that Trelford was keen to get in a report about Sir Ranulph Twistleton-Fiennes, a self-styled 'explorer' who was trekking to the South Pole. This might push out the Kenya feature, which was already set – complete with the editor's added reference to Cubans. After I had remonstrated, the decision was taken to jettison Twistleton-Fiennes. But Kenya would have to be cut and set down one type size. Puzzled and secretly affronted, I turned to writing about the efforts to stop President Kamuzu Banda of Malawi from hanging an ex-minister and his wife.

Headlined 'Lessons of Kenya's Abortive Coup', my leader-page analysis duly appeared that Sunday. It certainly had been carefully edited – almost to the point of blandness – and, in the cutting, Donald's insertion about the Cubans had been lost. I shrugged the whole affair off as a bit of a mystery, and went to spend the weekend in Oxfordshire. It was there that Rowland telephoned me.

I had never before been subjected to his passionate rage, and it was not a pleasant experience. His tone was so unexpected, his flow of hectoring invective so wounding, that I could hardly believe it or bear it. Some of what he said did not really make much sense. 'Anti-Americanism, anti-Americanism,' he repeated several times. 'Without the United States you would not have your job, I would not have my job!' (In retrospect, I could see that his new friends, Ludwig and Anderson, had much affected his thinking.) It went on for almost half an hour, and I could rarely find a chance to speak. Tiny's diatribe touched the whole gamut of emotions. At one time he muttered: 'Buying the *Observer* was an error of judgement – a complete error of judgement.' He finally exclaimed: 'I could have flown you out to see President Moi for an exclusive interview.' With some difficulty, I told him that hearing Moi's version of why there had been a coup attempt might not reveal too much, but this rejoinder was not to Tiny's liking. He suddenly demanded: 'What about the Cubans in Ethiopia and Angola?' I replied that something had been in the text about them, but it was cut for space reasons. 'Yes, but it was not in your original script,' he shot back. That told me everything.

As I mulled over Rowland's passionate monologue, the reasons for it grew more plain. Only eight days before the coup attempt, there had been a ferocious dispute with the Kenya government over a leading article in the *Standard*, Lonrho's Nairobi-based daily. The editor-in-chief, George Githii, had written a carefully phrased, but firm condemnation of the arrests and repression being conducted by Moi. This had led to a tirade of criticism of Lonrho in the Kenya parliament by government spokesmen: one junior minister had urged that Lonrho should be expelled from the country. Right away, Rowland had acted. Even as the debate was still going on, a special edition of the *Standard* appeared, and a notice on the front page read: 'The shareholders, directors and management of the *Standard* unreservedly apologize to the government of Kenya for the provocative editorial which appeared in yesterday's issue of this newspaper. The views expressed therein are considered by our shareholders, directors and management to be contentious, and do not reflect this newspaper's long-established policy of support for the government of Kenya. At a special meeting of the Board of Directors this morning it was unanimously resolved that the editor-in-chief, Mr. George Githii, should be immediately dismissed.'

I knew Githii as Kenya's most respected journalist, but Lonrho had thrown him into the street, just as the Aga Khan did earlier to one of his Nairobi editors who had upset the government. There was a similarity with the instant dismissal by Rowland of the 'Kenyatta clan' when Moi inherited power. I could see how my piece in the *Observer*, quite independently touching on some of the points Githii had made about the realities of Kenya, thoroughly alarmed Tiny. A renewed vision of the expropriation of Lonrho's considerable assets in East Africa must have swept before his mind's eye.

His telephone call remained a secret. I knew it would be futile to ask Donald Trelford to go to the barricades, since he had been ready to show my copy to Rowland for vetting. Moreover, it was a rule that the journalists should only speak to the owner with the knowledge and consent of the editor. This was, after all, little more than a year since the end of the takeover battle, and for me to admit having had one conversation with Rowland, albeit unpleasant, would arouse suspicions that there must have been plenty more. So apart from confiding to a few close friends that I was in Tiny's bad books, I kept quiet, and tried to ignore a sensation of walking on sinking sand.

A few weeks later, I was invited to lunch in the paper's boardroom. The guests were Eddison Zvogbo, Zimbabwe's Minister of Legal Affairs, and his nephew, a journalist named Godwin Matatu. The American-educated Zvogbo I recognized only by name and reputation, but Matatu I knew personally: some years before we had appeared on the same platform at a seminar about southern African politics. Zvogbo made all the running, with much wit and verbal attack. Not for nothing was he the publicity secretary of Robert Mugabe's ruling ZANU party, and furthermore a poet of some note. He argued that Zimbabwe was receiving a bad press in Britain, that the efforts of its government for development were not appreciated, and that there was a great deal of pro-Smith sympathy in Fleet Street. This irritated me, and I replied that Zimbabwe seemed to me to be getting an extremely friendly treatment, considering some of the reports now surfacing about atrocities in Matabeleland and the detention of Joshua Nkomo's followers. There was, I stressed, still a lot of admiration for Mugabe – and rightly so. My response seemed to amaze Zvogbo, clearly not a person who took easily to being contradicted. There was a silence around the table, and Trelford changed the subject. By the time we rose from the table, the bonhomie seemed restored.

Our guests had been sent down to the *Observer* from Cheapside House, overtly for quite unexceptionable reasons. It was always useful for us to meet foreign notables who were passing through London. But Zvogbo had an extra significance, because Tiny was still trying to reorientate Lonrho in Zimbabwe after the downfall of Joshua Nkomo. The political realities meant that the company had to get on closer terms with ZANU, the force of the future. 'Old Josh' had been dismissed a few months earlier from the Zimbabwe Government, after large caches of arms had been found on his farms in Matabeleland. So Eddison Zvogbo, one of Mugabe's most dynamic and articulate lieutenants, was a contact to be cosseted.

A week or so after the lunch, Trelford sent me a long typescript Zvogbo had handed him. The subject: Zimbabwe's bad treatment by the Western media. Although I disagreed with his basic assertions, Zvogbo expounded his ideas with much passion, and I read the article through carefully. After all, he had a right to be passionate, as a patriot who had spent seven years in detention under a white minority regime. (Those same whites, moreover, were still free to lead their agreeable, sun-kissed lives.)

In some countries, with a press that was more academic and saw itself as duty-bound to give outsiders a fair crack of the whip, the article could have had a chance. I knew papers in Scandinavia which might have taken it. But in Britain it looked a non-runner, even for the *Observer*. It was also extremely long. After some pondering, I sent a note to Trelford saying so, adding that our failure to use the piece would doubtless be regarded by Zvogbo as 'further proof of Western media hostility'.

Another week went by, then Donald appeared in my office. He described how he had been looking through Zvogbo's offering again, and felt that inside it was 'an article trying to get out'. He had decided to make cuts and find a corner for it somewhere.

Later he sent me a memorandum confirming this decision. I was rather touched. So the piece subsequently appeared, most sensitively trimmed down and edited, on the second page of the paper's review section. It was an odd spot, but even there Zvogbo did command some attention. Several readers wrote in, a few agreeing, but most disagreeing with his line of thought.

That was not to be the last of our Zimbabwean guests, however. We soon saw more of Godwin Matatu, who was living in London. Like his uncle, he was immensely quick-witted and volatile, but understandably tired of being in exile. For the moment he was working on one of the British-based magazines specializing in African politics, but it was an existence from which he wanted to escape. He had been back in Salisbury – as Harare, the capital of Zimbabwe, was then still called – at the time of its independence in April 1980; but that episode had ended badly. Now, at the end of 1982, he saw the *Observer* as his second chance. Of course, he had powerful patrons.

I became conscious soon after the New Year of 1983 that Matatu was hanging around Donald Trelford's office. He was regarded as a nuisance, and Trelford's efforts to avoid seeing him became something of a joke in the newsroom. Early in February, after Matatu had dropped in on me, I told Trelford that he was proposing to write something for us about Jerry Rawlings, the Ghanaian ruler, whom he described as a personal friend.

The picture then started to come into focus, because Trelford explained that Matatu was pressing to become our freelance correspondent in Zimbabwe. This did not strike me as a good idea, because we already had a man accredited there – Stephen Taylor, who also wrote for *The Times*. Much more discouraging was Matatu's involvement in the country's politics; I failed to see how we could be sure of his objectivity when he had a close relation in the Cabinet. It demanded too much of him. My suggestion was that Matatu should use Zimbabwe as a base, and write about all the countries around: Malawi, Zambia, Angola, Botswana . . .

However, I admitted to being a bit baffled as to how he would make a reasonable living. My bafflement was a mark of my naïvety, because although I realized that Matatu knew

Rowland, I never guessed what lay in store. Perhaps even Trelford was unaware, too. 'Well, we certainly won't be paying him,' he said breezily. Neither of us could have known that Godwin was so close to Tiny that he had already flown with him to Mexico in his executive jet.

Matatu faded from my mind in the days that followed, because I was engrossed in a fascinating story. After much investigation I was able to establish that an unknown white man who had blown himself up while trying to sabotage a railway line in Mozambique was an Ulster loyalist named Alan Gingles. A product of Sandhurst, with service in West Germany as a British regular officer to his credit, Gingles had held the rank of captain in the South African Defence Force when he died. This revealed beyond doubt what had long been suspected, that South Africa was directly aiding the anti-government guerrillas in Mozambique. The story must have been interesting to Rowland, because the line which Gingles was attacking – 300 miles inside Mozambique – ran close beside the Lonrho oil pipeline. What was more, the RENAMO guerrilla movement with which Gingles was co-operating had been founded by Tiny's old friend Jorge Jardim, who four years earlier had given the *Observer* its great scoop about the sanctions-busting by Shell and BP.

Uncovering the Gingles story had meant a trip to Ulster. I took with me a fragment of a novel the dead man had been writing in spare moments during his sabotage mission. Penned in a notebook found among his equipment, it was all about terrorism in Ireland. Alan Gingles's father brought out for me, not suspecting my motives, one of the last letters from his only son. The handwriting matched.

A few days later I was back in southern Africa, where a lot was happening. Zimbabwe now held the world's headlines, because of the grievous events taking place in Matabeleland. After reports of many atrocities by the Zimbabwe army, foreign correspondents were converging like vultures on Bulawayo. The blame for the killings was put on the Fifth Brigade, to which was always attached that grim label 'Korean-trained'. Some of the reporting was portentous, with the London *Guardian* proclaiming on its front page that Zimbabwe was 'close to civil war'. All this made a harsh rejoinder to Eddison Zvogbo's recent *apologia* in our pages.

My main aim in Zimbabwe was to interview Robert Mugabe. The third anniversary of his country's independence was a month away, and this was a good 'peg'. Before I left London there had been a virtual promise from his country's High Commission that I should see him, and I had submitted a list of questions. But in Harare, the climate was less sympathetic. In fact, not one minister wanted to be interviewed, knowing that there would be tough questions to answer about Matabeleland. Only Eddison Zvogbo responded positively to my call, by inviting me around to his office.

When I arrived, his Mercedes was outside, with the driver and an armed bodyguard in the front seats. Zvogbo invited me to climb into the back with him. 'I'm going up to Heroes' Acre,' he explained. 'We can talk on the way.' Feeling in luck, I accepted. Heroes' Acre was the new national shrine, still incomplete, built on a hill outside Harare to honour the 7,000 freedom fighters who had died liberating the country from white rule. Few journalists had been allowed a chance to see Heroes' Acre, although those who had said it looked rather Stalinist, having been designed by the ubiquitous North Koreans.

Zvogbo and I certainly did talk on the way. Hardly were we out of the city centre when he demanded: 'Why are you here?' I began to explain that Zimbabwe was in the news, but he cut me short. 'No, no,' he replied, 'you don't understand. You are the Commonwealth correspondent of the *Observer*, aren't you? Why are you not in Canada?' I was perplexed. 'Well, Canada has never really been in my bailiwick.' Eddison frowned. 'What about the Caribbean?' Hoping to lighten the conversation, I responded: 'There's nothing I'd like more than a trip around the Caribbean. But there's not so much going on there.'

He suddenly tired of beating about the bush: 'Don't you know that Godwin is now the Africa correspondent of the *Observer*?' The Mercedes had just halted at some traffic lights, and it seemed as though everything had stopped, waiting for my reply. 'No,' I said, 'I am afraid you are mistaken.' As the car rolled forward again, Eddison bared his teeth a little. His eyes glowed red. 'Has nobody told you?' he asked. 'Godwin has been appointed the Africa correspondent.'

'You have it wrong,' I answered. 'Where did you hear this?' Zvogbo spoke firmly: 'In London. It was settled before Christmas. They should have told you.'

At this moment I saw how unperceptive we had all been. With one move, Rowland could get me out of Africa, where I was writing unpalatable stories, and please Zvogbo by giving his nephew a good job. It was swift retribution for my views on Kenya. Waiting for my reaction, Zvogbo leaned back in the far corner of the seat. 'All right,' I said, 'when I get back to London, I'll ask.'

By this time we were nearing Heroes' Acre, which was well protected. The car was stopped by a soldier who stuck his gun through an open window. When he realized there was a 'big man' inside he stamped frantically to attention and waved us on. The visit was to give me the material for a feature in which I contrasted Heroes' Acre with Zimbabwe's other national shrine, the grave of Cecil Rhodes in the Matopos Hills south of Bulawayo. Even Zvogbo unwittingly made his contribution to the piece, because a party of Namibian freedom fighters were waiting for him on the top of the hill, and he gave us all a conducted tour. The Minister explained that Zimbabwe's white civil servants had been opposed to Heroes' Acre, with its monumental statuary and huge bronze relief. But they had been overruled. Zvogbo told his admiring audience: 'We are ruling now, so we said to these civil servants: "What about Nelson's Column and Trafalgar Square? All for only one man! With lions – and Britain does not even have lions."' It was such a fine sally that I quoted him verbatim.

From Harare I dashed up to Lusaka, my old home, to write a profile of Kenneth Kaunda for the paper. The following week he would be in Britain on a state visit, so time was short, and that remarkable conversation with Zvogbo was relegated to the back of my mind. Until there was evidence to the contrary, I would just have to assume that Africa was still my responsibility. (With more discretion, I might have decided to propose to Trelford that I should go on a long tour of Canada, Australia and the Caribbean.)

Back in London, I found out that Rowland was taking a key role in the big African story of the moment – the flight of Joshua Nkomo. A fortnight earlier, Nkomo had slipped across the Zimbabwe border into Botswana in the middle of the night, afraid for his life after Fifth Brigade troops had broken into his Bulawayo home while he was hiding elsewhere; failing to find him they had shot dead three people in the house. Tiny was the first person to contact Nkomo when he was known to have got across the border, and he advised him to go home again. Joshua said he did not dare. Only too well, he remembered Mugabe's words at a recent party rally: 'ZAPU and its leader, Dr Joshua Nkomo, are like a cobra in a house. The only way to deal effectively with a snake is to strike and destroy its head.'

Rowland then tried to mediate, by contacting various Cabinet members in Zimbabwe. Although he could not reach Mugabe, who was at a conference in India, he persuaded the deputy Prime Minister, Simon Muzenda, to send a high-level delegation to visit Nkomo. At the last moment, the delegation's flight to Botswana was cancelled, and 'Father Zimbabwe' did what Tiny least wanted. He caught a plane to London.

The part Rowland had played while Nkomo was still in Botswana only came to light later. But what went on in Britain was closely monitored by Fleet Street. Nkomo shut himself up in a West London hotel and would give no interviews. The British government said he was free to remain, but did not try to hide its wish that he had never come. There was speculation that Joshua wanted to lobby his old friend Kenneth Kaunda, who was staying in Buckingham Palace for the week of his state visit, to intercede with Mugabe. Indeed, the confluence of events was poignant, because these two men were once the closest of friends (as I knew from often having been together with them), and Kaunda had always assumed that Nkomo would one day become the 'fellow-President next door'. Now they were both in London, but were kept apart by the dictates of destiny. While Kaunda rode in state, and the flags of Zambia waved in the Mall, a tired and dispirited Nkomo was hiding behind the door of his hotel room.

Rowland's earlier attempt to fend off Nkomo, and stop him from flying to London, was understandable. After all, Kaunda was vital to Lonrho's prosperity in Africa – if he nodded approval, other black leaders took their cue – and Joshua's fugitive presence might well detract from the well-practised harmonies of the state visit. Since Rowland was known to have backed the ZAPU leader, any such embarrassment could easily rub off on him. It was widely assumed (and correctly) that Lonrho was paying Nkomo's hotel bill and keeping his wallet full. That was always the way when Joshua arrived in London 'without a penny', as he would put it. But this time there was a proviso: he must not make any public statements or cause trouble in other ways, until the earliest moment when he could fly home to Zimbabwe.

So, although Rowland was not reneging outright on an old allegiance, he was letting Nkomo understand that their relationship was at arm's length now. There were other plain hints, for gone were the days when Joshua could be the family guest in the Park Lane flat, or failing that be fêted in the Savoy. I recalled the last time I had seen him in London, less than three years before, when he was staying (on the Lonrho account) in a penthouse suite overlooking Hyde Park. Just before I went in Tiny had come out. An article I wrote after interviewing Joshua then had ended with a description of how he gazed from the panoramic windows of his penthouse in the general direction of the Houses of Parliament. The last sentence read: 'He knows that in Britain's former African possessions, events have not tended to follow the Westminster pattern.' So it had turned out in Zimbabwe. The opposition was now, quite literally, on the run.

I could not help thinking about Joshua in his misery as I dressed to go with my wife to a banquet at Claridge's. The host was Kenneth Kaunda, and the guests included the Queen, the Queen Mother, several other members of the Royal Family, and the leaders of the main political parties at Westminster. Although one wondered about the cost of such a lavish function, for a country near to bankruptcy, it was also one where Joshua would have been a hit, in his own avuncular style. But if 'Father Zimbabwe' was missing, all the rest of Kaunda's old friends in London had been marshalled for the occasion. When we went to look at the seating plan, we discovered that Tiny and his wife

Josie were to be at the same table as ourselves. This coincidence was going to give the evening an extra piquancy, since Tiny had been boycotting me since the row about the Kenya coup. (When the Ugandan High Commissioner came to the *Observer* to protest about a report, later confirmed to the hilt, that Obote's soldiers were committing atrocities, Tiny accompanied him. They saw Trelford, but I – who had written the story – was not invited to come in to defend myself.)

It was surprising in a different way to find ourselves sitting with the Rowlands, because the table was in such an also-ran position, right down by the serving doors. Waiters dashed by constantly. That was fair enough for me, a journalist, but must have been mortifying for the chief executive of one of Britain's biggest and most thriving companies. Us apart, Tiny found himself sitting with a Buckingham Palace factotum, a security man, a red-faced bore who helped Kaunda improve his golf, and a black official of the nationalized Zambian copper corporation – plus their wives.

I glanced at Josie Rowland; she looked as charming and unaffected as I had first seen her, sixteen years before, when I had come back with Tiny from Ghana and he had presented her with a huge pineapple as she ran forward to greet him at the airport.

Tiny spent much of the banquet giving the Palace functionary an account of his recent adventures in Angola, where he had been flying around in a helicopter with the guerrilla leader, Dr Jonas Savimbi. On the far side of the circular table, I could not hear properly, apart from Tiny's insistence that Savimbi was 'the greatest man in Africa'. This was pretty much in line with what Edward du Cann, the deputy chairman of Lonrho, had once remarked while introducing Savimbi to a meeting in the Carlton Club – he was 'the Mrs Thatcher of Africa'.

The man from the Palace did not seem to know much about Angola (a fairly common failing, admittedly), but laughed a great deal in a courtierly manner. I contented myself with chatting to the black mining official, who put on a knowing face every time he tasted the wines being poured for us. The security man was keeping a discreet watch on the various entrances to the banqueting room, and I instinctively thought what a story it would be if terrorists suddenly burst in and began assassinating people before the very gaze of Her Majesty and Prince Philip and Princess Anne and all the rest.

The fantasy was interrupted by Tiny, leaning across the table and saying, 'You should have been there.' Where? In Angola, with Savimbi. It was a direct challenge, but for several reasons I did not share his enthusiasm for Savimbi.

It was in the salon after the banquet that I realized how Rowland had changed. As the other guests circulated, we paused behind a pillar, face to face. He said, without smiling, 'I've had three offers for the *Observer*.' This laid down right away who was the master, seeing that I was on the staff of the paper, a hired hand.

In the old days, in Africa, he had invariably begun conversations with a lot of banter, pretending to ask my advice on matters about which he clearly knew the answers already. Now he was playing a harder game. He had no intention of selling the paper, as I was aware. It would have pleased him, for a start, if I had feigned shock or amazement – even curiosity – over the predictable names of the three bidders.

Beyond Tiny's shoulder, past his white bow tie, I could see the Queen standing with Mrs Thatcher. In close attendance was the evening's host, President Kenneth Kaunda of Zambia, nodding his white head genially. David Steel, in a kilt, was chatting with Michael Foot.

'Rupert Murdoch, Robert Maxwell and Goldsmith,' said Tiny, and switched on one of his smiles. Perhaps he was genuinely amused by my dogged silence. I noticed as of old the flash of gold in one of his teeth, the Continental touch.

'You know it would be outrageous to sell the *Observer* to Goldsmith,' I replied. That was a safe enough show of defiance, because Tiny hated Goldsmith and would never sell to him. In any case, Sir James had burnt himself so badly in Fleet Street that he was not a likely buyer.

Still, with the introduction of politics, we might have moved on to a discussion of the paper's 'great liberal traditions' (a somewhat dubious tradition, as it happens, if you look back beyond 1945). But Rowland was not ready to bother with that. He had another shot to fire: 'I get along well with Donald Trelford.' He stopped, triumphantly, knowing that would touch a few nerves, then added, 'He is very weak.' It was said casually, with the emphasis on the last word, like an actor's well-rehearsed line.

Tiny and I stood glowering at one another in our white ties and tails, resembling characters in a Dornford Yates novel or a 1920s advertisement for Du Maurier cigarettes. He had gone too far, I decided, in attacking Trelford in this fashion, just to see what I would say. After all, he knew the etiquette.

My duty was to defend Trelford, and I set about it as best I might. Rowland must have been amused. At the end I said, 'Well, you know it is hard for Donald to be on a man-to-man basis with you. After all those disagreements during the Monopolies Commission.' This was true, if double-edged. Trelford had never wanted Rowland to be the paper's owner, and Rowland had not wanted him as editor, but so intricate were the conditions of purchase that they had become stuck with one another, like a pair of incongruous Siamese twins.

Anxious to slide away from this thin ice, I asked Tiny what he had thought of my profile of Kaunda, which had been in the previous Sunday's paper. Secretly, I was very proud of it. It had been all right, Tiny conceded, then complained about the unkindness of the accompanying caricature. Mark Boxer had drawn it, and although Mark has an exact and devastating touch with royalty and members of the upper classes – indeed, many of those around us at the banquet – he certainly did have a tendency to make black men look like maniacs with staring eyes.

I wondered what Boxer would make of the great tycoon himself. Although now in his late sixties, Tiny was still a good figure of a man. He was gaunt about the throat, of course, and no longer lithe as in those distant times when I first met him – but that was scarcely to be wondered at, considering all he had been up to since then.

We were slightly more relaxed, so I ventured to admit regret that we had fallen out over Kenya – although I still felt that his reaction had been excessive. He dismissed the memory of that peremptorily, then added: 'President Moi wrote a most helpful letter for us to the Prime Minister of the Bahamas, when we wanted to buy hotels there. He cleared up suspicions about

Lonrho. We owe him a lot.' It was a glimpse into the workings of power.

Our talk at Claridge's ended with some exchanges about the outlook in Harare, and it was clear that Rowland was sparing no effort to cement his new friendships. I touched on my belief that Mugabe had to respond to the demands of rival groups within his ruling party, if he were to stay in power. That was why Zimbabwe was sure to become a one-party state, just like Zambia. Up to that point Tiny had not appeared to hear much I had said in response to his verbal thrusts, but now he picked up the topic.

'There is one man', he said, 'who could go up to Robert Mugabe tomorrow and tell him, "I want your job" – and take it.'

'Yes,' I replied. 'Eddison Zvogbo.' He just looked at me, and we parted. I found my wife talking to the Queen Mother, and Tiny went to be introduced to the Queen by Kenneth Kaunda.

Driving home after the banquet, I tried to weigh all he had said and hinted at. We had not mentioned Nkomo in our talk, and I wondered how the old man's visit was going to end. It must have been on Tiny's mind as well. But the denouement was not distant, because a few days later Nkomo gave a press conference. He wanted to endorse the report just released by the Catholic bishops in Zimbabwe about atrocities in Matabeleland. As soon as the first reports of his press conference came over the Press Association wire, one of Rowland's aides was on the telephone to tell him that from now on there would be no more financial help available from Lonrho. 'I was very, very angry,' said Nkomo later. 'At the darkest moment of my life, the man I regarded as my friend withdrew his help and left me without either money or a place to live, at twelve hours' notice. I understand why he did it. People were pressing him. If he went on helping, his investments in Zimbabwe might be threatened . . .' Despite this let-down, Nkomo still says how grateful he feels to Rowland for his aid in sunnier days.

Although I was not immediately clear about Tiny's 'abandonment' of Nkomo, it was obvious that the portly exile was in straitened circumstances. With some difficulty I traced him to a noisy, nightmarish hotel, and found him staring aimlessly in his room at a cartoon programme on the TV. He did not seem to know when he was going home, despite reports from Bulawayo that his wife Johanna was appealing to him to do so. He complained that her telephone calls to him were being monitored, and hinted that she might be under duress about what she said.

Nkomo left me perplexed. Even if he did think Bulawayo was dangerous, his place was surely with his people, now leaderless at a dire moment. Behind his bluster there has always been more than a hint of weakness. So I wrote a fairly unkind piece, saying that he had 'moved down to the commercial traveller ambience', and was lingering uncertainly in London while Zimbabwe was about to celebrate its third anniversary of independence.

It was round about this time that *Private Eye* learned that the squall over Godwin Matatu was blowing up into a full-scale storm. Under the heading 'Street of Shame' appeared the following item:

> The *Observer*'s proprietor, Tiny Rowland, is going to great lengths to restore himself to favour with Robert Mugabe. Having backed the wrong man – Nkomo – to win in Zimbabwe.
>
> Since Tiny has enormous business interests in Zimbabwe – he is the biggest private employer of black labour in the country – there is a great deal at stake. It is therefore no surprise that Rowland is sympathetic to the moves afoot to replace the *Observer*'s Africa Correspondent, Richard Hall, with a man 'approved' by Mugabe's party. This is one Godwin Matatu, a Zimbabwean journalist who is political editor of *Africa* magazine.
>
> Unfortunately, this attempt is unlikely to succeed since Matatu, who failed to win a senior post in Mugabe's party, is not particularly favoured by the Government. Unaware of the revolting Matatu's true status, Tiny is willing to take him on board the paper, and is now trying to decide what to do with the wretched Hall, long-time Africa expert and open supporter of Tiny during his takeover bid for the *Observer*.

This was the usual *Private Eye* farrago, with plenty of incidental errors and *non sequiturs*, but a kernel of truth. The story now became public gossip around Fleet Street. Friends started telephoning me, to say that Godwin Matatu was boasting in the pubs that my days were numbered. Within the *Observer*, Trelford was being asked if he needed help to withstand the proprietor's machinations, but assured everyone that Matatu did not really matter. 'He'll soon blow up,' he assured me. 'This is not something for which I need to go to the limit, like Conor Cruise O'Brien's column.' Clearly, Donald was 'playing it long', hoping that the problem would go away. But after my Claridge's encounter with Rowland, I was not equally confident that it would, that Rowland would be persuaded to back down from his promise to Zvogbo.

However, the show went on. In the middle of the year, at a moment when all was quiet on the African front, I was asked to mastermind a major 'demolition job' on an Arab billionaire named Mahdi Al-Tajir, who was also the ambassador in London for the United Arab Emirates. The justification was that Al-Tajir had insulted the Queen by failing to show up in the Commons during the opening of Parliament. He had also been brazen enough, this one-time dockyard porter, to turn down invitations to dinner at Buckingham Palace. For such *lèse-majesté*, no vilification could be too ruthless.

While I was scraping the dirt together, a message was passed down to me from Cheapside House. There was an Egyptian living in Park Lane who knew a lot about the terrible Al-Tajir, and he was ready to talk. The message came from Rowland, who had obviously been told that I was doing the feature; he was no longer willing to recognize my existence by talking to me directly.

I went along to see the Egyptian. He had been done down by Al-Tajir, I gathered, over some big harbour project in the Gulf, and was exceedingly forthcoming – so much so that the lawyers struck out a lot of his revelations. My informant was none other than Mohamed Al-Fayed, eldest of the three brothers who eighteen months hence would become the owners of Harrods.

12

A Lovers' Tiff

The Matatu dispute rumbled on all through 1983, with much anguish among the *Observer* journalists and some dazzling gamesmanship by Donald Trelford. For the moment, he and Tiny were on the same side, which flummoxed everyone who thought the independent directors should become involved. The *raison d'être* of Lord Windlesham and his colleagues was to protect the editor against the proprietor; but if the editor was not complaining, then everything must be all right. The independent directors were certainly not empowered to act in response to complaints from the rank-and-file that the men at the top were getting on too well together.

This façade of amity concealed a great deal, however. The object of all the tension, Godwin Matatu himself, suddenly wrote from Harare accusing me of being a racialist. 'I am fully aware that you have been engaged in a campaign of calumny, innuendo, lies and vilification against my person,' he wrote. 'This black man will not take it.' He sent copies to Rowland and Trelford. I scarcely knew whether to laugh or cry. The one precise charge Godwin accused me of was asking two African journalists in London about his character – but the first I had not exchanged a word with for a year, and the other I had never spoken to in my life.

Matatu's letter greeted me when I came back from another trip to Uganda, and I warned Trelford that if I chose to I could start a legal action. It was never my intention, of course, because I felt rather sorry for Matatu: he was an experienced journalist, who had rather naturally fallen for the offer of a large salary in Harare, a Lonrho car and house. Now he was coming to look like Rowland's poodle. When we discussed the letter, Trelford was distinctly uneasy. 'It certainly doesn't help,' he admitted. He left unclear, though, exactly what it was not helping.

We found ourselves in a stalemate, the cause of reams of memoranda, rustling to and fro between the newsroom and the editor's office. The foreign news editor, Nigel Hawkes, went with Trelford to see Rowland, to argue the issue through. Although I was not invited, the word was put around that Hawkes was only against Matatu through being egged on – and I was doing the egging. Trelford remained consistent, saying that the *Observer*, of all papers, should give a black correspondent a chance. In a long and defensive missive to the National Union of Journalists, he wrote: 'It seems unfair (and illogical) that the main charge against Matatu is that he is championed by our proprietor, when Mr Rowland's own knowledge of Africa is surely unsurpassed.' There was a drawing in of breath when this was read out to the editorial staff.

By the middle of the year I thought I had had enough, and looked around for another job. I was about to sign up with a multinational oil corporation when my family dissuaded me. 'Can't you see how it would please Tiny?' said one of my sons. 'He will have got rid of you, and Matatu will have a clear field.' So I telephoned the oil company to apologize for wasting everyone's time, and vowed to stick it out. After all, my endorsement of Rowland had largely ensured that he would get his purchase of the *Observer* past the Monopolies Commission, so it would be pusillanimous to scuttle away when he behaved the way I said he would not.

The whole affair was wretched. Matatu was sitting in Harare doing nothing, Tiny had no thought of retreat, and Trelford was 'playing it long', as he repeatedly put it. Matatu finally sprung the trap by sending a telex to say that he could get a visa to visit Angola, and offering to report for the *Observer* from there. It was almost as if he knew that I had been trying in vain for a visa for more than a year – ever since Rowland had thrown down the challenge to me after our quarrel over the Kenya coup. Trelford was quick to say that

Godwin's reporting should be treated 'on its merits'.

Various compromises were now aired, mainly based on the belief that if Matatu was fated to write for the paper, then it was better for him to do it as a proper member of the staff than as a hired hand of Lonrho. Nothing came of these schemes, then Nigel Hawkes resigned as foreign news editor and sent a letter to the paper's correspondents explaining why. One of the letters from Hawkes inevitably found its way back to Fleet Street, where it made news. Rowland responded ferociously: 'If Mr Hawkes no longer wishes to work for the paper, then he needn't. Nobody is begging him to stay.' Trelford tried his best to smooth matters over by naming Hawkes as the diplomatic correspondent. By this stage it was obvious that through our wish to avoid splitting the editorial staff, Hawkes and I had sold the pass; and Rowland had won his first campaign to put a man on the paper to serve his own political needs.

Three weeks later, Matatu's maiden story appeared in the *Observer*, and its significance was jumped upon by Alexander Chancellor, at that time the editor of the *Spectator*. 'Well Done Godwin!' wrote Chancellor sarcastically. He went on to point out that a week earlier there had been a full-page advertisement in the *Observer* by Eddison Zvogbo, Zimbabwean Minister of Legal Affairs; this defended his country's detention – after their acquittal – of some white air force officers. Was the advertisement fully paid up, wondered Chancellor? He also speculated on the idea that Rowland might be trying to promote Zvogbo as a rival to Robert Mugabe: 'I only ask because of Lonrho's record in this respect.' Chancellor recalled a conversation he had once had with Ian Smith, about the amount Rowland formerly paid Joshua Nkomo. 'Clearly Mr Rowland backed the wrong horse with Nkomo. Will he be more successful this time?'

The *Guardian* telephoned me to ask what I thought about Matatu's début. I told Alan Rusbridger, the paper's diarist, to call me back after half an hour. When he did, I read him over a few sentences: 'I can't deny being disappointed with Tiny Rowland over the incident. I feel it personally after having been a leading supporter in front of the Monopolies Commission. He never interfered when I was his first editor in Zambia, and I said so.'

I went on to say that I regarded myself as 'a sort of guarantor' for Tiny (a phrase I knew was going to madden him). My brief bit of heart-searching ended: 'I think we're all a bit wiser now and a bit sadder. Like the editor, I hope Godwin Matatu will prove a useful *Observer* correspondent.'

The reaction was not long in coming. In a letter marked 'Personal and Confidential' Trelford accused me of waging a 'public battle' against my own newspaper, of contradicting him and criticizing the proprietor – 'offences that would get you fired on many other papers' – and of helping the *Guardian* to damage the name of the *Observer*. This remarkable piece of sophistry was doubtless copied to Cheapside House (where the damage really originated). I wrote back to assure Trelford of my loyalty to the paper as I understood it, and point out that the Matatu dispute was, after all, a public matter already, involving an important issue of editorial freedom. My own position was central in more ways than one.

Worse was to follow a couple of days afterwards. As Trelford told me later, somebody sent the *Guardian* a plain manilla envelope, and inside was a photocopy of his 10,000-word memorandum to the Monopolies Commission, denouncing Rowland as an unsuitable proprietor. Whereas I would by now be more inclined to agree with the thrust of his memorandum, Trelford only wished it in oblivion. As he was to say to me: 'It is a time bomb ticking away.' Who could have sent it? Only a small coterie of confidants had seen the memorandum – the 'Gang of Six'. One of those must have so disliked his handling of the Matatu business that they had chosen to shop him.

Rusbridger was not slow to quote some unnerving sentences, with a strong hint that there might be more to come. That evening I was working in the office until after midnight on a story, and while I was in the midst of it a rather overwrought letter landed on my desk from Trelford. It ended: 'If you assist Rusbridger's campaign, you must expect to come under suspicion when he quotes from confidential documents, whether you are guilty of leaking them or not. That's what happens when trust breaks down between colleagues.' I clenched my fists for a moment. Donald knew perfectly well that I had never seen his memorandum. The next day he apologized.

One could say that we had fought ourselves to a standstill over Matatu. The only person who might have regarded it as a bit of sport was Rowland – and as matters turned out, the principle mattered far more than the practicalities, because Matatu's contributions were so sparse. It often fell to me to rewrite them. As several months went by, we let the bad memories fade, and there was only a little unease when somebody remarked that in the new Zimbabwe telephone directory Matatu had put the *Observer* after his name.

Events elsewhere were even starting to persuade those journalists among us whose work had a regular political element that we were lucky. The granite-faced Andrew Neil had taken over at the *Sunday Times* in the autumn of 1983, and the effects were soon calamitous. Neil was the authentic voice of the New Right, someone Murdoch could trust finally to obliterate the liberalism which the paper had become imbued with in the Harold Evans era. Life was being made impossible at the *Sunday Times* for those of the old brigade who had not resigned when Murdoch bought the paper in 1981. Neil was always drawing up hit lists of those who did not fit into his Thatcherite scheme of things, and his principal lieutenant was Anthony Bambridge, the managing editor (news). Many of us were shocked about him, because he was a former *Observer* man; but I could remember that Bambridge had played a key role in getting me sacked as magazine editor twelve years before.

So as Neil laid about him, the more admired became the subtle virtues of Donald Trelford. The two papers had by now diverged quite noticeably since setting out – almost simultaneously, three years earlier – under new owners. There had been times in the last days of Astor when the *Observer* looked rather to the right of its bigger rival, but now was conspicuously to the left. You could not say that it followed a doctrinaire socialism – that would have been provoking Rowland too much, now that he was a Reaganite – but the paper was undeniably displaying a caring and libertarian vision of the world. All post-Tiny recruits (leaving aside those destined for the business section, seen as a Lonrho plaything) had recognizable leanings.

Trelford knew the sort of paper he wanted to edit, but he went after it by stealth. Whereas Neil charged headlong forward like a mastiff – knowing that his master was right behind him – Trelford showed the subtlety of a fox. Had he been identifiable as a 'pinko' (as Rowland termed Allister Sparks, our correspondent in South Africa), his survival would have been more in the balance. Then the paper might have been subjected to the duress of one of those Fleet Street hardliners whose names were always being touted as Tiny's favourites to take over as editor.

That was how we rationalized it: Donald's wheelings and dealings could be the least disagreeable price to pay in so hostile an environment. Most of the time British journalists manage to avoid thinking about the realities of their industry – that it is owned almost exclusively by the kind of capitalist who will not tolerate 'hostile' ideas being aired. The only way of placating such owners is to make fat profits for them; and that generally means a lowering of standards. The miracle of the *Observer* in the 1980s has continued to be that it makes no profits, has an arch-capitalist proprietor, yet generally manages to stay somewhere on the left.

Although it was an open secret that virtually all my work on Africa was now being submitted to Rowland for his advance vetting, that did not matter much in practice, although it made me feel spied upon. I wrote as I wished and nothing was materially altered, apart from the insertion of a sentence or two. In any event, in late 1983 and early 1984 I was able to spend a month in the United States and two months in India, which got me out of Rowland's sights.

Soon after I was back in the office from India, Trelford told me he was going to visit Zimbabwe. 'Tiny has arranged for me to interview Mugabe,' he explained. I smiled, recalling my own unsuccessful efforts to see 'Comrade Bob'. Later it emerged that Donald was unhappy about having the interview 'facilitated' by Lonrho, since it made him feel compromised. As we all knew, Zimbabwe was particularly dear to Rowland's heart: not only was it the country where he began his African career, but it still served as a main prop for Lonrho's profits. It would be hard to interview Mugabe without feeling a presence at your shoulder. On the other hand, such a proposition could not be dismissed.

Thus was the die cast for one of the most astonishing quarrels in the history of British journalism. Some of the onlookers – who were to include millions of astounded TV viewers – thought it ludicrous and unreal, like an episode in some big business melodrama. But the issues did matter a great deal, and one of the protagonists was to gain a reputation that even his best friends thought quite a marvel. It also served to cover up a lapse in the recent columns of the *Observer*, a campaign to prove that Mark Thatcher had taken a rake-off from a big British contract in Oman, with his mother's help. There was a vein of truth, everyone knew, but several weeks of digging failed to lay it properly bare. A feeling had grown around the office that by allowing the investigation to run on and on, Trelford had given Rowland enough rope to hang him, if he wished (even though, in the early stages, Tiny had pointed him in the direction of information, and Lonrho's security chief had briefed the reporters concerned).

The Mugabe interview was scheduled for 11 April in Harare, a Wednesday, and Trelford flew overnight at the weekend to prepare for it. But on Tuesday morning he was told it was cancelled – Mugabe had instead to meet President Kenneth Kaunda at the Victoria Falls. Luckily, Rowland was in town, and he quickly showed his influence by persuading Mugabe to put off some other appointments and fit the interview in. This feat had put Tiny in high spirits by the time Trelford met him for lunch on the Tuesday, and he held forth about what was going to happen to his powerful friends all over Africa. Often, Tiny implied, their fates lay in his own hands. As usual, his utterances were full of amazing hyperbole. For instance: 'Colonel Qadhafi is merely a retailer in death – the United States is a wholesaler.' As he flung these extravagances around, like hand grenades, a clutch of local directors sat in reverent silence. A more sceptical listener was Neal Ascherson, a distinguished *Observer* writer. He happened to be in southern Africa to do a famine survey.

After the lunch Trelford and Ascherson had a private chat, partly about their dazed reactions to Tiny's conversation, but mostly about the next morning's interview with Mugabe. Then they discussed the growing number of accounts emanating from Roman Catholic missionaries about renewed atrocities in Matabeleland by the Fifth Brigade; after a lull the terror now seemed as bad as it had been a year before. Ascherson said he had the telephone number of a good contact. 'I'd like to have it,' said Trelford. All at once, he was more interested in discovering the truth about Matabeleland than in talking to Mugabe; and he was set on his collision course with Tiny.

In the weeks ahead there was to be endless discussion about what made Donald do it. People's motives are often more complex than they care to admit. 'He thought he was going to get the sack and a big golden handshake,' I was told. Although it was known that two of the five independent directors were hostile to him, this explanation struck me as improbable at the time, and still does; Trelford had seen the relative obscurity into which Harold Evans quickly fell after allowing Murdoch to bully and buy him out of the editorship of *The Times*.

Should Donald want deliberately to throw up the job he had clung to so very tenaciously, and exchange it for the fickle world of television, as rumour had it? Another idea was that he chose Matabeleland as the 'cause' to rally support among his own journalists, after the buffeting he had received over Matatu. This also seemed unlikely, because there was a general acceptance that Trelford was marvellously adroit in his handling of Tiny: somebody else, with less flexible principles, might quickly bring the whole house down. For Donald to take such a risk, just to make his staff love him a bit more, seemed far too quixotic.

The ultimate conspiracy theory was to come from a government-owned Zimbabwean newspaper, the *Manica Post*:

> Suppose Mr Rowland had some score to settle with Zimbabwe, or rather with our present government? He hatches a plot with his *Observer* editor, whereby the latter would make a token fact-finding visit to Zimbabwe, as a cover for an already made-up story, putting our government in the poorest possible light. Mr Trelford returns to London and publishes the story, which 'embarrasses' Mr Rowland. We suspect that Mr Rowland only wanted the story to gain more publicity by reacting to it.
> More harm to Zimbabwe. Mission accomplished. Our country deserves better from a man whose conglomerate is flourishing because of its operations in Zimbabwe.

The mundane truth must be that Trelford was mainly concerned to engage in some straightforward reporting. Journalists in Zimbabwe thought that he had set out with the idea of knocking down atrocity stories which had already appeared in the *Sunday Times*; but finding they were true, decided to trump them. It is easy to realize how he came to feel – that if the Mark Thatcher 'investigation' had proved a dud he would show them at home what the real thing was like. What was more, it would serve to prove that he was not merely Tiny's yes-man.

The first we knew back in London that something unexpected was afoot was on the Thursday. His Mugabe interview had not arrived – Trelford was too busy out in the bush for that. As it happened, he had Godwin Matatu as a companion. On the Thursday night, when they had retired in adjoining rooms in Bulawayo's Holiday Inn, a knock came on Trelford's door. A messenger was standing there. This was to be the start of a five-hour tour in the darkness by car and van to meet victims of the Fifth Brigade's excesses. Trelford got back to his room at 3.30 a.m., to have a few hours' sleep; the unconscious Matatu never knew he had been away.

After flying back to Harare on the Friday morning Trelford wrote his story, telephoned it over, then caught an overnight plane to London. On Saturday morning he was in the office, to check through the page devoted to his bombshell. The piece was enormously impressive – not merely the content, but the panache with which he told his grisly tale of murder in the bush. There was only a brief mention of Mugabe, presenting him as a decidedly sardonic and ruthless personality.

During the afternoon I went into Trelford's office to congratulate him. He looked worn out, but elated. 'What's Tiny going to think about it?' I asked. Trelford smiled: 'He's just been on the line. He said he might close the paper down if my story is published. I told him that I was simply not prepared to talk on those terms.' It was a remarkable change of style. 'Of course,' I replied, 'that's all you can do. It's a story that must be printed.' Trelford obviously felt that on a subject like this, his position was impregnable. The next morning he imperturbably flew off to the Channel Islands with his family for a short holiday.

Tiny's hurricane of fury over Trelford's revelations made his anger about some of my reports seem like mere zephyrs. He must suddenly have felt that all his efforts – costly efforts – to curry favour with the Mugabe government had come to nothing. (He had, for instance, handed out cheques for more than £1 million to educational projects in Zimbabwe, and given selected ministers free holidays at a Lonrho hotel in Mauritius.) Now Trelford threatened to wreck it all, even putting the company's enormous investments in Zimbabwe in peril. Tiny had felt the first repercussions from Zimbabwe on the Sunday morning, after reports of Trelford's story had been wired out to Nathan Shamuyarira, the Minister of Information. Telephoning straight to his Bourne End retreat, Shamuyarira said that this was going to cause him acute embarrassment, since he had been responsible for organizing the Mugabe interview, at Rowland's insistence. The unfortunate Matatu was even more alarmed and mortified, since he had been charged with the duty of keeping an eye on Trelford's activities in Matabeleland. Mugabe himself took the opportunity at a public rally to make an all-round attack on the mendacity of the Western media. On hearing that, Rowland telexed an abject apology.

The quarrel was about to become public, in a fashion which must have had Northcliffe and Beaverbrook, if they were looking on from Heaven or Hades, scratching their heads in wonderment. Tiny traduced his own editor as 'discourteous, disingenuous and wrong' in publishing his account of the Matabeleland conflict. Mugabe was invited to make this grovelling letter public – a step which he took with alacrity, since it seemed to support his own claims that the Fifth Brigade was doing nothing wrong in its 'search and destroy' sweeps. Tiny put it plainly, calling the article 'sensational', and saying that Trelford had 'taken advantage of his position as editor' to print a story which would have been thrown out if written by one of his reporters. Lonrho 'unreservedly dissociated' itself from the allegations. The papers in Zimbabwe gave Rowland all the publicity he could have hoped for, and made clear that they appreciated his motives: as Joshua Nkomo had said about the way he found himself ditched: 'I understand why he did it ... his investments in Zimbabwe might be threatened.' This was very much a repeat performance of Lonrho's behaviour in Kenya in 1982, even to the wording.

Just as speedily as the *apologia* had been telexed to Harare, so it was winged back to Britain. Once more, the *Observer*'s private life was making news. Even abroad, this was judged as a topic too piquant to ignore. A superb headline in the *Wall Street Journal* said it all: 'London *Observer*'s Article on Zimbabwe Raises Ire of Paper's Owner, Who Does Business There.' But it takes two to make a slanging-match, and the hunt was on to find Trelford, somewhere in the Channel Islands with his family. Would he come out fighting?

Up to now he had never spoken a public word of criticism about Tiny, so we were hardly prepared for his language. He called the letter to Mugabe 'ludicrous', 'defamatory' and 'inaccurate'. Then he touched that most sensitive spot: 'Mr Rowland is simply acting to protect his business interests.' By the Tuesday after his report appeared, the quarrel was already in full spate, and on the editorial floor we listened in astonishment to every TV and radio bulletin. Each exchange was more heated than the last. Did Trelford intend to resign, since the proprietor had lost confidence in him, speculated Sir Robin Day. 'Certainly not,' came the retort from Guernsey. If Tiny had any complaints he should refer them to the independent directors. That was Trelford's ace, because he knew what they would say: his position was impregnable.

The battle hotted up with a fusillade of letters. Trelford rejected Rowland's assertion that he was a failure as an editor, by quoting some shrewdly-selected circulation figures, and ended: 'I reciprocate your desire not to make this a personal issue. It was you, however, who chose to make a public attack on my journalistic integrity and competence.' Having acquired a taste for this David and Goliath encounter, he went on to ridicule Tiny's charge that he had been discourteous to Prime Minister Mugabe: 'I wonder what he thinks about the discourtesy of the Fifth Brigade in Matabeleland who have been bayoneting people and torturing them with electric shock treatment.'

Rowland was nonplussed. Never in his twenty-three years at the helm of the Lonrho clipper had he been so abused by one of his own deck-hands. He accused Trelford of imagining he was an owner-editor, like David Astor. 'You are not,' he said, rather truculently. It was left to Paul Spicer, the *faute de mieux* Lonrho spokesman, to stoke the flames: 'Here you've got a monster, careering out of control, being paid for by us and by our shareholders.' It seemed to Spicer that people on the *Observer* thought they could do 'whatever they liked'. Relations between him and Trelford never had been too good, ever since he had asked, in his arrogant way, whether Donald had any O levels. Now Spicer claimed that Lonrho had monitored 'every minute' of Trelford's visit to Zimbabwe, and did not believe he had spoken to all the people he said he had done; indeed, Trelford's main source of information – according to Spicer – had been a *Sunday Times* correspondent.

This was belligerent stuff, and Trelford was at great pains in the following Sunday's paper to give as much detail as he could, without endangering his sources, about where he had been in Matabeleland. At the *Observer* we all waited to see what would come next. As the *Guardian* neatly put it, Trelford had long been a 'canny buffer zone' between management and journalists, but was now in the eye of the storm. However, the *Guardian* diary scarcely helped Trelford in his hour of need by once again quoting from his confidential submission to the Monopolies Commission in 1981 about Tiny's likely proclivities as an owner, including one pithy sentence – 'Rowland is no saint.'

We did not have long to wait to see how Rowland would deal with a mutiny on board. He would make us walk the plank and take our chance with the waiting sharks. One particular shark had already surfaced in anticipation – Robert Maxwell, who at that time was still to make his great *Daily Mirror* coup. 'Bob is very interested in buying the paper and he doesn't put up with any nonsense,' said Rowland ominously. All his animus was aimed at Trelford: he insisted that with the right editor, he would not want to sell, and could happily make good losses of £5 million a year, not just the actual £1 million. With a fine show of nostalgia, he recalled that until the Matabeleland upset, 'Donald and I were getting along very cosily.'

If he had wanted to strike terror in us all, he certainly

succeeded by talking of a sell-out to Maxwell. Everyone who had ever dealt with 'Captain Bob' had their own horror stories. I personally remembered how he had been prone to telephone me, when I was editing the 'Men and Matters' column at the *Financial Times*, to seek publicity for the drab memoirs of some superannuated Soviet tyrant signed up by his Pergamon empire. That booming voice, that way of repeatedly calling me 'Mr Hall' at once fawning and menacing – gave the dire sensation of being trapped in a small field with a large bull. Was this where Donald's fling was going to take us?

In the aftermath it was asserted that Tiny never did mean to hand the paper to Maxwell. Their much-reported breakfast in the Royal Suite at Claridge's Hotel, on kidneys, scrambled eggs, bacon and toast, did not lead to any deal. Having played his part, Captain Bob just faded from the scene; even *The Times* dismissed it as a 'breakfast-table flirtation'. But much later there was a rather macabre proof that Maxwell, at least, had been serious. It came in a death-bed disclosure by William Clark, one of the original independent directors of the *Observer*. In his last hours, a victim of liver cancer, Clark told Anthony Howard that Maxwell had promised to appoint him editor-in-chief if the sale went through – just one of the editorial changes he had in mind. (It would have been an adroit appointment, because at one stage in his distinguished career, Clark had been the *Observer*'s diplomatic correspondent and was everywhere well respected.)

However there was no sale, which reduced Rowland's declared 'options' to two – either he would find a way of ridding himself of Trelford, or he would just shut the paper down and keep the title. The last seemed the least likely, since it would involve Lonrho in a heavy loss – including the £6 million it could expect from a share in the controversial Reuters sell-off. On the other hand, if Tiny felt piqued and frustrated enough, anything was possible – his wilfulness was legendary. So we waited, only faintly reassured by a sharp condemnation of Rowland by the independent directors. 'I am not affected by anything they said,' he responded, and threatened to slash their stipends from £4,000 a year to £1,000. They were, he said, 'plastic gnomes'.

The rest of Fleet Street treated this unparalleled case of dog biting dog as a daily delight. *Private Eye* had a cover picture headlined 'Observer Latest', showing Maxwell and Rowland jovially shaking hands. From Maxwell's mouth issues a 'balloon', asking, 'Is the atrocity story true?' Rowland replies, 'Yes, I'm still in charge.' Even *The Times* made fun of the wrangle, and suggested that it was just a Rowland ruse to 'have a new and more successful editor'. It claimed that Tiny had talked of selling the paper a year before, but had been warned off by Robert O. Anderson, the Atlantic Richfield boss. The story went that Anderson was displeased that Tiny was preparing to renege on his promise to treat the *Observer* as a long-term responsibility. Anderson thought that this would make him an outcast in American financial circles, just as he was in much of the City of London. According to an 'informed source', he warned Rowland to watch his step: 'You may think you're big, Tiny, but I'm bigger.'

At first it was thought that an intervention from Anderson had led to the astounding U-turn when the feud had gone on for a fortnight. Everyone was taken unawares by the strange events of Friday 27 April. At midday, Channel 4 television interviewed Trelford, who said that he was determined to hold on to his job, despite Rowland's threat to axe any investment in the paper, including the withdrawal of all advertising by Lonrho subsidiaries. 'It would be a betrayal to quit,' the editor declared. The journalists were valiantly getting ready to pass a resolution denouncing Tiny's behaviour (even though some of them had started to question whether the price of Donald's integrity was getting pretty steep). But late on Friday came the truce.

Explanations were never offered as to who had instigated the deal. But clearly, Rowland was forced to climb down – to accept that Lonrho would go on owning the *Observer* and Trelford would stay on as editor. 'It was just a lovers' tiff,' feigned Tiny afterwards. Donald spoke in the same amorous vain: 'We share three basic affections: for the *Observer*; for Africa; and for each other.' As one cynic on the staff asked: 'Can we expect that the honeymoon will be in Acapulco?'

The 'My Dear Tiny' and 'My Dear Donald' letters published in the paper to announce the end of the fight rewarded careful study. They were both drafted by Trelford himself, along lines agreed verbally. The most dramatic element was his resignation offer, no more than an artful formality. This gave Tiny the chance to reply: 'Certainly not. I support your editorship and I refuse to accept your resignation.' It seemed a mighty hostage to fortune on one side, and on the other a triumph for editorial independence. (Or, as put in an earlier comment by Spicer, the people at the *Observer* still had a mandate to do as they liked – 'Donald Trelford is in a position to stick two fingers up at Mr Rowland.') There was a modest expression of regret from Trelford about his charge that Rowland had only disowned the Zimbabwe report out of 'crude concern for commercial interests'. On the contrary, he now accepted that Tiny had a genuine conviction that the truth about Zimbabwe was more complex than his own interpretation of it. As for the threats that Lonrho would withdraw all its financial backing, there was a promise from Cheapside that more money would be siphoned in than ever before.

What was more, Trelford was now virtually a national hero – the brave little editor who had stood up for the truth and outfaced the wicked giant of capitalism. Politicians of all parties had come to his support. Soon he was in demand as a speaker on press freedom. His television performances acquired a new prestige. His name was put forward for international awards (in one instance, by one of his acolytes on the paper).

Such a feat would surely have been applauded by Houdini himself. Yet we soon wondered how firm the reconciliation was, after I had uncovered a story about Rowland's secret attempt to salvage President Gaafar Nimeiri's regime in the Sudan. By this time, Nimeiri was clearly at the end of his time: he was suffering from religious dementia, and displaying it by an orgy of hand amputations in Khartoum; he was also faced with a mounting insurrection by southern rebels, led by a renegade colonel named John Garang. But Tiny's old loyalty to this worn-out dictator remained strong; and he decided to involve President arap Moi of Kenya in some last-ditch diplomacy. They both flew up from Nairobi to Khartoum.

My lead into the story had come through Benjamin Bol, the London representative of the Sudan People's Liberation Movement. He lived rather furtively in a mews in Notting Hill Gate, and was to die mysteriously a few months later in Addis Ababa. Bol told me a lot – for example, how he had seen Rowland several times at a London hotel. 'How did he make contact with you?' I asked. 'Through the American embassy,' replied Bol. It seemed that the Americans, like Rowland, were engaged in a forlorn effort to rescue Nimeiri, and were putting a lot of pressure on the southerners to sign a truce. The idea was that Garang and his colleagues should go down to Nairobi for talks. 'Be careful,' I warned Bol. 'You might find yourself being handed over to Nimeiri.'

The detailed account of Rowland's manoeuvres was given the full treatment in the *Observer*. It was a fine show of independence – although Trelford did take the precaution of telling one of the Lonrho directors that the story was going in, and then making sure that Tiny saw the typescript. Nobody complained in advance, but immediately afterwards a furious letter landed on Trelford's desk. Copies of it had been sent to all the directors, and other interested parties as well. Although he had ignored it in the typescript, Tiny lighted on one mistake in my long and complicated story: I had said that President Moi flew to Khartoum in the Lonrho jet, whereas he went separately in an official Kenyan plane. 'This is an example', Trelford was told in the letter, 'of the inaccuracies being published by the *Observer* under your editorship.' It was a malicious blow, because the fault was mine.

Donald shrugged it off. There was a belief that Tiny had reacted so explosively because I had upset the Americans. My story had certainly blown the cover of a senior Central Intelligence Agency man in the Grosvenor Square embassy, and that might have been embarrassing. Yet the incident did give a hint that the hostility over the Matabeleland bust-up was still alive – had it, after all, been more than a 'lovers' tiff'? The puzzle remained: why had Tiny been forced to capitulate?

The underlying tensions were made more obvious by a boardroom dispute three weeks later, when owner and editor quarrelled noisily about the paper's financial outlook. Once again, Rowland suggested that Trelford was inadequate for the job. The meeting had been called for by Robert O. Anderson, who was shocked by the venom let loose and tried in vain to appeal for calm. Almost immediately, a detailed account of what had occurred in the meeting was leaked to the *Guardian*, with a bias that was all too visible. The report stressed: 'The latest confrontation inevitably raises fears that the Lonrho chairman is intent on getting rid of Mr Trelford.' That was exactly right, for Trelford had been cancelling any duties which might take him too far from London. 'I dare not leave the country at the moment,' he admitted.

Lonrho declared itself furious about the leak, and said there was plenty of evidence about who was guilty. 'He will be dismissed,' promised Spicer, 'for making mischief.' One newspaper asked Trelford how he saw the matter. 'I have absolutely no comment to make,' he said. But the point had been driven home. Once again, Lonrho went strangely silent.

And as the hot summer of 1984 softened into autumn, we saw the reason why. Rowland could not afford at this moment to stand accused of crude and unbecoming behaviour in his ownership of the *Observer*, because he felt himself coming closer at long last to his heart's desire – the ownership of Harrods.

13

'Step Into Another World'

It did look, in the spring of 1984, as if Tiny might have finally conquered all hazards in his pursuit of Harrods. He was like some explorer seeing before him at long last the source of the Nile, and he kept telling the Lonrho directors that the store would be 'in the family' by the end of the year. Forests of official bureaucracy, inquiry upon inquiry, had been doggedly endured. Now an investigation by a government-appointed QC named John Griffiths into possible malpractices in House of Fraser share dealings was almost over, and Rowland felt he had easily won the battle of charge and counter-charge. The volatile relationship he had struck up with Griffiths was curiously similar to the one he had had ten years before with Heyman, the QC in the Department of Trade inquiry. Like Heyman, in his turn Griffiths would criticize Rowland: but he would also call him a colossus.

So, although the 'lovers' tiff' with Trelford won far more headlines, it was in reality a sideshow for Tiny. He could not resist compiling a passionate rejoinder to the Griffiths Report, even before it was published. This pre-emptive tactic was again reminiscent of the way he had tried to forestall Heyman. But he was now much more extreme in his language, more outrageous in his allegations.

There was a conviction in the City by mid-1984 that, even if he won in the end, Harrods was taking possession of Rowland's mind and energies in a way that was harmful to Lonrho. Even his admirers felt he was neglecting the rest of his empire in chasing this one prize. A partner in a prominent firm of stockbrokers put it vividly to me at that time: 'Harrods is the jewel he wants, so he will be able to say, "You bastards, I have got it despite you!" But he has been fighting for it too long and has squandered his chance to become a real force on the British scene.' Then he added, prophetically: 'In any case, Tiny hasn't got what he wants, even yet.'

The endless preoccupation with Harrods must be correctly deciphered if one is to understand the emotional pressures deep inside Tiny. Enormous though it is, the money involved has become almost incidental to him. So has the ostensible reason for his campaign, the prestige that the acquisition of Harrods would have brought to Lonrho. To be nearing seventy, and to have a private fortune of around at least £100 million – to be more than a millionaire for each year of your age – must take the edge off cupidity. (This is not to say, of course, that Tiny could realize every penny of his wealth in cash, because he has loyally kept the vast bulk of it in Lonrho shares, and if he really began to 'unload', the company would crash.) It is asserted that with advancing years he takes less pleasure than once was the case in doing deals and seeing the graph of company profits soar. In material terms, he has little to strive for, and even if ideas come a little less quickly nowadays, he can fairly boast of having guided Lonrho into becoming one of the world's great conglomerates.

There have to be other reasons for his nine-year obsession with the Knightsbridge store. They are to do, of course, with power – but of a kind much more subjective than the 'merchant-statesman' role he likes to play in Africa. Something of a clue exists in the date when Lonrho first took a stake in House of Fraser, of which Harrods is the flagship. It was February 1977: that was only six months after the release of the massive Department of Trade inquiry into Lonrho – in itself a sequel to Edward Heath's remark about the 'unacceptable face of capitalism'.

Since the early 1970s, one must say, Harrods has acquired a certain flashiness, a dash of vulgarity; yet it very definitely remains a most acceptable face of capitalism. Capturing this citadel of the Establishment would have bathed Lonrho (and Rowland himself) in a borrowed light of respectability. That much was pretty obvious in the City, and the relentless growth in the holding of Harrods shares by Lonrho after 1977 was treated with a marked superciliousness. (While I was on the *Financial Times*, a stockbroker who was aware that I knew Rowland said condescendingly, 'Your friend is trying to climb on board.')

As I began to assemble the story of Rowland's career, it came to me that a part of the yearning for Harrods must be rooted further back, in his pre-Lonrho years. He has always looked a very paradigm of the vintage Harrods customer – seeming to have stepped straight out of one of those elegant Francis Marshall drawings of the early post-war years, advertising expensive clothes and the better class of London department store. More than that, for a brief spell before the war, he was on the fringe of the Knightsbridge world. He and his brother Raimund, in their bespoke-tailored suits, looked as though they thoroughly belonged there. But then Tiny was flung into a different world, that was harsh and hurtful. The depth of the psychological wound is manifested by his secrecy over that part of his life.

He manages to be rather dismissive about Harrods ('I called in once for a haircut') but there is no doubt that he dotes on it; and if he could become the owner he would doubtless feel a sly pleasure in the knowledge that the wives and mistresses of many of his detractors spend so much time and money in the place. Lonrho's Princess Hotels in the Bahamas and Mexico may be extremely grand, in an aggressive way; the gold and platinum mines in Africa give the shares 'glamour', as he once told me; but putting Harrods in his pocket would have been an incomparable symbol of triumph over the country about which he has such conflicting feelings – and where, when his name is mentioned at a dinner party, you can be sure that someone will say, 'Oh, didn't he start as a railway porter?'

Those hackneyed rags-to-riches myths about Rowland can be disposed of by quite rudimentary digging. But one must burrow far more deeply to learn why his behaviour appears at times to be so compulsive. This was brought home by the publication in the *Observer* and other newspapers of a full-page advertisement for Lonrho in February 1984. It was an illustrated summary of the results for the previous year (turnover well above £2 billion, pre-tax profits £113 million). In pride of place among all the company's assets, and given the only double-column display on the page, was a picture of Harrods. Yet Lonrho still had less than a 30 per cent holding in the store. Such prominence was both undignified and unbalanced, and was widely remarked upon in business circles.

Such examples have made me realize that any book claiming to offer a coherent account of the man has ultimately to venture into territory where he has most resented intruders – to relate in some detail the first thirty years of his life, before he made his fresh start in Africa . . .

The romantic moment to begin is right back in the spring of 1906, in a Register Office in Richmond, west London. His parents to be, both twenty-one, were married there by licence (meaning that the event was a close secret). Wilhelm Friedrich Fuhrhop put himself down on the certificate as a 'manufacturer's agent', with a father of independent means, and gave an address in East Sheen, just across Richmond Park from the register office. His bride, Muriel Flora Kauenhoven, described herself as the daughter of a shipping agent. There is a strong suggestion that the wedding was in defiance of parental wishes: although the Kauenhovens, prosperous Dutch people who had been in Britain for about thirty years, lived near the Register Office, the bride's twenty-three-year-old brother Reginald was the only member of the family to sign the register.

Wilhelm Fuhrhop had come to Britain from Hamburg, his native city, after leaving school. He had been learning the import–export business, and perfecting his English. Fuhrhop sprang from adventurous mercantile stock, and his ultimate destination was India, then a land of opportunity. Within two years of their marriage he and his diminutive wife had sailed for Calcutta; they left their first child, Phyllis, to be cared for in London.

Kipling in the 1880s had written with distaste about Calcutta's stench and vice, but by Edwardian times it was a perfectly tolerable abode for the thousands of white merchants. The administrators of the Raj and the officers of smart cavalry regiments also lived there, because it was still India's capital.

Calcutta had a grandeur and worldliness which marked it off from any other city in the Far East: 'Too European for my taste and not really Indian,' grumbled Queen Mary when she went there in 1912 with George V after his Delhi durbar.

It seems that the young Fuhrhops were happy in Calcutta. Wilhelm ran a firm named A. Janowitzer, which quickly expanded to embrace engineering and insurance; he was himself inventive, and fascinated by machines. The firm had branch offices around the Bay of Bengal, right down to Ceylon. Muriel Fuhrhop looked after their high-ceilinged home, in a mansion block overlooking the Hooghly River, while her tireless husband chased contracts. In 1913, when he was twenty-eight, Fuhrhop became a member of the Bengal Chamber of Commerce.

With his energy and acumen, he typified one of the factors that would launch faraway Europe into war. He was a product of the new, irresistible Germany, snapping up business all over the British Empire; there was resentment among the older companies in India at the inroads being made by newcomers such as Fuhrhop.

When the 1914–18 war began, all German-based companies were ordered to stop trading and go into liquidation. The Fuhrhops moved out of Calcutta and lived quietly in Darjeeling, on the southern foothills of the Himalayas. The general belief that the fighting in Europe would be over, one way or another, within a few months, soon proved a delusion. The mood darkened, the war propaganda became more vehement: and Wilhelm Fuhrhop was a Hun.

The bitter turn of events was especially galling for Muriel, since Holland, the country of her forebears, was a neutral in the war. In any case, she regarded herself as thoroughly British: her family in London had changed their name to Carton by deed poll soon after the war began.

The anxieties of the Fuhrhops must have been increased because their only child, Phyllis, whom they had not seen since she was a baby, was still in London. The Indian newspapers were carrying lurid accounts of the Zeppelin raids.

Six months after the war began, Muriel Fuhrhop became pregnant. Her first son was born in November 1915, in

Darjeeling, and christened Raimund Everest (the world's highest mountain can be seen from a hill a few miles outside Darjeeling). This happy event occurred shortly before orders were given by the Viceroy, Lord Hardinge, for the arrest and detention of all enemy aliens in India. The move was a reflection of the 'total war' psychosis created by the German U-boat onslaught and the stalemate on the Western Front.

The nearest fighting to the Indian sub-continent was across the sea in East Africa, but the Kaiser had his eye on the Jewel in Britain's Crown. He boasted: 'We shall not only occupy India, we shall conquer it, and the vast revenue that the British allows to be taken by the Indian princes will, after our conquest, flow in a golden stream into the Fatherland.'

The Fuhrhops, together with several hundred more subjects of the Central Powers, were rounded up and put on trains under guard. They were taken to Belgaum, 1,000 miles from Calcutta. This was to be the birthplace of the Fuhrhop's third and last child, Roland. Dominated by a nineteenth-century stone fortress, Belgaum is a dusty and nondescript place, two hundred miles inland from Goa, and on the railway line from Hyderabad to Bombay. Although 2,500 feet above sea level, it is malarial; eight German children are buried in the graveyard of St Mary's Church, Belgaum.

When Roland was born on 27 November 1917, his mother was thirty-two. The family was living in the cantonment in a handsome bungalow with deep verandahs. (It still exists, but is now used as a liquor distillery.) It is said that the new baby was given the name Tiny by the family ayah, or nurse. His birth was registered when he was three days old; against the item 'Nationality of Father' were the tell-tale words 'Of German birth'. But there was one invaluable birthright – Roland Fuhrhop had been born in a dominion of King George V, and that, together with his mother's nationality, gave him the right to be British as well as German.

Life in the cantonment at Belgaum was never too rigorous. The detainees were allowed books and magazines, and 'the ordinary food of persons of their class'. But the town was a staging post for troops going to fight the Turks in Mesopotamia, and this must have brought home strongly to Wilhelm Fuhrhop

– always proud to be a German – that he was a prisoner on enemy territory. For his wife there was a conflict of loyalties: her brother was by this time a colonel in the British Army.

The Fuhrhops still had wealth. Old government of Bengal political department papers mention a sum of 2,000 Swiss francs remitted by mistake in 1918 to 'W. Fuhrhop (*detenu* at civil detention camp Belgaum)'. It was noted that he wanted the money sent back to Switzerland.

By the end of the war the thriving businesses in Calcutta created by Wilhelm Fuhrhop before 1914 were only memories. He could not stay in India, nor could he return to Britain, even if he had wished. Back in Europe he had money saved up, and the best hope of retrieving his fortunes lay in defeated Germany. By 1920 he was back in Hamburg, and in November of that year he set up a trading firm called India Agencies. It had a stock capital of 50,000 Reichsmark and offices in the Spitaler Strasse. He was able to prosper by making good use of his old contacts in Calcutta and his complete mastery of English.

Just how long Mrs Fuhrhop and her two sons stayed on in India is uncertain. According to Tiny Rowland himself, he lived there until 1925, when he was seven. But the deed poll he signed in October 1939, when he changed his name, seems to contradict this. The document was accompanied by a sworn declaration by his uncle Cyril, the ex-colonel, who said he had known Roland Fuhrhop 'for nineteen years and upwards' – in other words, since 1920. So it seems more probable that his mother sailed home from India with her children when Tiny was two, to be reunited with her daughter and her parents in London, then later went on to rejoin her husband in Hamburg.

By 1920 the worst of the starvation in Germany was over: the Allied blockade was lifted after the losers had agreed to sign the Versailles Peace Treaty. But the country lay in economic ruins, and was to remain so for a decade. For all that, the Fuhrhops kept several servants and were able to live in the affluent Klosterstern district of Hamburg, close to the Aussen Alster lake, beside which there are fine places to walk and play.

Tiny was first sent to a local *Vorschule* (primary school); at ten he transferred to the highly regarded Heinrich-Hertz Gymnasium, where his brother was already a pupil. (Another pupil was Klaus-Michael Kuhne, who was to become head of Kuhne and Nagel, one of the world's biggest freight companies. In 1981, Lonrho would pay £19 million for a 50 per cent stake in Kuhne and Nagel.)

It was at the Heinrich-Hertz school that Tiny was enrolled in the Hitler Youth, along with most of the other boys. With his flaxen hair, bright blue eyes and athletic build, the teenaged Roland Fuhrhop must have well matched the National Socialist vision of a re-awakened Germany on the march. None the less, he was never an enthusiast for the Hitler Youth – his mother saw to that. So in 1934, a year after the *Führer* came to power, Roland Fuhrhop was sent to a school in England. He joined the fifth form at Churcher's College, near Petersfield.

Up to this point the facts that can be accumulated about his life are scrappy and impersonal. The only people still extant who might 'flesh out' the story are Tiny himself and his sister Phyllis. They prefer to remain silent. But living in Petersfield, and now in his eighties, is Edward Granger, one-time art master at Churcher's College. He remembers the tall young German arriving, being appointed as a prefect, and quickly winning a place in the 1st rugby XV. 'Fuhrhop was impressive in appearance,' says Granger. 'The other boys seemed to admire him. He broke several school athletics records. He was decidedly "out of the ordinary".' Granger is ready to admit, however, that the Fuhrhops might have made a better educational choice for their promising son.

Churcher's was a minor endowment catering for day boys and a few score boarders. The County Council gave financial support, since many of the local pupils came on scholarships. Although the school houses were named after naval heroes, such as Drake and Nelson, there was a strong military tradition. Most of the boarders, among whom the new boy Fuhrhop found himself, were sons of army officers. 'The fees were low enough to be covered by the education allowances of middling officers,' says Granger. He also recalls that the pride of Churcher's was its officer training corps: 'The school library was terrible.' (Fuhrhop did what he could to improve the library, in accord with the military bias of the place, by donating a biography of Field-Marshal Hindenburg, the German Army's supreme commander in the First World War.) Although Churcher's had been founded in 1722, the main buildings were in a forbidding late-Victorian manner. Petersfield in the 1930s was a humdrum place, and one of the few excitements was on Sunday mornings, when the Churcher's boys marched through the town behind the school band. It must have seemed to Tiny like the Hitler Youth all over again.

Why he should have been sent to so unpromising a place may be explained by the Indian connection. Churcher's was founded to train cadets for the East India Company, whose commerce had – until its dissolution in 1874 – fostered the greatness of Calcutta. It is also possible that the Fuhrhops had been friendly with some officer in the Indian Army whose offspring were pupils.

At the time when Tiny was at Churcher's it was rare for a boy to go on to university. In any case, Wilhelm Fuhrhop apparently believed that when his sons had completed their secondary education they were well enough equipped to start on business careers. By 1933, Raimund was already working in the family firm in Hamburg. So at eighteen, Tiny was destined to join the shipping company run by his uncle, Cyril Carton. During his last school term he was active in the debating society. According to the *Churcherian*, the school magazine, he carried the day when proposing that capital punishment was right because it saved 'trouble and money'; moreover, he said, life imprisonment was far more cruel than a quick end for a murderer.

Another glimpse of Tiny as a teenager comes from Cyril Carton junior, his cousin. 'I was twelve and he was seventeen when he first came to stay with us at our house in Shepperton,' he says. 'Tiny spoke English perfectly when he arrived, with a trace of a German accent. But it had vanished by the time he left Churcher's.' To that extent, at least, the school was ideal: it has always prided itself on imparting a 'good' accent.

A year after Tiny had started work, under the watchful eye of his Uncle Cyril, his parents moved over to London from Hamburg. This event was linked to the rise of Hitler and the growing militarization of Germany, for although the family was not Jewish they were not happy in the Third Reich. There were also sound business reasons, because Wilhelm Fuhrhop wanted to go back to India and resurrect his old agencies there, while his elder son set up a company in London. The offices of India Agencies in Hamburg's Spitaler Strasse were also kept going. Now in his fifties, the senior Fuhrhop was clearly still very ambitious and energetic, hoping to regain his pre-1914 prosperity. Perhaps he also looked to the day when the younger of his two sons would come into the family business.

Raimund Fuhrhop started a firm called India Produce in Lloyd's Avenue, just off Fenchurch Street, where the leading commodity brokers were to be found. He was, like his father, methodical and precise (although he rather flamboyantly listed himself in the London telephone directory as 'R. Everest Fuhrhop').

This was a happy time for Muriel Fuhrhop, back in England once more. Despite the long absences of her husband in Hamburg, or out in the East, she often had the company of Tiny, already quite a thirties 'man about town'. Her daughter Phyllis had married an Englishman working for one of the principal clearing banks. When Wilhelm Fuhrhop was in England, family holidays were spent in south coast resorts. Everything seemed rosy – until the Nazis marched into Czechoslovakia on 30 September 1938. The very day after the invasion Raimund reported for training as a conscript in the German Army, to do his twelve months' military service. He had dual nationality, and did not have to go at that moment. It seems that he felt strong loyalties to the Fatherland.

For Raimund it was to be a long farewell to England, but Tiny did not follow in his footsteps. While his brother was a conscript, Tiny made a visit to Germany: by his own account he got into some trouble, and was jailed for eight weeks in Berlin for his association with two prominent anti-Nazis. If it was to be a matter of choosing he preferred England.

In those years between his school days and the war, Tiny led a life which his envious young cousin, Cyril Carton, has called 'very carefree'. He was able to indulge his taste for stylish clothes and fast cars. Tiny has always been a superb driver, and in the 1930s was already a connoisseur of the more powerful Mercedes-Benz models (the kind in which Hitler and Goering liked to lead parades). There is a legend that shortly before the war Tiny arranged the sale of a Mercedes for Barbara Hutton, the American heiress. At that time she had a mansion in Regent's Park – now the residence of the American ambassador.

There was another side to his life. He enjoyed painting landscapes at weekends, attended classical concerts, played tennis and went rowing with the Thames Valley Skiff Club. From the descriptions of his many pretty visitors when he later became an 18B detainee, it can be deduced that he had no lack of girlfriends in those pre-war years.

In September 1939, when war broke out, he was living in a flat beside the Thames in Sunbury. His parents had a house in north London, and Wilhelm Fuhrhop was at the time back from India. They all knew that bad days were ahead, especially since Raimund was already in uniform in Germany. Almost immediately, Tiny decided to change his name, just as his Uncle Cyril had done at the start of the 1914–18 war.

Tiny's way of anglicizing himself was oddly half-hearted – almost flippant: he took the initial of his second name, and dropped it into the middle of his first name. Most foreigners going through the deed poll process tend to make a clean sweep, by choosing a complete set of thoroughly British-sounding Christian and surnames. However, there was no flippancy in his next step. He went back to Churcher's College to find his old headmaster, Graham Hoggarth. He asked whether Hoggarth could write a testimonial to help him get a job working in British Intelligence. According to a contemporary, Hoggarth was non-committal.

Three months after the war began, Rowland was called up. His options were immediately reduced by his background – and particularly because his brother was in the *Wehrmacht*. The army sent him to train as an orderly in the Royal Army Medical Corps. Recruits in the RAMC were given three months' instruction, half of which was mainly devoted to drill, route marches and anti-gas warfare; the rest of the time was given over to training in first aid and stretcher-bearing exercises. History does not relate how Private R. W. Rowland took to this course, but he doubtless still remembers the way to put a broken leg in splints.

Most of his army time was passed at Peebles, in the Borders. The 75th British General Hospital had been set up in a converted hotel, and shortly after he arrived there the war began in earnest, with the Norway campaign and the German blitzkrieg on France. Although he never said so, Rowland must have chafed at his drab routine, walking around the wards with a white orderly's smock over his khaki uniform. Not only was it a sharp come-down from his lively London ways, but he also knew that his former companions in the Churcher's sixth form must all be officers by now.

Yet he had other preoccupations. Both his parents had been arrested in the frantic round-up of possible spies after the fall of France. Although Wilhelm Fuhrhop was a patriotic German, there is no suggestion that he was ever a Nazi sympathizer; on the other hand he was an inventor, someone with natural engineering skills – and he also had one son in the *Wehrmacht*. His wife, despite being British, was branded by her connections through marriage. The Fuhrhops were by no means alone in being seized – more than 27,000 enemy aliens and their relations were caught in the net during the summer of 1940.

In the desperations of a war which Britain looked in a fair way to losing, there were few niceties. Many of the women arrested for internment were sent first to Holloway Prison: some were quite elderly, a few were even schoolgirls in uniform. Mrs Fuhrhop found herself locked in a Holloway cell – and by that time her health was dangerously frail. Conditions in wartime Holloway were harsh and inhumane; they are described vividly in her autobiography, *A Life of Contrasts*, by Lady Diana Mosley, who was detained there under Regulation 18B.

The exact date when Muriel Fuhrhop was moved from Holloway to the Isle of Man, where her husband was already interned, is not certain. But a welfare officer, Mrs Joan Cole, remembers her arrival at the Port Erin women's camp sometime in 1940. 'I noticed that Mrs Fuhrhop didn't look very well. Her report from Holloway said she was always complaining and the doctors there said there was nothing wrong with her. As she was English, I think they must have given her a bad time in Holloway.'

It is easy to imagine the effect on Rowland of the news about his parents. He was their only child still in Britain, for his sister was now far away in the West Indies, where her husband was working for Barclays Bank. So Tiny asked for leave from his commanding officer in Peebles to go to the Isle of Man. His application was refused – in the aftermath of Dunkirk there was a lot of work in the army hospitals. He went absent without leave, and was picked up by military police in Douglas, the main Manx town. The army sent him back to Scotland under guard, and he was sentenced to four weeks in jail. He served it in the military section of Barlinnie Jail, near Glasgow.

'Twenty-seven days,' he has recalled. 'It seemed like two hundred and seventy.'

Rowland never talked about his wartime years until forty years later, when he was buying the *Observer*. Then he was interviewed for the *Sunday Times* by a well-primed Charles Raw – only agreeing to answer questions so that he might be able to scotch some of the more malicious stories being spread. Allowing for lapses of memory, he gave a convincing account (apart from propagating the tale that he had had two brothers rather than one).

'I was angry and bitter with the authorities,' he told Raw. His father had been upset at being arrested, not grasping how much weight the 'vetting committee' had put in the fact that his elder son was fighting for the enemy. Both Tiny and his mother were terrified after July 1940 that Wilhelm Fuhrhop might be sent out of Britain, to serve his internment in Canada or Australia – because at the start of that month the *Arandora Star* had been sunk by a U-boat off Ireland, and more than 700 internees were drowned; the dead had included many Jewish refugees and some prominent anti-Nazi Germans.

Towards the end of 1940, as the fear of a German invasion receded, the internees were freed in their thousands. By the middle of 1941 only a quarter of the original 27,000 were still behind barbed wire in Britain. All that were left had been concentrated in the Isle of Man. Although his parents were now reunited in the 'married camp' at Port Erin, it was constantly distressing to Rowland to think that they were still inside at all.

His own version of what now happened sounds probable enough, given his renowned capacity for hounding any topic on which his mind has become set. He says that he never stopped appealing to the tribunals to look again at his parents' case, and tried to make representations through his commanding officer at Edinburgh Castle, where he was now stationed. He was told to keep quiet, and in response asked his superiors why, if his parents were not trustworthy enough to be freed, he should be thought sufficiently loyal to be in uniform. At that point it was decided that Private R. W. Rowland was more trouble to the British Army than he was worth.

He was discharged in January 1942 – but there was no chance that he would simply be given his liberty to return to civilian life in the middle of the war. As a British subject he could not be interned. There was, however, Regulation 18B, designed for use against citizens who might 'act in a manner prejudicial to the public safety or the Defence of the Realm'. It had mainly been used against members of Oswald Mosley's British Union of Fascists, and some men of Irish origins thought to be security risks. It was ideally suited to Tiny Rowland's case.

The main 18B detention centre was also on the Isle of Man, in the town of Peel on the west coast of the island. Nine months before Rowland was taken there, all the most dedicated fascists had been removed from various camps and jails on the mainland and concentrated at Peel. Originally there were 750 of them, but some of those most insistent about their desire to 'do their bit' had soon been let go to serve in the fire services or civil defence; a few had even been accepted in the army. As the number of fascists declined, their places were taken by 130 Germans and Italians regarded as high security risks, too dangerous to be kept in the internment camps; some of the Germans were fanatical Nazis.

Tiny Rowland's arrival caused a stir in this tense, suspicious community. Although 18B prisoners were allowed to wear civilian clothes, since they had the status of remand prisoners, he looked quite uncommonly smart. 'You would have thought he had just strolled in from Savile Row,' said Richard Reynell Bellamy, one of the dwindling band of survivors from the British Union. 'He was not very popular, because he had such expensive clothes and plenty of money.'

Rowland has never talked about his time in the Peel camp, and I found tracing any fellow-detainees still living far from easy. But he was put into one of the peacetime boarding houses being used as dormitories, and there made friends with two detainees named Ralph Dawson and Arthur Mason. Both of them were fascists, but of very different backgrounds – Dawson was an actor, 'Wakey' Mason was a tough East Ender. (In 1983, Dawson died near Canterbury, where he had run an antiques business after leaving the stage. Mason is still alive, retired in Australia.)

Reynell Bellamy remembers that Rowland was 'decidedly unsympathetic to the British Union'. Another former detainee, Robert Row, heard him forecast loudly that Hitler would lose the war. It seems that he kept well away from the pro-Nazi Germans. (Some of them, who knew him from peacetime, insisted on calling him Fuhrhop.) There was a rumour for a time that this affluent newcomer was a government agent, slipped into the camp as an informer. The camp commandant, a Colonel Clarence Paget, was concerned that attempts at a mass escape were being hatched – indeed, plans to steal boats and sail across to neutral Ireland were in the detainees' minds. So Tiny's belated and unexplained arrival as an 18B detainee naturally evoked suspicions. According to William Eaton, who was the British Union 'section leader' at Peel, one of the first ideas Rowland had was that he should take over the running of the camp canteen. 'It wasn't too readily accepted,' says Eaton. 'People were not sure about him.'

There is one point of agreement among all the 18B survivors – that Rowland-Fuhrhop had an enviable number of girlfriends. It was permitted for visitors to come over from the mainland, to bring food parcels to the detainees; nobody in Peel was so well cared for as Tiny. 'It was remarkable,' says Row, 'how many visits he received from well-dressed girls – he seems to have had several. I clearly remember the tall, lean, immaculately dressed Tiny strolling down to the main gate to collect the latest parcel of luxuries, following its minute inspection by military intelligence.' Quite independently, Reynell Bellamy recalled 'Rowland's string of damsels'.

Tiny must certainly have relished those visits. He had arrived at Peel in winter, when the winds were whipping off the Irish Sea, and the view from behind double rows of eight-feet high barbed wire surrounding the camp must have made his spirits sink. Apart from the faded memories of those detainees still alive and willing to talk, there is little to go on regarding conditions at Peel: the official records now available in the Public Record Office have been most diligently 'weeded', and some are still retained in Whitehall, away from prying eyes. The most graphic impression is given by a photograph taken a few months before he arrived. This shows the heavily defended perimeter, with armed guards, and a crowd of detainees looking out from the balconies and verandahs of the peacetime boarding houses converted into billets, behind the wire.

Another photograph shows a group of Mosley's followers (most were unwilling to be recorded on film). They are wearing corduroy trousers and heavy sweaters; but one is in shorts and knee-length stockings, and rather poignantly holds a kitten in one hand like a mascot. The emotions about the war being fought out on distant battlefronts varied widely among Rowland's fellow detainees. Only a minority of the British fascists wanted Hitler to win; but some of the Germans, the Italians and the Irish nationalists cheered every Nazi victory. Tiny was numbered among those Anglo-Germans who despised Hitler (partly for class reasons) and wanted only for the war to end with his defeat as fast as possible.

After more than a year of detention – during which he was regularly allowed to visit his parents at Port Erin under military escort – Tiny was transferred across to be permanently with them. Later still, his 18B order was lifted. By 1944 the possibility of an invasion from the Continent had faded away, for Nazi Germany was now being overwhelmed by the Soviet Union, and the security atmosphere became far more relaxed. Tiny found himself, however, in something of a limbo: the war was still on, but he could not go back into the army, having once been discharged; and with his record, he was only rated as suitable for a limited range of civilian jobs. It was illegal to do nothing. His friend Dawson was in a similar position, having been dismissed from the forces in 1940 when all Mosley supporters were identified as security risks. Dawson found work with a repertory company, and Rowland reported to a Labour Exchange.

It was then that Tiny was sent to Euston station to be a

temporary porter. Perhaps it is true, as legend has it, that he would find out from the signalmen where the first-class carriages were placed in the approaching trains, so that he could position himself for the biggest tips. Even if invented, it sounds right. But the Euston job was short-lived, and it seems that Rowland did a series of such manual tasks. Facts are scarce. However, he must have used his time to prepare for business opportunities that would exist in Britain as soon as the war was over, because in 1945 he was occupying a flat at 78 Brook Street, Mayfair, just two minutes' walk from Claridge's.

Every few weeks he would travel back to the Isle of Man to see his parents. The authorities refused adamantly to free Wilhelm Fuhrhop, who was 'camp leader' for the 3,000 aliens still held at Port Erin.

It is clear from the official records that Fuhrhop senior was trusted as a spokesman for the anti-Nazi internees: there was another leader, named Gutberlet, who spoke for the 'Reichsdeutsche'. In February 1944 the camp was visited by a representative of the International Red Cross, and his report lists a string of requests put by Camp Leader Fuhrhop on behalf of the inmates. These ranged from disputes about the shilling an hour paid to interned craftsmen for their work, to the non-arrival of food parcels, and from the fate of the British property of those Germans who might be repatriated to the need to allow internees to visit the cinema in the town of Douglas.

After more than four years of incarceration the tensions in the camp were approaching desperation. Some internees had attempted suicide, others were taken to mental homes on the mainland. Many of the women kept in a separate camp were described as 'extremely neurotic'. But Wilhelm Fuhrhop did not falter: another Red Cross report said he wanted his typewriter sent to the Isle of Man from Hamburg, by way of the Red Cross in Geneva, because he needed it for his work as camp leader. (At the height of the bombing raids on Germany by the Allies, this displayed remarkable optimism, and there is no record that the machine ever turned up.) Fuhrhop also showed his public-spiritedness by asking for 1,000 Marks to be sent from his personal account in Germany, for the camp welfare fund.

Fuhrhop was popular, both with the internees and the Manx

civilians employed at the camp. Mrs Kathleen Jones, who was in the accounts office, has memories of a 'fine-looking, courteous man with a handsome moustache'. Wilhelm Fuhrhop spent his spare time on his revolutionary design for a carpet-making machine, and Mrs Jones told me how he sent off complicated drawings to London, to apply for patents: 'It cost him a guinea a time.' (In later years he would complain that his patent, which he was convinced would have restored his fortunes, had been stolen by a company in Bradford.)

If Fuhrhop senior was popular, his son was more so, especially with the fifty or so children of the German internees. Sometimes when he was visiting his parents he would look after classes in the camp school; he would also show the boys how to make bows and arrows or join in their games of football. Gus Fehle has returned to the island where he and his parents were interned, and runs an optical company in Ramsey. He says: 'Tiny was always nice and friendly – interested in what we were doing. He would come and join us when we were playing in the gardens of an hotel in the middle of the camp.' Tiny was seemingly almost idolized as though he were a film star – and indeed, he had grown a Clark Gable moustache, which he would sport for some years.

Udo Krebs, now living in Holland, gave me this account: 'He was wonderfully dressed in beautiful sports jackets. I was only fourteen at the time, but I still remember his clothes. He was always cheerful and we looked forward to his visits.'

If Tiny was cheerful with the children, he was also hiding a harrowing time with his parents. His mother was now constantly unwell, and at his request an RAMC doctor gave her a careful examination. The diagnosis was cancer. Frau Grabau, one of the German internees, tells of her last months: 'She was so very ill, and I remember Tiny sitting with her in the hotel lounge, holding her hand.' The son she had given birth to in one internment camp watched her die in another. There is an official record of all the people who died in the internment camps. Muriel Fuhrhop is listed as having been cremated in July 1945, at Blackpool on the mainland, at the expense of her family. Almost all the other internees are recorded as having been buried in the Douglas cemetery at public expense.

That loss left Tiny with few family ties in Britain. He respected his father (and in later years supported him financially), but was never close to him. Moreover, Wilhelm Fuhrhop was remarried soon after the war to the formidable German–Swiss widow of another internee, and she was a painful contrast to her gentle predecessor. Raimund had survived the war, including a long stint on the Eastern Front, and was living in Hamburg. Their sister was still in Trinidad. Single-mindedly, Tiny gave all his energies to amassing money. As he told his friends: 'One good reason for being rich is that it makes you free.'

He had all the appearance of instant success. With two other young entrepreneurs, named Clements and Cleminson, he founded a company; they called themselves, with some bravado, 'manufacturers and exporters'. But the wartime years and the stigma of 18B surely left a carefully concealed scar on Tiny – a sense of being rejected and unaccepted in the country he thought of as his home. The emigration to Rhodesia in 1948 was an escape from that past, and he has said that he never wanted to return. Only Ian Smith and the UDI rebellion drove him back to Britain – there to be once more rejected and made into the 'unacceptable face of capitalism'.

After I had completed my efforts to appreciate Tiny better as a product of his background, the obsession with owning Harrods grew easier to understand. The place is, explicitly, a citadel for all those who deem themselves thoroughly acceptable.

14

The Egyptian Brothers

It is an astounding gallery of people who stand accused by Rowland of having played some part in denying him his last great prize. Prominent among them are Mrs Margaret Thatcher and two of her former Secretaries of Trade, Leon Brittan and Norman Tebbit. A clutch of senior British civil servants have likewise been the objects of his invective, plus a gaggle of Fleet Street financial journalists. The young Sultan of Brunei, reputed to be the richest man in the world, has been dealt his share of the blame – if not for being part of the alleged conspiracy at least for being a dupe of others more malign. A senior merchant banker whose stance in the affair aroused Tiny's fury was sent a bouquet of yellow roses every day for a week, with a card bearing a two-word message: 'Yellow Belly'.

The ultimate villains on the Rowland charge sheet are, however, without doubt the Fayed brothers, whose lightning coup in March 1985 brought Harrods and the rest of House of Fraser into their total control. It was they who became the targets of the most uninhibited vendetta mounted by a British newspaper in recent years – a campaign which caused upheavals inside the *Observer* and bemused many of its loyal followers.

So in the end it has not been the proprietor's interference in the coverage of Africa which has brought the real obloquy upon the *Observer*, but his imposing of 'stories' about the ownership of a very British institution.

Rowland's sustained onslaught on the three Egyptians has been interpreted in Arab quarters as a particular brand of racialism. He would deny that emphatically, and there is not one jot of evidence for it. Yet it must be said that while he has had Arab friends (most notably the Saudi entrepreneur Adnan Khashoggi), he has never got along with them as a people so easily as he does with Africans.

His private complaint about Arabs is that they sit talking hour after hour about any proposed deal (often in their own language, which he does not understand), then prove impossibly demanding when it comes to money. However, a conglomerate such as Lonrho cannot sensibly ignore the Middle East and its petrodollars. There was a phase, indeed, in the mid-1970s when Rowland actively sought Arab connections and the Lonrho board was well sprinkled with Muslims. 'We thought a sheikh might ride in any day on a camel,' joked one English director. The Kuwaitis proved a nuisance, although Rowland was grateful at first for their support during his 1973 struggle against the 'Straight Eight' rebels. 'They harassed me every day about the share price,' he said vexedly.

This all bears directly on the long fight for Harrods. The *nouveaux riches* of the Middle East have long been fascinated with the store, where they are avid customers (some South Kensington wit once dubbed it 'Harabs'), but nobody imagined until late 1984 that they would have ambitions to combine, or compete, with Rowland in buying it. On the contrary, Rowland might have seemed more likely to look for Jewish collaborators, because in the early 1980s he became a frequent visitor to Israel – there was a report, quickly denied, that Lonrho was angling for a big contract with the Delek oil company, controlled by the Israeli government. One of the few clues that he was keeping up his Arab business connections came in 1983, when I was told that Mohamed Al-Fayed could supply me with gossip about Mahdi Al-Tajir, the feckless billionaire diplomat.

It was, in fact, precisely at the time when I went to see Al-Fayed that John Griffiths, QC, was being ordered to investigate some unusual dealings in the equity of House of Fraser – and one of the 'mystery buyers' was Al-Fayed's sister-in-law. She had bought shares costing £2 million. Almost simultaneously, an Egyptian financier named Dr Ashraf Marwan had paid £4 million for a House of Fraser stake. It looked as though Rowland still had loyal and affluent friends in the Middle East, just when he was eager for more shareholders' votes in support of his plans to hive off Harrods from the rest of the Fraser group. Certainly, they did vote for him at an extraordinary general meeting called at his instigation – although the 'de-merger' idea was, to his chagrin, finally blocked.

The essential aim of the Griffiths inquiry had been to discover whether Lonrho had been secretly organizing what the stockbroking trade terms a 'concert party', a secret agreement among several buyers to combine their voting strengths to gain an advantage over a target company. In this case, claimed the House of Fraser board, these big new investors were merely the tools of Rowland's strategy to split off Harrods and bid for it. The evidence given to the Government by the House of Fraser chairman, Professor Roland Smith, had looked convincing enough for action. If covert tactics could be proven, this would show that Rowland was trying to circumvent the official ruling that Lonrho must stop buying into House of Fraser. (A Monopolies Commission team was simultaneously deciding whether it was in the public interest for Lonrho to be given freedom to seek full control of the group.)

Griffiths called 175 witnesses in his year-long search for a chink in the curtain behind which Rowland had allegedly assembled his 'concert party', his cabal of shareholders. Most of all, Griffiths kept interviewing that 'consummate wheeler-dealer', as he dubbed Tiny. The chink in the curtain was never found. As his 400-page report said downrightly, Griffiths regarded some of the witnesses as unconvincing, and he uncovered the strangest coincidences in their financial dealings. Several foreign 'suspects' whom he wanted to interview refused to attend – even though he offered to pay for them to come to London.

His account of his investigations was written up in a style which might almost be termed florid, and is often amusing. If Griffiths had been allowed to go on, would he have reached a positive verdict? We shall never know, unless one of the 'mystery buyers' decides to speak out one day. The questioning had to stop when the Government said that enough time and money had been expended. Official frustration was later vented in a proposal that Department of Trade inspectors should be able in future to confiscate the shares of recalcitrant overseas holders who refused to give evidence.

The buyers who had so solidly supported the Harrods de-merger scheme included a wealthy German speculator, Dr Joern Kreke, a Japanese consortium, and 'Union Jack' Hayward, the unorthodox British financier living in the Bahamas. The Japanese and the shadowy Dr Kreke both refused to speak about any possible 'concert party' with Rowland. As for Hayward, he told Griffiths that his decision to have a sudden £4 million flutter on the House of Fraser had been inspired by a brief Sunday paper report containing some bullish quotes from Jim Slater. Of course, Lonrho owned hotels in the Bahamas, but Griffiths ended up convinced that there was no secret understanding between 'Union Jack' and Tiny.

Much more exotic (and with hindsight, more intriguing) were the purchases by Dr Ashraf Marwan and Mohamed Al-Fayed's sister-in-law. Marwan was one of Rowland's foremost Arab friends: a son-in-law of the late President Nasser, and adviser to President Sadat, he was reputedly the contact man when Rowland was involved in some 'merchant-statemanship' that cleared the road to the Camp David agreement. For a brief period, Marwan had a stake in the Lonrho air-cargo concern, Tradewinds. Yet when Griffiths started asking questions about Marwan, it was startling how violently Rowland traduced him: 'I would not want to do business with Ashraf Marwan . . . I would never know from day to day whether he was still my partner, or whether he had sold his shares to a third party . . . in terms of business, Dr Ashraf Marwan is totally unreliable . . . I would not dream of asking a man like Dr Marwan to buy shares in House of Fraser.' Remarkably, the elegant Egyptian did not seem to take the slightest umbrage at this fusillade of insults, ultimately published for all to see. According to Marwan, he simply threw the Griffiths Report 'in the dustbin'. Events were soon to unite him and Tiny in mutual rage against three of his own countrymen, the Fayed brothers. It now seems likely that Rowland's denigration of Marwan was pure persiflage.

But at the time when Marwan was suddenly dabbling in House of Fraser, there seemed, on the face of it, to be a much closer rapport. Mrs Salah Al-Fayed, an Italian-born shipping heiress, became a shareholder only forty-eight hours after Marwan, both used the same stockbroker, both gave addresses abroad although they had London addresses, and when Mrs Al-Fayed sold out after seven months, her holding went straight into Marwan's portfolio. There were further complexities, Mrs Al-Fayed used her previous name, Adriana Funaro, by which she is known in Italy, when she took her brother-in-law's advice and made her £2 million gamble.

After groping around in this tangled web of circumstances, Griffiths ended up by declaring that nothing was proven. All parties most vehemently asserted their innocence. The QC did say, however, that some of Marwan's evidence did not ring true, and that often Rowland's wishes 'fathered his memory'.

For all of us at the *Observer*, the most intriguing incident cited by the report concerned a meeting between Rowland and Rupert Murdoch. The only thing both of them agreed on when giving evidence was the date when they met. For the rest, there was a total conflict about who asked for the meeting, where it was held, and what was said. According to Murdoch, he had been uncertain why Tiny wanted to see him – they had not met for four years – but the purpose that emerged was to urge him to buy 5 per cent of the House of Fraser equity. (This would have cost, at the current share price, at least £15 million.) In return, when the de-merger was achieved, he and Lonrho would divide the profits equally. It was a damaging statement.

When Rowland was questioned, he said this version was 'absolute nonsense'. On the contrary, Murdoch had made proposals to him – that Lonrho should buy the *Sunday Express*, *Daily Express* and the *Daily Star*. Then for certain 'help' – it might have concerned the *Observer* – Lonrho would shut down the *Daily Star* to give Murdoch's *Sun* a clearer run in the down-market tabloid field. When the Digger heard Tiny's version of their conversation, he shrugged it off as 'laughable'.

Griffiths gave a devastating verdict on this get-together by the two tycoons. He did not think that Murdoch had a sufficient motive to make him commit perjury, and he had been left with a 'compelling feeling' that the Australian (as he then was) had been telling the truth. Rowland had not given him that impression.

So the release of the Griffiths Report left nobody much further forward (although the QC must have gasped at what happened four months later), and Lonrho's ferocious response had merely antagonized the House of Fraser board still more. On the other hand, Harrods was still there, waiting like some huge ocean liner at anchor for a new captain to clamber aboard ... Estimates in the City put the cost of Lonrho's seven-year campaign at around £4 million. (In the middle of 1984, the House of Fraser showed in its own accounts for the previous year a charge of £1.16 million for coping with the de-merger plan.)

Both sides were now awaiting the findings of the third Monopolies Commission referral, on whether Lonrho should be freed to make its all-out takeover bid, from the powerful springboard of its 'frozen' 29.9 per cent holding. By the autumn of 1984, the result was expected any day. If Lonrho was given the green light, that long-delayed triumph was in the palm of Tiny's hand. His first action, as he had so repeatedly warned, would be to give the sack to Professor Roland Smith, the obstinate chief executive of House of Fraser.

Then, at the start of November 1984 came a volte-face which took all Tiny-watchers aback: Lonrho announced that it had sold its crucial 29.9 per cent. What could have happened? According to both Rowland and his mouthpiece, Paul Spicer, it was the 'last straw' when the Government agreed that the Monopolies Commission could have another three months to ponder the Lonrho case. So the sudden sell-out was interpreted as a spasm of pique by Tiny over yet more Whitehall foot-dragging. If that was the case, it was a gigantic pique, because the Lonrho shares fetched £138 million – one of the biggest City transactions of the year. The deal had been conducted in a melodramatic fashion: representatives of both sides sat facing across a table, and the shares and the cheque were exchanged like pawns in a game of chess.

Financially, it was an expert stroke for Lonrho. As Tiny told his shareholders in a special circular, the deal had netted the company a profit of more than £70 million – the difference between an average purchase price of 145p a share, and the sale price of 300p. Yet, as one knew, Tiny was not just into Harrods for a quick profit, however big it might be.

The buyers, of course, were the Fayed brothers – Mohamed, Ali and Salah. Given that Salah's rich Italian wife, Adriana Funaro, had until recently owned a large chunk of House of Fraser equity, and given that Mohamed had once been a senior Lonrho director, was not some new kind of 'concert party' being devised? That was how it looked, at the moment. After all, 300p was a high price for any buyer, hard to justify in terms of House of Fraser profits. But the Fayeds had been around for a long time, so were unlikely to be Tiny's stooges.

One subtle interpretation was that Rowland expected to be given the go-ahead to bid for House of Fraser after the extra three months' delay. When that happened, the Fayeds would sell him back his 29 per cent at a pre-arranged profit, and in the meantime Lonrho could start rebuilding its own shareholding at pre-bid prices. That seemed plausible, for within a week Lonrho had laid out more than £30 million of its profit from the Fayed deal to buy back into House of Fraser. It was assumed, therefore, that Tiny had a new trick up his sleeve. But then, events started to go horribly wrong. If Tiny had one purpose, the Fayeds had quite another: as Mohamed Al-Fayed insisted afterwards, 'We wanted House of Fraser all along. Why not?'

Later it would emerge that Tiny had been in contact with the Fayed brothers as early as mid-1984 to discuss selling his House of Fraser stake. At that time the idea had fallen away after discussions with merchant bankers. There were also other candidates in the field, including Alfred Taubman, the American financier who bought Sotheby's. While Taubman was staying in a castle in Ireland, Tiny phoned him several times to discuss a deal. Another possible buyer was the British entrepreneur Gerald Ronson. But in the end it was the Fayeds who produced the money, at forty-eight hours' notice and with every show of amiability on both sides.

The best temperature gauge was the business section of the *Observer*. That remark by Donald Trelford to me about giving Rowland some satisfaction in an area he understood had not been taken lightly. Lonrho now possessed excellent access to the business pages – sometimes offering leads to good stories, but occasionally using them to air its own interests. Ever since the Griffiths Report in the high summer of 1984 the Harrods saga had been given special attention. Now, as winter came, it was a prime topic. We all fancied that Tiny was winning.

At first, the Fayeds were treated like white knights. A profile of the family revealed how the £138 million cheque had been handed over to Rowland without the involvement of bankers or lawyers. After revealing that Mohamed Al-Fayed in the past year had made several approaches to buy the Lonrho stake, it stressed how close he and Rowland were. The article went a long way to explaining why the family had so much cash on hand. Apart from owning the Ritz in Paris, the Alfayed Investment Trust was in shipping, banking and property. The Egyptians' fortune was put by the *Observer* at that time at around £500 million; later it would be quite a different story.

On one point the *Observer* was emphatic: the Fayeds said they had no intention of bidding for control of Harrods. The impression was left of three good-natured Alexandrian gentlemen who just had a penchant for excellence. There was, however, a slightly more combative review of developments by the City editor, Melvin Marckus, called 'Harrods: Not Over Yet'. This touched on some rather curious reports that the brothers wanted Rowland and Lord Duncan-Sandys, the two Lonrho directors on the House of Fraser board, to resign. The response to this in Cheapside House was quoted as 'distinctly cool' – Tiny saying that he had just been re-elected with a massive majority. He and Duncan-Sandys did not want to step down.

Other newspapers reported Mohamed Al-Fayed as using far more forceful language: 'They will, of course, resign, on Monday. If they do not, they will be thrown off.' Rowland was quoted as replying: 'He must have been joking.' (In the event, although it took rather longer than Monday, the Lonrho pair had to go, despite protesting loudly.) The warmth with which Professor Smith welcomed the Egyptians as directors was by contrast striking. This, it seemed, was what he had long been waiting for; he stressed how courteous and thoughtful they were.

Early in 1985, the *Observer* reported that Lonrho profits for the previous year had hit a record £135 million. The 'quality' of its earnings was improving, with almost half of the profits coming from Europe and America – the inference being that there was no longer a need to see the group as overwhelmingly dependent on more vulnerable business in Africa. The report then mentioned that the Monopolies Commission verdict on Lonrho's right to bid for the House of Fraser was due out within a month.

Clearly, Rowland still believed that all would come right for him in the end. Lonrho had, right after selling its 29 per cent, acquired a new 6.3 per cent stake, costing more than £20 million, in House of Fraser; significantly this came from 'Union Jack' Hayward and Dr Marwan, who had earlier been acquitted by Griffiths of any involvement in a financial concert party. But on 4 March 1985 the thunderbolt struck. The Fayeds launched a £615 million bid for total control – and a jubilant Professor Smith welcomed it unreservedly. He and the brothers toasted one another in Ritz champagne, the Fayeds' own brand.

The timing of the bid was crucial, because only four days later the Monopolies Commission overturned its 1981 finding and said that a Lonrho acquisition of House of Fraser would 'not be expected to operate against the public interest'. All too late. The professor joked mercilessly at Tiny's expense. 'It is a bit like arriving at the right platform to find that your train has just gone,' he chortled. Smith had every reason to be in high spirits. Not only had the threat of the sack been removed, but the Fayeds had immediately doubled his salary to £100,000.

As the *Observer*'s business section fairly said, the wrath of Rowland was now 'fearsome'. A number of other newspapers pointed out that he really had been hard done by. But they also asked why had he granted the Fayeds victory on a plate in the previous November, by selling them almost a third of the equity at one shot? Something far more modest would have been logical. Equally puzzling was the way he had sold his 6.3 per cent to them in March, thus allowing them to consolidate their hold; it had also been a signal to other institutional holders to follow suit.

The most relentless critic of Rowland's tactics was the *Daily Mail*, which was rewarded with exclusive glimpses into the private lives of the shy Egyptians. It told how Dodi Al-Fayed, the Sandhurst-trained son of Mohamed by his first wife, had financed and produced the film *Chariots of Fire*, and how Mohamed had once worked for Adnan Khashoggi, the Saudi

Arabian financier, as manager of a soft drinks company. Most of all, oozed the *Daily Mail*, the senior of the three brothers – the 'King of Harrods' – loved Britain devotedly. Nowhere was he so happy as on his 32,000-acre estate in the Highlands.

Up to this moment, virtually nobody in Britain knew a thing about the Fayeds, and few would have chosen to be any better informed. The country was already saturated in foreigners of one hue or another. If they could afford to buy up the best country houses and displace the old aristocrats, nobody cared except a few Blimps. If Mohamed Al-Fayed was married to a former Miss Finland, splendidly blonde and suntanned, that was also his good fortune. It was like a joke in Nicholas Montserrat's *The Cruel Sea*, about how the hero had in peacetime worked in an advertising agency and written the slogan for a new brand of toffee – 'Rich and Dark like the Aga Khan'. That was it, the Fayeds were just rich and dark.

However, another version of the Fayeds' private life was now being publicized. Tiny had now found a role for the *Observer* which perhaps made all the former aggravation (and the continuing million-a-year loss) quite worthwhile. Week after week the journalistic feud was maintained, with writs and lawyers' warnings just brushed aside.

A first Lonrho demand, trumpeted by the *Observer*, was for the Fayed takeover to be referred to the Monopolies Commission. That seemed totally reasonable. If Lonrho had been forced to endure three investigations over Harrods, was it right that a family of uncommunicative foreigners should be 'nodded through'? The then Trade Secretary, Norman Tebbit, was bombarded with letters in Rowland's most vehement style, but remained unmoved. There were insinuations in the *Observer* that Mrs Thatcher had been influenced by having just entertained the Egyptian President, Hosni Mubarak, at Number Ten, with Mohamed Al-Fayed in attendance.

Another aspect of the campaign was to reveal that the Fayeds were hiding disreputable episodes in their past. A useful informant in this regard was none other than Dr Marwan, whom Rowland had so castigated before John Griffiths, QC. Already a writ had been issued against Marwan by Mohamed Al-Fayed for remarks he had made in the *Evening Standard*. But little personal mud seemed to stick on the brothers, and the most dramatic charge was that it was not Egyptian money which had bought Harrods, but funds supplied by the Sultan of Brunei. That was certainly credible, because the Sultan possessed untold wealth and not long since had snapped up the Dorchester Hotel, another grand old British symbol.

The Sultan denied it, the Fayeds denied it, and so did their merchant bankers. The City knew that the truth might never be discovered, unless some very private bank accounts in Liechtenstein and Switzerland were laid bare. When the *Financial Times* joined in the hue and cry, by suggesting that nobody really believed the Fayeds were the true owners of Harrods, the brothers deployed a battery of lawyers to extract a humble apology. They then moved against the *Observer* in a novel fashion, by asking the independent directors to stop the persecution from the business pages. This took the paper by surprise, since the independent directors had always been seen as there to defend the editor against the owner. They could only have a role if Donald Trelford complained that Lonrho was planting the Fayed stories against his wishes. He was not minded to do that.

The journalists had a meeting to discuss this conundrum, and agreed that if the business section believed – as it did – that there was something about the Fayeds that should be exposed, then there was nothing more to be said. But there was a certain anxiety that the paper had been in a situation like this not long before, over Mark Thatcher and Oman. That inconclusive hatchet job had been helped by Lonrho at the start with titbits of information; when the sources dried up, the long-term coverage had dragged on, to the paper's discredit.

Perhaps we did not think enough about a simple journalistic question: was it news – did the readers want to know? If the Asians could own half the corner shops in Britain, why should some Egyptians not own one big one? It came back to the changing nature of the country. Of course, Rowland might have a valid complaint, but would it not seem to be tainted if aired in a paper he did not own? But we suppressed such doubts, in the reassuring knowledge that the 'Harrods vendetta' was being contained within the business pages. It did not seem to matter so much there – we knew from market research that only a small minority of the readers ever glanced at that section.

There was, however, a flutter of amusement in November when Melvin Marckus, the City editor, printed an open letter – that well-tried device for pumping up a flagging exposé. It was addressed to Leon Brittan, the Trade Secretary. He assured Brittan that he was making his inquiries into the Fayeds' bona fides 'quite independently of the *Observer*'s proprietors, Lonrho'. Marckus ended his reiteration of the case by promising that if he was shown to be wrong in his allegations about the Harrods takeover he would tender his resignation to Donald Trelford. The parting shot read: 'I would like to think that, should you prove wrong, you would consider similar action.' Brittan treated the very idea with smooth indifference, for no Cabinet minister was more self-confident in his prime (although he would resign over a quite different takeover controversy, the Westland affair, less than three months later).

As 1986 began, journalists on the *Observer* hoped that the Fayed vendetta belonged to the past, that Rowland had expended all his ammunition. We were quite wrong.

15

When the Magic Was Gone

Tiny Rowland's income is now said to be £7 million a year —
mostly the dividends on his Lonrho shares, plus another
£300,000 or so from his emoluments as the company's chief
executive. But such wealth has made little difference to the
simple patterns of his private life.

One regular event is the New Year holiday in Acapulco with
Josie and their children. Tiny enjoys the beach and the sea; but
his telephone often rings and his mind is never idle.

He came back to London during the first week of 1986 re-
invigorated for the Harrods fight. His first action was to send off
a letter to the hapless Leon Brittan (by now deeply embroiled in
the Westland furore). This accused Mrs Thatcher of 'political
bias' in allowing the Fayeds to buy Harrods without any investigation by the Monopolies Commission. He asserted that the
Prime Minister 'was most certainly not at a proper distance
from Mohamed Fayed'. She and her ministers had allowed a
British institution to be taken over by a man 'whose record was
questionable and whose business experience minimal'. He then
sent letters in a similar vein to Mrs Thatcher herself.

These were just ranging shots. Tiny was now about to let fly
with his latest weapons; and for the first time he was going to
use the front page of the *Observer* as his arena.

A hint that something big was afoot came after Donald
Trelford returned from dining at Claridge's with Tiny, just back
from Mexico, and a somewhat rum assortment of guests. These
included Adnan Khashoggi and two curious Indians, called the
Swami and the Mamaji. It was soon whispered about in the

newsroom that Trelford had been given a sensational story by Rowland and was intent upon running it that Sunday.

We then heard that the nub of it was the assertion that Mark Thatcher had been on a secret journey, in Mohamed Al-Fayed's executive jet, to meet the Sultan of Brunei. This explained the mounting level of invective from Tiny aimed at the Prime Minister. But it also gave a lot of the journalists an uneasy feeling. Mark Thatcher again: we had reached an impasse over the Oman stories, so this one just had to stand up.

Then we learned that it had been ruled that there was no need to check the details, because Tiny's sources were so well supported by documentary evidence. (Some time after the event, Trelford confided that it had cost Rowland $5 million to get that evidence, such as it was.)

We were not happy. David Leigh, the paper's ace investigative reporter, expostulated to me in the *Observer* canteen about the dangers he foresaw: 'Unless we check, how do we know that Mark Thatcher wasn't in the Houston Astradome on the day in question?' I said I thought it just the kind of place where he might well have been.

The story went in willy-nilly. Donald wrote it himself, and personally saw it into the front page. He credited it to an anonymous 'Staff Reporter'. The events on that day were so extraordinary – they were such a watershed for the paper and Rowland's proprietorship – that I went home and immediately made notes of what had occurred.

This is what I jotted down:

> By Friday night it was clear that DT was going to put the story on the front, and memos began to fly. Howard [Anthony Howard, the deputy editor] sent a fierce one; so did Leigh. On the Saturday morning it became known that Tiny was in the building – in the boardroom to see the printouts of what DT had been composing overnight. This was unheard of.
>
> By lunchtime the newsroom was in a ferment, with people standing around in groups, asking what could be done. It was suggested that we might convene a chapel meeting to try to stop the story appearing, for the protection of the paper's reputation. Significantly, Adam Raphael, until

then DT's staunchest ally , was protesting as vigorously as everyone else.

There was no attempt to 'legal' the story, but a printout was passed to Stephen Nathan, the duty lawyer; and he was seen arguing with DT; as a result, some small cuts in one of Tiny's letters to Mrs T. [quoted in the story] were made.

During the afternoon DT sent around a response to his main critics. This declared that he had met all the 'principals' in the story. (What about Mark Thatcher and Al-Fayed? Perhaps he had, some time in the past.)

His memo admitted that the Ob. would be attacked. 'So be it.' He insisted that he was convinced of the accuracy of the story, and said that it was no use pretending that the paper was not owned by Lonrho. If people wanted to criticize that was their right, but he was the editor. He had decided that the paper should 'publish and be damned'.

I have been uncertain about making public that personal *aide mémoire*. But in retrospect, it seems worthwhile, not merely 'for the record' but also to convey the predicament journalists can find themselves in when time is short and issues of principle are involved. We might, admittedly, have had a chapel meeting to stop the paper – but how could we be positive that the story was either true or false, since nobody had been allowed to check it? In any event, the story of that Saturday ultimately became common gossip in Fleet Street. Nine months later when Donald Trelford launched a legal action against *Private Eye* over its allegations about his social life, the magazine responded by entering a defence detailing at great length what had happened, and thus implying that he had no reputation to lose. He withstood the assault.

As it turned out, there was a slightly eerie silence for some days about the *Observer*'s 'Brunei bombshell'. The dailies seemed to shun it. But the *Sunday Times* was working away, and the following week came up with denials by almost all sides. The Sultan issued a statement that he had never met Mark Thatcher, and Mohamed Al-Fayed said the same. The Fayeds as a family complained to the Press Council, and more writs began to fly. Downing Street was reported to regard the story as the

Observer's 'annual attack' on Mark Thatcher; only Mark said nothing, apparently on the instructions of his mother, who thought it would be politically damaging for her if he let himself be caught up in this vitriolic battle. (In recent years the Prime Minister has been at pains to keep her son out of the headlines and as far from Britain as possible.)

One other key figure also said nothing – the elusive Swami, who seemed to be both preposterous and slightly sinister. It took some digging to find out who he was; but to do so was important, since clearly it was he who had primed Rowland about the alleged meeting between the Sultan and Mark Thatcher.

This Swami had also given Rowland the alleged transcript of a long and rambling series of conversations he had had in Carlos Place, Mayfair, with Mohamed Al-Fayed; a copy of this transcript had been left on the newsdesk by Donald Trelford, but nobody could extract much sense from it.

We discovered that the Swami (who liked to be referred to as 'His Holiness') was a thirty-seven-year-old Indian from Hyderabad called Chandra Maharaj. He had started off some years before as an astrologer in New Delhi, but in the manner of such gurus had enjoyed a sudden vogue among the famous, leading to a meteoric rise in his wealth and fame.

The Swami had become the 'spiritual adviser' to the gullible Sultan of Brunei, and claimed that he had, for a considerable fee, introduced Mohamed Al-Fayed to him. Not surprisingly, the self-appointed holy man had been identified by Rowland as a likely informant about what had been going on between the Sultan and his arch enemy. The ubiquitous Adnan Khashoggi had doubtless provided some introductions. But the Swami and his amanuensis, Kailash Nath Agarwal – who called himself the 'Mamaji' – were soon going to rue the day they became Rowland's tools in the Harrods battle.

The transcripts they had handed him were based on tapes made secretly at the behest of the Sultan, apparently in the middle of 1985 when he was making a check on Mohamed Al-Fayed's negotiations to buy the Dorchester Hotel for him for £50 million. The Sultan was not well pleased when the front-page story in the *Observer*, with its oblique references to the

Swami, made it obvious that the transcripts were being bandied around.

Most explosive of all was the use Rowland had made of the alleged transcripts to brand the Fayeds as anti-Semitic, to deter Jews from going into Harrods and thereby hurt his foes financially. Another copy of the transcript had been sent to a lawyer in Tel Aviv – a trusted friend of Tiny's named Eliahu Miron. From there the document found its way to New York to a small weekly paper in Brooklyn, called the *Jewish Press*.

The *Jewish Press* had woven a long feature story around one alleged quotation from the transcript, in which Mohamed Al-Fayed called Jews 'terrible people'. The feature ended ominously: 'Next time you are in London, remember that the owner of Harrods hates Jews, although he is unlikely to object if they shop there. Business, after all, is business.'

The weakness of this latest thrust in the vendetta was that nobody seemed to have heard the actual tapes, because they were presumably in the possession of the man who had commissioned them, the Sultan himself. That had not deterred Donald Trelford from referring in his story to the charge – made rather obscurely in New York, only two days before – that Mohamed Al-Fayed hated Jews. Nobody in London had ever heard of the *Jewish Press*: the timing of its feature had been thoughtfully arranged, then made known to the erstwhile 'Staff Reporter' in St Andrew's Hill.

All this was fairly murky. It was one thing to accuse the Fayeds of using the Sultan of Brunei's money to buy Harrods, quite another to use transcripts of doubtful provenance to assassinate their characters. I also learned that huge sums were being offered to anyone who could penetrate the secrets of certain bank accounts in Liechtenstein or tap certain telephones in Mayfair.

Shortly after the vendetta had moved down to this new and distressing level I went off once again to Uganda, to report the victory of Yoweri Museveni and his guerrilla army. Between expeditions into the bush to look at mountains of whitening skulls, and the devastation of civil war, I sat in my hotel room and pondered over what to do. I decided that the moment had come to bid a final goodbye to both the *Observer* and Tiny.

It was not going to be easy, because both had separately been the dominant forces in my life for almost a quarter of a century. Their convergence (for which I knew myself to be partly to blame) had proved fatal to my relationship with each of them.

Then there was the matter of my book – this book. Ever since the great boardroom quarrel in the mid-1970s. I had tossed around in my mind the idea of a biography of Rowland – 'Rowland of Africa'. He appealed to me then as being a cross between those Victorian explorers I had written so much about and one of the great empire-building capitalists such as Cecil Rhodes (and I had noticed that even Hedsor Wharf, where Tiny has made his home, starts with an anagram of Rhodes). After the Lonrho takeover of the *Observer* the project began to crystallize in my mind: later events had made it more compelling, although less pleasant to confront.

When it leaked out that I was collecting material, my relationship with Rowland and Trelford was downhill all the way. Both were exceedingly nervous at the thought of being inside hard covers. My transgression was to be punished, most visibly when I was stopped from attending the 1985 Commonwealth Summit in Nassau, even though I was the paper's Commonwealth correspondent; Donald Trelford went instead and took the opportunity to write a warmhearted feature about the Prime Minister of the Bahamas (an island where Lonrho has an investment in luxury hotels). A few weeks after that Tiny had vetoed a special supplement on Kenya planned by the colour magazine; I had been asked to write it.

So, soon after I came back from a visit to Nigeria, I handed in my notice. A Trelford aide gave me a surprise: 'They will be displeased, up in Cheapside House,' he said. 'Our instructions were to keep you working here. Tiny would rather have you inside the tent pissing out than outside the tent pissing in.'

My last weeks on the paper were eventful, journalistically speaking. I was in charge of the foreign newsdesk at the time of the American raid on Libya, followed by the disaster at Chernobyl.

There were also distracting pressures within the paper, aside from the ever-rumbling Harrods affair. We had achieved a narrow victory at the Old Bailey when the Crown failed in its bid to have us convicted of trying to bribe a Ministry of Defence official to hand over confidential documents. But then came a disastrous clash with the printing unions – a ricochet from the Rupert Murdoch dispute at Wapping. The unions were intent on 'blacking' all journalists working for Murdoch, and reacted strongly against setting any copy by Bernard Levin, one of the *Observer*'s principal reviewers. He had been a most aggressive supporter of the move to Wapping.

I was attending a conference in Trelford's office when he was called out to talk to Rowland on the telephone. When he returned he said with a conspiratorial smile: 'That's the price of our principles – £850,000 worth of advertising.' It had been decided to kill a review by Levin in the face of a threat from the unions to stop the coming issue. (Six months later there would be a punishing sequel when Donald was severely reprimanded by the Press Council for his capitulation. The complaint had been laid by Ronald Spark, chief leader-writer on Murdoch's *Sun*; it was a sweet revenge for him because Peter Hillmore, gossip columnist on the *Observer*, had consistently made mock of Spark and his colleagues.)

At the end of my final day, after the first edition had been put away, there was the executives' ritual relaxation session in the editor's office. 'And so we say farewell to Richard Hall,' said Trelford, eyeing me quizzically from over his whisky. I smiled back, and remembered our first meeting on Addis Ababa airport, almost exactly twenty years before.

A fortnight after my departure there was another 'Staff Reporter' special in the *Observer* about Mark Thatcher and the Sultan. This time the Swami was brought right to the fore, with a picture of his bearded countenance alongside the reproduction of an immigration document purporting to clinch the charge that Mark Thatcher really had been to Brunei. Goaded into a follow-up by complaints that his original 'exposé' was just a ragbag of innuendoes, Trelford had thrown in everything this time.

The result was predictable. The Swami was now all too aware that by trying to please Rowland he had gravely upset the Sultan, who had already denied meeting Mark Thatcher. A firm of London solicitors was hired to protest to the *Observer* that the

Swami had nothing whatsoever to do with the fight between Rowland and the Fayeds. His Holiness had been woefully misquoted.

If the Swami and the Mamaji hoped to slip out of the firing line so easily they were soon to be disillusioned. Now they were squarely in Rowland's bad books as well – and would have to pay the price. An Indian magazine suddenly chose (with, it was rumoured, the active support of Lonrho) to devote itself to uncovering the Swami's past. He had, it seemed, been arrested in earlier years over some dubious deals in scrap iron; his mastery of tantric magic and astrology was proving of little value in fending off journalistic investigations.

Just as the *Jewish Press* had been quoted at the start of the year, so was the Indian *Illustrated Weekly* cited by the *Observer* in July 1986. This time, however, it was *in extenso* – across eight columns. Rowland had personally ordered this uninhibited treatment.

That Sunday, as I was reading the story, one of my former colleagues telephoned. 'Why should our paper be used to pursue a private quarrel with some bloody Indian fakir?' he demanded. 'What do the readers care?' Then he went on angrily: 'You've known Tiny a lot longer than anyone. Can't you tell us how we can persuade him to stop all this nonsense?' I thought for a moment, then replied: 'I just don't know, not any more.'

It was never my intention to end in such a way, because before the obsession with Harrods took over there was a different Rowland in my mind's eye. The one who had said in 1977: 'I am not a paper merchant . . . I believe in assets, in land, in factories and stores. It is very difficult to convince the City.'

However much his astounding career has been stamped with wilfulness, and his later years have been marred by one implacable fixation, nothing can gainsay his early vision. His monuments will be in the places he loves best, in Africa – in the tea and sugar plantations of Malawi, the wheat fields of Zambia, the cattle farms of Kenya, the coffee estates of Zimbabwe, the gold mines of Ghana. Tiny has his faults, sure enough, but the astounding story of Lonrho must prove that he is what the Africans call a 'big man', a real *bwana mkubwa*.

Appendix A

Lonrho in South Africa

When it was founded in the early years of this century, Lonrho inevitably had close ties with South Africa. The landlocked British colony of Rhodesia was always in some measure an economic appendage of the powerful country beyond the Limpopo River; matters have scarcely changed today, even though Rhodesia has become the independent state of Zimbabwe.

What is noteworthy is the extent to which Lonrho under Tiny Rowland has maintained, and even extended, its involvement with South Africa. Rowland was never a stranger in Johannesburg, the financial hub of southern Africa, in the pre-Lonrho days when he was looking for backing for his own mining ventures in Rhodesia. Ever since the early 1960s, when he began to spread Lonrho's activities throughout black Africa, he has been able to keep the two branches of the company's growth on the continent completely separate. Some African leaders remain unaware that Lonrho has any significant investments in 'apartheid territory'.

The Lonrho annual reports are far from illuminating at a casual glance. The Mining and Refining section speaks enthusiastically about platinum developments, without saying precisely where the metal is being produced. Likewise the references to coal mining do not say where it is being carried on. Only in the final pages, classifying Lonrho's principal overseas companies, is South Africa specifically mentioned. In fact, Lonrho has more than 10,000 employees in South Africa, mostly black miners. Its coal mines have an output of more than three million tons a year. But it is platinum mining which has been the spectacular success: according to the *Daily Telegraph* (7 April 1986) Lonrho's 50.4 per cent stake in Western Platinum in South Africa 'played a major role in the group's overall mining and refining profits for 1985 of £40.1 million'.

Mining, though, is only part of the activity conducted by Lonrho South Africa (of which Rowland is a director). It has more than one hundred subsidiaries, whose activities range through sugar production, vehicle distribution, avionics and printing.

It was reported by *The Times* (28 May 1986) that Lonrho was planning to sell off its entire South African interests to Anglo-American Corporation for more than £260 million. But if the idea was seriously considered, nothing came of it. Indeed, there were later reports that Falconbridge, Lonrho's Canadian partner in Western Platinum, wanted to sell out, and then Lonrho might exercise its option to buy 100 per cent; but this would involve a considerable outlay of freely convertible currency.

With the fall in the Rand, it may be too late now for Lonrho to get out of South Africa without suffering severe losses. But the political risks of staying in grow higher with the deteriorating political situation; investments in the rest of Africa have to be weighed in the balance.

Appendix B

Some Lonrho Projects since 1961

It was a witticism among Lonrho employees in the 1960s that Tiny Rowland would have a score of ideas before breakfast, discard ten by noon and still have one in play by sundown. It was that one which made all the difference. The following list is far from being exhaustive, but does show how Lonrho's interests have been diversified in the quarter of a century since Rowland took control.

MOZAMBIQUE: *Beira-Mutare pipeline*. When Rowland joined Lonrho in 1961, he brought with him this project, for which he had with unflagging determination extracted a concession from the Portuguese (then the colonial rulers of Mozambique). He later had to exert pressure on the oil companies to persuade them to build an inland refinery at Mutare – then called Umtali. But nine months after the oil began flowing, Rhodesia declared UDI and the 190-mile pipeline went out of action for fifteen years. Today it carries all of Zimbabwe's oil imports through the 'Beira Corridor', and Rowland has assessed its value as $75 million. However, after the death of President Samora Machel – with whom Rowland was on close terms – prospects for the pipeline had to be reassessed in the light of Mozambique's political development.

MALAWI: *Tea and Sugar Plantations*. During the early 1960s, Lonrho's first ventures outside Rhodesia were into Malawi (then Nyasaland). Rowland established good relations with President Kamuzu Banda, as a prelude to investing heavily in agriculture. Lonrho also has a textile factory in Malawi, run by

239

its David Whitehead subsidiary. Abortive efforts were made to develop bauxite deposits in the Mount Mlanje district. The output of the tea and sugar plantations helps to sustain Lonrho's claim to be the largest commercial producer of food in Africa. But Malawi is landlocked: with the worsening conditions in southern Africa, Lonrho has had difficulties in exporting its produce, so Rowland has taken a close interest in the rehabilitation of the railway running east from Malawi to the Indian Ocean port of Nacala. A Lonrho grant has helped finance a British-trained force to guard the line.

ZAMBIA: *Breweries and Building*. On the hard-drinking Copperbelt of Zambia, the Chibuku maize beer monopoly gave Lonrho the cash flow it badly needed during early years of rapid expansion. Subsidiaries now profitably make and sell beer in several African countries, although Lonrho has been reduced to a 49 per cent stake in Zambia's National Breweries. Sustained by his twenty-year friendship with President Kaunda, Tiny has branched out in Zambia into road haulage, newspaper publishing (now nationalized), farming, vehicle and tractor distribution, and mining machinery. Apart from the disastrous road haulage venture, all these prospered until Zambia fell into economic ruin through low copper prices. Lonrho also controlled a highly profitable amethyst mine in Zambia, but in recent years this has been the subject of tortuous legal proceedings against Tiny's former friend, the American dealer Daniel E. Mayers.

TANZANIA: *Sisal*. There was never any *rapport* between Rowland and Tanzania's President Julius Nyerere. A Lonrho-owned newspaper in Dar es Salaam was soon nationalized, then the company's sisal estates were expropriated in 1969 because of the Lonrho involvement in South Africa. In 1979 there were signs that Britain might be persuaded to withdraw aid from Tanzania because of the takeover. Although some compensation was agreed, Tanzania has always been Rowland's 'dead area' in East Africa.

KENYA: *Cattle, cars, and newspapers*. The newspaper publishing group owned by Lonrho in Nairobi has been the cornerstone of its activities in Kenya. The daily *Standard* has been at pains to keep close to the governments of both Kenyatta and Moi.

Lonrho now has a dominant position in the sales of cars and tractors throughout Kenya. It also has expanding agricultural interests. In the early 1980s, Rowland donated prime land for a new university to be named after President Moi. He has also repeatedly expressed interest in laying an oil pipeline from Kenya to Uganda (a country in which Lonrho's interests have been held to a minimum). Until 1984 the Lonrho cargo airline, Tradewinds, had ambitions to capture the important Nairobi–London freight route; but Tradewinds proved a liability and was abandoned.

SUDAN: *Sugar.* When higher oil prices attracted Rowland towards the Middle East, he decided to advance by way of Khartoum, where Lonrho's 'Middle East office' was established. Lonrho sponsored a huge sugar scheme, drawing on the group's sugar expertise in Malawi, South Africa, Swaziland and Mauritius. But the Kenana Project was bedevilled by disagreements between Rowland and the Kuwaiti backers; by 1977 the Lonrho interest was vestigial, although Rowland retains a sentimental interest in it. The scheme never looked viable and the capital investment has approached $1 billion. Not until 1985 did Kenana achieve its projected output of 300,000 tonnes of sugar a year. Rowland once also talked of building a Nile railway to link the Sudanese and Egyptian systems. Latterly his involvement in Sudan has been political: after the overthrow of his old friend President Nimeiri he has shown a close interest in the southern rebel leader, Colonel John Garang.

SIERRA LEONE: *Diamonds and Gold.* One of Rowland's first sorties into West Africa was an attempt to gain control of Sierra Leone's mineral wealth. Armed with a written recommendation from President Kaunda, he flew in to meet Siaka Stevens, the wily ruler of the one-time home of freed slaves. Rowland proposed a joint venture company to 'develop all known mineral resources of the country': Sierra Leone was renowned for its large, high-quality gemstones. Gold was also waiting to be exploited. But although a company was formed with Lonrho representation, the combined opposition of Selection Trust and the Lebanese diamond dealers proved too strong. This reverse was not unlike one suffered further south in Zaire; but although

Rowland has lately gone back to Zaire he has never in the past fifteen years tried again to find a foothold in Sierra Leone.

GHANA: *Gold*. As related in Chapter 4, the most conspicious triumph scored by Rowland in West Africa was the takeover of Ashanti Goldfields Corporation. The tribulations of successive coups in Ghana have been surmounted, although Lonrho now retains only 45 per cent of Ashanti. In times when the world gold price was high, the mine contributed more than 5 per cent of the Lonrho group turnover. Plans to expand the mine are in train with aid from the International Finance Corporation.

SOUTH AFRICA: *Coal and Anthracite*. Some of Lonrho's interests within South Africa have been detailed in Appendix A. However, the tangled affairs of Coronation Syndicate, Tweefontein United Collieries and Witbank Consolidated Coal Mines deserve mention. Lonrho first gained control of Coronation soon after Rowland took charge in Salisbury; throughout the 1960s these South African mining interests were closely intertwined with those in both Rhodesia and Mozambique. There was continuing discord with some embittered minority shareholders in South Africa, together with unproven allegations that one resurrected copper mine in Mozambique was being used as a cover for sanctions-busting during the UDI period. A Johannesburg stockbroker, J. P. Esterhuysen, began what was to be a lifelong vendetta against Rowland. The accusations made by Esterhuysen led to the arrest in South Africa of Frederick Butcher, Lonrho's financial director, and the issuing of warrants for the arrest of Rowland himself, Ogilvy and other Lonrho directors, during the second half of 1971. The charges were withdrawn, but the affair led directly into the great 'Boardroom Battle' of 1973 by compounding liquidity problems. Lonrho still has extensive coal interests in South Africa.

MEXICO: *Hotels*. Deteriorating economic conditions in black Africa, making it increasingly hard to get profits out, encouraged Rowland in the late 1970s to spread Lonrho's activities to other parts of the world. Interests soon embraced such diverse concerns as whisky distilling and steel making in Britain, wine growing in France, and freight forwarding in Germany (Kuhne and Nagel). One of the biggest of these new ventures was the purchase of the Princess Hotels chain from the billionaire recluse, Daniel K. Ludwig. By 1985 the book value of Lonrho's hotels, in the Americas and Europe, was more than £350 million.

BRITAIN: *Casinos*. A development which startled some of Rowland's admirers was the move into gambling clubs. By the mid-1980s Lonrho was operating a string of casinos in Britain, with the former Playboy Club in Park Lane as its flagship. These establishments saw their profits held in check by the fall in the oil price, which reduced the gambling propensities of the most renowned clients, the Arab sheikhs.

But Rowland has remained enthusiastic about the Lonrho casinos: others are attached to the Princess hotels in the Bahamas. In 1986 he made an unsuccessful bid to build and run the world's biggest casino-hotel complex in Australia.

UNITED STATES: *Oil and Gas*. Towards the end of 1986, Rowland began paying increased attention to investment possibilities in the US. Lonrho announced, as a first step, the launching of a £130 million joint-venture company to buy up oil and gas wells and pipelines in the American Mid-West and Rocky Mountains. This initiative (which some analysts thought daring in view of the turbulence in world oil markets) was in one way a product of Rowland's purchase of the *Observer* in 1981: the partner in the 50/50 venture was Robert Anderson, with whom Tiny had become friendly when Rowland bought the paper from Atlantic Richfield. At the start of 1986, Anderson had retired from the Atlantic Richfield chairmanship, and the assets acquired by the new company came from his former multinational 'empire'. Lonrho described the deal as the basis for further expansion in the US; it has also become involved with Atlantic Richfield itself in an oil exploration programme around the Bahamas. This further proof of Rowland's desire to reduce Lonrho's dependence on its African roots revealed at the same time his attachment to his early business instincts – the oil pipeline across Mozambique became a prize Lonrho asset after he took control in 1961.

The opinion of financial analysts at the end of 1986 was that although Lonrho had significantly moved away from its original

African milieu, it still remained excessively exposed to the decline in world commodity prices. One of the biggest successes of the past decade has been Western Platinum, but this is not something which Lonrho much cares to publicize, because it is in South Africa.

Indisputably, the conglomerate's greatest asset remains Rowland himself; in the twenty-five years since he took over, Lonrho has advanced to rank thirty-ninth among Britain's biggest companies (*Business* magazine, October 1986). But as he approaches his seventieth birthday there is speculation about what might happen to so heterogeneous a financial creation if Tiny were no longer in charge.

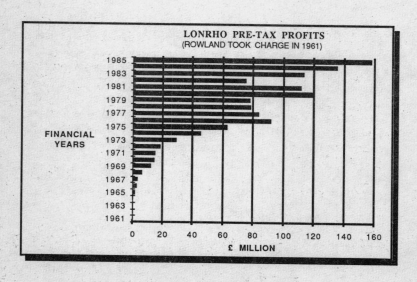

Index

117–20, 122, 133–4, 185–6
Guardian diary revelations,
184
in Congo, 43–5
in Ivory Coast, 31, 34–7
in Nigeria, 37–43
joins *Observer*, 49
Malawi Times, 32–4
Matabeleland story, 186–97
Matatu problem, 169–70,
180–3, 185
on TV, 157–8
publishes Zvogbo's article,
168–9
reaction to TR takeover, 140–2,
144, 146, 151, 159–61
relations with Anderson,
134–5
relations with RH, 92–4, 133
submission to Monopolies
Commission, 153–4
submits articles for vetting,
165–7, 186
TR dossier, ix–x
TR on, 176–7
union relations, 235
warning to RH, xiii
Tweefontein United Collieries,
242
Twistleton-Fiennes, Sir Ranulph,
165

Uganda, 33, 164, 175, 233, 241
Unilever, 70
Union Minière, 62–3
United Arab Emirates, 180
United National Independence
Party, 24, 29–30, 46
Upper Volta, 38

Varga, 8–9

Wall Street Journal, 117, 191
Wallef, Louis, 62
Wankel engine, 97–8, 101, 124
Warburg, S. G., 97
Washington Post, 123
Watergrade Shipping Company,
63
Watt, David, 118
Waugh, Auberon, 150
Wayas, Senator Joseph, xi
Welensky, Roy, 10, 14, 19, 22, 43
Western Platinum, 128, 238, 244
Whitehead, David, 70, 240
Whitehorn, Katharine, 78
Whitehouse, Mary, 147
Willoughby, Lady Jane, 92–4
Wilson, Harold:
Astor's opinon, 86
Biafran policy, 52
in Nigeria, 37–8
Rhodesian sanctions, 54, 116,
126, 129
Rhodesian UDI, 32, 115
Windlesham, 3rd Baron, 181
Witbank Consolidated Coal
Mines, 242
World Security Trust, 86

Yace, Philippe, 36
Yates, Ivan, 93
Yeoman Investments, 108
Young, Hugo, 145

Zaire, 44
Zambia:
African Mail, 23, 24, 25
Chartered, 11
independence, 25
Kaunda, 18, 24, 116
Lonrho, 33, 240
Monopolies Commission
report, 157

Peel, 80
RH leaves, 50–2
Rhodesian UDI, 32, 130
see also Times of Zambia
Zambia Times, 24

Zimbabwe, 132, 153, 167–74, 186–90, 195
Zvogbo, Eddison, 167–9, 171–2, 178, 180, 183